Advance praise for *Now and Yesterday*

"*Now and Yesterday* is both an up-to-the-minute dissection of contemporary Manhattan and an old-fashioned nineteenth-century novel with all its pleasures—big set pieces and a rich cast of characters. With great skill, intelligence, and emotional wisdom, Greco paints an indelible portrait of The Way We Live Now."

—Andrew Holleran

"An unexpected treat. Greco's big, juicy, triple-decker has love, sex, business, and death, as well as ethical and décor questions galore."

—Felice Picano

NOW AND YESTERDAY

STEPHEN GRECO

KENSINGTON BOOKS
www.kensingtonbooks.com

Excerpt from "East Coker" from *Four Quartets* by T. S. Eliot. Copyright 1940 by T. S. Eliot. Copyright © renewed 1968 by Esme Valerie Eliot. Reprinted by permission of Houghton Mifflin Harcourt Publishing Company. All rights reserved.

Excerpt from "The Death of Saint Narcissus" from *Poems Written in Early Youth,* by T. S. Eliot. Copyright © 1967, renewed 1995 by Valerie Eliot. Reprinted by permission of Farrar, Straus and Giroux, LLC.

Excerpt from "East Coker" and "The Death of Saint Narcissus" from *Collected Poems 1909–1962* by T. S. Eliot reprinted by permission of Faber and Faber Limited.

Der Rosenkavalier, Op. 59 by Richard Strauss © Copyright 1910, 1911 by Adolph Furstner, U.S. copyright renewed. Copyright 1943 assigned to Hawkes & Son (London) Ltd. (a Boosey & Hawkes company) for the world excluding Germany, Italy, Portugal and the formal territories of the USSR (excluding Estonia, Latvia and Lithuania). Reprinted by permission. Libretto by Hugo von Hofmannsthal. English version by Alfred Kalisch.

KENSINGTON BOOKS are published by

Kensington Publishing Corp.
119 West 40th Street
New York, NY 10018

Copyright © 2014 by Stephen Greco

All Kensington titles, imprints, and distributed lines are available at special quantity discounts for bulk purchases for sales promotion, premiums, fund-raising, educational, or institutional use.

Special book excerpts or customized printings can also be created to fit specific needs. For details, write or phone the office of the Kensington Special Sales Manager: Kensington Publishing Corp., 119 West 40th Street, New York, NY 10018. Attn. Special Sales Department. Phone: 1-800-221-2647.

Kensington and the K logo Reg. U.S. Pat. & TM Off.

ISBN-13: 978-1-61773-060-3
ISBN-10: 1-61773-060-2
First Kensington Trade Paperback Printing: June 2014

eISBN-13: 978-1-61773-061-0
eISBN-10: 1-61773-061-0
First Kensington Electronic Edition: June 2014

10 9 8 7 6 5 4 3 2

Printed in the United States of America

So here I am, in the middle way, having had twenty years—
Twenty years largely wasted, the years of l'entre deux guerres
Trying to learn to use words, and every attempt
Is a wholly new start, and a different kind of failure
Because one has only learnt to get the better of words
For the thing one no longer has to say, or the way in which
One is no longer disposed to say it. . . .

—T. S. Eliot: *Four Quartets* ("East Coker")

1975

When Harold first saw the apartment, the week before, it was painted in hideous colors that someone had obviously thought groovy. The living room and little alcove looking onto the back garden were electric yellow, while the bedroom, on the street, was neon orange and dominated by a five-foot-high, freestanding structure of two-by-fours and plywood, like a play fort, in royal blue. The previous tenants had kept their desk inside the thing, the realtor said, and their mattress on top. By the time Harold returned with Peter, two days later, the fort was gone and the whole apartment had been painted white. The place looked bigger and, while possibly less groovy, more like the charming abode that the boyfriends instantly agreed it could be—the parlor floor of a handsome old Brooklyn row house that was meant to be their home.

They were at one of the large windows facing the street, rigging up an improvised window treatment of old bedsheets and flimsy tension bars they'd brought with them from Ithaca.

"Steady, please," said Peter, standing on a stepladder, adjusting the tension bar to fit snugly inside the window frame.

"I'm *trying*," sang Harold, crouching below and holding the bottom bar in place.

It was early on a summer evening, their first in the new place. There were screens in the windows, and as they worked the sounds of neighbors walking by filtered in genially from the street. They'd spent the day moving and settling in with the few possessions they had—boxes of books and records, several lawn-and-leaf bags stuffed with clothing, a pair of mismatched director's chairs, a third-hand steamer trunk they planned to use as a table ("We can sit on the floor, Japanese-style...."), some kitchen items they'd picked up at a neighborhood stoop sale, and an old mattress that had been sitting unused at the apartment nearby where they'd been crashing with Cornell classmates who'd moved to Brooklyn before them, that spring.

Peter stepped down from the ladder and gave the improvised shades a final smoothing.

"So how long do you think we'll have to suffer this mess?" he said, regarding his handiwork. The beige-and-white-striped sheets, which had looked so sophisticated when new, a few years before, were now threadbare.

"Oh, c'mon, it's fine," said Harold, straightening up.

"Think we'll ever have real drapes?"

"Of course we will, eventually. Maybe even soon. I mean, if that's what you want. But what about blinds, baby—wouldn't wooden blinds be nice?"

Peter hooted.

"Can you imagine how much wooden blinds would cost for windows this big?" he said, slipping his arm around Harold's waist. "Probably a month's salary—and remember it's *your* salary we're talking about, sweetheart, 'cause I don't have one."

"One of those interviews will pan out, don't worry," said Harold. "Meanwhile I think it's extremely cool to use a trash bag as both a dresser and a chair." From the floor Harold grabbed the mug of wine he'd been sipping and flopped down on one of the bags full of clothing. To celebrate the housewarming they'd opened a bottle of Boone's Farm apple wine and were drinking from drabware mugs that Harold's sister had given them as a gift.

"Honey, *no,*" said Peter, pushing Harold off the bag and fluffing it back into shape. "That'll wrinkle everything. I hope those were *your* clothes...."

They laughed and Peter looked around for his wine.

"It's a very pop, very *now* way to live, don't you think?" said

Harold, moving over to the mattress on the floor in the middle of the room and making himself comfortable on it.

"Yeah?" said Peter. "Andy Warhol? You wanna live like that?"

"Could be cool," said Harold.

"Might get cold in here this winter, without drapes."

The stereo had gone silent, and Peter was about to flip over the record they'd been listening to, Judy Collins's *Wildflowers,* when Harold stopped him.

"Oh, play that last song again, please. It's so beautiful."

Peter set the needle down on "Lasso! di donna," Collins's take on a fourteenth-century Italian *ballata,* then he got down on the mattress beside Harold.

> *Lasso! di donna vana inamorato*
> *Son che pur mi lusinga con inganno,*
> *Dàmmi speranza non mi toglie affanno.*
> *Perch' è fallace 'l suo ben disiato.*

Kcch-pop.

> *I' mi doglo che tanto su' amor fello. . . .*

The track had a bad skip in it—the result, Peter thought, of his having lent the album once to a friend who, like everyone else, handled records far less reverently than he did. The skip always made Peter wince, though the expectation of it had become oddly satisfying by now, and he could almost savor the fact that perfection had given way to an experience of the song that was his in a special way. The embrace of flaws and particularities could apparently bring unexpected consequences that were welcome and sometimes even glorious. At least, that was the way he explained his relationship with Harold—how they had gone, during the previous year, from being acquaintances to friends to boyfriends, to this larger thing they were now exploring. They were committed to each other now, they said, and wanted it to last indefinitely—and they said this because they didn't know what else to do *but* say it, while moving in together and vowing to accept each other's particularities and make up life as they went along.

"The street is quieter than I thought it would be," said Peter lazily, in the silence after the song ended.

"Mm-hmm," said Harold.

The day's work was done, and it felt good to be temporarily beyond the reach of family and friends. The phone wouldn't be installed for another couple of days. They'd already decided against rushing out to a dance performance that Harold thought might be interesting, in favor of a quiet night. "Important things are happening," Harold always said, and that was exciting, even if some of those things, like the Lou Reed songs they'd heard a few nights before, at the latest incarnation of Andy Warhol's Factory, were a little scary for a couple of nice gay boys with middle-class dreams. Now that they lived in the big city and were gobbling up culture, they were encountering plenty of stuff that they admitted to each other was mystifying, even intimidating—avant-garde theater, experimental music, performance art and the like. Yet Harold, ever the advanced thinker and now a promising journalist, maintained that mystifying was good and exposure to it healthy. So they'd face it as a team. And it thrilled them that Harold was beginning to get comp tickets to these events, as a newly hired stringer for the *Times*—though it wasn't clear exactly what a guy who'd written his master's thesis on the "hagiographic, eremitic, and Biblical traditions" in an Old English poem about Saint Guthlac would bring to the coverage of contemporary culture, nor indeed how Peter, who'd never had a clue what to do with his life, could survive by writing poetry. They'd figure out something.

"What are we gonna do about dinner?" said Peter, propping himself up and setting aside his mug conspicuously at arm's length from the mattress.

"Well, let's think about that, shall we?" said Harold, setting aside his mug, too. "We could go to the falafel place."

"We could. . ."

But before they could decide they were kissing and pawing each other, and the sound of them laughing and rolling around on the mattress was echoing from the freshly painted walls of their empty new house. And as the day faded they realized they could still see each other's faces in the darkening room, since the old sheets did such a feeble job of shutting out light from the streetlamp that came on right outside their window.

"First fuck in our new home," said Harold, as he rolled on top of Peter and kept covering his boyfriend's face, neck, and ears with hungry kisses.

"I know," burbled Peter. "Consecration of the house."

"The first of many, many!"

Peter was giggling, pretending to shield himself from the barrage.

"Hey, hey, *Harry*—I'm referencing Beethoven over here . . . !"

"I know what you're doing. I love you anyway."

2012

CHAPTER 1

"Whaddya think?" said Peter, modeling a new gray hoodie underneath his Brooks Brothers blazer.

"You *could,*" said Tyler, looking up from his texting. They were at the agency, in Peter's office. It was just before lunchtime. Tyler was sitting in Peter's desk chair.

Peter tried to catch a reflection of himself in the glass of a window that looked onto the agency's multistory atrium lobby.

"It's good, right?" he said.

"I dunno. Simpler might be better."

"Do you ever put up the hood?"

"Maybe at the beach, if it's cold."

"I'm talking about tonight, Tyler—this thing I'm going to."

"Oh." The boy made a face. "I wouldn't."

Only in his mid-twenties, Tyler was one of the agency's brightest comers—a terrific conceptual thinker, a gifted copywriter. And it didn't hurt that he was shockingly blond, had electric green eyes, and commanded the megawatt smile of a born entertainer.

"No?" said Peter, trying the hood up.

Tyler shook his head.

"That *Mad Men* thing you've got going on today is fine," said the boy. "Don't mess with it. It's a good look for a man your age."

Peter smirked. It was a joke between them, his age. So was referring to Tyler as a boy, except in front of clients. The "thing" Peter was preparing for was a housewarming hosted by his friend Jonathan, whose circle consisted mostly of decorous homosexual gentlemen of his and Peter's generation, whom Peter sometimes referred to as "best-little-boys-in-the-world-of-a-certain-age."

"Note custom-made," said Peter, demonstrating the blazer's working buttonholes.

"Swell," said Tyler.

Back in the '50s, when he was a kid in a small town upstate, people wore sweatshirts to keep warm when they actually did something to work up a sweat, Peter said. The main references in his mind to sweat clothes were early-morning drills on frost-covered playing fields and after-school games in smelly gymnasiums echoing with the scuffle of boys and the bark of gym teachers who'd seen action in Korea. Back then, he said, the hooded sweatshirt was an immutable building block of American culture—resistant, like a Brooks Brothers blazer, to shifts in quote-unquote meaning.

"Well, that's just not right anymore," said Tyler, impishly. "It's not even wrong."

Peter smirked. It was like Tyler, who'd studied semiotics at Brown and found his way into advertising as obliquely as Peter had, to work a quote by a famous physicist into a conversation about fashion. And it was like him to do so flirtatiously. There was a bit of a crush between the two, the youngish fifty-nine-year-old and the precocious twenty-five-year-old, though Peter had decided that nothing romantic should come of it. He had scruples about fooling around with employees and reinforced these frequently by pontificating about a worker's right to be valued for his work, not his flesh—though flirting, he maintained, sometimes catalyzed the work because "it deepened the ongoing conversation among members of a creative team, who need to address not only a client's needs but their own feelings about those needs and the creative process itself."

"We love it when you talk fancy to us," Tyler once cracked, during a staff meeting.

Still wearing the hoodie, Peter continued to paw through the items he'd picked up that morning at Barneys—a knit cap with earflaps, a pre-wrinkled plaid scarf, a woven leather bracelet-y thing that was a little bit butch, a little bit femme. So many options! Peter tried to stay engaged with fashion's fun, but sometimes longed for a time with clearer rules. The whole idea of dressing right was like a religion back in 1961, when he first visited Brooks Brothers, he told Tyler. His uncle Malcolm took him there to buy his first suit; they came down to the city in a chauffeur-driven car. And Malcolm—a kind of gay godfather, who owned, with his wife, Aunt Ida, the fanciest hair salon in the Mid-Hudson Valley—had done nothing less that day than usher a boy into the palace of wisdom.

"He showed me what to prefer in a cuff and a buttonhole," said Peter, "took me to lunch at the Brasserie—which must have only just opened, at that point—and explained to me why Mrs. Oliver Harriman's book of etiquette was superior to Mrs. Emily Post's. Dear Uncle Malcolm. Oh, and he told me that a hairdresser he knew named Kenneth, who was 'a great artist, only a few blocks away,' had pulled off 'the culture-shaking triumph of big hair over hats.' Can you imagine?"

When Tyler giggled at this last bit, Peter recommended he look into the history of modern millinery and the career of one Mr. John. The agency was scheduled to pitch a luxury fashion brand the following week and the information would come in handy.

They were always talking about small but seismic matters like this, Peter and his team, and Peter knew that many outside the industry, including the worthies of Jonathan's crowd, looked down on this type of inquiry as trivial. Yet he found it natural to puzzle over questions like "What should I wear?" and "What should I drive?" as practically philosophical matters and some of the biggest questions of the age. How *do* you construct a personal look that says everything you want to say about yourself—or at least *enough* about your taste and personality to be specifically *you*—while avoiding clichés determined by, for lack of a better word, class? It was a question at the root of a certain discomfort that Peter felt with Jonathan's crowd, despite his falling squarely within their class, since they seemed to embrace every cliché that grown-up, well-mannered, best-little-boys could—cultural, political, sartorial. And the question was central to Peter's career, too, since the boutique agency he founded and ran required a leader who both saw beyond old-fashioned class boundaries and *appeared* as though he did.

Especially now that Peter had become a star in the world of "creative," appearances mattered. He was the celebrated author of a series of video spots for a talking car that had become a national mascot, and of a campaign for a new energy drink whose tagline had gone globally viral. High-profile clients paid well to absorb wisdom in Peter's presence, which meant that in meetings and presentations, and even in videoconferences, he was expected to wield his entire persona like a Broadway star does during a performance, fusing the right lines with the right moves, in the right costume.

"Are we done, boss?" said Tyler, tucking away his phone. "I gotta run—Damiano's downstairs."

"OK, go," said Peter. "Thanks, Ty."

"You look terrific," said Tyler, bolting up from Peter's chair and scooting for the door.

"Mr. John!" said Peter.

"I'm on it!" sang Tyler.

OK, so maybe I do do just the blazer tonight, with no funny business, thought Peter, trying to find his reflection again in the window. *It would be sort of ironic to go decked out strictly in Brooks, if I'm not just to* fit in *with a bunch of old men, but to* explore the idea of my fitting in.

He smirked.

Anyway, drag is fun, whether it's Brooks or Patricia Field.

That evening, when Peter turned onto Twenty-fourth Street and saw the elegant green canopy, he immediately knew which building must be Jonathan's.

Oh, that *place,* he thought. Once, long before Jonathan moved in, Peter had endured a tedious dinner party there, seated next to a thin-lipped know-it-all whom he realized, midway through the broiled trout, had been specially invited for him. For three hours, the guy stifled conversation with opinions delivered like proclamations. The host seemed disappointed when Peter left early and alone.

Great apartment, though.

The building was a well-cared-for, prewar pile of brick and limestone with a restrained Moderne feel, designed by an architect Jonathan called "the Candela of downtown." On either side of the revolving door was a neat boxwood in a tapered, cast-stone planter. Jonathan, in fact, had referred to his new home only by the address number, the way people sometimes did with iconic buildings on Park and Fifth Avenues—740, 820, 960, 1040—and though the number didn't automatically summon an image in Peter's brain, it reminded him that West Chelsea had its iconic addresses, too. And it made sense that one of these would be where his fancy friend would relocate after years of renting a small but spectacular East Tenth Street penthouse, now an overpriced co-op.

It was a mild October evening. A motley *paseo* of dog walkers occupied the sidewalk—mostly gay men and straight women in after-work mode, chatting amiably with one another and/or their pets, while a stream of sharply dressed, decidedly on-duty types strode through on their way to dinner on Tenth Avenue or a gallery opening beyond. The fall was still gentle enough for people to go without coats and everyone was talking about that—New Yorkers being often more focused on protection and shelter than on the elements themselves.

It was 7:30 on the dot. Peter always timed his arrivals carefully. For fashionably late events, like the fashion week after-parties and cool-cause benefits he attended regularly as a New York fast-tracker, he still had to remind himself to translate the time stated on an invitation into a real hour at which an arrival could be made. Sometimes nine o'clock meant midnight. For this party, though, 7:30 meant 7:30. Jonathan and his crowd were not late-nighters. They were media execs and entertainment lawyers, mostly, whom Jonathan knew through his work as a documentary filmmaker, mixed with survivors of that original circle of artsy rebels in which Peter and Jonathan first met, in mid-'70s New York. The two had arrived in the city back then like so many other newly out young gay men, after a spin through college and grad school, ready to pursue serious agendas suddenly made possible by adulthood and revolution. For most, it was the start of a comfortable rut in law, or academia, or arts administration. And for some it was a historical moment that ushered in destiny.

For Peter, it was destiny. Having come to New York to be a poet, after the publication of some overheated verses about life up-state, he quickly moved on to fashion journalism and eventually to advertising. Immersion in these fields had rendered him more fashion-forward than anyone else in Jonathan's crowd—which is why, as he approached Jonathan's building in his sober blue blazer, gray slacks, and white shirt, he felt an odd kind of pleasure in knowing that for once he'd be dressed absolutely right for a party. That pleasure was rare for Peter, since the hip that was required of him was anything but effortless. Some evenings, before going out, he had to think long and hard about just how young-and-trendy to go with his look. For a man of his age and position, the clothes should be neither too disheveled nor too put together, the accessories neither too fun-junky nor too fuck-you expensive—though, no, a perfectly formulated mix of Prada, J. Lindeberg, Y3, and Hello Kitty, donned in response to a constantly fluxing set of cultural meanings, never made him feel totally, absolutely, unflappably right when he stepped out of a taxi at the door of a happening nightspot. That line between right and pathetic was blurry, even for Peter, which is why he relied on Tyler for help.

He passed through the revolving door, nodded at the doorman, and approached the desk.

"Hi, there," he said.

"Good evening," said the receptionist.

Peter stated Jonathan's name but before he could say his own, the receptionist nodded.

"Penthouse 2-A. Elevator to your right."

The elevator was fitted elegantly with an upholstered bench. Peter's late boyfriend, Harold, used to make it a point of lighting gracefully upon such benches, when available, even for short trips. When Peter, with a silent glance, would remark on his need to sit, Harold always responded with a face that made him look both content and quizzical, his lips pursed like Tony Curtis's as Josephine in *Some Like It Hot*. It was the kind of subtle exchange, below the radar of elevator operators and most other people, that Peter missed keenly now, even twenty-three years after Harold's death. In fact, this was exactly the kind of party that they would have gone to together—and going together would have been the right way to do it, since many of the guests would undoubtedly be long-term couples.

Peter was single now—"famously single," according to Jonathan—but he'd always thought of himself as the marrying kind. He and Harold were together for seventeen years. In another era, black-tie evenings together at the ballet or opera, and dressed-up dinner partying and entertaining at home, in couples, were *de rigueur;* then AIDS fund-raisers and memorial services were; and then that whole way of life passed into eclipse. Harold and Jonathan's partner, Roberto, died the same year, as did fifty-three other men whom Peter knew well—men who might have become tennis partners, or housemates at the beach, or fellow members of a benefit committee. An entire foreground of assuring, if only penciled-in, history-to-come was erased in an instant, leaving everyone in that generation of gay men not only to mourn individuals but to scramble for entirely different, assuring histories-to-come. Peter scrambled all right, right into a new profession that allowed him—well, required him—therapeutically to reinvent himself.

For a long time he kept track of the dead by carrying around a list of their names, meant to honor them, but also to help him remember who was alive, including himself. In fact, Peter now sometimes thought of jacket-and-tie gatherings like this one, perhaps ungenerously, as reflective of a list *not* written down, of the men who'd survived not necessarily because they were lucky, but because they were indifferent to the pleasures and heresies of their own social revolution. They squeaked by and went on to become model gay boomers, and they paid their taxes and voted for the right candidates and were now really getting married; and that was all perfectly lovely. Yet their very respectability sometimes struck Peter as tinged with a certain smugness resulting from their choice of a new, safe, penciled-in history over things like pleasure and heresy—a choice that Peter inoculated himself against defiantly with fashion, as well as with continued, if modified, erotic adventure.

Famously single. The thought made him chuckle. He was secretly proud of being known for showing up at parties with men half his age. His hair was still dark; his face and body looked much younger than his age. (*Thank you, Uncle Malcolm's side of the fam-*

ily!) But he was also sad to be exiled from the kind of respectable-*and*-adventurous life he had carefully designed with Harold and expected to have forever. He had tried to recapture that life subsequently but to no avail, for two decades, with a string of guys he dated during his Merry Widower phase, which started a year after Harold's death; then with Nick, a nice man he partnered with for nine years, who developed problems with alcohol and drugs; and now with a whole new crew of sweeties, who tended to be younger, because, well, that's who was out there and available.

And that included Tyler, who went out with Peter sometimes "for fun" when his current boyfriend, Damiano, a fitness model, was out of town—though Peter well knew that a gig like Jonathan's would hardly be fun for anyone of Tyler's generation, which is why he'd decided to go alone. Jonathan's crowd registered genuine boyfriends and boyfriends-designate, and authenticated exes, and just-plain-friends of an appropriate age. Younger persons were seen as boy toys, or fashion accessories, or hustlers—generally not as peers, at least not until demonstrably on the path to a suitable career and/or a solid relationship with one of the clan.

When the elevator doors opened Peter found himself standing in a little hall where Jonathan was greeting arrivals.

"Darling!" said Jonathan, noticing his friend and sending a couple into the apartment. He was shorter and heavier than Peter, and had started shaving his head a few years before, when he began going gray. And he was looking a little more tired than usual. Peter chalked that up to the move.

"Welcome to my little shack!" Jonathan was wearing a green velvet jacket with pressed jeans, and an embroidered red cap that looked customary for the tribesmen of some mountainous region of Central Asia. He was enveloped as usual in a resinous and smoky-sweet fragrance that had been his favorite for the past few years.

"Wow, gorgeous," said Peter, stepping with Jonathan into the foyer and looking around. The walls were finished in persimmon enamel and hung with a series of Donald Sultan prints of black lemons. Beyond, through a graceful archway, was the living room, crowded with guests—a sea of gray suits and dark blue sport jackets. The room itself was elegant and inviting. Pieces of Jonathan's collection of American antiques were mixed with understated midcentury basics, upholstered in soft celadons, mosses, and jades. The rugs were contemporary.

"We did what we could," said Jonathan, in mock-exasperation. "What can I get you—some wine? I want to hear all about this 'brand mind' business." *W* had recently published a piece on Peter, calling him "one of the most persuasive architects of the planet's emerging 'brand mind.' "

Then the doorbell rang—more guests.

"I'll find the bar, baby," said Peter. "You go. We can do the tour later, when I'm fortified."

"Connor's here," added Jonathan. "Say hello to him."

As he entered the living room Peter was embraced by that sense of well-being associated with so-called "good" prewar buildings; a feeling enhanced, certainly, by expensive decoration and lighting—and Peter knew that Jonathan had splurged on both—but created in the first place by architects like Candela through the subtle play of volumes, the careful planning of circulation, and the canny deployment of details. Together, these help express the difference between affluence and mere money. Jonathan's place was as different from the comically indeterminate, open-plan apartments in the shiny new glass tower across the street as a poke in the ribs was from a nice massage, and perhaps the New Yorkers who lived in each kind of place were as different from each other, too.

The party was already bouncy. Two dozen conversations mingled in a gauzy din, while the recorded piano stylings of Oscar Peterson jazzed away in the background. Among the artworks were several large abstract paintings by Connor Frankel, a world-renowned artist in his eighties who was a friend of Jonathan's. Outside the double-glazed windows a glinting city shone resplendently.

With practiced geniality Peter began greeting people—men he rarely saw now, whose names he sometimes misremembered. "Sam, good to see you." "Charlie, how's that pretty puppy?" "Draper, congratulations—I saw you were nominated." "Kevin, hi! Gimme a sec so I can grab a drink—I mean 'Keith,' sorry! What am I saying?" The crowd included a lawyer for a large bank, the development director of an art museum, the vice president of an orchestra, several people from the film community, a few authors and journalists, a poet from a long-prominent family. It was early in the evening and navigation was still easy. As he squeezed through the crowd Peter nodded cordially at Connor Frankel himself, who was seated on the sofa with a much younger man. The two were talking with a small group of very respectful-looking people standing in front of them. Peter wasn't clear if Frankel saw him, but he wasn't going to intrude. He had met the artist a few times before and found him intimidating. There was Frankel's lofty spot in history as one of the grand masters of twentieth-century art and also the fact that he'd always been somewhat closeted, which Peter had mixed feelings about.

"Good to see you," said an art dealer Peter had known for years.

"Hey, Lawrence, you too," said Peter.

"Isn't your boyfriend with you tonight—the blond?"

"Tyler? No. And he's not my boyfriend."

"That's what you always say about your boyfriends!"

Peter gave the man's shoulder a warm squeeze and kept moving.

I keep coming to these things thinking I'll meet someone "appropriate" who's available and hot, he thought. *But I never do.*

He was grateful when Tyler did accompany him to events like this. With his young friend at his side, Peter felt less trapped by the habits of his generation; he had a conspirator against the thundering babyboomerishness of it all. He'd been thinking a lot about the baby boomers lately. They were looming large in a brand audit and study of "relevant signs in the mediasphere" he was doing for a client hoping to target the aging-but-active-boomer market for a body wash that was already a best seller among twentysomethings. Where are we with concepts of "young" and "clean" these days? Does clean mean fresh? Is fresh still sexy? Is sexy still good? Good in what way? And what about Canada? This is what Peter had been thinking about all day.

"All I wanted to do was look at her hair!"

"It was the star of the movie."

"And the wardrobe!"

"The off-the-shoulder thing?"

"*Brill*-iant."

A foursome was discussing *Charlie Wilson's War.* In passing, Peter attempted a contribution.

"And then ten minutes later she's wearing a burkha," he said.

"Yes!"

"You know," continued Peter, "I've always marveled at the way he uses that rich-lady Texas Baroque style to create the character *visually. . . .*"

One of them took a sip of wine.

"He?"

"Mike Nichols," said Peter. "The director."

There was a second-and-a-half of silence, then genial laughter. The discussion was about stars, not directors.

Peter smiled, nodding.

"Excuse me," he said. "Bar."

OK, got it—no one here for me tonight.

Through another archway was the dining room, where an elaborate buffet had been laid out, and beyond that the bar, which had been set up in the kitchen's breakfast nook.

Then again, he could be here and I wouldn't even know it. Harold always said I have this oblivious side. . . .

The bartender was a tall, dark-haired young man in his mid-twenties, dressed in a black button-front shirt.

"Hi, there," said Peter.

"Hey, what can I get for you?"

"A vodka would be terrific, please—ice, twist of lime. Actually, make it a double. I won't have to bother you so soon."

"No bother."

The bartender made the drink and handed it to Peter.

"Brilliant, thanks," said Peter. It was the slight awkwardness Peter was feeling at the party that kept him from registering the warmth of the young man's smile and the sparkle of his gray-blue eyes.

"Enjoy," said the bartender.

Peter peered across the crowd.

"The, uh, library?" he asked.

"Just on the other side of the living room," said the bartender, pointing.

"Ah, thanks," said Peter, raising his glass in a little toast. "I'm on the tour. I know there's gonna be a quiz."

That was a lame thing to say, thought Peter as he walked away.

Why did I say that? It sounds so ungenerous toward Jonathan—not that the guy was really listening to me or would even take it seriously. Why the hell do I say these things?

Twenty-plus years after Harold, Peter still found socializing as clunky as he had before Harold, when he was a small-town teenager with scant social grace. Years of experience had done little to make him any smoother, he felt, especially in gay circles like this. And the gay men of his age who were single? In addition to incurious, most of them were wounded, exhausted, or bitter, settled into an imperturbable equilibrium of self-acquaintance that seemed to preclude the mad, transformative ardors and intoxicating, pop-music highs that he still craved. He remembered, too, the shock, one day before meeting Nick, of realizing he knew essentially nothing about men—certainly not what everyone else seemed to know: that whether straight or gay they could be untrue. Before Harold, Peter had not dated at all, not even a high school sweetheart. He and Harold met in college, in the early '70s, just as both were coming out, and it was love at nearly first sight—"a marriage made in heaven," as his grandmother had always described her own long and storied marriage. And Peter and Harold's relationship did turn out to be a kind of heaven—not unbumpy, but elevated, resonant in a metaphysical way that made it feel, then and since, like myth. They framed pictures together, read Foucault together, attended protests together, boiled lobsters together, traveled to Machu Picchu together, blessed newborn nieces and nephews together. And still, in memory, Harold was the great love of Peter's life, his seductively wicked smile caught in the halcyon glow of an undying late-spring afternoon in Venice, the saint and prince with whom no mortal, perhaps, could ever compete.

Certainly not Nick, who craved drugs more than love, and certainly not the boys whom Peter saw now. And about the future, who could say? Failing heaven's help, Peter would gamely soldier on, trying to do what he imagined other people do: talk about yourself when asked, ask questions about the other person, find points of mutual interest, like Mike Nichols—or rather, Julia Roberts.

More greetings, as Peter kept navigating, then he entered the library, a gentleman scholar's retreat lined with custom-made bookcases holding artwork and objects, as well as books upon books.

Displayed beneath two large windows on a bank of built-in cabinets, spot-lit from the soffit above, were some of Jonathan's prize possessions: a commedia dell'arte mask, a miniature window from a Victorian dollhouse, a collection of antique Japanese pots; on a table nearby was a draft manuscript of T. S. Eliot's *Four Quartets,* mounted under a Plexiglas cube. While most folks in the room were chattering away about things like Broadway openings, beach houses, and skin treatments, some were focused on a TV newscast flickering from a screen tucked into a bookshelf, showing the fleshy, college-boy face of Henderson McCaw, the nation's newest demagogue. It was a broadcast that had been promoted for days in the media. A radio-talk-show-host-turned-TV-personality-and-populist-hero, McCaw had recently emerged a self-appointed champion of what he called "America's God-given right to listen to itself." He was interviewing a newly elected conservative senator from the Midwest, a former beauty queen who was rumored to be considering a run for the presidency.

"I don't mind using the word 'abomination' to describe same-sex marriage, because that's what I think it is," said the senator.

"And that's why we love ya," said McCaw. "You tell it like it is." He smiled and lit up the screen with a parody of cheer that seemed as needy as it was undergrad.

Not that McCaw was stupid or unsophisticated. His quick rise to prominence proved he was anything but. Somehow, more effectively than anyone else since McCarthy, McCaw had been able to exploit that enduring strain of the American psyche that is sometimes truly revolutionary, sometimes merely cranky—a strain that seeks always to get some real or imagined oppressor off the backs of decent people. He claimed several million followers and had begun appearing at rallies that were more revivalist than political in feel. "Shove it!" was McCaw's take on anything established, though the last thing he and his people seemed to call for was systemic thinking about social or economic realities, or careful analysis of exactly what to shove, and where, and how far, and why. McCaw's power was to mobilize a single emotion: the nostalgia for a simpler America that was either long gone or never existed. And that was more than sophisticated—it was priestly.

"And you go all the way, don't you, Senator?" said McCaw.

"You want to roll back civil unions and the legal benefits that go with them."

"That's right, Henderson, and for the same reason," said the senator. "I just feel—well, you know a lot of us feel—that we have to take America back." Some of the guests in Jonathan's library booed, in a light, party-friendly way.

The senator was wearing a red suit; McCaw was in dark blue. Behind them, through a large window, across a body of water, was the Statue of Liberty. The interview was apparently being televised from a makeshift studio or visitors' center on Ellis Island or somewhere in New Jersey.

"What does that mean, 'Take America back'?" declared one of the guests, a gray-haired lawyer in a suit and bow tie whose name Peter couldn't remember. "Take it back from whom, from what?" Some of the others laughed. "From the present day? From a nation of 320 million people? Why not take America back to the Stone Age?" More laughter. Then the lawyer turned to his partner who, like him, was wearing a bow tie. "It sounds like what hawks used to say about Vietnam: 'Bomb them back to the Stone Age!' "

The lawyer saw that Peter had overheard this last remark.

"Right?" he said. "What a dope."

Peter smiled back.

"You're right," said Peter. "But he *is* a dope with an audience. He's reaching people."

"With pure ignorance," said the lawyer.

"Well, yeah. But ignorance is *real,* sadly," said Peter. "It's powerful."

"Look at him," continued the lawyer. "Where is that, Liberty State Park?"

"It's actually the golf course *at* Liberty State Park, they said," said the lawyer's partner.

"Oh, perfect," said the lawyer.

"Look at the way that shot is composed," said Peter.

"I get the creeps when those people use the phrase 'Lady Liberty,' " said the lawyer, suddenly in a lighter mood. "Actually, I get the creeps when anybody does."

Peter snickered.

"Me too," he said. "But I wouldn't take this populist thing too lightly. God knows, the Europeans don't. It created Reagan, derailed Clinton—you know. . . ."

"At least we've got some smart thinkers on our side," said the lawyer's partner.

"I wish we had some killers on our side, too," said Peter. "If we expect to hold our own, we need some of that shit our fathers brought into World War Two."

The word "shit" made the partner wince.

"Ooh, baby!" said someone else nearby, in a campy accent. "Save some of that for me."

A round of snickers.

"Excuse me," said Jonathan, suddenly appearing. "May I flip this off?" He switched off the television before anyone could answer. "People, you are here to have fun. Eat, drink, and be merry, please! Inspect furniture."

The lawyer and his partner drifted off, while Jonathan pulled Peter close to him.

"Party, darling," said Jonathan.

"Yes, of course. Sorry," said Peter.

"Have you said hi to Connor?"

"I'm too scared."

"Don't be ridiculous. He's a pussycat. And now that he's decided to come out he's a changed man."

"Really? Details, please."

"All shall be revealed," said Jonathan, taking Peter by the arm. "But first you must see what we did in the master bath. I found some tesserae in Rome that are the absolute *point* of existence—recycled, seventeenth-century."

Two hours later, Peter was home in Brooklyn Heights. He was standing at his bathroom sink, drying his face with a white terrycloth towel and studying his reflection in the medicine cabinet mirror.

The hairline, stabilized for the moment. No further receding or thinning through the crown. And still no gray—except for a few in the sideburns, though only one or two new ones this year. More of those whiskery things in the eyebrows, which need more frequent trimming. And the nose hair, of course. Still—it could be worse.

He peered more closely, in a magnifying mirror mounted to the wall on an accordion arm. The light in the bathroom was bright white.

No wrinkling, even around the eyes—that's something! But a distinct fleshiness of the face that was never quite there before. Tiny new bumps on the forehead that probably admitted no pathology other than age. And, yes, some sag around the jaw and upper cheek, which a bit of gentle pushing, as in a surgical consultation, could momentarily counteract. What was that, a muscular issue? How much worse it would be, without the regular facial massage during bath time that Uncle Malcolm once recommended to a fascinated little boy!

It was still early. There was time for a nightcap in the garden, one of Peter's favorite things to do after a party, in all but the coldest months. He applied some moisturizer.

In all, still plausible. And with a few drops of the expensive facial serum and the right haircut, completely possible.

Somehow, though he could also afford face work and knew plenty of men who'd taken that step, Peter had never seriously considered surgery. He knew that the flesh had matured a bit, but saw no reason to stop conceiving of himself as essentially the same person who had moved into the apartment thirty-odd years before. And even when a random reflection or cell phone photograph clearly showed *diminishment* and reminded him of the kind of aging that was in force when he was a boy, which made all his aunts and uncles go elderly years before Peter's age now, he never thought, *Gee, I'm old.* Peter knew that that kind of aging no longer applied to a huge swath of the population. Demographics said that old people were staying fitter and living more healthily; psychographics said that they were embracing greater expectations about their later years—the expectations themselves serving partly to protect people from certain effects of aging. Wouldn't anybody who could naturally cling as long as possible to some of the same expectations they'd always had, whether noble—"I will one day write a novel," "I will once again fall in love"—or silly—"I will grow my hair long next fall or maybe even go blond"? Though Peter knew that falling in love again probably belonged in both categories.

Conceptually, he had no problem with aging. As a child he always envisioned himself at the exciting age of fifty, which since he'd been born in 1953 meant just after the year 2000—the Future!— and which, for the first two decades of his life, meant a golden age promised by science fiction, when everyone, at least according to comic books like *Mystery in Space* and *Strange Adventures,* would go about in flashy jumpsuits, weirdly exhilarated. Then later, in college, fifty began to look like a different kind of golden age, when one might live quietly in a shack on a lake, with a shaggy lutenist and a couple of Labrador retrievers. Personally, he'd always found that aging made most men more attractive, and he believed, knowing himself to be not particularly handsome, that he might well have benefited from the process, while also going to the gym every day, taking his vitamins, and learning what worked for him clothing-wise, year after year.

He was aware, of course, that American culture and gay life were pitilessly youth-oriented, but he'd never suffered from this professionally or socially. And any lingering concerns that might have been developing about taking his clothes off with younger men had been dispelled a few years before, on Fire Island, at the Pines beach house he shared every summer with Jonathan. Three visitors arrived one weekend: a friend of Jonathan's, a distinguished surgeon who was around their age, and two cute, skinny, muscular boys, both in their early twenties—the surgeon's boyfriend and the boyfriend's best friend. Both boys were fun and warm, both had real jobs and career goals; and over the weekend the single boy and Peter hit it off. Then on Sunday, after the guests departed, Peter confided gleefully to Jonathan that he'd had sex with the boy, but confessed surprise that the boy had been so into him, physically. Jonathan replied adamantly. "Dope! The boys who want older men want you because of your body, not in spite of it."

Peter decided to make the leap of faith. After that, he allowed himself to accept the term "daddy" for himself, if someone used it. He decided to ignore his Freudian-based objection to the term and the specter, from an ancient newsreel, of a venerable, white-bearded Ezra Pound striding over the heath with a walking stick.

Also, the cock is great and the feet are in good shape—that's something, too. Old men can get such grossly gnarled feet.

Peter changed into sweats and heavy socks, and poured himself a drink. He opened the door to the garden and stood there, letting the cold night air stream in. It was probably too cold to go out and sit.

"My little house," he said out loud, in a kind of baby talk that he and Harold used to share. Outside, a few steps from a small iron porch led down to a sizable garden with a patio, which his landlady tended diligently but rarely used. As a joke, Peter liked to tell people that he lived in a single-family house with his live-in gardener. The garden, now mostly bare, still looked inviting in a late-fall way. The hosta was all gone, leaving patches of bare earth and slightly stranded-looking shrubs, but the hydrangea along the back wall were still blooming, and yellowed leaves still clung to the dogwood that dominated the part of the garden nearest the house.

It was a one-bedroom apartment that occupied the parlor floor of a hundred-and-fifty-year-old Federal brick row house, the top two floors of which were occupied by Peter's landlady of thirty-seven years. The place was best described as shabby chic. Boasting immaculately restored original details like plank floors and plaster moldings, and thoughtful improvements like the bank of multi-paned windows and a glass door onto the garden, the apartment had been his and Harold's home, and then Peter's alone. Harold died there, having returned to more loving surroundings after a yearlong decline in the hospital. Though the apartment was modest in comparison to Jonathan's, it boasted what Peter always called "good bones"—and a garden that, in Peter's book, was worth two or three extra rooms anywhere else. Over the years he'd made the place more comfortable, shifting out most of the inexpensive basics with which he and Harold had set up house and bringing in more adult furniture, serious cookware, and custom-made wooden blinds. The place had been Peter's home now for longer than any other place he had ever lived—far longer than the house he grew up in, a modest subdivision split-level built by his father in 1954, where Peter lived for sixteen years, before going off to college. The Brooklyn apartment had thus seen the vast bulk of Peter's life unfold and also acquired a certain psychic heft, as now, on some nights, in primal dreams where mysterious forces repel and attract a dreamer along pathways of shadowy spaces, the place seemed to warp itself, by some cellular logic, into Dad's split-level castle and even, Peter suspected, the womb.

It does mean something that we wound up here—that I stayed here, Peter thought.

It was only the third place that he and Harold looked at, and the nicest house on the block.

"That's it," said Harold, when they were still several doors away. The realtor had shown him around once already and told the landlady he and Peter were "very nice and very interested." Harold clasped Peter on the shoulders and did a little dance as they sped up to approach the stoop.

"It *is* nice," said Peter.

It was a steamy day in June. They'd arrived in Brooklyn only two weeks before, to stay with friends until they found a place of their own. Harold was starting a job at the *Times*—which would undoubtedly lead to better and better jobs there—while Peter was still writing poetry. Both were wearing T-shirts and cut-off jeans. Peter's shirt was appliquéd with a pink ice cream cone and Harold's proclaimed "Cabbage Is a Good Thing" in Russian.

The landlady, Angela, showed them around. Everybody liked everybody else and agreed that white was much better for the place than the shocking yellow and orange of the previous tenants. The dogwood hadn't even been planted in the garden yet.

"But can we afford it?" said Peter, afterward. The rent was $25 a month more than the budget they'd agreed on.

"We have to look at this in the long term, Peter," said Harold, beaming. In this and in all other things, his boyfriend's determination, which balanced prudence and optimism, made Peter so proud—to love such a man!

And the place was still a rental, decades later, though at ten times the original rate. Peter, thus far in his life, had been perfectly content not to own a home and to remain in this one, even if it wasn't gigantic or lavish—though his recent financial success had opened up the question of a place, perhaps, upstate.

Would Harold have been pleased to know that Peter was still living in the same place, years later? Peter smiled—and wondered if he would have been anything like the man he was now, if Harold had lived. Would he and Harold have slipped into the same kind of gray-flannel adulthood as Jonathan's crowd, buying property, consolidating security? Maybe. And of course it wouldn't have been so terrible to go on taking care of each other and of their little segment of society, the way those men did—though adultness itself had evolved so astonishingly, over the decades! Peter realized that since first laying eyes on his garden at twenty-two, when he was already an adult, he and the rest of the world had effectively lived at least three additional lifetimes, from childhood to adulthood, with the coming of three technological game-changers—computers, the Internet, and cell phones—each of which had forced a full mental cycle that began in naïve excitement and finished in smug sophistication. The resultant shift, personal as much as cultural, was far headier, he thought, than the one his grandfather used to describe, between the horse and the automobile. The same period, of course, saw the ebb of space exploration, supersonic transport, and network television—civilization, in fact, being a lot like himself: the same as before, but different.

He stood at the door, letting himself relax. The garden was as quiet as it got, in its annual cycle. During the other three seasons, across neighbors' fences at night came the sounds of air conditioners, or friends enjoying an al fresco drink, or the little kids down the block who should be in bed, playing in their yard. But starting then, in mid-October, the garden echoed at night only with the whisper of chill and rustle of sharp winter stars, and for Peter this had always been a kind of music, both exciting and terrifying. Would it ever be warm again? Would the sun and sunny times ever return? Could we really protect ourselves from the barrenness we feel encroaching at this time of year? He had heard this music first as a child of seven or eight, when asked by his parents to take the garbage out, one dark late-fall night after dinner; walking with no coat across the yard to the garbage can, the sound of a dog barking coming from several houses away, a vast precariousness thundering above and beneath him, above and beneath them all; his subdivision being the farthest extent of their little upstate town, before miles of thick woods and a mass of dark hills that crashed up against the sky. And he heard the music again when he stood with Harold at Machu Picchu's *Intihuatana* stone, the "hitching post of the sun," to which Inca priests ritually tied the sun to halt its dangerous progress away from men; instantly and with a shudder Peter felt the power of ancient sun worship. And even now he found slightly distasteful the cheer of weathercasters who bantered lightly about the coming end of daylight savings, a time when the slow and comprehensibly steady slide into life's precariousness takes a stupid, man-made jerk forward, for reasons no one seemed to understand anymore.

Yet there was ecstasy in those chill harmonies. Tuning into planetary cycles felt like liberation from the strictures of civilization, even if it was civilization that kept us alive.

"Now this is more like existence as I understand it, eh?" said Harold, as they stood in the roofless ruins of the Inca temple, looking out over the Urubamba Valley, shading their eyes with their hands, squinting.

" 'High reef of the human dawn,' " said Peter, quoting Neruda, from one of the scores of books they'd devoured in preparation for the trip to Peru. It was early morning, before the day tourists arrived; they'd spent the night at the site's tiny guesthouse. Morning brightness pressed down to meet the jutting peak they stood upon.

"We've always been here and we always will be, Peter."

That moment did feel eternal—and moments are perhaps the only places where one can look for eternity. Peter knew from the start that Harold had heard the same thunder in Elmhurst, Queens, that he had heard in the mountains up north, and that was the bedrock of their bond. And that thunder was in bed with them that night in Peru, as they made love beneath overlaundered blankets on a squeaky bed in a drafty hotel room in Aguas Calientes; and it was with them on all the other nights they ever spent together, including the last, when Peter sat up faithfully past midnight with a nurse and Harold's sister, in that same room in Brooklyn Heights where he now stood, and Harold, shortly before the end, mute and skeletal, woke from a nap and looked at Peter in wonder, still in command of some vital bit of knowledge, though the rest of his faculties had slipped away weeks before.

When Peter confessed to Jonathan, at the housewarming, that he'd been feeling lonely, despite all the dates with young men, Jonathan nodded gently.

"Look," he said, "it will take a while to find someone on your wavelength."

"It's been twenty years."

"Yes, and it may never happen again."

They were in the new bathroom. Peter ran his fingers over a band of golden antique tesserae that had been set into a wall of watery green glass tile.

"I feel . . . exiled from my own life," he said.

"Coraggio," whispered Jonathan.

Peter gave Jonathan a little kiss on the cheek and marveled how good his friend smelled. The fragrance was Black Tourmaline, Jonathan said. It had been designed to encapsulate the talismanic qualities of the mineral black tourmaline, which was used to ward off evil energies. Peter hoped the talisman would work. Among the other things that Jonathan told him as they chatted in the bathroom was that a couple of recent PSA tests and a prostate exam—his first, now that he was in his early sixties—had "turned up something." A bit had been snipped and was being biopsied. Jonathan was hoping for the best. He was going in for a scan the very next day.

CHAPTER 2

Even before the party was over, Will had tidied up Jonathan's kitchen. When Jonathan appeared to announce that the last guests were gone, Will had finished turning the bar back into a breakfast nook.

"Golly," said Jonathan. The sink and counters were clear and the dishwasher was churning.

"The leftover food's in the refrigerator," said Will. "I stacked all the glasses in their trays, back by the service door. And . . . you recycle, don't you?"

"Oh, yes."

"That's what I thought. So the bottles are in the trash room, in that big blue bin." Will looked around. "I think that's everything."

"Awesome. You're the best bartender ever," said Jonathan. "Sorry people stayed so late."

"No problem," said Will.

It was just after midnight. The housewarming had gone on much longer than Jonathan planned for. He pulled off his cap and rubbed his head.

"Sure I can't give you a few hors d'oeuvres to take home?" said Jonathan. "Some crab?"

"Oh, no—but thank you," said Will.

Jonathan handed him a small white envelope.

"I stuck in a little extra. You did a really great job, Will."

"Thanks, it was fun."

"Thank *you*. I was so glad to get your number and the glowing recommendation."

"Yeah, he's a great guy."

"You know, he always throws this little Christmas party. Maybe he can use you. . . ."

"He's already asked me—you know, to bartend."

"Wonderful, wonderful."

"You have great friends."

"Thanks, yeah, they're a good bunch. I'm a lucky man."

"How long have you been in New York?"

"Ooh—thirty-some years, now. Since the seventies."

"I guess it takes time to build up a network of friends like that."

"Well, sure," said Jonathan tentatively, not sure where Will was going. "I mean, friends happen. All you have to do is be ready."

Will made a mock-cowering face.

"I *guess* I'm ready," he said. "I just got here, in New York."

"Oh, from where?"

"L.A. I went to school in San Francisco. My family's from Santa Barbara."

"Uh-huh. And what are your plans?"

"A job, a life."

"Perfect. In that order? What kind of job are you looking for?"

"Magazines."

"Editing?"

"Editing, writing. I did a few things for *San Francisco Magazine*."

"What kind of things?"

"Movie reviews, restaurant reviews. Celebrity interviews."

"Oh? What celebrities?"

"Music, mostly. People who played the big venues—Beyoncé, Carole King, Ringo Starr."

"Hmm, cool. Well, with those clips you should certainly be able to find *some*thing."

"I hope so."

"You will. Just keep pushing."

* * *

Thirty minutes later, Will was standing in RecRoom, a lounge-y gay bar in Hell's Kitchen, themed like a '60s suburban basement recreation room. A stop there was technically on Will's way home to Astoria, since he had to go up to Times Square, anyway, to catch the 7, and RecRoom wasn't all that far away from the subway. He was tired and craved some lively company after the gig at Jonathan's place.

He had gotten a beer and parked himself in a strategic position across from the bar, at the end of a high wood-paneled counter, near a vintage ceramic lamp with a grasscloth shade. The place was indeed lively but not packed, since this was a weekday night, and the crowd was as expected: no one over thirty-five, everyone in neat shirts and sweaters, sporting neat-but-not-too-neat hairdos. A Rihanna remix, cranked up to the max, was working hard to displace every cubic inch of space not already occupied by people, furniture, and drinks.

"Hey," said a skinny boy wearing a narrow tie, who was suddenly standing next to Will.

"Hey," said Will, smiling.

"Scott," said the boy.

"Hi, Scott, Jonathan," said Will.

"Hi, Jonathan."

"I like your tie."

"Thanks! I love this song!"

"Yeah, it's great!"

And they said nothing further to each other, as Scott was suddenly off chatting with another boy, and anyway, Will was focused on a handsome guy with longish hair, at the bar, with whom he had shared a look a few minutes before, when they were both ordering drinks. The guy, who was chatting with friends, knew Will was watching, and Will knew that lots of other guys were watching him.

Will stood out, even in a crowd like this. He was more than cute; he was handsome in a square-jaw, strong-nose kind of way. Just over six feet tall, with a shock of styled-but-not-too-styled black hair, he possessed a bright, easy smile that dimpled his cheeks and made him look approachable—like he was having fun. Having pulled off, in the cab on the way to RecRoom, the button-front shirt he'd worn for Jonathan's party, he was now in a tight gray T-shirt that emphasized the gray-blue of his eyes and revealed the differential between his broad shoulders and narrow, athletic waist.

And he *was* having fun. After only six months in New York, he still found gay life in the city *lots* of fun, even the parts of it that were glitzy, or tawdry, or palpably bridge-and-tunnel. He liked the energy in New York, and, at twenty-eight, he was ready for anything.

"Hi!" screamed a boy in a little hat, holding a tumbler with a straw.

"Hello," said Will.

"Hi, hi! Aren't you Romy's friend?" The friends whom the boy had been talking with, nearby, watched eagerly for the outcome of this exchange.

"Umm, nope," said Will.

"Romy—Haitian Romy! Romaine!"

"Sorry."

"Oh—OK." And the boy went back to his friends.

Will took another sip of his beer. He liked the vibe at Rec-Room—it was relaxed, unforced. He liked that the place seemed designed to make you feel at home, among family and friends, which was much better than the supposedly super-hip gay bars that made you feel like you were part of a performance installation in an art gallery or trendy retail establishment; or the ones that were so popular with the older generation and had become a kind of national gay-bar vernacular, the garages, warehouses, and bunkers that made you feel like you needed an anonymous hookup, even if that wasn't necessarily what you came for. Will had heard that there were even a few bars of an earlier vintage, from the '50s and '60s, still grinding away, somewhere in New York: the Village piano bars peddling good times behind semi-closed doors, gin-and-Judy-style, and the clubbier, uptown establishments with discreetly unmarked doors, that were more like old-school cocktail parties, for the jacket-and-tie crowd. Will had no idea what kind of feelings those places might evoke, but they did sound like weird fun—living history! The city as museum! Will wasn't quite sure, in fact, what he was looking for, when he went out—friends? Fuckbuddies? A boyfriend? At least this was a real place to go, instead of the computer.

"A life and a job" is what he had told Jonathan he was seeking, but a boyfriend was somewhere in there, too. Will had grown up in the sunny embrace of upper-middle-class comfort in Santa Barbara, and through college and afterward had remained close to his tight-knit family, especially his mom and two younger sisters. After graduating with a degree in English, he had stuck around Berkeley and drifted among a series of genteel but not precisely career-track jobs in magazine publishing. He went out with other gay guys sometimes, but often preferred to hang out with his girlfriends or spend time with his family—that was fun, easy. And it had been easy to drift on like this, year after year, since the parents were always happy to help out with some rent, or a car, or a skiing trip. Yet during the previous year Will had begun to feel a sort of disturbing compression between his current life and whatever was supposed to come next, as well as an alarming decompression between his sunny childhood and the present, which was distinctly cloudy. His most recent job, the one in Los Angeles he had left to come to New York for, had put a question in Will's mind and focused it with a clarity that felt both exciting and scary: *Where the hell am I supposed to be going with my life?*

It was a job that Will aced: executive assistant to the very pressured head of a magazine publishing company, a woman he liked and respected, who took a liking to him. Though full of tense moments resulting from huge responsibilities, the job allowed Will to "overdeliver," as his boss liked to say, through good judgment, attention to detail, and willingness to remain on-duty after hours. The boss valued Will's efforts, and he came to value the opportunity to serve and observe someone so fiercely dedicated to her company and its mission—someone whose own personal mission seemed fused with the arc of her career. Working for this woman, Will came to think he should have a mission, too—but wondered why he didn't already have one, and if twenty-eight was too late to discover one.

Once, Will asked his boss if she had always been so driven.

"No. I was always smart," she said. "I had good habits—you know, work hard, keep your promises, all that. But I remember clearly, one day on my first job, at a company in New York, going up in the elevator with some coworkers—we were all entry-level—

and somebody joked about 'Who cares how good that report is? Let's just get it off our desks by noon.' And I said, '*I fucking care*'—and it felt like such a powerful thing to say, so adult. And that thing above all, Will, is the key to success."

"I see," said Will. The ideas were not new to him; his parents had told him as much. But somehow, in the passionate words of his boss, the ideas took on urgency.

"And I look for this quality, now, whenever I do a deal or hire someone," she continued.

"You do?"

"Absolutely," she said. "And I saw it in you."

"You did?"

It was a powerful moment for Will, and he planned the move to New York as a kind of catalyst for his life, even if he had no exact plan to follow.

Later, when his boss asked if he was moving to New York "with anyone or to be with anyone," he felt sad to say no. It suddenly felt odd, though he'd already attended the weddings of several high school and college friends, that he had not yet been in love himself, really *in love*. During his mid- and late twenties he'd dated two or three guys semi-seriously, but wound up wondering, months later, what he had ever seen in them, besides good looks. Still, no sweat, nothing lost. Then there was a relationship that lasted for two years, with a handsome man slightly older than Will, a movie studio executive with a glass penthouse in Century City and a fifty-five-foot Ferretti docked at Marina del Rey. They were trophy boyfriends for each other, and Will understood that, and then the excitement of the first few months gave way to more domestic concerns and questions about the future. When he and the movie guy broke up, that *did* seem like a loss, though Will couldn't figure out exactly why, beyond the generic reason of incompatibility he gave his sisters and girlfriends. It should have worked, Will thought, and he didn't know what directions might be open to him, other than trophyism, until he started interviewing music stars for his magazine assignments. Many of these were true artists and big spirits, despite all the celebrity, who were telling Will that love did matter, that it was possible and changed everything. It wasn't only about looks and it started with *you*.

Did people still have that kind of love? Was it possible for him, or had his generation been programmed away from it? The laxness of his California gay friends in finding "the one" finally proved too annoying. "Oh, something'll happen, someday," they laughed. "Eff love, anyway—who cares?" Which sounded wrong to Will. Happily echoing his boss he said, "*I* fucking care."

The music in RecRoom shifted from R&B to trip-hop to classic disco. Will felt himself happily swaying along.

> *I'm not just another crazy bitch*
> *To have an itch for you, baby*
> *I'd rather take a cap than see you turn your back*

The long-haired guy, still over by the bar, caught Will's eye again, then moved off, with a knowing look, toward the hallway where the phones and restrooms were. Will followed, and found the guy in one of the small one-at-a-time restrooms, the door to which he had left ajar. Will slipped in and shut the door behind him. Without a word Will pressed the guy into the wall and the two began kissing. It was a warm, hungry embrace, amplified by the groping of pecs and crotches, which quickly led to cocks out and then a brief turn each, on knees, with cock in mouth. Then, after more kissing, the other guy took hold of Will's cock and jerked him off, in less than a minute.

Cum flew onto the floor, and there was a moment when the two bodies relaxed. Will's halfhearted attempt to get the other guy to let him jerk him off fizzled. Silently, the guy put away his cock and wiped his hand with a paper towel, then gave Will a quick pat on the shoulder and walked out.

And Will felt fine about all this. He'd scored the cutest guy in the bar and could now go home, as he had been dying to do—though on his way out of the bar, a few minutes later, he saw several other guys he would have talked to, if only it hadn't been so late and he weren't so tired.

When he arrived home, around two, Will found his roommate, Luz, still up.

"Hey," he said.

"Hi, hon," said Luz. She was sitting at the kitchen table, tapping away on her laptop.

"Writing?"

"Big day tomorrow."

Luz was in law school. She was a few years younger than Will. They'd been friends since Berkeley and were living together now as an economy measure. The place they found for themselves was a five-room, second-floor apartment in a large, formerly single-family home on a tree-lined street in Astoria, still owned by the original family. The landlady, a middle-aged Greek widow, liked her new tenants, and visited them frequently with gifts of dolmades and baklava.

Will poured himself a glass of club soda.

"How was your gig?" asked Luz.

"Easy," said Will.

"And long. You just getting out?"

"I went for a drink afterward."

"A big gay drink?" It was a phrase they used when Will invited Luz, who was straight but between boyfriends, to join him for a cocktail in Chelsea or Hell's Kitchen.

"Exactly."

"I thought the party *was* gay."

"It was—*way*."

"But?"

"No but. Just older guys. I needed to see some younger faces before coming home."

"Working tomorrow?" asked Luz. Will was currently temping, through an agency.

"Nope—day after," he said. "Tomorrow, I'm sleeping in."

"Bitch."

The next morning, Peter was busy in his office, working on a tagline, when Tyler appeared at the door. He was dressed sharply in a brown Prada jacket, skinny blue jeans, and good shoes. He and Peter were pitching a client, later in the day.

"How'd it go?"

"The party? Fine." Peter waved Tyler in.

"Yeah? Did I miss anything?"

"Cracked crab, baby."

"Oooh!"

"But it was dull. Not *dull,* but—well, you know what I mean."

"How'd you look?"

"Like everybody else."

"What a triumph."

"Anyway, are we set for the meeting? The projections?"

"The tech guy's setting up right now in the Den."

"And the video—the new edit?"

"Done, in my office."

Actually, "office" was not the way their work spaces were referred to, in the agency's official jargon. They were "executive pods." It was the parent company's idea. Peter had sold his agency, the year before, to one of the big global advertising conglomerates. He and his team now were housed in a complex of work spaces in the company's newly renovated headquarters, on five floors of a boxy office building on Madison Avenue. For years, the headquarters took the form of the usual warren of offices and cubicles; then it was transformed, by gutting all five floors down to the structural steel, into a "three-dimensional hive of supercharged creativity," as *Ad Week* described it. Now, when the elevator opened onto the twenty-first floor and a visitor stepped off to approach the expansive, white plastic, sculptural installation that served as a reception desk, she looked up into a vast, multistory atrium that unified several levels and was crisscrossed by an erector set of stairways and ramps, punctuated with landings and balconies, and studded with a variety of seating pods and large-scale, cutting-edge artworks. On the periphery were more private meeting and work spaces, with names like "Temple," "Nest," and "Arena." There were even a few plain-old offices, for the company's big bosses.

Peter's part of the complex was designed to be "like home" and had the formulated realness of a sitcom set. Comprising a kitchen, "living room," and gym, in addition to work pods and the Den, the place wrapped around a loggia halfway up into the corporate maze, chiefly on what had been the twenty-third floor. The aerie looked out into the atrium, affording views of people going between levels, clients waiting, way down *there,* whiz kids taking a moment to clear their heads, way over *there*. Throughout the hive, people spoke quietly. Every so often laughter could be heard echoing through the atrium, and when there was no human sound at all there was the barely audible *whusshh* of massive amounts of air being circulated by a dramatically exposed system of ductwork.

As Peter was chatting with Tyler the phone rang. It was Laura, the company's vice president for business development. She had one of the few conventional offices, on the twenty-fifth floor.

"I have to take this," said Peter.

"Hey, are we on for tonight?" said Tyler.

Peter nodded yes and mimed texting, and the boy took off.

"Laura, darling." Peter swiveled around in his chair, to gaze out the interior window in back of his desk, into the atrium.

"Wanna hear something funny?" Her voice sounded perpetually, if superficially, cheerful, and she never started phone calls with a greeting, as if a conversation were already in progress—a habit that put the other person in the somewhat defensive position of having to know instantly who was calling and what it was about.

"Always," said Peter.

"I just got off the phone with McCaw's people."

"Henderson McCaw?"

"He's leaving Fox and starting his own media company. They're looking for someone to rebrand the whole thing—TV, Internet, radio, documentaries, live events."

"Amusing idea. So?"

"You'd be perfect for it."

"I doubt that very much. And how are you today?"

"And they wanna start deep with the DNA, Peter."

"Whose DNA?"

"Their message, their thinking—and the national mood. And the global mood. They're not just thinking national; they're thinking global."

"Like the Taliban."

"I'll have their plan in my hands by the end of the day."

"C'mon. Don't you think they should have someone who likes the guy?"

"I don't know—don't you like him?"

"I think he's—Laura, he's basically Satan."

"Now..."

"He's completely ignorant, for one thing."

"No, he's anything but that and you know it. The point is, this could mean millions of dollars in billings. It would be one of our biggest accounts."

"You can get somebody else, easily. I'm not the only genius in this joint."

"You're the one he wants to talk to, Peter."

"Me? Specifically?"

"Apparently, he loves the talking car."

Laura said she was going to meet with McCaw's people preliminarily and get a clearer idea of the scope of the project. Peter agreed to think about the assignment, but said he wasn't promising anything. Good advertising involved the ability—and willingness—to think exactly like a client, to feel his hopes and fears as symbiotically as possible, while mapping these emotions dispassionately onto a) market realities, and b) the collective unconscious. Going deep in this way—into the individual's quest for wellness through personal hygiene, as Peter did for a facial tissue, for example, or her birthright of easy breathing and clean air, as he did for a sinus medicine—could be an interesting venture and a rewarding one; at times, it even felt noble. But diving into the panic McCaw was stirring up felt dangerous to Peter. The values McCaw espoused on Fox were backward and hateful, yes, and success in the assignment would probably mean the propagation of those values. But the underlying dissatisfactions McCaw exploited—including, perhaps, a certain existential rage at the limits of life itself—seemed deeper than Peter wanted to go, personally, for any assignment.

Yet that limit alone, now that it had arisen, was also slightly intriguing.

Peter went on with his morning—writing copy, returning calls, making some notes for the afternoon's client meeting. Then, just before noon, Jonathan called. He was in the neighborhood. Could he take Peter to lunch at Fred's or somewhere?

"What are you doing up here?" asked Peter, cheerfully. "Shopping?"

"My new urologic oncologist is on Park."

"Oh," said Peter. Alarm clutched his stomach.

"Yeah," said Jonathan. "Not good."

"Shit."

"Listen, if you're busy, we can talk later."

"No, no—I'm good. This is a good time," said Peter. "I'm glad you called. I've been worried about you. I do have a thing here at the office at three, but—you wanna meet now? I'm walking out the door."

Barneys was empty and Fred's still quiet when Peter arrived. The hostess, a gorgeous dark-haired girl in big heels and a little black dress, took Peter straight to Jonathan, who was installed at one of the tables by the big windows along Madison Avenue.

"Your e-mail was so sweet," said Jonathan.

"It was a fantastic party," said Peter. "I just hope *you* had a good time."

Jonathan barely rose and the two men kissed. Peter silenced his iPhone as he sat down.

"Why do I know I'm also going to receive one of those delicious Pineider cards of yours in the mail?" said Jonathan.

"Because . . . I wasn't raised in a barn?" said Peter.

With a flourish he unfolded the napkin and draped it over his lap.

"Everyone wants to know why you showed up alone," said Jonathan.

"I'm a lonely old bachelor, that's why," said Peter. "And I doubt anyone was paying attention to me."

"You're not that lonely. You do have your young ward, after all."

"His boyfriend is in town."

"I thought you were sweet on him."

"Tyler? Jonathan, I'm not even attracted to him in that way. He's just fun. A valued coworker."

"You like his *energy*."

"Exactly. God knows, I haven't had real sex in I don't know how long."

"No?"

"I talk about boys, I go out with 'em, but I'm not gettin' any love anywhere."

"Well, maybe we should do something about that."

"Like what—get me a hustler?"

Jonathan made a squeaky "maybe" sound.

"No," continued Peter. "I have to face the awful truth that my standards have gotten stratospherically high, in my old age."

He instantly heard his words about the "awful truth" in context and felt a pang of regret. Normal chitchat was suddenly over.

"Don't worry," sighed Jonathan, as a pair of stylish women sailed past, following the hostess to a table. "*Oh,* this is so exhausting."

"Tell me everything," said Peter.

"OK." Jonathan took a breath. "From boys to cancer. It might be stage four. It looks like it is."

Peter winced.

"No."

"Yeah."

"Damn."

"I was at Sloan-Kettering all morning."

"And?"

"You can see it in the scans. It's gone into the bone—you know, the spine. It's 'aggressive'—that's the word they're using. And remember I was having this little ache in my back . . . ?"

"Ugh."

"I thought maybe I pulled something in the gym. My trainer gave me some stretches for it." Jonathan shook his head. "Funny, huh?"

"What's the next step?"

"Chemo, radiation. They're figuring it out. But we're going to start doing something fast." Jonathan managed a wan smile. "We're going to be aggressive, too."

"Good."

"There's this place in Cleveland—superspecialists—where they want to send me for a consult."

"OK."

"It's not gonna be much fun, this next year."

"No."

"And they're clearly not too optimistic, either—though there's such a reassuring language around all this."

They were silent for a moment, then Jonathan continued.

"The word 'options.' There are always *options*—apparently even for people who will be dead by next summer."

"They're making advances all the time," said Peter quietly.

"Are they? In prostate cancer?"

There was anger in Jonathan's voice, and fear.

"I'm totally here for you, no matter what," said Peter.

"I know you are, darling—thank you," said Jonathan, attempting to brighten. "Could you possibly go through the treatment for me and pay for it, as well?"

Peter smirked.

"I'm sorry," said Jonathan. "That came out wrong."

"It's OK," said Peter. "I know you have insurance."

"Oh, yes—a million-dollar cap," said Jonathan. "The doctor says I probably won't burn through that, in one bout of anything. Very comforting—the thought being that I might not need insurance after that."

Jonathan shook his head. Just then a waiter arrived, with two enormous menus.

"Can I get you gentlemen started with something? A bottle of water?"

"You sure can," said Jonathan. "A bottle of Fiuggi, please. And do you have any dry sherry? I would kill for a few sips of Manzanilla."

The waiter smiled slyly.

"I'll see what I can do," he said. "For you, sir?"

"Better not, thanks," said Peter. "Oh, wait—on second thought, make it two sherries."

"Very civilized," said Jonathan.

"Yeah—if they have it," said Peter. "Watch him come back and ask if Dry Sack is OK."

"It's so funny," said Jonathan, sitting back in his chair and slightly repositioning his silverware. "You live through AIDS, Vietnam, 9/11; you eat well, you take care of yourself—all so you can live long enough to start facing the diseases that are waiting out there for old men, anyway. . . ."

"We're not invulnerable, are we?"

"But, darling, I thought I was! What's the point of buying a new house and doing it up, if not to live there blissfully and safely, forever and ever?"

A spray of midday sun, tinctured with a steely glare reflecting off the glass building across the street, was fingering through the latticework screens covering the windows. Traffic on Madison pushed uptown sluggishly.

The waiter arrived with the water, took their order.

"Did you know that Michelangelo was cured of kidney stones at Fiuggi?" said Jonathan.

"I did not," said Peter.

"He was. Wouldn't it be nice to have the kind of ailment that one went to a spa to cure?"

Besides being a filmmaker and a collector of pots and manuscripts, Jonathan was a war vet. As a young man he'd been drafted and sent to Vietnam. He told Peter about it once, soon after they first met, in the '70s, without many details, and never mentioned it again. Jonathan had come from a poor family from Queens with low expectations. They hadn't been able to avoid the draft, like richer, better educated people did, and Jonathan vowed, once he returned home, to go back to school and find a path through life that exposed him to less risk and more of the blessings of American liberty. A thread running through all the documentaries he did, especially a well-known series probing the lives of living artists, explored themes of self-invention, self-permission-giving—self-liberation.

"I take it you didn't have any symptoms," said Peter.

"Well, the back stuff," said Jonathan. "And I've lost a little weight recently, felt a little under par. I chalked it up to work."

"How's it going, by the way?"

"The film is going. We're set to start shooting in January—we *were* set. I suppose it's anybody's guess what's going to happen now."

"You'll see how it goes."

"Sure, but I've got to get this done, Peter. It took me twenty years to talk him into it."

Jonathan's current project was a profile of Connor Frankel, the painter who'd attended his party the night before. A homosexual gentleman of the old school, Frankel was extremely private and had never come out publicly. He and another well-known artist had been lovers in the '50s, yet history books took little note of this fact, let alone of the influence that an emerging gay imagination might have had on the artists' revolutionary work. Frankel, now in his eighties, was finally willing to talk.

"You'll figure it out. You'll get some help. It's a very important project."

The waiter delivered the appetizers and wished the men *Bon appétit*.

"It's interesting," mused Jonathan, picking up a fork. "My next film turned into my last film, this morning—*if* I'm lucky."

In the hour that followed, the restaurant filled up, lunch got noisier, and one sherry turned into two. The two friends talked of politics, space exploration, and the number of cable TV cooking shows devoted to cake. The conversation raced from subject to subject, perhaps a bit more rapidly than usual.

Afterward, on the sidewalk, they hugged and said good-bye.

"So we'll talk," said Peter. "I'll call you later."

"Thanks, Pete—thanks for listening."

"You're a prince and I love you," said Peter, over the din of traffic. "We know how to take care of each other, don't we, our generation? We learned it the hard way."

Jonathan nodded.

"Promise me one thing," said Jonathan. "Help me do this right. I want to leave something behind."

"Your work."

"Of course, my work. But I need your help to do something else. I've been talking to friends in philanthropy. I'd like to endow a prize for film or some kind of institute. I'm going to need a board of directors."

"Of course," said Peter. "Anything I can do."

"I don't want to be morbid, but they're already talking to me about this hospice that's associated with Sloan-Kettering. It's a very homey place, apparently—for when they're done being aggressive with me. Or maybe I'll go upstate—I don't know."

Peter shook his head.

"No, really," said Jonathan. "I wanna leave some mark, as my mother would have said. A few months is not enough time to do everything I wanted to do in this world. As of yesterday, I was still looking for someone to get married to and adopt kids with."

"We'll figure something out."

"Good."

Peter put Jonathan in a cab, then began walking back to the office.

"My next film turned into my last film."

The windows of exclusive Madison Avenue shops quietly beckoned with suggestions for a more comfortable life, expensive merchandise that had been freshly created for the season—not just fall, but *that* fall. An upscale cookware shop was showing some Thanksgiving china in a particularly fresh-looking shade of burnt orange. It occurred to Peter that he might stop in and pick up four dessert plates. And then he thought, *Poor Jonathan! Will this Thanksgiving be his last?*

And suddenly Peter found himself wondering whether he, himself, would ever enter that store again. Of course he would; there was no reason to think he wouldn't; it was one of his favorite stores. Yet what if the previous time he was in there, a few months before, had been the final time—if, for instance, he was about to be clobbered by a bus on his way back to work, or die in a subway crash on his way home? Wouldn't that be sad—a middle-aged gay man, on an August afternoon, contentedly comparing pepper mills for the last time and not even realizing it?

Even before reaching the corner of Sixtieth Street, Peter was thoroughly unsettled by the onrush of old memories. The idea that the next anything, or the previous one, could be the last had been a panic-point for him ever since the '80s, when people got sick on a Friday and were dead by Monday; when author friends told him that the books they were working on were turning into their last ones; when Harold realized that the job he was aiming for and being groomed for at the *Times* would never be his. Those days!— when Harold was home again after his long ordeal in the hospital and Peter wondered whether *this* would be the last time Harold tasted his beloved yakitori or *this* the last time he heard the overture of his favorite ballet, *Giselle*. With a sting of sadness mixed with thrill, Peter remembered the last time he and Harold made love, just before Harold got really sick. They didn't know it would be the last. It was on a long weekend in London, where they'd gone to see the Royal Ballet. They'd napped in their hotel room, after shopping and tea, and were dressing to go out, when a squeeze past each other in the bathroom turned into a kiss that overtook them thunderingly. He remembered thinking that Harold was as sexy that day as when they'd met, almost twenty years before—his eyes as true, his laugh as entertaining, his touch as reassuring.

And a walk down Madison Avenue could always be one's last, too.

Peter stopped for the light. He noticed that a perfectly coiffed gray-haired woman in front of him was sobbing lightly as she spoke on her cell phone. He couldn't hear what she was saying. She was dressed like an executive, in a black suit, and carrying a briefcase. She was wearing a pair of gold earrings in the shape of turbo shells—a gift from someone? A splurge for herself? Then the light changed and he moved on with the crowd.

It was beginning again, the oppressive awareness.

And this time it's for keeps. We're all going into our sixties, those of us who managed to survive.

It helped, back when people were dying, to know that the thrum of mortality was premature, forced by too many deaths out of natural sequence, like those of a plague or war. Plans and dreams dissolved, but not the ability to plan and dream. People were young. The ones who didn't die recovered. Yet Peter had always known the thrum would return, on the day when deaths were expected to arrive more seemly, in sequence. And here it was again, that thrum, which, quiet as it was, threatened to drown out—what a laugh!—the hope for Husband #3, whom Peter dreamed of so fervently.

CHAPTER 3

Tyler was performing that night at a place in Bushwick called Rico's Party House, and Peter had promised to attend. So around ten, Peter stepped out of a cab in front of what looked like a decommissioned church, on a desolate block lined with one- and two-story warehouse buildings, fenced vacant lots, and a run-down brick apartment building whose original window openings had been plugged by smaller windows bricked into place with unmatching bricks. The church's door also looked like a replacement: a battered glass-and-steel thing that had seen long service at a supermarket or gas station. Over the entrance was a spotlit sign that said "Rico's" in a graffiti-like typeface, with a halo over the R.

Peter paid the $10 admission and went inside. There was no line and the place seemed fairly empty and lifeless, which somehow made it seem wrong to mention to the door guy that he was on the list that Tyler said would be at the door. Actually, if Rico's was always this empty the place didn't need a list, Peter thought. It was a dark and cavernous space in which only a handful of people were walking or standing about, holding plastic cups, doing their best to vibe with the Latin house sounds that were blasting from giant speakers. The choir loft was the DJ booth, the sanctuary, a stage. On the arched wall in back of the stage a rotating projection of the haloed R cycled slowly through a spectrum of gaudy colors. Above the entire space, soaring rafters were picked out in flashing spotlights of blue, pink, and purple.

It was only when Peter got a vodka and checked a flyer at the bar that he saw ten o'clock was the "doors open" time for the event. Had Tyler mentioned this? Had Peter misunderstood? The bartender said the show would probably be starting around eleven. Since Tyler was backstage, preparing, Peter resigned himself to hanging out for a while in a corner and trying unobtrusively to return a few e-mails.

Like a lot of young men and women of his generation, Tyler maintained an artistic practice in addition to a professional career. Having studied dance and performance while he was up at Brown, Tyler was currently a member of a performance art collective run by a friend, and he performed with them once or twice a year, in places like Rico's. The group's work combined visual art installation with elements of theater and dance; it was high on concept and grounded in a queer-inflected, nouveau burlesque aesthetic. It was play and it was cool. And doing art on the side like this was not at all uncommon for kids at the agency or in other creative professions around New York; Peter heartily approved of the practice. Far from detracting from Tyler's work at the agency, the exploration of concept and performance only enriched it, and made Tyler better as both a person and a worker. For Peter, the situation was not so very different from that of his own generation during the '70s, when so many well-educated, middle-class twentysomethings with respectable but low-paying jobs maintained sidelines as hustlers, call girls, and drug dealers. It wasn't talked about very much, and business was conducted in quite a genteel way—there was no truck with street people or tawdry stuff like weapons. It was all for the fun of it and, of course, for the money.

Was his performance artwork one reason why Tyler was so good with clients? Earlier that day, when they were pitching their prospective client in their Den, Tyler had shone and probably won the account. The product was Triumf, an artisanal vodka made on Long Island. Present at the meeting, besides Peter and Tyler, were Triumf's CEO, a rich, young immigrant from Russia; his marketing director, who acted a lot like his girlfriend; and a few other members of their team. The brand traded heavily on the idea of "Russian revolution." Tyler went through the usual PowerPoint slides, unpacking concepts like "subversion" and "seduction," then he paused the presentation, stepped away from the head of the conference table, toward the clients, and spoke with fervor about social progress and how smart brands today did more than move units, they fomented positive social change.

"And really," he said, "this is where commerce merges with progress, which is what the twenty-first century is going to be all about."

The Triumf people were all nodding enthusiastically.

"*This* is why we started the company," trumpeted the CEO.

"It's about the passion for a better world," purred the marketing director.

"We get that, because we have lives outside this office," said Tyler, gazing just over the heads of his audience, as if out into the expanse of a great arena, then making eye contact with each of them. "We get it because we're paying attention."

The words might have come from a script being used anywhere to pitch clients on Madison Avenue that day, but it was the way Tyler delivered the lines that added the punch. And the slide where he had paused had been cannily designed to serve as a backdrop for this specific point: no words, just a dynamic abstract design in black, white, and red, with a neo-Constructivist feel. It looked as if Tyler had tossed aside the script in a fit of inspiration, but the whole moment had been conceived as theater. His posture, too, at that moment, had been choreographed to subtly echo the dynamism of a Constructivist sculpture: a little curvy and a little angular. And the entire performance led deftly into Peter's well-oiled spiel about why his agency was the right one to do this work, blah-blah-blah.

The handshakes that concluded the meeting felt ardent, conspiratorial. As the clients went off toward the elevators, Peter whispered "Well done!" to Tyler, and the boy rolled his eyes heavenward, with a shrug.

And Tyler had something else, too, that worked for him, in meetings and out of them: a vibrant girlishness that had never hardened during youth into bitter, defensive flamboyance, the way it had done for many men called "effeminate," of Peter's generation. Neither did this quality obscure a scrappy, can-do masculinity that Peter always associated with Tyler's upbringing in a small midwestern town, where the boy's dad had both served as mayor and owned an automobile repair shop. Tyler bragged of driving a pickup truck at fourteen, the engine of which he had rebuilt himself. Perhaps the ability to grow up with slightly less need to defend your sexuality was producing new generations of boys in which gender qualities coalesced in interesting new ways. Some of the top-or-bottom warriors among Peter's friends found this confusing; Peter found it delightful—even if it rendered the constructs of his generation, by comparison, sadly monochromatic.

Slowly, Rico's began to fill up. When he was done with his e-mail, Peter grabbed another vodka and began to loosen up, smiling at people, swaying with the music. He was the oldest person in the club, by far, but the place had an extremely friendly vibe and there was nothing to suggest he didn't belong. Occasionally, he felt the need to pull at the tight shoulders of his Ben Sherman jacket—purchased a size too small, because Tyler said it looked better and "you won't be doing any gymnastics in it."

It was nice to be out. Late-night club scenes were less and less Peter's thing, anymore. In the old days, he had gone out five or six times a week, sometimes to four and five events a night, often with celebrities who were part of his fashion-y crowd. This was just after Harold died, during his Merry Widower phase. Back then, he might start at midnight and stay out until dawn or later. It was a time when Elton, or Mariah, or Gianni, after partying all night, might suggest jumping on someone's private plane, so they could all be on a private beach in the Dominican Republic by lunchtime— the kind of invitation that Peter always declined in favor of heading off to work by way of Barneys or the Gap, where'd he'd pick up a new shirt to replace the sweaty one he'd been dancing in. Nowadays he felt a little less loyal to the ongoing party scene and sensed a bit of Fabulous Old Timer syndrome setting in, a condition he'd first observed years before among Andy Warhol's playmates, just after Andy died. You're nostalgic for the fabulous parties they used to throw back then and dubious about the music they're playing nowadays, yet you're game to keep going out and pretty sure that some of your great old party clothes still look timeless. But for the first time you don't mind missing some of the supposedly essential parties you hear about in the media, even if you *are* a bit lonely. You have a theory about why social life in the city peaked ten years ago, which may or may not have something to do with the fact that your work is more important to you than ever—which means you like to get to bed at a reasonable hour and may even watch more TV than you've ever watched since childhood. And sometimes you find yourself telling people that "television writing is getting better and better . . . !"

Rico's entire bill that night was devoted to nouveau burlesque, gay- and tranny-style. It looked like Tyler's crew was scheduled to go on last. The show opened with Foxy Love, a group of girl and girl-like dancers working hard to keep their Vegas-tribute-type moves synched with the naughty energy of Kelis's "Got Your Money." Sloppy dancing begged the question of unison and symmetry. Then came a tall, leggy male diva named Momus, who did a kind of strutting and posing routine to Jonté's "Bitch You Betta." A backup duo of dancing twins, a boy and a girl in matching miniskirts and pageboy wigs, did a series of tight, angular moves that paralleled a noisy, electrically colored anime that was projected on the wall behind them. Then there was Mister Mad, an act led by an angry ringleader-type character in a black plastic helmet and boxy yellow suit emblazoned with expletives. With the help of some henchmen in black suits and shades, Mister Mad cleared a runway from the stage into the middle of the club's floor and "punished" a series of selected guests by making them dance to jagged excerpts of vintage German electro. Then there was Cherie La Bête, a squad of tawny fembots in total-body-workout gear, who parodied a Jane Fonda–type aerobics routine from the '80s, accompanied by a vocodered version of "Life Is But a Dream."

All quite diverting, in a way, thought Peter.

By then, Rico's was buzzing and the place was packed. Peter was about to head to the bar once more when a cute Asian girl standing next to him asked if he was gay.

"What?" he said, beaming. He had just been thinking that it

was nice to be in a room with so many cute girls who looked like they were having fun. Some of them would look at him, occasionally—a man standing alone.

Who knows? he thought. *Maybe some of them find an older guy attractive.*

"My friend thinks you're hot," said the girl, indicating a slender twink who was dancing with some of the other girls in their group. The kid was pretty, in a high-school-student way, but Peter hardly knew what to say.

Maybe it's a joke? he thought—and then he wondered if he should feel flattered, though the kid himself didn't seem aware of what was going on.

"Let's talk later," said Peter. "He's cute but I need to be drunker."

Then Tyler appeared onstage. The troupe he was performing with was called Davidsbündler. The stage was set with cardboard flats depicting the fountains, balustrades, and topiary trees of a formal garden. Characters in a low-budget sort of eighteenth-century French royal attire entered and milled about, greeting each other with bows and curtsies; then they were joined by a towering, ten-foot-tall gentlewoman—part performer and part puppet—in panniers and a powdered wig. This was Tyler. The lady paraded, ponderously, greeting the audience and those onstage with gracious arm gestures—controlled with two sticks by Tyler from underneath the massive skirts. Then the lady lowered her arms and turned her back to the audience; she bent over, hiked up her skirt, and revealed a mammoth vulva, lovingly articulated, puppet-style, in quilted pink satin and tufts of shiny black ribbons. The lips moved, of course—somehow Tyler was working them. With her vagina the lady lip-synched the aria "O Mio Babbino Caro." Afterward, the lady stood up again, smoothed her skirts, and bowed.

The crowd went wild. They applauded madly, then the DJ went back to the Rico's house groove.

"You were awesome," said Peter, when Tyler came bounding up to him, half an hour later.

"I was? Did you like me?" Tyler gave Peter a peck on the cheek. The boy was in jeans, T-shirt, and a scarf—far more casual than Peter had ever seen him. And he smelled both sweaty and clean.

"Brilliant," said Peter. 'The best singing vagina I've ever seen."

"Isn't the costume amazing? I want you to meet Mandy—she's the genius behind Davidsbündler. She'll be out in a second."

"I kinda actually better get going, Ty," said Peter. "It's late."

"Oh, no you don't, mister," said Tyler, playfully. "You have to have a drink with me."

"The most amazing thing happened to me, just before you went on," said Peter, when they were at the bar. "Some girl came up and asked me if I was gay."

"Was she into you?"

"No. It was for her boyfriend. She said he thought I was hot."

"Are they still here?" said Tyler, looking around. "I wanna see."

"I don't know where they went."

"Was he hot?"

"Not really."

"I'm jealous."

"Right."

"I am."

"Tyler."

"No, really," said the boy, getting closer and attempting to plant another, more serious kiss.

Peter noticed a couple of other men standing nearby—gay and somewhat older, too, than the rest of the crowd. They saw the attempt at a kiss and appeared to find it charming.

"No, c'mon—we're not doing this," said Peter, pushing Tyler away gently.

"We're not?"

"No. Are we?"

"*Are* we?"

"No. But you know I adore you and think you're the biggest star in the universe."

"Well . . . OK," said Tyler, pretending to pout. He took a sip of his drink and surveyed the crowd. "Oh, there's Mandy," he said suddenly, grabbing Peter's hand. "Come with me."

In fact, Peter had lots of affection for Tyler and was not unresponsive to the boy's feelings for him. But even more important than his well-publicized scruples—which were, in fact, newly minted, dating to the time when his agency was sold to the conglomerate—Peter was lonely, he was looking for love. He had increasingly little inclination toward hookups with cuties, friendships with benefits, even harmless, romantic flings intended to go nowhere. Not that the light sexual recreation that had become a vernacular for Tyler's generation wasn't entertaining; it *was*. It was just that Peter was looking for a mate, hard-core, and Tyler, he knew, was not.

Jonathan called the next day to say he was starting treatment—a bout of chemo, followed by radiation. It would take a few weeks, and then he and the doctors would see where things were at. The survival rate for his scenario was not good, Jonathan said. Fewer than a third of patients were still alive after five years.

"OK—a third," said Peter, with optimism in his voice.

"Those are *appalling* odds," countered Jonathan. "But there it is."

"Still."

"The idea is to keep it from going to places like the lungs and the brain, which it apparently wants to do."

"Ooof."

"So we're going to nuke the hell out of it."

"Good."

"And I'm also thinking of taking another step—sort of drastic."

The words chilled Peter.

"Now, Jonny . . . ," he said.

"What?!" said Jonathan.

"We should talk, if you're even *thinking* about doing something like that. . . ."

"Something like . . . ? Oh, sorry! I didn't mean suicide! Darling! I meant hire a hustler. That's a kind of therapy, too—sex without all the . . . you know."

"Oh." Peter snorted. "You mentioned hustlers the other day. Now that's something I never knew about you, Jonathan."

"Never done it before. Never had to, never thought about it. But suddenly, I thought, 'Hey, it's a kind of massage. One step I can take for my own well-being, especially now.' "

"Absolutely."

"Can you recommend anyone?"

"*Nooo.*"

The moment he said it, Peter was afraid his emphasis had sounded judgmental.

"I mean, no," he continued. "I don't happen to . . . know anybody."

Jonathan laughed.

"Don't worry, I'll figure it out," he said.

Peter had never paid for sex, though he had nothing against it. He had often wondered, in fact, whether his continuing quest for love wasn't simply a parody of what might be a more seemly pursuit for a single, older gay man of his station, paying for companionship. Yet what kind of boys did that, and what happened to them? Questions of purpose, not payment, had always proved a solvent to this kind of sexual interest, for Peter. A young guy he'd known years before, Adam, a strikingly handsome photographer's assistant who lived mysteriously above his means, was always jetting off for long weekends with unnamed friends and coming home with expensive gifts like a gold Rolex and the first PowerBook Peter ever saw. Peter had a little crush on the guy until one day when Adam broke a lunch date to keep "an appointment that just came up" with a well-known publishing mogul who was said to be secretly gay. Adam later confessed it was a sex thing. He said he'd met a member of the so-called Velvet Mafia at a fancy party the year before; that led to introductions and more invitations and his current role as a favored plaything of three or four gay big shots.

The stories Adam told were amazing: penises large and small; sexual tastes infantile and brutal; affections that were lovely and nasty at the same time. But the drugs, he said, were always the best, and anyway the job was better than cater-waitering for helping make ends meet.

Peter liked Adam's intelligence and affability—qualities that were clearly as important to a successful rent boy as looks and prowess—but he was never again attracted to the guy, sexually. He found it odd that Adam was never interested in advice on parlaying his lofty contacts into career advancement in photography—which raised the question of what Adam wanted his career, ultimately, to be. In the end, it was drugs that ended the party. Adam crashed and burned and went home to his family in the Midwest. After rehab he found a boyfriend, put on some weight, and started shooting for a local newspaper.

That day, Peter was having lunch with Laura, to talk business. The restaurant was a fancy Italian place near the office, where the company had an account. Peter thought the place too self-important and rarely went there. The tables were too large and too far apart. Laura, as usual, was in an eye-catching suit—this one of black-and-white stripes.

"Hi, hon," she chimed, as Peter slid onto the banquette with her.

"Looking smart, as always, Laura."

"You're always so sweet," she said. "Don't you *love* this place? I told the waiter to let Jackie know we're here." The restaurant's chef, whose name was Jacqueline, was a rising star in the New York food world. Laura always referred to celebrities by their first names, whether she knew them well or not.

She was around Peter's age—overweight, with dyed blond hair that was limp and overprocessed. Though witty and connected, she wasn't particularly pleasant to be around, because of a bitter edge that seemed to come through the brittle laugh she ended half her sentences with—the result, apparently, of a determination to remain vivacious. She'd never married and had terrible luck with boyfriends. She'd said no in college to a guy who became a software billionaire; then there was a criminal lawyer who drank and made scenes, a real estate guy who cheated with bimbos, and a personal trainer who wanted money to launch a line of workout gear. Peter knew all this because Laura confessed such stuff freely and had done so since the day they met. But she was smart and high up the ladder on the business side, and Peter respected her for that.

"And you look great," Laura said, with a laugh.

Peter knew he looked a bit deflated. In truth, he was hungover. He hadn't gotten home from Rico's until around three.

"A friend is going through chemo," said Peter. "You know."

"Acupuncture," she said.

"Well . . ."

"No, I'm telling you," continued Laura. "That's the thing. It helps the body counteract all those toxins."

"Ah."

"I know the best guy in New York."

There was no real conversing with Laura—only listening, reacting, then eventually finding a way to cut it off. Lunch would last ninety minutes. Peter had prepared himself for that, in the interest of business. The only variable was whether or not the two of them would walk back to the office together. In that case, there would be squiring to do—doors to be opened, attention to be paid while negotiating crowded sidewalks at a painfully slow pace.

Acupuncture led to Laura's manicurist, who wanted to study acupuncture, which led to Laura's current exercise routine and diet, and then to northern Italian cuisine, which somehow led to Bronze Age migrations from Asia to Europe—all of which led to Henderson McCaw.

"Talk to him," said Laura. "He's really very charming."

"I couldn't. I simply couldn't be in the same room with . . . that face."

"Oh, now, don't be so gay." Laura felt she could make remarks like that, since she was such a good friend of the gays.

"He's clearly not our only prospect, is he?" said Peter.

"No," said Laura, "but he's one of the biggest. This could be a hundred million in billings, over the next five years. Look—what's the problem? Talk to the guy."

"Ecch."

"He's really smart. He really knows who he is and what he's doing. And, Peter, you can't deny he's onto something, cultural."

"I cannot deny that."

"And that's where the new business is. And you like that kind of challenge, don't you? And frankly, Peter, we need you to play ball on this. We didn't acquire the agency because of its cute name. We have numbers to meet—numbers we all agreed on."

"I know. It's just . . ."

"Look, you're not a new business guy, hon—you're not. You're creative, and you're the best, full stop. So you go and do creative, and let me bring in the new business. See how easy that is?"

She laughed in a way that was once probably meant to be flirty. Just then Peter heard the *dink* of his iPhone—a new text.

u in the office? It was Tyler.

Gimme a sec, said Peter, typing a reply. *back in 20*

need to run triumf by u b4 sending

"They're lost without me," said Peter, smiling.

sure. will come and find u, he typed.

were n farmers mart

Peter tucked away the phone. Tyler and the team he had put together for the vodka proposal were gathered in a little community-square-ish corner of the atrium, where fresh produce and homemade soups and baked goods were available each day.

"Triumf," said Peter.

"Your boys?" said Laura.

"Well—boys and girls. We're an equal opportunity shop, as you well know, darling."

"Are you? Just be careful with the boy toys."

"And what is that supposed to mean?"

"Relax. You know I'm your best friend. But this kind of thing, it can blow up in your face—that's all I'm saying. Some clients might not be so comfortable with it."

"There's nothing to blow up, Laura. I'm a saint. God knows, my sex life is a barren wasteland. My kids are saints, and they're all hugely talented. And we're going to keep making tons of money."

"Good! That's what I like to hear!"

Later, as they walked back to the office, Peter kept wondering what, if anything, was in back of Laura's crack. Knowing her, it could have been some concern about women in advertising and the enduring glass ceiling. More likely, it was a reservation about something she thought was standing in the way of a juicy new client.

Or something that actually was *standing in the way,* thought Peter.

"Vodka cran, please, twist of lime." Tip.

"You have any scotch? How about bourbon? OK, rocks—make it a double." Tip.

"Hi, there! Can I get three white wines, please? No—four. Wait—no, three. Sorry." Tip.

"Do you have beer? Any Belgian beer? Miller is all you have?" No tip.

"Hey, what's in the rum thing? Is it any good? OK, can I get two of them?" Tip.

For almost three hours Will had been on his feet behind the bar at a large and lavish party in West Chelsea. A leading style magazine was launching its fattest-ever December issue, and fifteen hundred people had come to celebrate in a mammoth, multispace photography studio that occupied a full floor of a former factory building. The building featured two elevators as large as some New York apartments, built especially for trucks, which once were hauled up to loading docks on every floor. The elevators were now used chiefly to carry guests, by the score, up to events like this.

The entire studio was white—floors, walls, ceilings—and the décor of the party capitalized on this with a winter wonderland theme. Suspended above the crowd's heads were thousands of tree branches that had been painted white and dipped in iridescent sparkles. Positioned strategically throughout the space were six open bars, each thirty feet long and manned by four bartenders with as many barbacks; the bars were draped in sparkly white fabric and preset with a ridge of glassware, lined up in neat ranks. There were two DJs—one for the main space, a central area that the loading dock opened into, and another in the big room at the far end of the floor.

The crowd was the usual thing for this kind of event—editors, associate editors, and assistant editors, with assorted designers, stylists, and photography types, plus people from fashion, beauty, music, and art, and a sprinkling of modishly dressed venerables of both genders, who'd clearly been upping the city's festivity quotient for a long, long time. A few film and music stars were said to be attending, but Will was too busy to care about that. He was working his butt off, dressed in a tight white T-shirt emblazoned with a special graphic incorporating the magazine's name and the logo of the rum brand being used in a special cocktail they were serving, the Winter Wind: rum with mango juice, mint, ginger, and sugar.

"The special, please. Oh, no, wait—do you have wine?" Tip.

"I said no ice—sorry." No tip.

"Ketel One? Stoli? Christ—whaddya got?" Tip.

"Excuse me, where are the bathrooms?" No tip.

"Vodka and soda, please. Maybe some lemon." Tip.

Will had rushed to the party from his temping gig at a downtown law firm. He'd devoted a full day, already, to standard office labor, and was exhausted, but the party gig was a good one, for an event company that used him often, and he hadn't wanted to say no. Besides, he needed the money. The three other guys he was working with at his bar—all of whom could have stepped out of the pages of *W* magazine—he'd hardly talked to beforehand, as they changed clothes and set up; and now that things were busy there was barely time to utter a word, unless it was about the supply of ice or mango juice. Even Brent, a really nice guy he'd worked with before, at other gigs, with whom he'd bantered a bit as they were setting up glasses, now was concentrating only on the guests. And of course, Brent's tip jar was loaded.

Will was getting some good tips, too, but he found it harder to work for them than Brent did, with fast service, flirty smiles, and witty exchanges. In fact, despite its supposed glamour, the entire party—his tenth or twelfth such gig since coming to New York— was hell, and being there reminded Will just how dissatisfied he was with the catering/bartending lifestyle. Scrambling hard for subsistence living was now officially charmless. His periodic searches on craigslist and Mediabistro for editing and writing jobs had not turned up as many leads as Will had expected, and none of those he did spot had led to an interview. Was there some other way to go about it?

Most of the other bartenders were actors or models, so the hopes on which they pinned their escape from this life of servitude lay on the screen or the stage. If they didn't have a sense of where they were going, careerwise, at least their agents did. And the guests, Will felt, must have a sense of direction, too—but where did they get it? Will knew he fit in with them, in terms of looks, and style, and temperament, but what exactly did those people do, anyway, and how exactly did they come to do it? Were they all editors? The kind of editors who write, and choose their subjects, and have lunch with writers, and produce photo spreads, and plan issues? Did they come from literary backgrounds? Journalistic backgrounds? How did one become an editor? Who taught that kind of editing? How did you talk about your aspirations in the field of editing, in an interview? Was there anyone at the party, among those fifteen hundred souls, who might have read the interview Will did with Beyoncé—who might appreciate the skill and charm it took to get the star to reminisce about the smoothies she used to have for breakfast as a child?

It was nasty business, serving people. True, everyone in the room understood that cute bartenders were all bound for something else, that by the end of the following year half the party's bartenders might well be talking about some new project from the couch of a late-night talk show. Yet until the couch, what did they say and think about themselves? Nothing in Will's twenty-eight years—nothing in his comfortable upper-middle-class upbringing—had prepared him for this. God knew, he wasn't looking for anything fancy, just survival with dignity. As much as he liked New York, he resented this quality of the city that seemed to be both goading him to find himself and preventing him from doing so.

"Hey, buddy—four specials." No tip.

"Beer." No tip.

"Hi, there! Three white wines and one red, please—thank you. Eew—is that the end of the bottle? Could you open a new one, please? Is it a French wine, do you know? Is it very sweet?" No tip.

"Hey, Brent!" shouted Will, slamming down his corkscrew. "Do me a favor? Cover me for five minutes? I gotta pee. Literally—back in five."

Will walked across the floor, down a roped-off corridor, and into the staff men's room. He washed his hands at a sink, then went into a stall and just stood there, breathing. The room was empty. He needed a moment to himself. From outside the men's room echoed the pounding DJ music and the roar of a thousand conversations. After a moment, Will peed, then checked his messages. He wasn't expecting anything; it was just an excuse to enter his private iPhone world and push a few buttons. On a whim he checked his Facebook newsfeed. Nothing special—then he saw a new picture from his sister, who was on vacation with some Italian friends of the family, in Paris. Will "liked" the photo and made a breezy comment, then he checked for any other Paris pix, of which there were a few.

Damn—I was supposed to meet them there, he thought. *Why did I say no?* Then he remembered: He'd never really intended to go to Paris, this time. He'd decided that he had to concentrate on landing the job he'd come to New York to find.

Will kept scrolling. Also among his sister's shots were several from the previous spring, when Will's family had visited the vacation home of their Italian friends in Ischia. The friends had a large boat that was staffed both with hired help, for the sailing, and family retainers, Marta and Claudio, for the serving. There was Will, shirtless, in the sun, with Chiara and Sarah; Will, shirtless and squinting, on the beach of one of the tiny islands they stopped at; Will with Sarah and Elisabeth, on the beach; Will's parents with the Italian parents; all the kids gathered for lunch on the boat's aft deck over a fresh seafood salad, with Marta and Claudio in the background, beaming. The tablecloth was striped blue and white.

OK, great, so now I've joined the servant class, thought Will, with a silent chuckle.

For some reason, he suddenly remembered a moment from that trip—the gracious answer their friends' mom gave when his mother asked, at the end of their stay, whether tipping Marta and Claudio was appropriate.

"Yes, it is done, if you like, and they will be so grateful," the lady said. "They like you all so very much. But may I suggest . . . well, we have something in Italy we call *bella figura*—um, good form, I suppose you might say. This means you might select a little gift for them, something very small, and then also give them an envelope with some bills, if you choose. You see?"

Just then, someone entered the men's room, with the bang of a door, and Will put away the phone.

Back to work, commendatore.

Back at the bar, Will noticed that one of the guests was shooting smiley glances at him—a good-looking man in his late thirties or early forties, surrounded by a crew of younger cuties. He had the air of someone important, with prematurely gray hair and a pair of clunky, retro-style glasses. Will knew that at parties like this it was par for the course for the handsome bartenders to be flirted with and maybe invited to after-parties and such, but no way! Will's feet and lower back were screaming for help, and he was already dreaming of the steaming-hot eucalyptus bath he was going to sink into, the moment he got home.

The man stepped over to the bar.

"You guys are doing a terrific job tonight," he said.

"Thanks," said Will. Underneath the man's gray sport jacket was a tight purple sweater that showed off an obviously worked-out body.

"Busy," said the man.

"That's the way we like it," said Will.

"Oh, I'll bet you do."

"Drink?"

"Got one, thanks. Say, are you an actor, or a model?"

"Sorry?"

"An actor, right?"

"Oh—sorry, no."

"Damn, that was my best guess. May I ask what it is you do or intend to do when you grow up?"

"This," said Will, chucking out an empty wine bottle and opening a new one with pretend disgust that wasn't so pretend.

The man made a frowny face.

"When you're not here, I mean," said the guy.

"Sorry, I don't mean to be a jerk," said Will. "I'm looking around. I just got to New York."

"Oh, yeah? What are you looking for?"

"Something in magazines, I guess."

"You guess?"

"No—in magazines. I write; I've done some editing."

"You have clips and strong references, I assume?"

"Sure, why?"

"This is magazine world, my friend," said the man, with a gesture indicating the entire party.

"I know," said Will, "but . . ."

"I happen to know someone in HR. Have you been over there yet?"

"No."

"Well, what's the delay? They should see you."

"OK."

"Maybe Condé Nast has made you a better offer?"

"No," laughed Will.

They introduced themselves and shook hands.

"Here's my card," said the man. "Call me tomorrow."

"Thanks," said Will, examining the card. "What's an 'editor at large'?"

"I hope, my friend, that by this time next year, when you are making six figures and wielding vast power, you will find a question like that comically naïve."

Will was confused, but he giggled.

"Sorry," said the man. "I do a little bit of everything. But seriously—call me. We'll see if we can hook you up with something."

"I will."

"Magazines always need good people. Are you good?"

"As a journalist?"

"Of course, as a journalist."

"Yeah."

"Great. So call me tomorrow. E-mail me, too, OK?"

"Thanks," said Will, as the man walked away.

There was still a huge throng of guests at the bar, all waiting for a drink.

"Excuse me, can I get a vodka with tonic?" Tip.

"The rum thing, please. Actually, no—can you do just the rum, straight up?" Tip.

"Club soda. One ice cube. Twist of lemon *and* a twist of lime." No tip.

CHAPTER 4

The law firm where Will was temping was a relatively small one: just three partners and a handful of other counsel and associates, headquartered in a generically modern building in lower Manhattan. Will was filling in as executive assistant to the head partner, while the regular assistant took a brief matrimonial leave. The duties were simple—answering phones, running the office, and receiving clients and other visitors—and the boss was pleasant. He was an older man with a milky complexion and white hair, whose mildness underlay a fiercely competitive intelligence that Will enjoyed observing in action when he happened to overhear the man's phone calls. As temp jobs went, this was heaven. The desk even had a view of the Brooklyn Bridge and the beautiful borough that lay beyond.

At around ten-fifteen on the morning after the magazine party the caterer arrived—fifteen minutes late!—with coffee and platters of pastries and fruit that Will had ordered for an eleven o'clock meeting the partner was hosting in the conference room. Will signed the bill and scurried around the room, setting things up and making sure the chairs were neatly arranged around the large oval table. He was just about to zip away and make a call when the partner looked in.

"Are we set?" asked the older man.

"We are," said Will.

"Good. We'll only be an hour, an hour and a half."

"All right."

"Shouldn't be much blood. These are the folks who serve with me on the board of the dance theater I told you about."

"OK," said Will. "I'll be ready."

On his way back to his desk, Will ducked into the file room, which was relatively secluded, and made a call from his cell phone.

"Stefan Turino's office," said a British man's voice.

"Hi," said Will, and he gave his name in a hushed voice that was meant nonetheless to sound confident. "Is Stefan in, please? He asked me to call today." Will was holding the card that Stefan had given him at the party.

"I'll see if he's in. Please hold."

Will had wanted to call just then, around ten-thirty, which he felt would be not too early, which might seem desperate, nor too late, which could look lax. The seconds ticked away, then the British man returned.

"Will, please hold for Stefan."

"Hello, Stefan?"

"No—please *hold* for Stefan."

"Oh, sorry."

More hold. Then Stefan came on.

"Hey, buddy. How's it going?"

"Hi, how are you?"

"You survived our little party. I hope you didn't stay out too late."

"I went straight home to bed. It was a school night."

"Oh, too bad. There was a thing afterward and I thought about calling you. Then I realized, Wait, I don't have your number. You have mine."

"Yeah."

"Yeah."

"So . . . since you were kind enough to offer, I thought I'd ask you about . . . we spoke about an interview, or . . ."

"Oh, absolutely—very good. Will, tell you what. E-mail me your CV right now, will you, and let me get back to you very shortly?"

"Yeah, sure." Will was glad he had stored a copy of his resume in his Gmail account not long before, when he started looking for jobs.

"Will you do that for me?" said Stefan.

"Of course, right now," said Will.

"Good. Buddy, listen, I'm glad you called but I'm getting pulled away here. Let me go, but I'll get back to you very soon. Promise."

Back at his desk—surreptitiously, while his boss was on a call—Will looked over his resume before sending it.

Not too bad for a guy in his twenties, he thought. He'd been meaning to check Mediabistro for some advice on whether or not to mention your prep school on a resume. Will decided to leave it for now. *And what's the difference between a CV and a resume, anyway?* But there was no time to check.

Also in his head were other questions that the call had prompted.

He thought about calling me last night? Is he always that familiar with strangers? His assistant used my name right away, as if I were a known quantity. Do they do that for everyone, in that world? But is it real thoughtfulness or just a trick?

A little before eleven the dance theater board members arrived. Will took their coats and showed them into the conference room. They seemed a lovely bunch of somewhat older people, nicely but not formally dressed. One of them asked where the ladies' room was and thanked Will graciously.

They reminded him of his parents and his parents' friends: cultivated folks who were obviously affluent, but genial, unpretentious, understated. Will was glad to know there were enough people like that in New York to comprise a social stratum. Sometimes it seemed the city was all flash—money and accomplishment detached from taste, modesty, service, and other higher values that Will's parents observed and tried to teach their children. His father was an aerospace executive with big defense department contracts, and his mom the head of the English department at the prep school he'd attended. They were active in Santa Barbara politics and donors to the arts, and had always encouraged Will to do and be anything he wanted. Even their brand of Episcopalianism was warmly permissive. And indeed Will had come out as gay without drama practically as an adolescent, and was never encouraged, particularly, to go into aerospace or education. He often wondered whether this amiable, laissez-faire up-bringing had left him lacking in a certain kind of pushiness, or just clarity of purpose, that people needed in New York. People always asked, "What do you do?" with such fervor; and when he told them, "Temping and catering-waitering and looking around," and they asked what he really wanted to be doing, career-wise, he always felt the question premature. Though of course it wasn't. He was almost thirty.

As another of the ladies asked for the ladies' room, Will felt his phone vibrate. It could be Stefan. Quickly, he surveyed the conference room and saw that his boss and guests were installing themselves smoothly at the table, then he sped back to his desk, managing to grab the call as he went.

"Will here."

"Will, Stefan."

"Hey."

"You're in luck. Can you come in on Thursday morning, nine-thirty sharp?"

"Uh, yeah—Thursday morning?" If Will sounded tentative, it was because he knew he was scheduled to work that day at the law office.

"I suggest you just say yes, buddy," said Stefan. "It only sounds like a question." He went on to tell Will whom he'd be meeting with, and where.

"Thanks a lot," said Will. "I really appreciate it."

"Cool, cool. We'll see where it goes."

The Paul Smith store on Greene Street in SoHo was one of Peter's favorite shops. It was a temple of cool. The cheeky merchandise; the store's elegantly quirky design, incorporating quaint artworks and vintage fixtures; the whole smarty-pants-British-art-school point of view—all was in synch with Peter's reverence for tradition and standards but devotion to wit. For some, shopping at Paul Smith entailed as sincere a form of worship as existed in the twenty-first century, and Peter had long been a member of the cult.

Often, during the '80s, when Peter and Harold spent long weekends in London, to see ballet or theater, they would make it a point to visit the original Paul Smith shop on Floral Street. They were always amused by the sharply seasoned-up versions of the menswear classics they found there, and sometimes would pick up a striped plastic belt or woolen scarf on sale—the kind of small purchase they could comfortably afford then. Later, Peter began buying shirts and suits at Paul Smith's first New York location, on lower Fifth Avenue, and then, on returns to London, at the new flagship store in Notting Hill. To this day, Peter continued to wear a cherished pair of socks he splurged on in 1985—in navy blue, with a woven-in grid of white Bodoni numerals. They must have cost $30 or $40—then an absurd amount that Peter paid willingly, thinking the socks so very cool, and bolstered by a vague impression about the value of design and workmanship. Twenty-five years had done much to strengthen that impression, as good design and workmanship had proved enduring and were now the kinds of things that were more important than ever to Peter.

He had felt a little twitchy in Rico's, in his slightly undersized Ben Sherman jacket. Besides, that jacket was a year or two old. So a few days later Peter went to Paul Smith in search of a few things to help him through the coming round of holiday parties. Tyler came along to help, as usual. The two of them stopped in after a meeting not far away, with a graphic artist who was helping them create new visuals for a client.

"You could do this," said Tyler, plucking a boldly striped jacket on a hanger from a hook and holding it up to Peter's body. "Hmm, no, maybe not."

"No?" said Peter, inspecting the jacket, after Tyler stuck it back on the hook.

"Crazy, but not the right kind of crazy," said Tyler, already looking elsewhere. "How about this?" He had another jacket, in a vibrant green herringbone—a nice twist on tweedy.

"Huh," said Peter, as Tyler pushed the jacket upon him.

"That's hot," said Tyler. "You're trying that on." Tyler added the jacket to the armful of garments Peter was holding and moved on. "Sweaters, shirts—we'll look at those later. OK, let's see what we have. Dressing room."

The store was not particularly busy that day. Five or six customers were milling about, looking at things in a casual way, or chatting amiably with salespeople. Inside the dressing room Peter put down his briefcase, hung his things on some antique hooks, and decided where to begin. When he stepped out of the room in his first look, the green jacket, with a green T-shirt and a pair of black jeans, Tyler was a few steps away, looking at sweaters.

"Ty, what do you think of this?"

Tyler came over and they both studied Peter's reflection in the dressing area's mahogany cheval glass. The image had the power of a page in *W:* The right silhouette and the right background brought everything into focus for *right now,* even as the mind felt connected to a truth about life that one yearns to hang onto—something that's larger, more important, *eternal.*

"Awesome, I knew it," said Tyler, holding a sweater. "You should definitely get it—the jacket."

"And the jeans?"

"Ehh. I'm just not seeing you in a black jean—sorry."

The jeans had been Peter's idea. Black jeans had been one of the staples of his first decade in New York.

"I know they're showing them and all," continued Tyler, "and they're really well done, but I'm just not feeling it."

"Meaning . . . Paul Smith made a mistake?"

"Meaning . . . I'm just not feeling it."

"He's just not feeling it," said Peter to the salesperson, a slender, dark-haired young man, who was standing nearby, watching.

"I'm not feeling it for *you,* mister," said Tyler, pointing with the hand that was still clasping a sweater. "I could get away with them *easily,* no doubt." And Tyler tossed the sweater at Peter playfully, which amused the salesperson and a straight couple who had also been looking at sweaters.

To a stranger, they might have looked like boyfriends—or some modern version of uncle-and-nephew, or perhaps call-boy-and-client. A few months before, at a charity concert that Peter took Tyler to, they had run into a former fling of Tyler's, a tattooed, puppyish young stylist who not long before had been the boyfriend of a famous fashion designer. The kid was also, notoriously and somewhat proudly, a hustler; the fashion and media press had been full of stories, nominally celebratory but steeped in contempt, about the bad boy who'd captured the designer's heart. Before the concert the boy barely acknowledged Peter as he chatted and giggled with Tyler, and during the concert he continued to text Tyler. Afterward, they met again on the sidewalk and Tyler declined to go off with the kid and his friends, to some supercool after-party.

"He says he wants to hook up again," said Tyler, as he and Peter strolled off to dinner. "I have no idea why."

"Because you're such a hottie," said Peter.

Tyler clowned a smile.

"But you're not into him," continued Peter.

"There's not enough *there* there."

"Cute, though."

"And extremely sincere."

"Oh, that's nice."

"Hung," said Tyler.

"Of course," said Peter.

"He asked me who the john was, who I was with."

"What?"

"Yup."

"Me?!"

"I said you were my friend."

"And your boss."

"Well, I didn't say that."

"He thought I was a john?" It was the first time this picture of himself, though he often went out with younger men, had entered his mind.

"What about me?" said Tyler. "That kinda makes *me* a hustler."

"Yeah! And you're a fucking important creative director."

"Not that I have anything against being a hustler."

"Nor do I against being a john—I guess. Though shouldn't the kid know better? Is that the way he sees the whole world?"

The incident made Peter realize exactly how uncharted the waters were that he had been sailing into, by dating such young men and purposefully looking for love among them, as he had been doing since the breakup with Nick. There were new balances these days among love, money, manhood, adulthood, and the like. To overlook these new balances or neglect to account for them in one's behavior—to ignore the fact that everything had shifted in the previous generation—could make the going treacherous. On the other hand, Peter was as curious about these new balances as he was about new developments in art, fashion, and music; and in this way he had felt for a long time more in synch, taste-wise, with people under forty. As an editor, early on, he was expected to stay in touch with the new. And as with committing to the gym, he simply got into the habit of listening regularly to new pop music and taking seriously what he saw in store windows. Then the loss of Harold and all the rest of his friends within twenty-four months jolted him free, in a way, of an entire generational trajectory he'd been programmed for, and the new was all he had. He was free—or lost, depending on how you looked at it.

The men of his generation—the ones who were left—disdained new music, except for official icons like Madonna, and new styles, except for those sanctioned by the *Times* "Thursday Style" section. They were stuck in overcurated bubbles defined by things like classic Callas performances and 1977's idea of a sexy tweed: "It looks gray from far away, but up close it's pink and blue and purple and green. . . ."

Please.

Nick was a *bit* younger—fifteen years younger than Peter. When they met, fifteen years before, Nick had just come out of his twenties and seemed to be entering a kind of prime. Peter wasn't thinking consciously about younger men, at that point—only that Nick was cute and had lots of a new kind of gay energy: fun, open, but connected to the world in ways that didn't constantly reference gay in a political way, or reference it at all. And not referencing it any longer felt as dangerous as in the old days! They'd met at a party and gone home with each other that night. The sex was great—for Peter, the best since Harold—and for a few years the relationship built in an organic way: They attended each other's family events, mixed with each other's friends. Then Nick started mixing with new people whom Peter didn't like much—club people, whose existence, though they had jobs and lives, revolved around clubs, which meant drugs. Peter was naïve, at first; he didn't understand the drug part until it was too late and Nick was in too deep.

Over the years, Peter had tried this or that drug, and enjoyed the experience without feeling the need to repeat it immediately. A certain sacramental quality of drug taking, and the insights attached to it, made the experience special, and Peter always wanted to take some time to honor the specialness before repeating it. And there was always a voice in his head when he took drugs—the same voice, his father's, that arose when he was tempted to do things like divert money from savings into an investment: "Be careful."

Things went downhill fast. Nick continued to deny he had a problem, accused Peter of not being cool, not really A-list. They argued constantly, though still followed through on social commitments with family and friends. Then Nick started going absent for important events, disappearing for days at a time, and coming home exhausted and needing to sleep for twenty-four hours. When the arguments threatened to morph into physical violence—a possibility that changed everything for Peter—they decided to part.

Officially, they were now best friends, or family, as a wise old queen suggested they say. Nick finally got some help and maybe wouldn't slide again. Mercifully, he'd managed to hang on to his job, his health, and his bank account.

They were together for nine years. After that, Peter's preference for younger men was even more entrenched. And though Peter had gotten older, the men who interested him—the ones who weren't already taken, that is—were still around thirty: old enough to know they weren't the only creatures on the planet, but not yet bitter, or disillusioned, or curated into a bubble. The "team" idea had come from Jonathan, when Peter confessed one day that he was afraid that some of the guys he was seeing felt too much pressure to become Peter's third husband.

"I think I can be a little intense for people," said Peter. "I'm a pretty open and unblocked human being, you know. I just feel that if there's a connection, it should be explored, like, *now,* and a little thing like age shouldn't matter."

Jonathan chuckled.

"Little to you," he said.

"Thirty little years," said Peter, knowing how absurd the idea was, even as he found it perfectly normal.

"Look at them as members of your team," suggested Jonathan. "You're not dating," he said with a lilt. "You're hanging out with each other, having fun. If someone turns into something special, you'll know it. Meanwhile, keep it light, easy."

"I know, I know," said Peter. "But I'm stuck with this sense of fate that I felt with Harold. *It's* supposed *to be this way. So we must rise to the occasion and let destiny be fulfilled.* That's what kept me with Nick for so long, I think. I couldn't imagine having made a mistake."

"No, Peter—no fate," said Jonathan. "Just happy. Fun. Light. That fate thing—comes across as Lonely Guy. I'm being honest with you."

"But happy, fun, light—aren't I just enforcing my own loneliness, unless I push for something deeper?"

"You can't really push these things, darling. You can't when you're twenty-two and have all your looks, and you can't when you're sixty and a master of the universe."

Peter sighed. He *was* lonely—even if, at times now, because he was an adult, he was able to enjoy solitude more than ever. Something else was going on, something he didn't have a word for. His hunger for bonding with another soul had always felt cosmically urgent; now, since Nick, it had ripened into a kind of starvation. Peter once explained to Tyler that he felt he possessed more than just the knack for couplehood. He said he felt he could breathe comfortably only on that elevated plane of existence where relationships were pure, true, divinely purposed—a thought Peter had hoped at the time might help dissolve Tyler's infatuation with him, but apparently didn't. Playing fast and loose with affections was like suffocation to him, said Peter, even if it did make him popular with young guys who were looking for a cool daddy or something. That was fetishization, objectification, whatever. Instead, Peter wanted to be known by another man specifically and completely, and was willing to know that man just as specifically.

Sometimes when he was home alone, Peter found himself desperate simply to share his apartment, since it constituted a form of such personal expression for him. The harmoniously odd bits of furniture and haphazardly acquired art collection all seemed to require more witness than one person could offer. A gag gift that Tyler gave him one day, a beautiful book entitled *The Pleasures of Cooking for One,* by the legendary food book editor Judith Jones, left him mysteriously enraged. It was unacceptable, the idea of this marvelous woman, cultivated and sensuous, now a widow and dining alone on a little gratin, at the table she and her husband might have found together at an antiques shop one marvelous day in Sag Harbor. As was the idea of Peter living alone in the home he'd thoughtfully fitted out to nourish body and soul—a refuge from city stridence that could gratify the mind with its sensible arrangement of books and objects and files, and feed the soul with the well-ordered flow of dry goods and fresh produce. The delight Peter took in the apartment was so strong that even the dark memory of his losing Harold there—in a wheeled-in hospital bed that scratched the floor—couldn't dim it.

What happened to delight like that, if not shared? Did it accrue interest, like money in the bank? Or rot, like food on a supermarket shelf?

Of course, beyond the apartment, it was happiness that Peter most wanted to share. He had never been happier! It was the pleasantly predictable result, perhaps, of looking inward and working on one's self for five decades, after being encouraged to do so in elementary school by well-meaning child psychologists, in high school by radical, Vatican II–inspired nuns, and as a wannabe adult by the entire spirit of the 1960s. At the age of almost sixty, Peter had finally managed to shut down most of the spirit-sucking shame and doubt programs that had once occupied his mind. He was confident now, even buoyant. Sure, it was enjoyable simply to be this way. It was better to share it.

Worshipping with Tyler in a temple like Paul Smith was a small part of the sharing that Peter had in mind—vibing over sweaters meant to re-center you in the redeeming splendor of optimism. Only with Tyler, dear boy, there was no chemistry. Fun, yes, and maybe a little lust. But no real chemistry, and Peter needed chemistry. He always had. And this was a quandary, because Peter had little taste anymore for the maneuvers of lust that gay men used to deploy instantly in their search for chemistry with another man. That jump-into-bed thing felt outmoded now; anyway, Peter couldn't do it anymore. In this way he felt he might have something in common with younger guys who were contenting themselves with occasional hand jobs in the men's rooms of their local gay bars, even if it meant that neither he nor they were locating much chemistry.

*   *   *

"You're going to meet with him?"

"Sure am."

"The guy is pure evil."

"Yeah, unlike the rest of our clients, who are only partly evil."

In a cab, on their way back to the office after Paul Smith, Peter and Tyler talked about Henderson McCaw.

"I just don't know what it would feel like, to work on an account like that," said Tyler.

"It would feel like getting paid your usual six-figure salary, wouldn't it?" said Peter.

"You know what I mean. I came to work for you for certain reasons—we all did. You stand for something—your work does."

"Look, I'm not going to get us caught up in the wrong thing. I'm only gonna talk to the guy. It's my corporate responsibility, really."

"Now there's a phrase I haven't heard until now."

"Nothing wrong with money."

"Since when have you only been about money?"

"Tyler—enough. You'll be the first to know what happens."

"OK," said the boy, backing down with politeness that was meant to be conspicuous.

It was only a little after noon. Traffic was light. It took both men a second to figure out how to shut off the cab's backseat video screen, which was blaring nonsense.

"Anyway, on a lighter note," continued Tyler, "are we going to do the holiday party or not?"

"Oh, shit—yes, we are. Thank you. On that date we spoke about. Hold on." Peter fished out his phone. "Just us," he said, tapping in some numbers. "No clients. Let everybody know?" And then he held up a finger to pause the conversation with Tyler. "Jonathan—sorry to disturb," said Peter. "How are you doing? Mm-hmm. Mm-hmm—good. Mm-hmm—great. Well, listen, I won't keep you. The bartender you used for your housewarming party—was he any good? Mm-hmm. He seemed good. I need someone for an agency thing I'm doing at my house. Mm-hmm. Can I get his number from you? What did he charge you? Mm-hmm, mm-hmm. And he was thorough and on-time, and all that? Mm-hmm. OK, great. Text me the number. You're a rock star. I'll call ya later. Big hug."

"Yay," said Tyler.

"Yeah, good," said Peter. "Agency staff and plus-ones, OK? I want to keep it under fifty. People, that is."

Will couldn't believe his eyes. It was the fanciest, if tiniest, New York apartment he'd yet seen.

"Whoa," he said, stepping into the minuscule entry hall and looking around.

"Take your coat off; make yourself comfortable," said Enrico, stepping away with a little squeeze of Will's wrist. "There is a closet on your left."

It was late, around midnight. Will had met Enrico at G, in Chelsea.

The entire hall, tiny though it was, had been painted in *faux marbre* to look like the interior of an ancient temple. Doorways leading off to the kitchen, where Enrico slipped away, and to a sitting room, opposite, were framed by trompe l'oeil Corinthian columns and classical pediments. The door to the coat closet was painted with a trompe l'oeil niche featuring a statue of Cupid.

"I'm just getting us a nibble," said Enrico, from the kitchen.

A delicate console and bijou of a mirror, flanked by two fragile-looking chairs, upholstered in pearl-colored silk that harmonized with the blue-gray of the "marble," clung decorously to one wall. Surrounding the mirror, which was framed in a band of gilt scroll-work, was a collection of scallop shells in different sizes, carved out of something that looked like ivory, hung in a pattern that appeared at first to be symmetrical, but on closer inspection proved subtly asymmetrical. Then the lighting altered. In a gentle cascade, the wall sconces and chandelier in the hall dimmed, and a little lamp on the console came on. Beyond, in the sitting room, done dramatically in black, lights came up to half, creating a warm, inviting glow. That room looked spectacular, too, though also quite small.

"Go on in," said Enrico, reappearing with a plate of cheese and nuts.

Will proceeded and tried to take it all in.

"Please feel free to sit, or of course look around," said Enrico.

"I don't think I've ever been in a black room before," said Will.

Enrico chuckled.

"Aubergine, please," he said. "I told you I am a designer." Enrico spoke with a light accent that Will had learned in the bar was Argentinean.

The room could have been no larger than twelve-by-fifteen feet, yet there were no surfaces or corners that had been left unembellished. The walls, moldings, and floors had been enameled in a lustrous, semi-matte finish that resembled onyx. Such a finish, which draws the eye to every bump and imperfection, would have been disastrous on an old surface, but Will noticed that every bit of wall, molding, and floor in the apartment appeared to have been newly renovated. Even a close look into a corner or at a joint betrayed no messiness.

Impressive, sort of, thought Will.

A writing desk, draped partially with what looked like a tapestry and topped by a life-sized plaster bust of someone agitated, with wind-tossed hair, occupied one corner of the room. Over the desk was a large oil painting of a nude, muscular man who had fallen down or been injured. A large window, festooned heavily in black silk, had been scrimmed over with some high-tech and unobtrusive-looking material.

"There's no view and not even much light," said Enrico. "Sit—please." There was a small black fauteuil, upholstered in yellow with gray medallions, but Enrico indicated the large settee that was the centerpiece of the room. "I think you will be comfortable there."

The settee was framed by ornate, built-in wooden bookcases with glass doors and set off by a dramatic baldachin suspended above, in black-and-purple-striped draping that hung down on either side of the settee, to create a plush, upholstered nook. Covered in purple striped damask, the settee was topped with silk and velvet pillows and bolsters in purples, grays, and yellows. In front of the settee was a mammoth hassock covered in a black-and-white hide that looked like palomino, which was topped with two piles of overscaled art books and, on a mirrored tray, some mismatched candlesticks and something that looked like an ostrich egg.

"There we are," said Enrico, placing the plate of cheese down on a book about Derain. "Comfy? How about some wine?"

Will nodded and Enrico, with a touch, opened a disguised door in one of the few blank spots on the wall, to reveal a mirrored bar that sparkled under concealed pin spots with glints from decanters, bottles, stemware, and glass shelving. The inside of the bar door was decorated in three little trompe l'oeil still life paintings, frames and all.

"Burgundy OK?"

"Sure," said Will.

Will wasn't quite sure how to be in such a room: remain attentive to all the details clamoring for attention, or ignore them in favor of some cumulative enjoyment of, what, luxury? Delirium? Will decided to do what was recommended in a certain sexual situation that was said to be pleasant but which he'd always found difficult: He tried to relax and open himself to the experience.

"Chin-chin! Welcome," said Enrico, insinuating himself onto the settee near Will, and pulling up a bolster on which to semi-recline.

"Cheers," said Will. The only place he could find to put his wineglass after taking a sip was on top of an art book. It looked precarious, but he promised himself to be careful. The fear of staining palomino with burgundy was not far from his mind.

"It's my little zone," said Enrico.

"How long have you been here?" said Will.

"Two years. Half of that was renovation."

"It's beautiful."

"Thank you."

"Do you own? You must."

"Yes."

"How many bedrooms do you have?"

Enrico made an expansive gesture, to indicate the room they were in.

"This is the bedroom," said Enrico. "There is only one."

"No. Really?" said Will.

"Yes. This is the bed—we are on it. This comes off"—he pulled up a corner of the damask, to show that it was a large spread—"and I push away the ottoman. Easy."

"You do?" said Will. "Every day?"

"Every day, every night."

"Hmm." Will noticed that hidden among the folds of baldachin drapery was a flat-screen television, mounted to the wall by a hinged arm.

"Yes," said Enrico. "And the hall becomes my dining room. I can do sit-down for six—eight, maybe, if we are all very good friends."

"And that's it—the whole apartment? I mean, it's gorgeous."

"Yes, the galley kitchen, you saw where that was, and the little bathroom is over there." Enrico pointed to another hidden door, the handle of which Will now recognized. "My printer and all that is in the bookcase."

"And what do you call this style?" asked Will. "I just don't know very much about décor—design."

Enrico giggled.

"Good question," he said. "In school we called it 'Louis Louis'—which means, mmm, French, classic, but loose. Oh, but you should have seen before the renovation, when I moved here— before I planned this. It was modern, *Moderne,* and mod, all mixed together! I had a lot of junk, but it was fun, I think!"

Enrico spoke in an animated way that Will found appealing, and he was handsome in a classic sense—with dark hair and eyes, and features formed with almost mathematical precision. His teeth were perfect. And Will knew from various cues—the smoothness of the neck, the muscularity of the hands, the tautness of the waist, all gleaned from some light snogging at the bar—that there was an amazing body underneath the neatly pressed exterior.

"Where did you go to school?" asked Will.

"Well, I was preparing for law in Argentina," said Enrico. "But then I went to Paris, and apprenticed with one of the big decorators there—very high society. "

"Out of the blue, you started apprenticing?"

"The decorator—we met at a party."

"Oh, uh-huh."

It was clear Enrico came from a good family, or money, or both.

"Then I became very serious and went to a school called Ecole Boulle—very well respected," said Enrico. "And then I came to New York, to be with a boyfriend, but . . ."

"It didn't work out?"

"No."

"Sorry."

"It's better this way."

Suddenly, Enrico seemed like such an adult. Will had assumed he was no older than his mid-thirties.

"May I ask how old you are?"

"Yes. I am twenty-seven."

"Ah."

"And you, if I may ask?"

"Same."

"Exactly?"

"Exactly."

It wasn't such a huge lie, Will thought, as they raised their glasses in a toast to the age of twenty-seven.

"And may I ask what you do, Will?"

Enrico took Will's hand and began to stroke it gently.

"I, uh, am temping right now at this law firm," said Will. "And I'm doing the cater-waiter thing, you know. I just arrived in New York, six months ago. But I'm transitioning into magazine editing. That's where I want to be. I just had an interview this morning, in fact."

"Oh, very good," said Enrico, expressing delight when Will told him the name of the company. "I know some people there."

"Yeah, I'm hopeful," said Will.

The interview had gone well, after a shaky start. He had gotten up early and arrived at the building half an hour before his appointment. He wore his only suit, and made it a point to polish his shoes.

"Come in, please. Sit down," said the head of HR.

"Thank you," said Will.

The office was small and surprisingly free of personal touches— no pictures or little objects. The desk was clear. The head of HR was apparently a legendary lady who had been in the position for decades. Unlike every other woman who worked at the company, regardless of age or station, the HR lady was distinctly unfashionable. She was dressed in a shapeless blue jacket and collarless white blouse that would have been too plain even for a '50s Hollywood parody of a librarian. Her short grayish hair was lifeless.

"What brings you in today?" the woman asked.

"I am very eager to work here," said Will.

"I see. And why here?"

"Well, because you publish the best magazines, and I believe I can contribute in a significant way."

One of the lady's eyes was strabismic, and at first Will was extremely self-conscious about where to look. He was uncertain as to which eye to focus on, and tried to look toward the one that was looking most directly at him, and hoping his disconcertment was not obvious.

"And I gather you know Stefan," said the lady.

"We just met the other day . . . or, night," said Will.

"He's one of our most valuable assets. And that's what this company has always looked for, in all economies—assets."

"That's awesome. A company is its people."

It was only after a few exchanges that Will's panic about looking at the lady subsided. She seemed to be kind, and Will began to feel as though they were actually having a conversation.

She can't be unaware of the issue, thought Will, *especially if she's been here for decades and decades. Clearly, handling this appropriately would be part of an interview.*

"Your clips are impressive," said the lady, shuffling through some printouts.

"Thanks," said Will.

"What was it like to speak with Beyoncé?"

"Beyoncé? Oh, remarkably easy. She's a very down-to-earth person, very forthcoming. We talked about a million more things than we could put in the interview."

"Really? Were you alone in the room with her?"

"Yes."

"Where?"

"Where did the interview take place? In a hotel room—the Saint Francis, I think. The publicist got us started, then she left us alone."

"Uh-huh. And how long did you have?"

"Well, they allotted twenty minutes, but we wound up speaking for two hours."

"Ah, so Beyoncé liked you."

"I think so."

"Good. Did you prepare your own questions?"

"Yes, pretty much."

"No guidance from your editor?"

"Actually, none at all. He didn't know much about music."

"And you do?"

"Pretty much."

"Did you record or take notes?"

"Both."

"Who landed the interview?"

"I did, actually. I had worked with the publicist before, for some of her other clients—you know, musical acts. She pitched me, and I pitched the magazine."

"Why you?"

"Because I'm . . . good?"

"Stars like you," said the lady gently, in a way that combined certainty with conjecture.

"Maybe," said Will, modestly.

"I can see why they would."

They talked a while longer, about Santa Barbara, hip-hop, and a new movie that was said to be an Oscar contender, then the interview was over. The HR lady stood up and extended her hand.

"It was a pleasure to meet you," she said, as she and Will shook.

"A pleasure to meet you, too. Thank you very much for your time."

What would happen next?

"We'll call you, one way or another, in a day or so. The next step would be for you to meet an editor who needs someone."

"OK."

"Let me think about it."

"Of course."

Will was jubilant as he left the building.

She wouldn't even be talking about next steps unless I had a chance.

"So you think it went well," said Enrico, still stroking Will's hand.

"Yeah, I do," said Will.

Enrico drew himself closer to Will and kissed his hand tenderly. Then he started caressing Will's neck and shoulder.

"That's good," whispered Enrico, kissing Will on the ear and cheek, and then on the lips. Will relaxed into the kiss and leaned back with Enrico, and the two men stayed that way, locked in a constantly evolving kiss, for several minutes—tongue giving way to little pecks, giving way to a kind of mutual heavy breathing and looking deeply into each other's eyes, with the stroking of hair, which led back to tongue kissing. Then Will pulled himself up onto one shoulder.

"Enrico . . . you have to forgive me. This is so nice, but I can't stay," he said.

"No?" said Enrico. "Are you sure? I thought we were . . ." In a friendly way, Enrico let his hand wander over Will's crotch, which betrayed an erection.

"I'd love to," said Will, "but it's later than I thought, and I have to be up so early. And I am just . . . finding myself so distracted. I'm a little overwhelmed. Can you forgive me?"

"Yes, of course," said Enrico, sitting up. "No worries. But, Will, I think you are a lovely man. I hope we can see each other again. Soon."

"Oh, definitely," said Will. "I would like that."

After collecting himself and a few more kisses with Enrico, Will was outside, on a sidewalk in the West Village, near Seventh Avenue. The air was chill and felt clean, and Will thought the scent of something like grapefruit might be clinging to his clothing, though he hadn't been aware of any fragrance in the apartment.

It was like waking up from a dream. And Will was truly tired, after having risen early for the interview and worked at the law firm much longer than usual, to make up for coming in late. He really shouldn't even have gone to G at all—and trompe l'oeil was just a bit too much to deal with.

Why do I do these things? Will thought. It seemed clear now, in retrospect, that all he'd really wanted to do after work was go home.

On his way to the subway, Will saw that he had two messages: one from Jonathan, and one from an unknown number.

"Will, Jonathan. I just wanted you to know I gave your number to a friend of mine who's looking for a bartender. A small holiday party in his home. His name is Peter. So he'll probably call you. And listen, when are we getting together again? Lemme know what your week looks like, OK? *Ciao* for now."

The next message was from Peter, who explained what he was looking for and when.

"It'll be supereasy, I think—wine and water for fifty, max. Some hors d'oeuvres to serve and clear, but they'll already be prepared. Whole Foods is delivering. So if you can do it, and you can do it for the same rate as Jonathan's party, I've love to talk. Lemme know?"

Now which one was Peter? thought Will. He didn't remember meeting a Peter, and all the guests had kind of looked alike.

CHAPTER 5

New York itself—that ludicrous creature—was one reason why Peter was now in advertising and not the field he thought he wanted in 1975, poetry. This was a thought he often had while sitting on the Promenade in Brooklyn Heights, as he liked to do occasionally, contemplating life and the postcard view of the lower Manhattan skyline rising over the East River.

Cities may affect a geological mode of existence, since they are solid and constructed of essentially the same materials as the caves they superseded, but they actually function more biologically than geologically. Cities are given birth by the human species—they're laid, or spun, or excreted—and then they grow and/or strengthen and/or fester through a life force of their own. Sometimes a new city will sprint along for a millennium or two, like Babylon, then find itself exhausted and need to rest. Sometimes a city won't find its stride for centuries, like London, and then, when it does, it will gallop for a while, only to trip on a stick and fall in the mud. On any given day cities seem permanent, as befits their sacred role as vessels of civilization, yet cities evolve over time like species do, adapting to new conditions of climate, commerce, and the like, in order to survive in changing ecological niches. And as cities evolve, civilization budges forward in a direction we call progress, once it proves dominant.

Sometimes the aspect of a city that best allows it to survive a great ecological shift is precisely its impermanence. Think of Troy, rebuilt again and again. Yet the story of how the permanent and the transient function together is never quite visible to a city's inhabitants, who can spend a lifetime walking its streets and contemplating its towers, laughing in its sidewalk cafés and sunning themselves on the steps of its marble-columned museums in springtime, poring over books of historical maps and beholding the urban countenance thousands of feet above the top of its tallest towers, from airplanes, and still not see enough. The full story is discernable only at the end of history, when the reasons why a city was born and died can be fathomed in perspective—which is why a city can be dead before it knows it, like ancient Rome, or more alive than it realizes, like New York today.

In the almost forty years since Peter arrived there, New York had changed profoundly. Unlike more decorous capitals, New York embraced new historical moments eagerly, even recklessly—a frenzy of maritime trade, an industrial revolution, an era of immigration, a belle époque, a jazz age, a great depression, a postwar imperium—which meant that while the rest of America was lingering at the victory bash of the 1950s, New York in the '60s was latching onto something new, once again. The city was famously poor in 1975, yet just beneath the graffiti'd crust of that moment was a forge of new wealth fueled by the work of bright young idea workers in the burgeoning sectors of media and advertising. So when America woke up to the fact that it was no longer manufacturing the fastest trains or most advanced cars, or supplying the best education or most comprehensive medical care, it found it had branding, a new-improved thought grammar that was chief among a whole suite of made-in-New York, consciousness-2.0 goods and services for a brave new world in which more people needed more things that were more essential to their well-being than train service and education.

It was branding that allowed new creeds to tendril into the gaps in American life left by the withering of old creeds devoted to Mom, apple pie, and Sunday dinner. *And people saw that it was good.* Would the stratum of remains left by this era be the one that in 10,000 years archaeologists stabilized as representing New York in its true golden age? *Who knew?* Wouldn't the stratum even just beneath, representing an age of bustling automats, lively theaters, and GIs kissing dames in the street, be judged less golden, less mythically American than the present age? *Maybe—if current trends prevailed.*

Peter often mused on questions like these, on the Promenade. There were no answers—only the pleasure of knowing that the view of the Manhattan skyline revealed something in motion. Once there were twin towers, then there weren't; now there were new towers. Peter was grateful that his aimlessness earlier in life had allowed him to make the most of the speed bumps he encountered during the '80s, which jarred him into better sync with the newest of New Yorks—even if advertising did sometimes seem nuts and the connection between now and yesterday had become obscure. He wondered if archaeologists of the future would envy those who were walking around the city now, during its current heyday, when so many mad, exciting, unprecedented things were being done and remained to be done, and created and imagined. . . .

Will called back the next day.

"Peter? This is Will. The bartender from Jonathan's party?"

"Oh, hi."

"I got your message. Sorry it took me so long to respond."

"Oh, no problem. Thanks for getting back to me."

"Sure. You're doing a party?"

"Yes—a holiday thing for my agency. Just some wine and hors d'oeuvres. Maybe forty, fifty people. At my place in Brooklyn Heights."

"Great."

"So you can do it?"

"I'd love to."

"Sorry for the short notice."

"No problem. I'm free the night you mentioned."

"OK, good. Well. And you can do it for the rate you charged Jonathan?"

"Yeah, absolutely."

"I'm calling it for six to nine, and let's say you come an hour early—that's five o'clock—and stay a bit afterward, tidy up—so ten, at the latest. Five hours?"

"Sounds good to me. What do you want me to wear? Black, like I did at Jonathan's?"

"Uh, yeah, if you're comfortable in that. I have a chef's apron, too, if you want."

"OK."

"And I told you I'm in Brooklyn Heights."

"Right. Nice."

"You'll see my place is pretty small. It's an open kitchen. You'll probably be able to plant yourself at the counter and cover the door, as well."

"Sure. I used to run my family's parties all the time."

"Good. I know it will be totally manageable. So why don't I e-mail you some directions?"

They exchanged e-mail addresses.

"Forgive me, Will," said Peter, "but my memory of Jonathan's party is a little hazy. We didn't talk that night, did we?"

"I don't remember," said Will. "I don't think so."

"I mean, I probably asked for a vodka and you probably gave it to me, right?"

"Probably. Earthshaking, wasn't it?"

Peter laughed.

"Epic," he said.

"So will it be some of the same people?" said Will. "I'm just wondering."

"Oh, no, no," said Peter. "Lord, no. Very nice men, that whole crowd—dear friends. But this is a little thing for my company. I have an ad agency. So it'll be my staff and some of their friends. Very mixed. But cool. A bit younger than . . . Well, mixed."

After speaking with Will, Peter called Jonathan, to thank him for the recommendation.

"He seems like a very nice guy," said Peter.

"Oh, good—it worked out, I'm glad," said Jonathan. "He's a nice kid—intelligent, curious, funny in a dry way."

"You realize I'm only asking him to pour the wine and answer the door."

"I'm just saying."

"And, Jonny, I hope you can come, too. Think you're gonna be up to it?"

"Well, we'll see. Can I let you know?"

"Of course."

"I just don't know what shape I'll be in. That'll be a little after my first course of treatment. I may be flat on my back, nauseous and weak, eighty-eight pounds, with no hair."

"And . . . not in the mood for a party, you're saying?"

"Maybe," said Jonathan. "If I find the right shirt to wear, at Barneys."

Peter giggled.

"That's my boy," he said.

"Seriously," Jonathan continued, "I don't know how to plan anymore. I don't even know how to think about the future. And I'm not trying to be poetic here. I just get up, see to my work, see to my cancer, period. I put one foot in front of another. And in one way, it's all very easy. And no bullshit. I don't give any, I don't take any. It's all for real, all for the record. I don't know what's going to happen— but the thing is, that's the way life is *anyway,* right? Nobody knows anything about the future. Yet we operate as if we do; it's so comfy that way. It's like I'm in recovery from this delusion that tomorrow is going to be just like today. Which it fucking may not be."

"Recovery is an interesting way to look at it."

"Seriously, Peter. One day at a time."

The house where Will lived, in Astoria, was two blocks from the N line, which runs on elevated tracks out in that neighborhood. The grittiness of Thirty-first Street, a perfectly safe and serviceable boulevard of shops and small businesses directly underneath the tracks, immediately gives way to tidy residential side streets lined with oak, pear, and maple trees. The neighborhood, which had always been modestly middle-class, stands on ground once home to Indians, then owned by Peter Stuyvesant, then part of one of the farms that occupied the area for two centuries, then developed, in the early twentieth century, into single family homes for the immigrants who were arriving in Queens in successive waves. Built in 1920 for a second-generation German American who worked in the nearby Steinway factory and eventually moved with his family to Westchester, the house was bought by the father of Will's land-lady, who had arrived in the U.S. with his family and thousands of other Greek immigrants just before the First World War. Shortly before the landlady's father died in 1968, he converted the house into two apartments, in one of which, on the ground floor, the land-lady, now a widow, still lived.

The original contours of the house, a standard, two-story box with minuscule front and back yards, had been swallowed by cum-brous improvements, like an expanded kitchen and family room, and an exterior stairway to the now-independent second-story apart-ment. A wrapping of white plastic siding unified the house's entire accreted bulk, which was both joined to and kept separate from the street by an elaborate growth of red-and-white-brick fencing, steps, and porch. And the house was the single remaining, formerly one-family residential structure on the block. Jammed onto properties once occupied by similar houses on either side of the house, and on most of the rest of that block and surrounding blocks, were now undistinguishedly bland three-story apartment buildings built in the '70s, just as the neighborhood's population was plateauing.

Will and Luz frequently told friends how lucky they felt to have found the place. The house was just a five-minute walk from their N train stop, only the fifth stop in Queens, which meant it was only twenty-one minutes from Times Square. The place was a lot more convenient and a much better value than the supposedly supercool Lower East Side, they said. Astoria, in fact, was the new "secret" discovery of a large segment of young New York professionals, who couldn't afford the high rents in Manhattan and wanted to avoid the lower living standards in the affordable parts of Brooklyn. If Astoria did have some environmental issues due to traffic conges-tion and the nearby Con Ed plant, which contributed to rising local asthma numbers with record-level air pollution, this was still the neighborhood Will felt was more him than any other he'd seen, in-cluding others with burgeoning gay enclaves like Bushwick and Windsor Terrace.

Of course, nothing in New York—not even what he had seen of Park Avenue, that parade of limestone fortresses—was as much Will as the five-bedroom, Mediterranean-style villa in Santa Barbara where he grew up: a fifteen-acre, so-called "in-town ranch" at the edge of Los Padres National Forest, built by his parents the year after Will was born, complete with terraced pool, a producing avocado orchard, and views of the Pacific and the Santa Ynez Mountains. Will missed home and the easy lifestyle he shared with friends and family, which had continued through the time he was in school in San Francisco and afterward, when he moved to L.A. He would return often for parties and hiking and swimming, and there was never a worry of asthma or traffic congestion on San Roque Road. Will had never felt particularly privileged until he moved to New York, and was now, truthfully, not 100 percent comfortable being made constantly to think of himself that way, as he went about his life in the city among reasonable people so apparently unconcerned about lacking basic comforts and pleasures. Nor did it feel right to bond with someone like Enrico, who had clearly come from a privileged background, solely on the basis of, whatever, class expectations.

The apartment's renovation had probably been expensive and was clearly meant to be luxurious, but the result was nonetheless cheesy. The look was generic Home Depot's best: Sheetrock walls, painted linen white; laminated hardwood flooring in pecan; double-hung, vinyl windows of the energy-saver variety. New ceiling fans with the look of brass and walnut contributed a "heritage" touch, while the kitchen proposed "Mediterranean" via faux-rustic cabinet doors and a ceiling lamp in faux-wrought iron and faux-stained glass. The lamp hung directly over the kitchen table, one of the pieces of furniture that came with the place.

"Sometimes I have to wonder if I'm looking for something that really isn't here," said Will to Luz one night, shortly after they had arrived in New York. "I mean, I'm here now and I'm going to give it a year or so, but sometimes I think I'll wind up back in California. Or, I dunno—Switzerland."

"Switzerland?!"

"Yeah, one of those beautiful cities on Lake Geneva, or one of those amazing mountain towns. We used to go to Zermatt every year, to ski. My family rented a house there. Did you know they only have electric cars in Zermatt? They don't want pollution to spoil the view of the Matterhorn."

"Doing what, may I ask? With whom?"

"What do you mean?"

"How are you supporting yourself in the Zermatt scenario? Are you working? Are you in a relationship?"

"Oh. I don't know."

Luz smirked genially.

"Minor details," she said.

"I know," sighed Will. "It's a dream."

"More like a fantasy."

Luz was an East L.A. girl, originally. She and Will met at Berkeley and then saw each other on the Hollywood party scene, but they hadn't been particularly close until moving in together in Astoria, and then a deeper friendship blossomed—something like what Will had with his sisters, but more challenging, in a good way. Will liked Luz's directness, her talents for frank discussion and intelligent compromise—good qualities for a lawyer, which had also proved themselves useful when the two of them were moving in and needed to figure out how to deploy their personal items among the pieces of furniture that came with the place, and what new pieces needed to be bought. But Luz was also warm, caring, real— and she was that way constantly, and never seemed to fake it or waver from it. Their friendship felt healthy to Will, mature. He and Luz began referring to each other jokingly among friends as "my gay husband" and "my straight wife."

"Must not live in fantasy world," said Will, punctuating each word of the resolution with a poke to the side of his head with his forefinger. "Guess we can live without that."

"Yes, we can," said Luz.

They were hanging pictures. Luz had a set of three abstract silkscreens she had done as an undergraduate, that they were installing on the wall of the living room, above a Crate and Barrel-ish sofa that was another of the pieces of furniture that came with the apartment.

"Case in point—Rob," said Luz, while continuing to play with the exact position of the silkscreens. Rob was the movie studio executive with the penthouse in Century City. She had never liked him.

"No, you're right. It's a fantasy."

"Two fucking years! That man wasn't good enough for you, sweetie."

"I know."

"You know *now*. So enough. You need to find a man who's worthy of you. Stop wasting time."

"Ouch."

"You know I adore you, *mi amor*."

"Worthy of me—what a concept."

"Of course, worthy of you. I learned this from my family. My dad's a tailor; my mom is a cook. Self-respect was the name of the game. Otherwise, you know how jerked around I would have been, just because I am this beautiful woman you see before you?"

"You're saying I'm spoiled."

"Not spoiled."

"Lazy."

"Just not in the habit."

Will had begun to worry, in fact, that he lacked the habit of personal growth that others seemed to possess. Everything he knew he should be doing at this stage of his life with jobs and men seemed unnatural to him, and everything that came naturally, especially with men, seemed more or less a dead end—an attractive dead end, perhaps, but dead nonetheless. Everyone else seemed to be finding their so-called next levels, as if they'd been taught to do so, but for Will, so far, the quest was largely theoretical. He tried to mimic what he saw other people doing, but knew he wasn't doing it very well: go to New York, find job, date men—are we adults yet?

And in back of this worry was something worse. Luz had actually named it once, as if it were the easiest thing in the world to name, accept, control, and surpass: fear. Will had begun to be afraid he wouldn't be able to find a next level, that there was no next level for him; that he might actually be kind of content at his current level, and that this complacency was something like a blessing and damnation all in one. This had been a nagging feeling even when he was in L.A., with Rob, who was so supermotivated. Now, in New York, it had become truly unpleasant. Whenever people spoke about their passions and projects and intentions for the coming year, Will felt embarrassment and shame. That was new for him. Luz had helped him name those feelings, too. Sometimes Will found himself exaggerating the passions and intentions he did have, because suddenly they felt vague and juvenile. Sometimes he heard himself dwelling on them too much in conversation—". . . supposed to be meeting my sister in Paris . . . ," blah-blah-blah—and that made him feel even worse.

Luz was right: He *was* spoiled. Why else would every day in that apartment feel like exile from his real self? Two blocks from an elevated train! A two-family house with no landscaping! Exile was a persistent ache, if a manageable one. And what if the next level were even lower than the current one, if he were sliding down toward something truly abysmal? Like moving into his parents' guesthouse.

A few days after his visit to Enrico's apartment, Will was sitting at the kitchen table with Luz when Enrico called. He went to his room to take the call, then came back to the table.

"He wants to do something this weekend," said Will.

"And?" said Luz.

"He texts me, like, ten times a day."

"You gonna see him?"

"I guess so."

"But?"

"No chemistry."

"I thought you went home with him."

"I did."

"*Why* did you go home with him?"

"I thought he was hot, a nice guy."

"OK."

"I told you about the apartment."

"He fell into your trap."

"What do you mean?"

"You see a guy, he looks hot, you do that thing, Will—with the sparkly eyes and the big smile. I've seen you do it a hundred times, and it always works. 'Cause you're the designated Cutest Guy in the Room."

"Oh, now . . ."

"Right? You've always been. You learned it around eleven, right? By the time you were, like, fourteen—*pfft*. But then what?"

Will sighed.

"Exactly," continued Luz. "Those are tricks, sweetie. Believe me, I know all about it, because we girls, we have our own tricks, as you may have heard. Only some of us are smart enough, we know when to give it a rest."

"Oh, come on," said Will. "You know I know better than that."

"Oh, yes, you do. But you're gonna tell me that, walking down Eighth Avenue, you don't feel like you can get anybody you want?"

"Well . . ."

Will's smirk gave him away.

"That!" said Luz, pointing at him. "You see? That look says everything."

"What look?" said Will, giggling.

"You're so proud of yourself! That's, like, your superpower. Dope, you need to hang up that shit."

"No walking down Eighth Avenue? No talking to other men?"

"Did I say that? No, sweetie. You just need to find the rest of your power. It's not all in those *ojos azules*."

Will was silent for a second, thinking. And then Luz finished her thought.

"Because you're almost thirty, mister. You wanna be rocking those tricks when you're fifty?"

Peter's get-together took place a week later. It was just before Thanksgiving, when New York's seasonal parry against the on-slaught of short, sunless days was coming into full swing, with in-cessant inducements to shop, party, celebrate.

On the sidewalk in front of Peter's house in Brooklyn Heights, just before five, Will stopped to answer a text from Enrico.

How did the interview go?

Fine, thx—the ed. was cool. But lemme call ya later. Going into a gig.

It was almost dark, and the evening was cool and clear. Will felt a little shivery, having chosen to wear a jacket that was lighter and more stylish than his heavy coat; the jacket would be easier to man-age, should he want to go out after the party. He double-checked the address in his iPhone against the number on the door in brass numerals, then mounted the stoop and rang the bell.

Once again, the *blerp-blerp* of an incoming text sounded from his pocketed phone.

Calm down, buddy, thought Will, without checking it.

Peter came to the door in jeans and a polo shirt, looking unlike any of the older gentlemen Will remembered from Jonathan's party.

"Hi, hi—c'mon in," said Peter.

"Hi," said Will.

The house was much more charming than any Will had seen in New York—an old house in great shape, warm and homey, without the interpolation of too much modernness. The architectural elements in the hall looked more restored than renovated—the wide planks of the floor, the original turned-wood banister of the stairway leading up to the second floor. Hanging on the wall, echoing the muted red, white, and yellow in the Persian rug at the foot of the stairs, was a fifteen-foot-long sign proclaiming MURRAY'S CUT-RATE CIGARS, in faded, hand-painted letters. Peter's landlady had rescued the sign, years before, from the demolition of a building on the Lower East Side.

Peter showed Will through a large door into the parlor floor apartment, where he lived.

"Very nice," said Will, taking the place in. "Eighteen forty-three, huh?"

"Yeah—oh, the plaque outside?" said Peter. "My landlady just put that up. We're one in a row of four brick houses—maybe you noticed, as you came in? All sort of small-scale. They were built twenty years before the real so-called brownstones."

"Cool."

Peter walked Will through the place, showed him the bedroom, the bathroom, the back door and, from the porch, the garden beyond. He pointed out the original moldings, several of the artworks. Lights were low and votive candles flickered from little sapphire-colored glass cups, all around the apartment.

"Put your stuff in the bedroom," said Peter, "and I'll show ya what I've done."

Will was taller than Peter remembered, and much better looking. Why had such a handsome guy failed to make an impression on him? Peter wondered. Vainly, he tried to remember him from Jonathan's party, behind the bar, but drew a blank.

"I see you've got everything set up," said Will, surveying the kitchen, which was open to the living area. Peter had come home from the office early, to prepare. Arrayed on the counter, under tiny spotlights hidden under the cabinets, were several bottles of wine, a phalanx of stemware and tumblers, a cutting board with a knife, some lemons and limes, and a corkscrew. Also on the counter was a platter of shrimp; and set up around the apartment were baskets of crudités and dip, and platters of *meze* appetizers.

"Yeah," said Peter. "And here's what I was thinking about, for the hot hors d'oeuvres." He produced a printed schedule that noted the times when the baking sheets he'd lined with canapés should go into the oven and come out, and be passed among the guests. One sheet was already in the oven, heating up, and three more were waiting in the refrigerator. Peter also showed Will where the rest of the wine and soft drinks were.

Will was amused by the written schedule.

"I do the same thing for parties," he said. "It's good to stay organized."

"It helps, right?" said Peter. "Anyway, poke around, see where everything is. I have to answer three more e-mails. Oh, and people can put their coats either on the hooks out in the hallway or on the bed."

"How long have you lived here?" asked Will, when Peter returned to the kitchen. He was opening one of the bottles of red wine.

"Thirty-seven years," said Peter. "My late boyfriend and I moved here pretty much directly from college, and I've been here ever since. He died in 1989."

"Oh, sorry," said Will.

"Works *much* better for one person. Sorry, Harold!" When telling people about the apartment Peter sometimes added that Harold died right in the spot where the daybed was; in this case, he thought better of it.

"And you said advertising, right?" said Will.

"Right," said Peter. "And may I ask what you do—I mean, besides this?"

"It's a long story."

"Bartending-as-well-as."

"Exactly. Actually, I had an interview this morning for a job I'm up for, at a magazine—my second interview. Fingers crossed."

"An editor thing?"

Will named the magazine and told Peter about the interview. The editor in chief who had seen Will had "turned the magazine around" and run it for the past few years; he spent a large portion of every evening, apparently, going to parties and being photographed with leggy babes. He seemed a nice enough guy in person, but didn't always look directly at Will when speaking to him; in fact, he had let his managing editor, a gay man with a shaved head and big glasses, pretty much run the meeting.

"We're going even more in a celebrity direction," said the managing editor.

"And we're taking more of it online," said the editor in chief. "Just in case print is, you know, dying."

Will didn't know if the remark was supposed to be funny or not, but tried to look as if he thought it was at least wry.

"Onscreen interviews?" asked Will.

The question seemed to surprise the editors.

"Those, too, probably," said the editor in chief.

"You'd be great onscreen," said the managing editor.

"They've been trying to figure out what to do online for years," observed Peter. "Maybe you can help them solve it."

As Peter and Will were talking, Peter poured himself a club soda.

"Lime?" said Will.

"Sure," said Peter.

Guests began arriving around six-thirty. Deftly, Will managed the door and the coats, and got people started with their drinks, while Peter, after putting on some music, began chatting with his guests. It was forty-five minutes later when Peter realized what a good time he was having and how effortless the hosting was for him. Will was handling the mechanics beautifully. Peter, while enjoying the company of friends and coworkers, noticed Will across the room, filling glasses and plating hors d'oeuvres; and then there he was, right next to Peter, with a platter of phyllo-parsnip-and-gruyère puffs, encouraging people to try one.

He's so smooth, Peter thought. Will was better than any of the other guys he'd ever hired for a party—realer, warmer, noticeably more competent. And though the party's small talk touched flatteringly on the fact that poor Peter lived alone in that beautiful apartment, without a boyfriend to share it with, Peter, in fact, was enjoying the evening hugely. He saw himself, at one point, in the movie moment when the chatter in a room full of people goes distant and the music swells, with a close-up on the leading man's happy-looking face, meaning, "Me in my lovely home, with my lovely friends, with this lovely young man running my kitchen."

And then suddenly Will was standing next to him, as a friend might do—only Will, in his apron, was bearing a fresh club soda with lime, and took away the old glass, which he had spotted as empty from across the room.

When Tyler arrived, the party, already in gear, kicked up a notch. He greeted everyone elaborately and introduced everyone to his date, a glossy young man named Matt, who ran a PR company representing entertainment types.

"G-Star and Lindeberg," said Tyler, looking Peter over appreciatively, when they found a moment alone. "Very good."

"Your work here is done," said Peter, wrapping his arm around Tyler's waist and pulling the boy closer. "No, Tyler, it isn't! What would I do without you?"

"I always love your place. It works so well for a party!"

"People are having a good time, right?"

"Matt's boyfriend is coming, by the way. I told him to meet us here. Is that OK?"

"Of course. So you're not seeing this guy?"

"I haven't decided yet."

"Tyler!"

"No—they're probably splitting up! The boyfriend is much younger."

"But Matt's only your age."

"Jacob is, like, nineteen. He's a model."

"How long have they been together, four minutes?"

"Yes, four minutes." There was no talk of Damiano.

They were joined by Frank, a straight guy from the production side of the office.

"By the way, Petey, I gather that guy is not your boyfriend," said Frank, gesturing toward Will.

"Oh, no, no," said Peter.

"We all thought he was," said Frank.

"He's helping me out for the evening."

"You should have said that."

"What do you mean? I introduced him."

"You said his name was Will, like we should know him."

"Oh, I don't know how to do these things."

"You should have said, 'This is Will. He'll get you a drink.' "

And the party chugged on, happily. Even the arrival of Jonathan, who looked noticeably fragile and was showing a bit of rash on his face, didn't deflate the evening. Jonathan installed himself in a chair, and Peter tended to him for a while, before leaving his friend in the hands of a little group who wanted to know all about the new film and Connor Frankel's coming out.

"Everything OK?" said Will, as Peter poked into a kitchen drawer for a couple of paper napkins.

"Absolutely," said Peter, shutting the drawer and squeezing past Will, to wet the napkins in the sink. "Will, I can't believe what a fantastic job you're doing."

"Nice crowd," said Will.

"No spills, either," said Peter.

Will laughed; there actually had been a small spill that Will cleaned up before Peter could notice. The crowd *was* nice, thought Will—attractive, smart, and mixed in a way that seemed to be exactly what he had been looking for, socially: gay and straight, men and women, young and old—though Peter was probably the oldest person in the room. Yet Peter didn't seem that way at all. He had a certain energy that fit right in with this mix—that seemed to spark it up, in fact.

He seems like a nice guy, Peter thought. *Organized, yes, and there's something great about the way he moves—negotiating the limits of my little kitchen, making his work look easy.*

It was an unexpected pleasure for Peter to squeeze so smoothly past Will in that tight space—to make just the right moves in coordination with the guy, to notice that their synched moves meant they were on the same wavelength about how a body should move in those circumstances. It was a pleasure as visceral as in a dream. With a flood of emotion Peter realized he hadn't had that feeling of being in someone's wake like that since Harold. He'd been close to other men, of course—danced, had sex. He and Nick had even shared that same kitchen, though with Nick there was always bumping into each other and never quite moving together in a way that felt natural. It was something special, Peter realized, to co-inhabit close quarters with someone gracefully; to coexist chore-ographically; to know always where the other body was and what its trajectory might be; to sense its progress, not just by visually tracking its parts but by detecting the movement of air surrounding it, triangulating the sounds it made, processing the molecules of sweat or fabric softener emanating from it—one per billion being enough to let you know if you're a bit closer to it or a bit farther away.

Peter had taken this smoothness between Harold and himself as organic proof of their compatibility, but he hadn't remembered this in a conscious way until that evening. Suddenly, he felt that with Will he was once more speaking a native language that he hadn't spoken in decades.

Wow, interesting, thought Peter.

People ate all the food and stayed late. They started leaving around ten. Jonathan made a date with Peter for the opera, as he was leaving. He also made a point of saying good night to Will, giv-ing the guy a little hug—which Peter thought odd. Tyler, on his way out, asked Peter to join him and "some crazy people" at a bar in Williamsburg, but Peter declined.

"I'm sticking right here," he said.

"Then see you at the office," sang Tyler. "Thank you very much. Fantastic party." Then he whispered, "I hope you two will be very happy."

"I'm glad you could come, Tyler."

"He's so into you."

"It's his job. I'm paying him."

"Alrighty."

After the last guest had gone, Peter was delighted to see that the house had been returned to normal, and the trash and recycling taken to the cans out front.

"You were wearing a suit, weren't you, that night at Jonathan's?" said Will.

"Yeah, I guess I was."

They were standing at the end of the kitchen counter, equidistant from the front door and the two armchairs where Peter liked to sit and talk with friends. Will had already tucked away the envelope Peter gave him.

"Is a suit more your work look?" said Will.

"Actually, no, it isn't," said Peter. "I doll up in Brooks Brothers only for very special occasions."

"It's a good look. Men should wear suits more often."

"I agree. I remember once on a Nile cruise we met this older gentleman—a dealer of antiquities from San Francisco, Louis Pappas. He wore strict Brooks Brothers and nothing else. Blue blazer, gray slacks, period. Lovely man—white hair, very courtly. He spotted us at dinner on the first night of the cruise and invited us to join him at his table. He ordered wine and he insisted we dine together every night. It was three or four nights, I think. I remember he was looking for a head of Alexander, to buy for a client."

"This was you and your late boyfriend?"

"Yeah, in, like, the early eighties. So check this out. One morning we're supposed to go for a ride in a felucca—you know, one of those Egyptian sailboats—and Louis tries to get into the boat—he walked with a cane, by the way—and he falls into the Nile, right in the mud. I mean, it was only two feet of water and he was fine—all of these cruise people jumped into the water to save him—but he was a mess. Mud all over his blue blazer and gray flannel slacks! They found his cane and helped him back to the ship, and Harold and I went on the felucca ride alone. And don't you know, when we returned to the ship, later, there was Louis in *another* blue blazer and another pair of gray slacks. The first outfit had been sent out for cleaning. That was all he ever traveled with, he told us—blue and gray. It made it easy."

"Amazing."

"Can you imagine? That world? Kind of great. But I think we may have moved on."

Nile cruise. Dead boyfriend. Peter heard himself slipping into that thing he did with young men he was interested in. Only, until then, he hadn't known he was interested in Will, nor was there much foundation, he knew, for him to *be* interested, beyond the boy's looks and five hours of employer-employee communication. Peter wanted to ask Will to stay for a drink but couldn't find the courage. The choreographic ease between them had somehow morphed into a field of gently repellant energy. Will looked quite ready to be dismissed.

"Hey, well—thanks again," said Peter. "Your great, great work totally helped make the party a big success."

"You're welcome. It was fun," said Will. "You know, being new in New York, it's nice to be able to visit a party like this, with really cool people, even if I'm still, you know, the bartender guy."

Peter felt touched, suddenly.

"Well, then, Will . . . the next time I do one of these things, you'd be perfectly welcome to come as a guest, if you want. I mean, I'd like that. People enjoyed talking to you. . . ."

"Oh, that would be nice—thank you."

"Great."

"Cool."

"And, you know," continued Peter, "I get invited to tons of events all the time, big parties and such, and I hate going alone and love to spread the wealth. So maybe, I dunno, sometime, you'd wanna come along. . . ."

"Yeah, maybe. Cool."

They agreed to talk further, then said good night—with a handshake, instead of a kiss, though in New York's kiss-everybody circles, even the mention of possibly attending an event together put the two of them squarely in kiss-each-other territory.

There were several more texts from Enrico for Will to read, on his way to the subway. It sounded like Enrico, too, had been at a party, but bored. Will went straight through the turnstile and put away his phone, without answering.

Him, I'll deal with tomorrow, he thought. *Right now I need to get home and into the bathtub.*

CHAPTER 6

"Mortality just isn't the horror it's cracked up to be. Though it's certainly no picnic thinking you might not be around next summer."

"No."

Jonathan was on the phone with Peter, updating him on the Connor Frankel film project.

"It's partly a gift, I think, mortality," said Jonathan, "an opportunity for comfort, even joy—if you embrace it. Do you know what I mean?"

"I think so," said Peter.

It was late on a weekday morning. Peter, with the earbuds of his iPhone stuck in his ears, was walking through the bright, spacious aisles of the largest Walgreens in suburban New Jersey, fifty-five minutes from Manhattan. He was doing reconnaissance on the design and display of mass-market body and skin care products, in advance of a client meeting with the makers of a line of organic wellness products. He was taking pictures of shelves and displays, gathering products to purchase and take back to the office for discussion, and generally letting himself take in the big-box store vibe. A car and driver were waiting outside in the parking lot.

"But you have to embrace it," said Jonathan. "That denial-of-death thing we remember from Psychology 101 was only the beginning. America's gotten completely cut off from the natural flow of life and death. *You* know. Most people today know as much about death as they do about sex, which is nothing, of course, except for what they see on TV—and that's pure entertainment. This commitment to entertainment is blotting out our humanity, Peter."

"I know."

"These are notes I make for the film. I'm on my laptop. Anyway, I can see all this much better now. Thank you, cancer—thank you very much."

Peter had been looking at the label on a bottle of shampoo. But when Jonathan called he tossed the bottle into his cart and wheeled to the end of the aisle, out of traffic, in order to concentrate on his friend's call. In a way, he thought, many of the store's products hoped to build sales on consumer emotions deriving from exactly the life-and-death urgencies Jonathan was talking about. From the shelves behind Peter came kind word of real benefits from scores of well-meaning brands, along with the loud and sometimes comically crude blandishments of other brands more interested in higher profits than the well-being of their consumers. Even seemingly small choices that go into product design—imagery, typeface, color, texture, material—determined what would fly and what would nose-dive as the result of deeply rooted consumer responses that Peter was paid to diagnose. Did the image of the sun on this tube of skin cream say "warm and life-giving" or something more akin to "scorching and carcinogenic"? Did the particular shade of green on the packaging of that shower gel resonate as "earthy and natural" or "bio-hazard from Mars"? Was the plain, sans-serif typeface on a vial of "complexion clarifying serum" more about purity or sterility? Some brands seemed to represent real souls who genuinely cared about the human beings on the other end of the supply chain, while other brands clearly stood for robo-execs programmed to know how the choice of a color called "process dark spring green," printed on high-density polyethylene and seen under electronic ballast fluorescent lighting on the shelf of a big-box store, would affect the bottom line.

"It's precisely because mortality is this ultimate failure that we don't want to think about it, we Americans," continued Jonathan. "Mortality is a kind of anti-achievement. It's all about the flesh, like obesity, so an obviously mortal person, say a cancer patient, is thought to be—well, may even think himself to be—weak or stupid or out of control. Which of course we *all* are with death, aren't we?"

"Mm-hmm."

"Denying mortality is denying the body, which is exactly what we did when we transformed sex into entertainment, so we could control it, right? I mean, happily we deny visceral pleasure, even experience itself. Not so much gay men, but there, too. Where are the new sexual explorers to replace the ones we used to know? Gay men are having sex like straight guys nowadays. They need it to be over in a flash, because prolonged pleasure and joy would mean losing control, which no one really wants to do. . . ."

Jonathan paused.

"Sorry," he said. "I know I'm going off here."

"You go, girl," said Peter.

"Anyway, I'm making notes and having the most incredible conversations with Connor. He says he doesn't feel he has to be in control of 'that side of things' anymore. Can you imagine? Coming out at eighty-three? Oh, and listen. We've had to adapt the process to fit my delicate condition. We'd been hoping to visit a few of his former homes together and shoot there, but I just can't bop around the way I used to. So now the interview part is just him and me sitting in chairs, talking, thinking out loud."

"Interesting," said Peter. Jonathan was simply going to talk on camera with Frankel *My Dinner With André*–style, session after session, until one of them couldn't do so any longer—presumably, this would be Jonathan—at which point the assistant director and editor would take over and shape the film.

"Yeah, it'll be great," said Jonathan. "He's letting us use some personal photographs."

"Nice."

"Petey, Americans just don't want to think anymore. Why is that?"

"I dunno."

"They have preferences instead. Would you like nonfat milk in your Frappuccino? Whole milk? Soy milk? Two-percent? Extra shot of espresso? Drizzle on your whipped cream? Most people don't know how to go any deeper or even that deeper exists. Tell me, Petey, did you get any logic in high school? Any statistics?"

"Logic—I got a little in math. It was 'the new math.' "

"Me too! They used to teach stuff like that, didn't they? How to think. But they don't anymore. Do you think people who like Henderson McCaw can tell you the difference between induction and deduction?"

Peter snorted a little laugh.

"And if they can't handle thinking," continued Jonathan, "forget about thinking *through*."

"It's funny," said Peter. "Your job is discussing life and death with one of the world's greatest living artists. Mine, apparently, is having lunch with a scumbag like Henderson McCaw."

"What?"

"That's right—next week."

"Oh, Peter. Business?"

"Could be. Big cross-platform branding thing."

"Really."

"My superiors are pressuring me to consider it."

"Why?"

"Why else? Money."

"Well, good luck."

"Thanks. But wait—can I ask you to hold a sec?"

With his friend on hold, Peter sent himself a two-word e-mail: "serum" and "McCaw." He needed to remember to ask Tyler to prepare a dossier on Henderson McCaw and also to work up a little study about whether the word "serum" was doing the same work in the consumer's mind that it was thought to be doing until then. Previously, the word sounded expensive and clinical-in-a-good-way, when used in the context of skin care. But did "serum" now, because of growing talk about bioterror and pandemic, carry a stronger whiff of world annihilation?

"Sorry, I'm back," said Peter. He noticed a shopper—a well-dressed, middle-aged woman, undoubtedly within the wellness client's target demographic—watching him as if she couldn't figure out why a man in a black Prada suit would be pushing a cart so full of toiletries through a Walgreens on a weekday morning.

"Listen, we can talk another time, if this isn't good," said Jonathan.

"No, no. Now's good. I'm just shopping."

"I'll let you go. I just wanted you to hear what we've been up to."

"Sounds like good stuff."

"It's just that—thinking our way up to death, trying to think beyond it, is so crucial to our species. To be able to do that was an evolutionary advantage—as important as language itself, in my view. 'Hello, death' is possibly *the* most important thing we can say to ourselves. Embracing death becomes this huge advantage to survival—not the individual, the culture. You know the way they say that microbes that wiped out practically the entire human race, thousands of years ago, became part of our genome and made us stronger?"

"Like you just said—adaptation."

"Exactly," said Jonathan. "Accepting death brings a usefully heroic dimension to everyday life."

Peter often said he'd never have achieved his current state of fulfillment, personal and professional, without the loss of Harold. Before it, he was a longtime companion who wrote a little poetry. Not a dishonorable role, yet he wasn't aware of wanting more until suddenly he had less. After Harold's death, Peter had to become more focused on earning a living. He started in magazines and saw he could make ends meet, which was nice—though the need to do so proved its own reward. A life need not be long to be whole, as he and Harold used to say. Without Harold, it seemed the only thing to do was try to make his own life *more* whole.

Conveniently, though Peter had lost no loved ones during childhood, he had been well trained to face death and keep going. He had grown up with the Bomb—the constant threat of sudden nuclear annihilation. It was a dogma, that threat, and religiously taught. At one point he and his schoolmates were ducking-and-covering at school at least as frequently as he was receiving communion in church. And there were other lessons, too—from actual religion, Catholicism, which told him that he'd witness the glory of the Second Coming after rising from a death he was thus fervidly to await; from social studies, which taught him that he might be called to risk his life one day in war, as his father had done; from science fiction, which reminded him weekly at the movies that aliens from space could be preparing to ray-gun his village or devour his brains. And then an impressionable boy's quandary over death blossomed into a usefully self-examined neurosis, with adolescence and Freud's gabble about *eros* and *thanatos,* which he came across in the little public library he visited regularly with his mother.

"Anyway . . . ," sighed Jonathan.

"Yup," said Peter, focusing back on the call after watching another shopper, an elderly gentleman, inspect an end-of-aisle display of multivitamins targeting "go-go seniors."

"We're charging ahead," said Jonathan.

It was such a boomer thing to do, thought Peter—Jonathan's letting the battle with cancer become part of the process. The plan reminded Peter of performances during the 1980s by choreographers with AIDS who decided to incorporate their physical and even mental decline into their work, appearing sometimes solo, sometimes with loving colleagues, in performances that didn't so much exploit the ghastly situation as explore it in an unprecedented way. The results were sometimes thrilling, even if hard to watch. The good artists made good work, and the bad ones at least made something interesting. Jonathan said he was glad for the opportunity to "take the project away from a standard documentary, into the realm of Bach's *Art of the Fugue,* an almost theoretical exploration of a theme. . . ." Peter only hoped that his friend could pull it off and avoid the cinematic equivalent of paint drying.

Meanwhile, said Jonathan, there were sessions with Connor Frankel to schedule and further medical treatment to endure. Apparently, the first phase of treatment had been gruesome—more so than Jonathan had originally let on. He'd had radioactive metallic seeds implanted in his perineum and begun a kind of chemical castration to reduce the hormones thought to be fueling the cancer, all of which left his body rashy and tender. The doctors were going to keep this up for a while and monitor the results. On the night he attended Peter's party, Jonathan had just started to feel the side effects of the castration drug—chiefly, hot flashes and "breast tenderness." The back pain from the cancer itself was also increasing. Yet other than this, he said, he was "fine."

"This may well be my first comedy," said Jonathan.

"I wonder if I could be as brave as you are," said Peter.

"Brave has nothing to do with it. You just get on with it. By the way, I'm hoping to get you up to the house in Hudson this spring.

Maybe in March or April? I wanna spend some time up there, if this hormone thing doesn't flatten me, and even if it does I'll definitely want some company."

After the call, Peter returned to the body-and-bath aisle. He was examining a bar of soap from Brazil, listening to dZihan & Kamien's *Freaks & Icons,* and thinking about botanicals, when the woman he'd noticed earlier approached him.

"Excuse me, are you thinking about buying that?" she asked. She was a pleasant-looking woman with a gentle manner.

"Yes, I am," said Peter, removing his earbuds.

"May I tell you? You should get it," said the woman.

"Oh, yeah? It smells amazing." He was hoping she might say something further that could be useful in his research.

"That's tangerine, I think," said the woman. "I use that soap all the time."

"You do?"

"I like a bath sometimes, instead of a shower. Very soothing. I don't know why, there's just something about that scent that really sends me."

"Nice. Tell me, where does it send you?"

The woman laughed.

"Straight to heaven," she said.

This delighted Peter. The woman wanted nothing but to offer a friendly observation, and Peter was touched by her kindness, instantly enchanted by her generosity in sharing such a personal pleasure.

People can be such treasures, Peter thought. *I must hang on to that! What a beauty! I hope she's as happy as she seems.*

"Have you been to Brazil?" the woman asked. "My husband and I try to go every year and see something different. This year we went to Curitiba."

"Interesting. I've been to Rio a few times, but that's it. My loss, I'm sure."

"There's always next time. You should really see more of Brazil, take it from me. They're amazing people—it's an amazing culture."

"Thank you so much," said Peter as the woman began walking away.

* * *

Thanksgiving was cold and rainy. Peter spent the day at the home of one of his straight friends from the office, for an annual dinner the man and his wife gave for folks who happened to be in town. It was a fun gathering, but Peter was attending alone for the first time since breaking up with Nick and felt a little odd-man-out-ish. It was still cold and rainy on the following Monday, when Peter and Laura were scheduled to have lunch with Henderson McCaw. Over the weekend Peter had read through the dossier Tyler had compiled and was surprised by a number of items—McCaw had studied law at Yale, his father had been a friend of Jesse Helms, he and his wife were big supporters of the arts, he played the cello—though of course there was no reason why any of this shouldn't be so. Peter felt prepared, but arrived at the office that morning definitely not looking forward to the meeting.

The lunch was to take place in the company's private dining room on the twenty-fifth floor. Both Laura and McCaw's people thought that was a better choice than a public place, though Laura was thinking about privacy and McCaw's people about security. Among the reasons why Peter liked the plan was the tiny convenience of not having to walk seven blocks in bad weather, wearing a pair of good shoes.

Like the rest of the advertising company's complex, the executive dining room had been designed with a theme meant to be amusing and provocative—in this case, something out of *Brideshead Revisited*. The room was a modern paraphrase of English-country-home splendor: a double pedestal dining table in mahogany with ten chairs, a polished brass chandelier, striped wallpaper. On the wall hung a vast painting of a naval battle, which for presentations, Peter knew, slid aside to reveal a flat-screen TV. Touches of cheeky irony were supplied by the decidedly nontraditional color scheme—bold blues and browns, with a touch of burnt orange—and a colorless Plexiglas replica of a first-century Roman statue of Diana, on a Plexiglas pedestal.

When Peter arrived in the dining room five minutes early Laura was already there, with her assistant, checking on details. Four places had been set at one end of the table, with traditional china, silver, linen, and stemware.

"Right on time," said Laura. "Very good." She was dressed in a crisp black suit, with black heels, and seemed in a buoyant mood.

"You look terrific," said Peter. "Everything ready?"

"Absolutely. I hardly ever use this room, but I think it's going to be great fun."

She gave some instructions to a waiter, who then disappeared into the kitchen. Then the assistant, on her phone, announced that McCaw's car had just pulled up in front of the building. Laura sent the girl down to the lobby, to meet him.

"They're early, too. Goody!"

"It's just him and his strategist, right?"

"That's all. And you and me, kid. Just a little lunch—easy! Meet and greet."

"We're not presenting, they're not presenting."

"No, no. We just wanted to chat and get to know each other a bit."

"Oh, charming."

"They want to meet our star player."

"Oh, well."

"It's ours to lose, Peter. All we have to do is listen."

"Lunch with America's favorite demagogue. What a treat."

"Let's be nice, shall we? This could mean a hundred million in billings."

"Has he told you any of the broad strokes yet?"

"On creative? No. Only scope of work–type stuff, which I showed you."

Peter took a breath and exhaled.

"Let's see what the man has to say," he said.

They chatted about another client for a minute, and then, in a great sweep of energy, Henderson McCaw strode through the door, accompanied by two of his people, all in gray suits. One of them, an assistant, proceeded immediately to the kitchen, accompanied by Laura's girl.

A food taster? thought Peter. *Really?*

"You must be Laura," said McCaw, extending his hand. They hadn't yet met in person.

They shook, then Laura presented Peter, and McCaw introduced Sunil, his strategist and adviser. They had just flown up from Raleigh, where McCaw lived.

"Good flight?" said Laura. "It looks nasty out there."

"No problem at all," said McCaw. "My pilot is a Gulf War vet. As long as there's no enemy fire, we're fine."

Everyone laughed.

"Are you staying in town for long?" asked Peter.

"We go back tomorrow. My wife is seeing a matinee this afternoon, and tonight we've got this big fund-raiser, over at the Waldorf."

"Ah, yes," said Peter. "We've been hearing a lot about that."

McCaw looked squarely at Peter.

"And I've been hearing a lot about you, my friend," he said.

Peter smiled modestly. McCaw was much taller and better-looking in person than he appeared on television. What seemed fleshy about his face and neck onscreen was, in person, more like the muscularity of a linebacker going gracefully to seed. He looked younger, too, than his forty-seven years.

"Good things, I hope," said Peter.

"Enormously good things."

Laura seemed happy to hear this.

"We're so grateful you could make the time," she said.

"We had to meet the guy who made a talking car more American than Uncle Sam," said Sunil.

"Is that what we did?" said Peter.

"The seventh most successful campaign of all time, according to *Advertising Age*."

"OK, it was catchy," said Peter.

Everybody laughed again.

"It was genius," said McCaw. "Listen, I have to tell you a funny story about one of those cars, same make. We were up at our lodge in the Adirondacks, one winter, cross-country skiing, with my family. We had a driver, but at the lodge my dad did all the driving. I heard about this party I wanted to go to, but didn't want anybody to know, so I asked our housekeeper if I could borrow her car, and she said yes. I must have been, oh, fifteen. I had my learner's permit, thought nothing of driving around Winston-Salem, where we lived. Anyway, wouldn't you know it? I smashed up the car, coming home from the party, and was damned lucky to survive."

"Ooof," said Laura.

"My dad was furious. He had to go out the next day and buy the housekeeper a new car, and charged me monthly payments for two years, until I paid him back."

"Lesson learned," said Laura.

"Lesson learned, indeed," echoed McCaw, chuckling.

"I never heard that," said Sunil.

"And how was the party?" asked Peter, silencing everyone for a second.

"See, that's why I like this guy," said McCaw. "He's got his eye on the ball."

McCaw gave Peter a warm clasp of the shoulder.

"Seriously, I'd like to know," said Peter.

"The party was great, Peter," laughed McCaw. "I got the girl—Aggy McClatchy. Well worth the monthly installments."

It was a dubious point, but somehow McCaw made it seem charming. And Peter immediately grasped the essence of McCaw's personal appeal. He was kind of a bully, though a friendly and mannerly one. He had a big personality and wanted to be persuasive, and was able to be so because he seemed so affable and open. He was ready to engage anyone in his purview, which somehow came across—even as he clearly expected to dominate that purview—as generous, rather than peremptory. The habit of smiling and locking people into a sincere gaze with blue eyes helped.

"Shall we sit down?" said Laura.

As they approached the end of the table where the settings had been laid, McCaw noticed the chairs.

"Are these really Hepplewhite?" he said. Neither Peter nor Laura knew whether the furniture was reproduction or real, or part of some corporate patrimony inherited from one of the core company's founders, both legendary, old-school ad men.

"Are you a collector?" asked Laura.

"No," said McCaw, "but my grandparents were. Strictly American is what they were interested in—Duncan Phyfe, Samuel McIntire. It's all in a museum now, but it was neat to learn about that stuff when I was a kid."

McCaw's dossier had said that his family had been rich for generations—tobacco money—but it had neglected to characterize them as patricians. His wife came from old East Coast banking and mining money. It was key, Peter thought, that McCaw didn't come off establishment in the media and he must be making an effort not to do so.

Clever, Peter thought—*to come off like a raging populist.*

The waiter appeared with the appetizer, a carpaccio of yellowtail with crispy shallots. At first, conversation ambled amiably from the high cost of taxis, to the amount of office space in lower Manhattan, to the large number of trees per capita in the city of New York. Then McCaw turned to take in his surroundings.

"This is such a cool room," he said. "It's right out of those sixties New York movies—you know, where Tony Randall or Gig Young plays the neurotic executive."

"God, remember neurotic?" laughed Laura.

"Are you a movie fan, Mr. McCaw?" asked Peter.

"Absolutely," said McCaw. "Please—call me Hendy. I love those movies. What always impressed me was that so many of them were about the media and advertising. The message seemed to be how much fun life would be, if we could all just grow up and get with the new, cool ways. And look—we grew up! We're all part of that world, now. It's all there is."

"Interesting," said Laura.

"That's kind of why I'm here, having lunch with you nice people. I need your expertise. Look, I know advertising has become more sophisticated than it was in the days of Mr. J. Walter Thompson, but your industry is still telling stories people want to hear. What did you call it, Sunil?"

"Creating discourse around desire," said the strategist.

"That's all I do," said McCaw.

McCaw paused for a moment. Peter, remembering they were there to listen, decided against jumping in.

"What's really changed, profoundly, are people," said McCaw.

Laura nodded her head.

"How so?" she said.

"We've evolved, as a species," said McCaw. "Desire itself has evolved—I'm not the first person to say this. Wanting is a kind of thinking, and human beings have definitely evolved some new ways of thinking—better ways, I think."

"Adaptation," said Peter.

"Bingo!" said McCaw.

"Man, and I thought we were going to be talking about motherhood and apple pie," said Peter.

McCaw laughed good-naturedly and went on.

"We've adapted to our ecological niche, and that niche has shifted drastically in the last generation, and continues to do so. Our lungs can't breathe car exhaust—not yet, anyway—but in response to this barrage of new ideas and messages and information, we *have* become comfortable with doublethink, which is not nearly as bad as George Orwell made it out to be. We *have* cultivated the ability not to think at all, as in meditating, and exercising, and focusing on the inner self. All good, good stuff. And all of which, in my view, frees us to enjoy more kinds of knowing than ever before."

"I'm not sure what you mean by that," said Laura.

McCaw placed both hands on the edge of the table, palms down.

"When we tell a good enough story, we change what people know," he said.

The look on Laura's face showed she was trying to process the thought. Peter found the statement a distortion of the truth, but again decided to merely listen.

"This is an enormous stride for humanity, if we are to survive, these new kinds of knowing," continued McCaw. "I'm not saying it's a *better* way, on any absolute scale. I mean, Christianity wasn't *better* than being a Roman citizen; it simply worked better for people, psychologically. Faith answered more questions about a world that was changing massively for them. What I'm saying is that if we expect to survive in a world of ten billion people, we need to get beyond the, like, four original, caveman ways of knowing something. I'm sure Peter would agree with me."

"Well—I agree that the brain is evolving and we're thinking differently . . . ," said Peter.

"But?" said McCaw.

"But, well, who gets to tell people what they quote-unquote know?"

"We do," said McCaw.

"But doesn't everyone have that power nowadays?" said Peter. "My mother has a blog."

"Some people tell better stories than others."

Peter shifted in his seat.

"All right, then," he said, "so let me ask you what stories you propose to tell."

"I am hoping you will help me figure that out, Peter. I mean, I have a few ideas to put out there—you've probably heard many of them—but you're the guys who can create the most powerful platforms for them, the most powerful engines. I came to listen to you."

Was this flattery? Was it true? Laura seemed to take McCaw's statement as a good sign, and looked confident as she took a demure bite of a cheesy breadstick.

"Listen," said McCaw. "Some people call 'Don't tread on me' stupid. Fine. Some people call me stupid. Fine. But some people call the folks who listen to me stupid, and that's not fine, not at all. Because I happen to know that America is intelligent in about seventeen new ways. And that's what I call a real opportunity for our culture, and for us, here in this room."

It was a shock for Peter to see how canny McCaw was. People looking inward, acting on what they "know," rather than some external "truths"! It was exactly why his form of "take back America" populism was so popular, Peter thought, and what made it so close to the fundamentalism of Islamic terrorists. The entire conversation couldn't have been farther from the common-denominator talk that Peter and Laura had agreed to stick to, when they went over their goals for the lunch. Specific truths and doctrines? Completely extraneous to the conversation—and Peter could just hear Laura reminding him that this was the case, too, with plenty of other clients.

The main course arrived: steamed branzino, with oyster mushrooms, scallions, ponzu, and cilantro. The presentation was worthy of a photo shoot.

"They told me you like seafood," said Laura. "So we got one of the chefs from the Lure Fishbar to come up and cook for us today."

"Looks yummy," said McCaw. "Is everyone as hungry as I am?"

Polite enthusiasm burbled around the table, as they tucked in.

"Your point about new kinds of intelligence intrigues me," said Peter, presently. "I saw the interview you did a week or so ago, with the senator."

"Ah," said McCaw. Laura opened her mouth, then closed it without saying anything.

"Now, with all respect, Hendy, this is not a very intelligent woman," said Peter. "She has very few solid points to make, and she can't seem to make them in any detail."

McCaw smiled.

"I know she is extreme," he said. "But I felt it my duty to let my audience see that. The senator and her positions are actually very compelling, though she may have a ways to go yet, as a candidate for higher office."

"Higher office? The only thing higher is the presidency, and she's completely unqualified for that."

"By what standard?"

"By any standard. Could she negotiate a trade agreement? Can she handle the subtleties of foreign policy?"

"She might not have to, is the point. She might be more effective as a symbol, like Reagan. Or Obama. This is one of the seventeen new kinds of intelligence that I'm talking about."

"OK, so . . . you want us to help you find better ways of making Senator Miss Congeniality look good?"

"Peter, what I think we're hearing . . . ," began Laura.

McCaw stopped her by pressing a hand gently on her arm.

"I need help in putting across my messages in as fair and persuasive a way as possible," said McCaw. "That's all. Why? We're expanding into print, cable TV, the Web—with an integrated media complex, just like Oprah and Martha."

"Also retail and events," added Sunil.

"So strategy and branding," said Peter.

"Strategy, branding, content, programming, product development and design," said Sunil.

"It's a bold initiative," said Laura.

"I just . . . wanna make sure people *get* it," said McCaw. "If we can just speak their language."

Peter chuckled.

"You know, in a way," he said, "what you're saying is a variant of that old saying, 'Nobody ever went broke underestimating the intelligence of the American public.' "

McCaw nodded.

"That's right," he said. "I am saying that. And I embrace that statement with love and respect for the American public—which is, by the way, not how Mencken meant it or anything else he ever said."

"Mencken was a cynic," said Peter.

"Yes, and I am not," said McCaw. "And, Peter, I venture to say that you're not, either—when you so ably assist a client like Procter & Gamble to sell a hundred million units of a shower gel that makes people smell like good, clean sex; when you make them realize they *want* to smell like good, clean sex."

"Uh, true," said Peter.

"All I wanna do is rent your brain, my friend," said McCaw. "Can I ask you to think about that?"

The comment made everyone laugh and lightened the mood at the table.

The chef looked in briefly when dessert was served—a lemon soufflé tart. They thanked him warmly, then went on talking, over coffee. They agreed to talk again, in a few days. The aim was "a passionate new media brand with a clear point of view." They were still arranging the money; March first was their deadline for having a plan in place. When they all said good-bye at the elevator, Peter realized that over the course of the lunch he'd come to see McCaw as a human being, which might prove useful in helping him decide whether or not to work with the guy. He'd even begun to have some respect for McCaw, though not, of course, for his politics— yet even McCaw's choice of steering largely clear of politics in an informal meeting like this seemed smart. What was most interesting was that McCaw welcomed provocation—it seemed to make him even keener to work with Peter.

"Like I said," said Laura, a few seconds after the elevator doors closed, "ours to lose."

"Are they talking to anyone else?"

Laura shook her head.

"Just us," she said. "They want you."

"So I gather. He's not what I expected."

"I know."

"He's smart."

"Clearly."

"It's a big project."

"I've been working on numbers. You need to be thinking about your key hires."

They started walking back to their offices.

"What he does in public is a performance, isn't it?" said Peter. "He plays a character."

"Not unlike the rest of us," said Laura.

"He seduces people."

"I know! Did you see those hands?"

"Quite large."

"Yes, large. And strong and gorgeous-looking."

"Laura!"

"I think we both learned something today."

CHAPTER 7

Will started working at the magazine a week after Peter's party and soon found himself acclimatized to life in New York's media lane. In fact, by the time the office started emptying out for the holidays, a week before Christmas, he found he was completely addicted to the stream of unprocessed cultural news that poured into the office and onto his radar every day, via press kits, calls, and e-mails from folks wanting editorial coverage for the fab phenoms they hoped to position as hot and happening. A new movie! A new album! A new fashion collection! A new art show! And beyond the possibility of actual coverage was Will's new membership in the city's influencer elite. A score of invitations came across his desk every day, providing welcome fuel for his calendar, which was suddenly jammed with parties, dinners, openings, launches, previews, and the like.

The people behind these invitations were press and marketing types, who ranged from new-best-friends to full-on monsters. Though Will found them loud and pushy, he always tried to respond politely, evaluating requests for his presence or attention fairly, in terms of what could be best for the magazine. Most of his fellow editors, however, responded in a different way to supplicants: They promised nothing and demanded everything—entrée to the best parties, free gifts and travel, special access to stars and top models. Entitlement seemed to be their biggest talent, intelligence and creativity being optional, and Will suspected more than one highly placed coworker of some degree of incompetence or fraudulence. There was Olivier, the party-going and always-too-fashionable editor at large, whose pronouncements on style sounded weighty and empty at the same time; Sebastian, the extremely good-looking assistant to the editor in chief, who referred to the celebrities who called his boss by their first names; Kitten, the fashion director, who had once been a rock star's girlfriend and was now, thirty years later, styling herself exactly the way she did then; and Herman, the managing editor, whose calm and tact concealed a doggedness that emerged whenever deadlines were threatened—a quality that had earned him the nickname "the human pit bull."

The editor in chief, Colin, was out of town so much—"he's with Karl, on Barry and Diane's yacht in the Aegean"—that Will had barely spoken to him since arriving. Will was determined to observe the lot of them without making judgments, before deciding who was actually human and who was not—though he did have a hard time imagining that someone as horrid as Herman could ever have cavorted barefoot and carefree, as a child, through a sprinkler on a lawn, on a late-summer afternoon, under the doting gaze of a mother. Whether life in the media lane required or produced such personalities, Will couldn't tell yet, so he kept his head down and worked hard. For the issue they were working on, April, Will had been assigned, in addition to his other responsibilities, a page on rain gear. Which meant working with the market editor to figure out what kind of great rain gear there was out there; and making sure the fashion director was happy with their choices; and getting a concept for the photograph and an idea for the breezy paragraph to go with it—several ideas, since the first few could be shot down—and then making sure that the plan could be adapted easily if, all of a sudden, someone decided to go with a hot young actor instead of a model, in which case the photo would need reshooting and the breezy paragraph would need turning into a mini-interview.

As New Year's Eve approached, Will found himself invited to several parties by people he didn't know. A fashion designer was hosting a thousand people at the Chelsea Piers; a recording executive was taking over the Rainbow Room; an aging party queen was re-creating the Roxy circa 1991, all of which sounded like fun. But the party Will chose to attend was the one hosted by Stefan Turino in his penthouse on top of a new tower on West Forty-second Street, which everyone said was spectacular. Stefan said he was inviting the crème de la crème of New York's scene and social types, plus a sprinkling of celebrities, which sounded great to Will—like something he could bring Enrico to. Will owed Enrico a fabulous party or two, since Enrico had taken him to events like the benefit opening of the Winter Antiques Show and the housewarming of a fifteen-million-dollar loft in SoHo that Enrico had decorated. Moreover, Will just wanted to have fun that night, with no strings, and Enrico was good party company, especially because he wasn't utterly fascinating or the next forever boyfriend.

"He's kind of a placeholder," Will told Luz, when she asked what was up with their relationship. "I like him, he's a nice guy. But friend chemistry, not boyfriend chemistry."

"He on the same page about that?" said Luz.

"He kinda likes me, I guess—maybe more than I like him. But it's not about sex at this point, and he seems fine with that."

Stefan had said his party would be a *real* party—that is, not a corporate function. And sure enough, when Will and Enrico arrived, around eleven, at the sprawling, glass-walled duplex penthouse that Stefan shared with his lawyer boyfriend, the place was abuzz with three hundred well-cared-for gay men under forty who clearly knew each other and seemed intent on making a memorable evening for themselves. Will led the way through the foyer and into the double-story living room, which boasted massive, can't-look-away, sixty-sixth-floor views of the thicket of skyscrapers that bristled just beyond, in Midtown, glittering for the occasion. Stefan's interior lighting was dim and club-like, which served to accentuate the views and flatten the guests standing in front of them into silhouettes. Low, minimalist furniture made the place look like the sky lounge of a new four-star hotel in Shanghai, as did the DJ balcony that overlooked the living room, halfway up a stairway that was thrillingly yet frighteningly free of any sort of banister.

After finding Stefan and making introductions, Will and Enrico circulated. They passed by the bar and buffet, said hello to a few acquaintances, and wound up in a corner of the living room that overlooked Times Square, a block away. The scene down in the square looked anything but scary. From the sixty-sixth floor—an elevation more than twice as high as the tower from which the ball was dropped—the mess of tourists, police, and broadcast trucks at street level looked magical, like an incandescent, three-dimensional simulation of Times Square Land, shimmering with coruscades of photo flashes and glowing under wheeled-in TV lighting. The scene looked like a stellar explosion, a slow-motion supernova.

"Great, huh," said Enrico.

"Yeah," said Will.

To the north, beyond sleek avenues shooting into the distance, was the George Washington Bridge, draped for the evening in diamonds.

"Think we can see thirty miles?" said Enrico.

"I dunno, I guess so," said Will.

"So maybe there is some teenager up in the hills there, in the attic of his parents' house, gazing out the window, over the treetops, at the skyline of New York, and dreaming of a party like this?"

Will looked quizzical.

"I thought we said no drugs tonight," he said.

Yet it was fun for Will to be at the party, even if his awe of Stefan's home was mixed with distaste. He was reminded of the New Year's Eve party, two years before, that Rob had hosted in the Century City apartment. By then, the relationship had gone sour and all of Rob's fake-nice, fake-important Hollywood friends had begun to grate on Will. That life was just one big reality-TV show.

Will had never taken to glass-walled living, either. He didn't feel relaxed, up in the sky. Being there felt more like air travel than being at home. Underlying the fascination with views was an unpleasant consciousness of movement, departure, threat—resulting, in part, from the greater distance from one's home planet and a forced trust in the skill of engineers who build towers and the competence of bureaucrats who write building codes. It was exactly like the trust you need to fly in airplanes, Will thought, which draws on quite a different emotion from the primal comfort of curling up on the tamped-earth floor of one's tidy grass hut.

Each tower is its own universe, thought Will, gazing at Midtown.

It was a view of many such universes, entailing a subconscious acknowledgment of all the other people in all the other towers, and the practically astronomical journey by which those others could be reached: by descending to earth, navigating the perils of people-choked streets, passing through another membrane of security, witnessing another corrosive show of lobby luxury, and ascending into another part of the sky. Living like that was a permanent spacewalk. Will didn't care for it at all. He'd grown up on a ranch—well, a luxury estate that was called a ranch, because it was on the edge of town, on land that had once been part of a real ranch. He was no farmer, but he had grown up with feelings about the earth and its cycles, which was another reason why he'd never clicked with Rob. Century City always felt generically urban, generically luxurious. The relationship felt generic, too.

"Decorating a place like this is always about the view," said Enrico.

"You can't fight it, can you?" said Will.

"It becomes a theme, but you have to use it the right way, or the apartment winds up looking like every other apartment."

A guy with thick black hair and a flashy smile, standing next to Enrico, said he agreed. He had overheard Enrico's comment to Will.

"It *is* a very commanding view," said the guy.

"Yes," said Enrico.

"Great jacket, by the way," said the guy. Enrico was wearing Commes des Garçons.

"Oh, thank you," said Enrico.

Will craned to get a glimpse of their new friend, not knowing what, if anything, to do. Introduce himself? Expect Enrico to present him? Ignore the guy?

"Are you from the city?" said the guy, in a way clearly meant for Enrico alone.

"Not originally," said Enrico.

The guy's sparkling eyes and body language said it all: He was totally into Enrico, and either unaware of Will or uninterested in the fact that Will and Enrico had been talking together.

What's up with that? thought Will. *We're not boyfriends, but we could be.* Was the guy being flirtatious or merely friendly? Rather than threatened, though, Will felt curious.

What are *gay men, anyway?* he thought. *Do they just sniff around randomly, like puppies?*

It was Century City all over again. Stefan's party was a portal to exactly the kind of trophy life that Will was determined to avoid. No more Robs!

"You OK?" said Enrico, after a word or two more with the smiley guy, then an emphatic turn toward Will. "What are you thinking about?"

"I'm thinking about portals," said Will. "Parties as portals—as in, the portal to hell."

Enrico smiled in a quizzical way.

"Now who's on drugs?" he said.

Meanwhile, fifty blocks south of Stefan Turino's party, Peter was spending the evening with Jonathan, at a three-star restaurant in Tribeca that did a festive, price-fixed New Year's Eve dinner for forty people. Both friends wanted to be with each other that night, and had sent regrets to exes and others who proffered various invitations. Moreover, Jonathan had told Peter that he wanted to be with someone who understood his need to be absolutely in the moment that evening, while Peter, for his part, wanted to make the most of the time he had left with his friend, which he knew might well make this New Year's Eve more memorable than the ones he'd spent with Nick on the beach in Bali in 1999 and at Madonna's mansion in Beverly Hills in 1991, or the one with Harold aboard the Orient Express, somewhere in Switzerland, en route from London to Venice, in 1985.

Jonathan was moving slowly that night because of the various pains and tenderness he was suffering—he said his clothes hurt!—but in spite of that, he said, he had been looking forward to a night out. He and Peter had decided to dress in black tie, and found that most of the other men in the restaurant were dressed that way, too; the ladies were in nice dresses or fancy jackets and pants. It was an older crowd, obviously, and as on past evenings in the restaurant Peter and Jonathan noticed that theirs was not the only same-sex table. Across the room was a table of two venerable-looking women, one of whom Jonathan recognized as the head of cultural giving for one of the nation's top charitable foundations.

"So," said Jonathan, once the first glass of champagne had been poured and initial toasts made between them. "Clintonian." He was making a valiant effort to keep the conversation going, despite his discomfort.

"That's the only way I can describe it," said Peter. "He's this big guy who commands the room. He's razor sharp and totally seductive, and there's this need, this urgency, in back of all that skill and intelligence, to be believed, to be liked."

"Huh."

"It was so weird to find someone not evil, whose views you believe to be, in fact, evil."

"I'll bet."

"And like I say, we didn't talk politics at all, practically."

"No home schooling? No Texas seceding from the Union?"

"It was as if he'd decided to steer clear of all that."

"Mm-hmm."

"And what we did talk about—you know, the nature of credulity and mass-media messaging—it was as if he'd cooked up those bullet points just to engage me, ya know?"

"To fool you or something?"

"No—I think he believes it." Peter took a sip of Pellegrino. "No, it was more to snow me, or seduce me into working with him."

"Really?"

"I definitely felt my buttons being pushed, in a nice way."

"He knew that much about you?"

"I'm sure his guy Sunil did a file on me, just like I asked Tyler to do one on him."

"OK, so *are* you going to work with him?"

"I'm thinking about it."

"You are."

"It could mean a million a year for me alone, Jonathan, on top of my salary. For two or three years. The company's billings would obviously be many times that."

"You think you *can* work with him? I seem to remember you claiming to revile the guy."

"I don't know that I revile him, exactly. I do regret the conditions that make someone like a McCaw possible—fifty years of decline in American intelligence, for one thing. I was sitting there at lunch thinking that the citizenry who bought the soap our company was built on, in the twenties and thirties, are like nuclear scientists compared to the public today. I can't very well blame McCaw for that."

"But you don't have to help him exploit it."

Peter frowned half-comically.

"No, I know," he said.

"Three million bucks. Sounds like you guys are a team already."

"You wouldn't revile me if I were to work with the guy?"

"We do what we have to do. I'm feeling very live-and-let-live, at the moment."

"I guess I *am* a little curious about being able to influence him, since we seem to be at least partly on the same wavelength. That's a powerful inducement. I just . . . don't know where it could all end up."

Jonathan smiled wanly.

"Do we ever know that?" he said.

Though Jonathan was eating and drinking modestly, he presently found the evening too much for him. Shortly after the main course was served he said he was feeling dizzy and sick, and asked Peter if he would mind leaving. Of course not, said Peter. On the way out of the restaurant, clutching a gaily decorated goody bag of holiday confections prepared by the dessert chef, Jonathan tripped on the foot of the receptionist's lectern and fell, narrowly avoiding hitting his head. At the curb they ducked into the car that Peter had booked for the evening, and on the way home Jonathan remained quietly slumped against his friend, half holding on to him. They were sitting like that, not speaking, when, stopped at a traffic light only a few blocks from Jonathan's building, they suddenly heard the people in the streets cheering and singing, which meant that midnight had come.

"Happy New Year, darling," said Jonathan feebly.

Peter and Jonathan had plans to see *Der Rosenkavalier* at the Met during the first week of January, but Jonathan canceled, so

Peter asked Tyler. Tyler couldn't go, so then Peter called Will, who said yes.

The night of the opera was cold and clear. They met in the lobby, ten minutes before curtain time, greeting each other with a handshake that turned into a huggy collision of overcoats, but no kiss. What with shuffling toward their seats with four thousand other operagoers, past ticket takers, bag inspectors, and ushers, they barely had time for snippets of "How was your day?" and "Glad you could come!"–type exchanges before the lights went down and the curtain went up.

The performance was radiant. Though Peter had heard the opera many times before, he found himself particularly caught that night by the Marschallin's first-act aria about the passage of time. It's morning and the great lady is in the lavish bedroom of her Viennese mansion. She's dismissed her elaborate levée and is alone with her much younger lover, who has spent the night and is about to part, reluctantly. Still lovely, but knowing that loveliness is bound to fade, she warns the lover that physical love is not always a reliable measure of happiness.

> *Die Zeit, die ist ein sonderbar Ding.*
> *Wenn man so hinlebt, ist sie rein gar nichts.*
> *Aber dann auf einmal, da spürt man nichts als sie.*
> *Sie ist um uns herum, sie ist auch in uns drinnen.*
>
> *Time—how strangely does it go its ways!*
> *First we are heedless—Lo! 'tis as nothing!*
> *Then a sudden waking and we feel naught but it,*
> *All the world tells of it, our souls are filled with it. . . .*

The aria was unutterably beautiful, and somehow its sentiment percolated into Peter's soul more deeply than ever before. Some joys, even love, must be let go eventually; knowing that becomes its own joy.

Yes, thought Peter, *but when?* As he listened to the soprano— herself a great diva of a certain age, whose voice was fading and time in the spotlight was nearing its end—he found himself breathing shakily and then, as the aria ended, shedding a few tears.

During the intermission they headed up to the Grand Tier bar, where Will bought them some champagne and they found a spot to stand near the glass doors to the terrace.

"Great seats," said Will. They were in the middle of the orchestra, on the aisle.

"Yeah," said Peter. "We've done a bit of work for the Met, so they're always very kind when we ask for tickets."

"You mean they're comps?" said Will.

"Yes."

"Cool. It was so nice of you to ask me."

"I really love this opera," said Peter. "You know, it's funny—it grabbed me the first time I heard it. I was maybe, what, twelve? I just knew *Rosenkavalier* was what life was about."

"Hmmm."

"Whereas I've seen, oh, *Marriage of Figaro,* just as many times, and maybe that's even a greater opera, but somehow it's always an ordeal to sit through."

"I've never seen *The Marriage of Figaro.*"

"*Rosenkavalier,* it's like I wanna eat it with a spoon."

The bar area around them quickly filled up with other patrons, some of whom were dressed better than others. Gaily, Peter and Will critiqued a saggy velvet pantsuit they saw on one of the ladies, trashed a man's egregious toupee, and shared a moment of love for Chagall's kitschy *The Triumph of Music,* which commanded the bar from far above.

Peter found Will even brighter than he had thought, and slightly bitchier, too, in a good way. The Chagall brought the conversation back to the opera.

"I love that it pretends to be this light confection, but it's really about very serious things," said Will.

"The painting or the opera?" said Peter.

"I meant the painting, but the opera, too, now that you mention it," said Will. "The opera is both frothy and philosophical, all at the same time."

"Strauss and Hofmannsthal knew what they were doing."

"I know, I Googled it earlier," said Will. "Hey, and I noticed that you were kinda touched during the part where the princess was singing about . . ."

"Age," said Peter.

"Yeah," said Will. "That must be a section you really like."

"Well, it's powerful stuff. I am, shall we say, really relating to that subject matter nowadays."

"I know," laughed Will, adding, with drag-queen emphasis and a toss of imaginary tresses, "the clock just *won't* stop ticking."

Peter smiled.

"Says the guy who's, like, twenty-four," he said.

"Twenty-eight."

"Same thing."

The way they could banter genially so soon after meeting surprised Peter—and thrilled him.

"C'mon, who cares about age?" said Will. "Like my grandmother says, 'It's only a number.'"

"Of course, and it's always the eighty-year-olds who say that."

Will gave Peter a playful push on the shoulder.

"Well, look," he said. "So . . . what number are you, if I may ask? *I* told *you.*"

Peter smirked. Had he nudged the conversation toward this question?

"I'm fifty-nine, thank you very much," said Peter.

This question had been arising more frequently, in discussions with younger men, Peter noticed, and he knew what came next—and both enjoyed it and dreaded it, the latter because he had no idea what it meant that he was beginning to enjoy such a low pleasure so much.

"Wow, I would not have guessed that," said Will. "You're in great shape. You don't look a day over forty."

Ahhhhhhhhh! Peter heard his inner Elaine Stritch screaming a little. For some boys, even forty meant unfathomably ancient.

"Thank you," he said.

"What's your secret—champagne, right?" laughed Will, raising his glass.

Yeah, Peter thought, *when I can drink it with someone like you.*

As Peter took a sip of champagne he found himself savoring a delicious lilt that seemed to brighten Will's laughter. He'd heard it several times during the evening when he tended bar at Peter's home, and several times already that evening.

The conversation rolled on to popular music, which was just as well. Peter didn't really want to talk about why he had wept, though there was a lot to say about that, and perhaps he would have said it, if he had been at the opera with Jonathan or someone else his own age. Yet Will was diverting. He was enthusing about the debut album of a young new R&B singer when, on their way back down to the orchestra, they ran into an acquaintance of Peter's, a member of the Museum of Modern Art's board, an elegant lady in a long dress, and her husband.

"Regina, good to see you," said Peter. "Harry, how are you?" Peter introduced Will and couldn't help noticing, as he spoke briefly with the lady, how smoothly Will swung into light conversation with the gentleman. The kid had not been raised in a barn, Peter noted. So many young men couldn't pass the intermission test. Will had also worn a sport jacket, too, for the evening, which also scored points with Peter.

For the second intermission they returned to the Grand Tier, where Will, in a quick bout of texting as the lights went up, had arranged to meet a friend of his who had seats in the balcony with a bunch of friends.

"There they are," said Will, as they approached a group of boys that looked like a high-school field trip. Everyone was in sweaters and chinos, or jeans.

After introductions and comments on the performance, Will and his friend started chatting and included Peter nominally, though Peter, of course, knew no one they were talking about and realized he didn't particularly care to. Meanwhile, the other boys talked among themselves.

Who were these boys, Peter wondered—young opera queens? If so, why weren't they better dressed? Were they the kind of boys who went to sports bars? They didn't even look gay. Were they academics or scholars of some sort? Were they trying to make some statement, by dressing down?

Just when Peter thought he needn't be so preoccupied with how the boys were dressed, Will's friend asked him why he was "dressed that way."

There are a thousand ways to answer that question, Peter thought, including a reminder that one might always run into a museum board member with whom one has worked on a multimillion-dollar benefit.

"I had a meeting," Peter said automatically, still trying to fathom what the boy could possibly mean. The Prada jacket? The Paul Smith shirt? The Berluti shoes? The fact that these pieces were selected to act together in harmony, in something known as an outfit, appropriate for this particular time of day and social milieu? Rather than get all dudgeony, though, Peter let the moment pass. It was only after Will told the boys where he and Peter were sitting that Peter felt them looking at them in a somewhat different way.

After the opera, Peter and Will decided to go for a bite at Fiorello's, even though it was late. Braced by the fresh, cold air they walked quickly across Lincoln Center's plaza, chattering about the opera's luminous final trio and the lovely bit of business at the end, where the Marschallin's little servant Mohammed scurries back into the room his mistress and the others have just left, to retrieve the handkerchief dropped by young Sophie, whom the lady's former lover will now marry. As Peter followed Will in a dash across Broadway, he found himself braced, too, by the cinematic long shot of a tall, broad-shouldered young man, stepping quickly over the pavement with athletic grace, in a long, dark overcoat that swept behind him rakishly, because he'd neglected to button it. This was the man he was with! Somewhere in Peter's brain, the shot was accompanied by a sexy line of jazz sax, arcing propulsively over a matrix of future beat, on a track laced with gauzy-vibey echoes—meaning that life in the city was sometimes splendid.

Fiorello's was welcoming, warm. Even at midnight the place was still crowded and convivial, and they were shown directly to one of the red leather booths. While waiting for their drinks, instead of examining the menu, they clucked over the brass plaques on the wall, that identified the booth as "belonging" to a variety of New York boldface types.

"So if they show up, what, we get kicked out?" said Will.

"I think it's more of a memorial," said Peter.

"Golly," said Will, reading some of the names aloud. "Yeah, some of these people are dead, aren't they?"

"Yes, they are," said Peter. "We're sitting on their remains."

They laughed. The waiter delivered the drinks. Suddenly, they knew that the antipasto sampling platter for two would be the perfect thing to order. Five selections were made with telepathic ease.

Will asked for the life story and Peter agreed to give him the short version: the small town upbringing, coming out at Cornell, moving to New York with Harold, AIDS, the merry widower, Nick, the breakup with Nick, the merry widower again—only this time not so merry. Will seemed especially impressed by all the traveling Peter had done, both with Harold and afterward, for his ad agency.

"Well, in a way, I was groomed to ingest the world and everything in it," said Peter. "And when you think about it, life as a gay baby boomer is the result of a perfect storm. Our parents survived the Depression, saved the world by winning a righteous war, perfected the backyard barbecue, and raised kids who expected to have more happiness, abundance, pleasure, and truth than anyone else in human history. It's an ethos of entitlement."

"Huh," said Will.

"And we're still rockin' it—the information superhighway, social networking! This is only what we were promised. Listen, when my family got our first TV—it was literally as big as our refrigerator—I remember my father saying that this little glass screen—smaller than a laptop screen, mind you—would bring the whole world into our living room. So I was hugely disappointed when I saw this pathetic, grainy, static-y, black-and-white piss-stream of a picture that couldn't even stay tuned in. I mean, I had imagined, like, a three-dimensional holograph in the colors of the fucking jungle, with roaring elephants, in surround sound. Only *now* are we getting to where I thought we were supposed to be then, with technology, when I was, like, two."

"Interesting," said Will.

"Literally, we expected everything," said Peter. "And we still do—jobs, peak experiences, love."

"I just can't imagine that level of . . . My friends and I hardly expect anything out of life."

"No?"

"Well, if our parents are rich, I think we expect them to stay rich—and for us maybe to continue to benefit from that, like we always have. But as far as our own fortunes are concerned?" Will grimaced. "Pretty iffy."

"Really?"

"Most of my friends have a pretty vague idea about all that."

"What about ambition? Jobs? Careers?"

"Iffy."

"But you have a new job, yes?"

"Yes, and I like it, and I think I'm good at it. . . ." Will paused.

"But you don't know if you want to be doing the same thing in twenty years," offered Peter.

"Right," said Will. "Though I'm not a complete idiot. I'm working through some of these issues and, you know, making some progress."

"Of course, of course. We all have to go at our own pace."

Peter asked Will about his family. He was the oldest of four children, Will said. He had two sisters, whom he loved dearly, though they could be a bit bubbleheaded; and a brother, who was the baby and on and off a drug fuckup; so Will had often found himself, with his parents' blessing, in the role of family organizer. Planning outings, trips, and parties had been his thing since he was old enough to wield his parents' credit cards.

Will told of heading off to L.A., after Berkeley, without quite knowing what he was looking for; then, when Peter asked about love, Will told him the story of Rob.

"So now," said Will, "I'm trying to be a little more, um, discriminating."

"Amen to that," said Peter.

"Though I'm sort of seeing somebody."

"Oh. Cool."

"It's not love, not even sex, really. But it's nice for now. He's a good guy. So maybe I'm, you know, seeing where it goes."

"OK. What's his name?"

"Enrico."

"And is this the guy who's been piling up text messages all night on the phone that you're so politely not checking?"

"Yeah, probably," laughed Will. "And what about you, Peter—are you in a relationship, seeing anyone?"

Peter was tempted to use the phrase "barren wasteland" to describe his love life, as he sometimes did when someone in Jonathan's crowd asked him that question, but before he could answer, Will went on.

"At your party, that blond guy, very cute—I could have sworn you and he had something going on."

"Who—Tyler?"

"Is that his name? He came with that PR guy. He really seemed into you."

Peter snickered.

"Tyler works with me," he said. "Well, *for* me. He's a very talented guy. We're close, for sure. I adore Tyler. And we do go out a bit—not in a date-y way, but in a New York, professional, workin'-the-room kind of way."

"Ah-hah. But no . . . ?"

Peter pursed his lips and shook his head.

"Not even a little . . . ," said Will impishly as he spread a bit of eggplant caponata on a crostino and took a nibble.

"No," said Peter, with exaggerated delicacy. "I'm lucky enough to have my health—which is some kind of miracle, given, shall we say, the exploits I took part in during the seventies and eighties. I'm saving myself for true love. I go to the gym every day, drink in moderation, take my Lipitor—oh, God, now I sound like an old man. . . ."

"Good for you."

"I dunno. I just feel a little blessed just to be here, so I wanna . . . you know, do it right."

"And you never got sick? That's amazing."

Peter shook his head.

"But your partner . . . ," said Will.

"Right," said Peter. "He did, and I didn't. Am negative and intend to stay that way."

"I can't imagine what it's like to lose someone you love like that."

"It's no day at the beach, lemme tell ya. But seriously, you go on. You try to be better—a better person."

"So . . . you guys weren't monogamous? And please tell me if this is none of my business and I'll shut up. I've just never known anybody personally who . . ."

"No, not at all, Will," said Peter. "I don't mind talking about it. Although when I know ya better, I'll give you the full version. Basically, we were totally committed to each other, forever—but this was way before the idea of gay marriage was even talked about, among gay men. In fact, the so-called revolution required just the opposite: We were *not* going to do love and marriage the way mainstream society did it. This was the seventies, yo! We thought that being true to each other—and to gay culture or whatever—meant allowing each other certain freedoms. We were gay boomers and we wanted it all. So we made rules to detail what the freedoms were."

"Rules?"

"Like having to spend at least four nights a week together. And on the other nights, no staying out all night, which meant past two a.m. No threesomes, because we tried threesomes and they didn't work for us. Everybody had different rules, you see. Harold traveled a lot, so we were both allowed to hook up when he was out of town—but no hookups ever in our apartment."

"And you didn't think he would ever fall in love with someone else?"

"Not at all," said Peter. "Absolutely never a doubt about that. We totally trusted to love each other until death did us part." Peter paused. "And then death did us part."

Will thought about that for a moment.

"I just find that amazing," he said. "You guys were very lucky to have had that."

"We were indeed," said Peter. "And, Will, we did it all in totally textbook, trailblazer style. Our families knew and liked each other. We were the cool uncles for all our nieces and nephews. We went to weddings and kids' birthday parties as a couple—the whole thing."

"You must miss him."

"Every day. But life goes on, right?"

Will nodded.

"Makes me angry to think about how slowly the world reacted to AIDS," he said. "I did some queer studies at Berkeley."

"It was war," said Peter. "I'd always heard about World War Two, as a kid, from my father, but I knew I'd never go in the army. I protested Vietnam, like everybody did. AIDS was my war."

"My dad just missed Vietnam."

"Remind me to tell you my antiwar stories."

"Protests? Demonstrations?"

"Some snowy night by the fire."

The antipasto had been devoured. When the waiter arrived to clear the table, they decided to have one more glass of wine, instead of dessert.

"Have you always been out?" Will asked.

"Pretty much," said Peter. "You?"

"Pretty much."

Will explained how accepting his parents were, how liberal his childhood friends. His parents did worry about sexually transmitted diseases, though.

"Of course," said Peter. "And you're careful, right?"

"Oh, sure," said Will. "Probably too careful."

"I know," sighed Peter. "People can go too far, trying to stay safe. The utter rapture of a sexualized world! The thrill in this heightened, primal awareness of other men, that I think Mother Nature gave us for hunting or whatever, that we just don't tap anymore! We don't have to totally chuck all that, just because of a flew fuids...." Peter stopped and tried again. "A few fluids ..."

Will hooted, and Peter shook his head.

"Oh my goodness, two drinks—that's all," said Peter.

"No worries," said Will.

"We'd better get a check."

It was around one-thirty. Will wanted to take the check, in gratitude for an evening at the opera, but Peter suggested they split it, and Will graciously acceded.

As they headed for the subway, Peter felt a thousand conversations in his head that he wanted to continue, but he only suggested to Will that they get together again sometime soon.

"Sounds great," said Will.

They took the 1 train south to Times Square, where Will had to switch to the 7. Peter had decided, in the interest of a neater parting, to wait until Fourteenth Street before switching to the express. As the Times Square stop came, Will, before rising from his seat, leaned into a little kiss on Peter's cheek—"Thanks again; get home safely"—which Peter reciprocated once he understood what was going on. This took a moment, because he had decided to be a good boy and not *expect* a kiss. Yet after Will was gone, as the 1 rattled southward, and Peter sat there in the glaring subway light—reaching for his iPhone, inserting earbuds, pulling out the *New Yorker*—he thought that he had actually gotten surprisingly close to Will over a little antipasto, and a kiss on the cheek didn't feel inappropriate at all.

CHAPTER 8

The next day brought one of those New York moments when everyone is talking about the weather, though the weather itself was hardly extreme enough to account for all the buzz. Skies were gray, it looked like snow—simple enough. The real storm was people's engrossment in the media's extremely calculated frenzy over an approaching nor'easter that might drop a ton of snow on the city and paralyze it—or might not, as was often the case with such storms. Either way, a looming nor'easter was a reliable cue to trigger latent fears that New York copes with every day but rarely moans about—plunging elevators, crashing subway trains, falling skyscrapers!—so why not moan endlessly, when you can, about how you're going to get to work in ten feet of snow, what you're going to do with the kids if school is cancelled, and whether or not the sanitation department is ready with the plows? Living stoically with constant unseen threats, New York loves to seize now and then on storm clouds as the opportunity for an urban ritual whose necessity mounts with every passing plunge- and crash-free day: the public display of vigilance, an aptitude required of all citizens here, perhaps even more than the cleverness and ambition we usually associate with the city.

Standing at his office window, looking out onto Madison Avenue, Peter wondered how differently the people scurrying below might process the weather from the way country people did. The sky—at least, as much of it as he could see—looked low and heavy, the light leftover and stale. Since moving into his present office the year before, Peter had always wished the window faced west, instead of east, country boy that he was. Western skies tell so much more about the coming weather than eastern skies do. And though Peter enjoyed the city's storm frenzy as much as anyone, at that moment he envied those upstate who faced greater actual danger from a nasty winter storm. He wondered what people might be doing at that very moment in his hometown or in the hills thirty miles north of there, where Jonathan had a house on the other side of the Hudson River, in a town called Hudson. Those folks would be checking their supply of salt for the front steps; calling a neighbor with a snow plow, to arrange for clearing the driveway; checking the pantry for enough food for a few days or simply the ingredients of something wonderful to make after the world had become immobilized. He remembered how the morning light upstate, on a clear day after a snowstorm, seemed to radiate both down from the sky and up from the fresh snow on the ground, revealing something essential about the trees and buildings you thought you knew; and how well this view, from the window of a cozy house, married with the aroma of a roasting chicken or a baking apple-cinnamon cake.

The view out the other window in Peter's office, the one that looked into the atrium, revealed coworkers buzzing about as usual that morning.

I wonder what frenzies buzz in those *little brains,* he thought. As usual, the agency was in the midst of preparing several new business pitches. There were big presentations the following week for their vodka and skin care clients. And then there was McCaw.

Peter had tried to make some notes, earlier that morning, on the basic terrain of the McCaw assignment and some directions that might be promising, but he had gotten nowhere. Was the job a play on the irritation of a certain segment of the populace, and their seduction into a cult of personality? What were the irritants? How large was the segment? How could personality help? Was it about the formation of a political movement and thus attached to the trajectory of "America," the idea; or perhaps something more religious, building on the human habit of faith? Instead of notes and diagrams, Peter had come up with a series of singularly inert-looking doodles. To shake himself up, he decided to grab his laptop and go sit in one of the semicircular balcony pods that overlooked the atrium. *That's what the god-damned place is for,* he thought.

Floating above the gentle ambient buzz in the atrium that day were the sounds of a team of workers installing a new sculpture there. Already suspended from the roof of the atrium was half a spray of artificial clouds, which seemed to be made of transparent plastic, framed into great puffs by concealed ribs. On the floor below were the rest of the clouds and a brand-new, bright yellow boom lift—itself, with its curiously expressive extendable arm, looking like a sculpture. After securing several wires attached to one of the clouds on the floor, a worker stepped into the bucket of the lift and was boosted to the top of the atrium, under the direction of someone whom Peter guessed was the sculptor. The finished installation was going to look great, Peter thought. The clouds looked somehow classically Japanese, like those surrounding Mount Fuji in a Hiroshige print. Peter made a mental note to introduce himself to the sculptor.

"Prepared for the storm?" said Laura, whom Peter had run into on his way to the pod. Rather than her usual suit and heels, she was wearing jeans, a turtleneck, and a pair of hiking boots of the Madison Avenue variety. The look placed Laura in the early 1970s, when she would have been in college.

"Hat, scarf, and gloves," said Peter.

"I'm supposed to be in Paris on Thursday," said Laura. "Now I'm wondering if I can get there."

"You'll be OK."

"Sunil called again."

"Uh-huh."

"Just checking in."

"We're on track for the fifteenth."

"I know."

"Look, I know how good a job this would be—believe me. But I wanna make sure we know what we're saying yes to."

"Besides the money."

"Besides the money and besides the stories that *Business Week* and the *Journal* are gonna run about us being in bed with Henderson McCaw."

"Could be good, honey. There is a way to spin it."

"Of course there is. I just . . . have to look at the thing as a whole. And, I mean, purely on the work level, this office cannot just pull the creativity out of the freezer, thaw it out, and serve it up. We have to grow the stuff out in the fields, Laura—cultivate it, then harvest. . . ."

Peter paused.

"Sorry, I'm getting a little fancy," he said.

"I know, but I'm buying it," laughed Laura, continuing on her way. "Just keep going."

In the pod, Peter made some notes and paused. Then another cloud was in place and the worker in the lift returned to the floor, to start on the next one.

"Constructing the weather," "building a climate" . . . hmmm. Was there anything in there? Peter wondered. He made more notes.

McCaw was trying to exploit and further goad a massive shift in the American psyche, which would fail miserably if not synched with the planet's alternative weather system, the collective unconscious. That much was clear to Peter.

And there's twice as much of the stuff these days as when Jung coined the term, he thought, *since there are twice as many people in the world. All that meat, all that spirit—it either counts for something or it doesn't. It either changes what we're doing, in the media, or it doesn't.*

And especially now, with massive, instant interconnectivity, the clouds and currents in all that unconsciousness were fluctuating faster than ever. Fashion people knew this very well and happily tapped into it. Sometimes on a runway, amid the usual notions of Soldier, Whore, Ballerina, and Russian Peasant, you'd see an acrid shade of green or beguilingly graceless bump of silhouette—a true surprise!—and you'd know you were receiving news of some important shift in human thinking. And though there was no better way to apprehend shifts like this except to venerate fashion and, perhaps, to wear the clothes themselves, the news was exactly as important as $E = mc^2$ and "Beauty is truth, truth beauty."

Peter stared at the clouds. Vigilance paid off. Everything is a tell, he knew, if you just know how to look at it.

"There you are. What are you doing?"

It was Tyler, at the entrance to the pod. Peter waved him in.

"I like the view," said Peter. "What's up?"

"I know you're busy, but can I get sixty seconds? I need a jolt on the Royal Caribbean pitch."

"Shoot."

Tyler plunked himself down on the pod's curved banquette. He, too, had dressed in honor of the approaching storm, in a funny amalgam of Williamsburg, Brooklyn, meets Freeport, Maine: layers, flaps, and the knit wool skullcap that all the boys were wearing that season.

"OK," said Tyler, "they want to hype their spa services, and I'm trying to unpack the logo. I am thinking crown, royalty, service, pampering, hot-and-cold running staff. And then maybe there's something in the blue—though their blues are standard process royal and navy, and I don't know if we can get away with overlaying a bunch of azure thinking. . . ."

Tyler broke off, and Peter thought for a moment about what he'd heard, before raising a finger.

"Let me suggest another direction," he said, crisply. "Here's what I see: ocean, limitless horizon, out beyond the sight of land, the infinite frontier, peace but danger, this little cork bobbing up and down on top of water that's three miles deep, the passenger threatened but available for comfort, the voyager discovering simple pleasures that could be the last but in some ways are the first. Water, rebirth, the presence of infinity—am I getting anywhere?"

"Gee, boss, I think I just got a boner," said Tyler. "Thanks." The boy stood up and was ready to dash away.

"Which of course brings us to the body," continued Peter. "Floating, suspension . . . See if that gets you anywhere. Oh, and Ty—also? Those little maps of the decks."

"Ooh, I love those maps—floor plans. The Lido Deck!"

"Right? Like porn. You can get lost in them. Remember porn. Don't condescend to that."

"I won't. You're a champion," said Tyler. "Say, how was the opera?"

"It was lots of fun, thank you," said Peter.

"You took your new friend."

"I did, indeed."

"And?"

"We had a great time. Dinner afterward—talk, talk, talk."

"You gonna see each other again?"

"I hope so. Maybe."

"Yay for you."

"Thanks. I think I might be a little obsessed. I'm actually having a hard time concentrating today."

"Really? After one date?"

"It wasn't a date."

"But you're obsessed."

"I think there was chemistry. I love his laugh and his sharpness; I think he might find me a little interesting. But . . . you never know."

"Never know what?"

"Never know if you're, you know, cute enough or whatever."

"Are you serious?" shot Tyler. "Don't worry, Charlie. You qualify on that score."

Peter's expression squeezed into a grimace.

"Tyler, please," he said quietly. "Can't you see I'm fragile over here?"

"I'm sorry, boss," said Tyler, seeing that Peter did look a bit upset. "Omigod, you're so vulnerable."

"That's exactly how I'm feeling."

"I'm so sorry. I didn't mean to be a jerk. I was just being me. So do you think this might be serious?"

"I don't know."

"You've only seen each other once?"

"Yeah, and so why am I suddenly obsessed with him? I can't figure out how I'm supposed to think about it."

"Don't think about it. Just do it. I can't believe I'm speaking in taglines."

"It happens to all of us, eventually."

"Go out again. See what happens."

"Right."

"I'm completely jealous, of course," said Tyler. "But I am here for you totally, as a friend. Anything I can do to help."

"Talking helps," said Peter. "Thank you."

"OK—then, seriously? It's not about what you think of as cuteness."

"No?"

"I guarantee that's more in your mind than his."

"Hmm."

"And it's not about your age or your generation—and, believe me, I know how absorbing you find all that. That's just not the way he's thinking about it—I guarantee it. I suggest you *don't* torture him with any of that."

"Define 'torture.' "

"Mentioning it."

Peter smirked. Tyler knew him well.

"I already did, a little," said Peter. "So my plan to dazzle him with my insight about the collective unconscious—the way some older gay men resist new archetypes like Lady Gaga because they feel they already own Madonna and Barbra Streisand—that's not a good idea?"

"Uh, no."

"But I talk about that with you."

"Because we're friends, and we work together and that's our world. If you're really interested in this guy, you wanna go easy on that. For real. Can't you just *talk* about Lady Gaga?"

Peter nodded.

"Yes, but," he said.

"Look," said Tyler. "You're both unique human beings. You're not defined by your ages, or your generations, or your salaries, or anything else."

"That's another thing—money."

"Of course it is. He's not making a million dollars a year."

"Neither am I, but no."

"Two different, unique human beings."

"Thank you, Tyler. This is very helpful. We *are* friends, aren't we?"

"Bestest ever."

"You know, most people bore me," said Peter. "You know that, right? Most men bore me. But when you and I do things, I have a really good time. Our friendship has come to mean a lot to me."

"Boss, that's the nicest thing you've ever said to me."

"I really value being able to talk about things with you."

Tyler nodded his head once, decisively.

"Well, that is my honor," he said.

"To be continued," said Peter.

"Yeah, I should scoot."

"Go in peace."

"Thanks for the . . ." Tyler mimed an explosion and made the sound of a bomb going off.

"It's the pod," said Peter, gesturing toward the vast space beyond them.

After Tyler left, Peter jotted down a few more McCaw thoughts that arose from the line he'd been pursuing for Royal Caribbean: *faith vs. heresy, orthodoxy vs. revealed knowledge*. Politics and social change were sometimes explained in such terms. Then he closed his laptop and sat back. Another cloud was in place.

If only he could do the boy-toy thing, Peter thought. It would be lovely to be content, as many successful, single gay men of his generation seemed to be, to play around in what Colette or Oscar Wilde would probably have called the demimonde, with adorable, expertly styled young men who spoke earnestly of becoming actors, yoga instructors, or fashion directors. Yet Peter had found that so many earnest party pretties have nothing else on the ball, and that any interest generated by a turn of phrase or a curl of lip usually dissolves before dinner is over. He was still cursed by the lofty intellectual goals and high romantic intentions that were driving his desires forty years before, when he met Harold.

Ah, Harold! Unlike Peter's first encounter with Will, which apparently had taken place without Peter even being aware of it, at Jonathan's party, the first encounter with Harold was the proverbial thunderbolt. It was cloudy that day, Peter recalled—a Saturday morning in early fall, which in Ithaca meant that the days were already cold enough for the boys on campus to be wearing bulky sweaters, scarves, and down vests, though many were also still sporting shorts, which they wore with boots and thick socks. A new recruit to the town's first food co-op, Peter was picking up his friend Shira, who'd cofounded the co-op, and her friend Harold, whom she knew from folk dancing, for a drive in Peter's thirdhand Dodge Dart to a farm twenty miles away, to collect fresh eggs for distribution at the co-op's repurposed storefront, in Collegetown. Peter pulled up in front of Shira's house, a shambling old mansion on the edge of campus that had been converted into apartments, and found Shira and a cute guy with long hair and a scraggly beard waiting on the porch. As the two of them clambered down the wooden steps and into the car, Peter thought it was odd that his friend should volunteer to duck into the backseat and let the cute guy sit up front. Shira later admitted this was a setup.

As they drove, they laughed as the car was buffeted by strong gusts of wind blasting in from the lake. Desperately, Peter tried to stay on his side of the smallish country road while keeping up with small talk about the coming snow, the co-op's new commercial food scale, and the folk musicians who were scheduled to appear on campus that fall. He also tried to steal glances at Harold for whatever clues could be gleaned about his body from knees, hands, and the shapeless brown cable-knit sweater he was wearing. Yet the road was twisty and hilly, and Peter was forced to keep both eyes on it. But then, at the farm, while waiting for Shira to conclude dealings with the farmer, Peter feasted as he and Harold chatted. Harold gestured as nobly as an ancient senator in a painting by David; he shifted his posture with the casual strength of an astronaut on a television newscast. Even as Peter squinted and shielded his eyes from the sun that was trying to stay out, he gorged on details like eyes that were not brown but greenish-brown and hair that was not brown but brown-that-had-once-been-blond. It would only be a few years later, after Peter and Harold had moved to New York, when Harold would lose the beard and trim his hair. By the time Harold was working for the *Times* he'd lost most of his hair anyway and was shaving what was left.

Shira directed the loading of the backseat and trunk with crates, and at the storefront she directed the unloading. They all put in a few hours slicing cheese and weighing vegetables, then went home to Shira's place for dinner, where they made a mushroom-and-shallot frittata with the fresh eggs they'd brought back to town and a spicy cabbage salad with peanuts and toasted tofu. Harold was studying

English lit as an independent major, Peter learned—which meant smart. He was from Queens and, like everyone else, didn't smoke. His voice was deep and slightly breathy, like a movie star's, and though he'd asked how many cylinders Peter's Dodge Dart ran on, he scarcely knew any more about cars than Peter did. In fact, as the evening went on, Peter saw that Harold was just as dreamily poetic as one might hope—political but not nearly as strident as the otherwise admirable activists of the Student Homophile League, as it was then called, and seductive but not whorish, like the townies Peter was meeting in the county's one gay bar that wasn't even gay until ten p.m. on weekend nights. Instantly, Peter felt chemistry—or *something* more thrillingly inertial than anything he'd ever felt for a human being except the brother of his high school girlfriend, a boy whom the girlfriend often half-jokingly complained saw more of Peter than she did.

And Peter's attraction for Harold was amplified by the headiness of those times, the early '70s, when epoch-changing antiwar protests and historic civil rights demonstrations—revolution as a collective act, not a theory—made every day feel like the stuff of legend. Why not throw personal liberation into a fall weekend centered on post-supermarket food activism? Harold knew that Peter was gay, because Peter talked about it all the time and because Shira, at least then, was a lesbian; and Peter knew that Harold, who was supposedly seeing a woman named Jane, was not likely to be hemmed in by big, bad, bourgeois, capitalist-patriarchal norms. So when Harold's sweater came off after dinner, as the three of them sipped roasted barley tea and compared the diaries of Anaïs Nin with those of Virginia Woolf, and Peter glimpsed a promised land beneath the rumpled collar of Harold's plaid flannel shirt, open to the sternum, he grew bolder. Peter said he didn't see why men couldn't share erotic friendships, too, irrespective of sexual identity and society's judgments; Harold and Shira agreed. Then, from inside Harold's shirt, Peter caught his first whiff of a clean-but-potent funkiness that would intoxicate him for decades to come, and he flipped into high gear.

"Wow, look at the time," said Peter.

"Mercy," said Harold.

It was past one. Shira invited them to stay the night, offering the living room and bringing in a pile of mismatched pillows and blankets. Then she retired to her own room, gently drawing shut a pair of glass-paned doors that were draped in pink-and-orange Indian cotton bedspreads. Peter and Harold flipped a coin, which yielded Harold the sofa. Peter made himself comfortable in a nest of blankets on the rug just in front of it, and the two of them fell asleep holding hands, which Peter suggested they try, whispering that it was OK for their bodies to be close and their spirits to soar around the universe, while dreaming, like twin shooting stars.

Peter's dreams that night came true within weeks. He and Harold were kissing by Thanksgiving and had plunged into full-on sex before the holiday break. They read books to each other—Harold hadn't read *Eros and Civilization,* Peter hadn't read *Middlemarch*—and traded stories of childhood. Peter hadn't realized he'd grown up "in the country," and Harold hadn't thought it odd to be able to sneak into the 1965 World's Fair every day, for free. They ran into few of the trip wires that can deactivate a young relationship—Harold was neither a hothead nor a wimp, nor overly suspicious or under-demonstrative—and by spring, everything about Harold was dear to Peter. Even Harold's nipples, which had looked a bit small and flat to Peter when he first saw them at a folk dance gathering, came to seem the most perfect nipples God had ever created. Same for chest hair and toes.

It was chemistry, it was luck, it was a rare alignment of stars, Peter mused. That's why thinking about it explained so little and was of no value in predicting the future. You're caught by someone's laugh, or the look of him dashing across the street, and that's it. It's only an observation, a memory, perhaps a motivation to pick up the phone.

Tyler was right: It wasn't about cuteness. But then what did Will see in Peter? A smart guy? A successful guy? A guy with comps to the opera? A guy who was, wait, vulnerable? Until Tyler mentioned it that day, Peter hadn't actually embraced that side of himself as anything but ordinary.

Sure, I'm vulnerable, he thought. *Everybody is.*

Yet the news, as delivered by Tyler, was as much of a surprise as Harold's remark about growing up in the country.

Really? I never thought about it that way.

Peter's reverie was broken by some shouting from the floor of the atrium. A client from the waiting area had wandered in front of the lift, thinking it was, indeed, a sculpture. The workmen were protesting.

"Acapulco Sand?" said Luz.
"Too pink," said Will, testily.
"White Marigold?"
"No, too green!"
They were standing in Schatz's Hardware on Steinway Boulevard, in front of a panoramic display of Benjamin Moore paint chips—three broad panels of wood cabinetry on a wall in the back of the store, lined with hundreds of color strips in graded intensities, arranged by hue. The lighting on the panels was brilliant but warm.

Will was agitated and Luz was trying her best not to be. For days they had more or less been arguing about what color to paint the living room. Will was being difficult about the choice, vacillating among mossy greens, dusty blues, and muted golds, without really being able to say why. They'd amassed a thick file folder of sample colors torn from magazines, and decided several times on a final choice, which then, a day later, Will would contradict. And though Luz was perfectly amenable to almost any color, she did expect a dialogue around its choice, and was interested in knowing why Will would prefer the colors he did and how he thought they would play in their house, against their belongings.

"Can I help you?" said a saleswoman.
"Yes, please," said Will. "We're looking for a nice tan."
"For a living room," said Luz.
"Something between a tan and a burnished browny-gold," said Will. "But not too dark. Not as pink as sand, not as yellow as khaki. Maybe paper bag?"
"Paper bag," said the saleslady.
"Paper bag, but with a hint of sun," said Luz, echoing a phrase Will had used on their way over to the store.
"The yellowy tans are in here," said the saleslady, zeroing in on a narrow patch of color wall.

Will pulled out a few strips and pointed out shades to Luz: Henderson Buff, Yorkshire Tan, Dunmore Cream.

"Can we look a bit?" asked Will.

"Yes, of course," said the saleslady.

"How do they even think up this many names?" said Luz. "Look, and they're not all stupid." She showed Will a strip of blue chips. "This is exactly what I would have thought Athens Blue would look like."

"Mmm."

"Nail polish names are the worst. I saw one the other day called Jizz."

"Can we focus, please?" said Will.

Luz picked up another strip and showed him.

"No, Luz, yuck. Those are beige."

"How come Enrico isn't helping you with this?"

"Oh, please. He'd have to mix his own color. None of these would be right. Besides, we're giving each other a rest."

"Oh?"

"It was turning into the same thing, all over again—superficial, whatever."

"You said he was a nice guy."

"He is. But he takes the whole A-list thing way too seriously. And I know he thinks I fit into it perfectly."

"And you don't."

"I don't know what I fit into," said Will gloomily.

"So you guys just aren't talking?" said Luz. "That sounds brutal. Then again, you *are* men."

Will had told Luz he felt lost, when he returned home from his New Year's Eve outing. The life of a trophy boy was no longer for him, he said, but he didn't know what else was out there. Did he have a good time? asked Luz. Yes, said Will, but it wasn't about having a good time anymore. Did he like Enrico? Yes—no. Well, maybe.

"Sag Harbor Gray?" said Luz.

"Maybe," said Will.

"Northampton Putty."

"Ooh! No. What about the one just below it?"

"Crown Point Sand."

Will exhaled.

"I can't tell," he said.

About his date with Peter Will had said little, only that it wasn't a date.

"We were just hanging out," said Will. "His friend got sick and he had an extra ticket."

"So what's he doing, going out with younger guys?" Luz asked.

"He's cool. He had a partner who died, like, years ago. He survived the whole AIDS thing."

"He wasn't looking for action?"

"We just talked. It was fun. I thought he might try to hit on me, but he's not like the rest of those A-list guys. Sorta shy, actually."

"What a line! He's got you wrapped around his little finger."

"No way, Luz," said Will. "It's just a friendship."

"Are you attracted to him?"

"Not really."

"No?"

"I mean, he's attractive for a guy his age."

"See? I'll bet he likes you."

"I'll say this: He takes me seriously—more than Enrico. I mean, he runs this big ad agency and still wants to know all about my family. I really don't think he cares about getting into my pants, which is itself kind of attractive."

"Omigod, this guy is good."

"I think he's more damaged than he realizes. He says his partner's death was the making of him, but it's clearly also this huge weight around his neck."

"You don't get over that kind of thing," said Luz.

"He talks a lot about the past. He told me that in 1964 he thought he had, quote, seen the future of mankind when he heard Barbra Streisand sing 'People' for the first time. You know that song? According to him, 'Some queens are still living in that same future.' Not him, of course. 'Western culture keeps making new futures.'"

It took Luz a moment to process this idea. She blinked in a comically exaggerated way.

"I know," Will continued. "I had to think about it, too."

"Have you made a choice yet?" said the saleslady.

"What about Danville Tan?" said Luz.

"I don't know, I don't know, *I don't know!*" whined Will, suddenly throwing the chips he was holding down on the counter in front of them. The outburst surprised both Luz and the saleswoman.

"Calm down," said Luz. "It's only paint."

The saleslady slipped away.

"Sorry," said Will. "I'm fine, don't worry."

"Don't be such a princess," said Luz.

"Sorry. It's just that what if . . . I don't wanna make the wrong choice!"

"Then we'll stick with what we've got."

"Landlady White," snapped Will. "We didn't even choose that. It's the absence of a choice."

"It's all right."

"But what if we do the tan instead of putty and the whole room comes out *too* yellow?"

"Jesus, Will—life goes on."

Will drew close to Luz.

"Peter said something that's been kicking my butt," he whispered. "He said that as a child he expected to be at home in the world, and that as an adult he had *made* himself at home in the world."

"Uh-huh," said Luz. "And?"

"It reminded me of something my boss in L.A. once said to me, about taking yourself seriously."

"OK."

"Have you ever felt that?"

"What—serious?"

"At home in the world. Comfortable with your life."

"I don't know. I suppose so."

"I've never felt it—about anything. I thought I did, but I don't."

"Some people don't have that particular feeling," said Luz. "But they still have lives."

"It made me feel like I wasn't equal, or something," said Will.

In a corner of Will's mind was a thought about how easy it had been for his parents, who started their family and built their house just as the prosperity of the '80s was cranking up. Family pictures showed his parents looking like young movie stars back then: His dad was the Tom Cruise of aerospace, the deceptively casual boy entrepreneur in designer jeans, a polo shirt, and Armani sport jacket, all in "relaxed" proportions; his mom was the Brooke Shields of private education, always perfect in a *Dynasty* hairdo and pumped-up interpretation of a classic suit or dress, finished with a tasteful array of big jewelry. Even the design of their multimillion-dollar, in-town ranch was pumped up with faux-Mission arches and fountained patios. Nothing in Will's life until New York—not school, nor religion, nor any of the jobs he'd ever held—had shown him how to keep up that kind of largeness or formulate another kind that allowed for new times and his own personal preferences. That it could take some effort to maintain a scale of living his parents found effortless came as a frustrating surprise.

Will took one of the strips from Luz—the one she had been looking at, with Danville Tan.

"Excuse me," he said, summoning the saleslady. "Does this come in both flat and semigloss?"

"All of these come in flat, semigloss, and high gloss," said the saleslady, stepping over.

Will gave the saleslady the dimensions of the room and she calculated the amount of paint needed, as well as the price.

"Eight gallons? That's insane," said Will.

"I think you're going to need two coats," said the saleslady.

"I could get to Paris for that kind of money."

"This is a premium product, sir. Now, I can show you some other choices. . . ."

"No, no thanks," interrupted Will. "We want the best—'cause we're, you know, *us*."

CHAPTER 9

Sometimes after a long day crammed with work and socializing, Peter would come home, sit quietly in his darkened living room, and listen to music on his iPhone. This was the extension of an older habit, of flopping down on the daybed and watching TV or listening to music on the stereo, in an effort to decompress—though somehow the intimacy of listening by way of the phone and a pair of earbuds, combined with sitting up, helped make the experience more of what Peter was looking for: a reconnection with his deepest thoughts and feelings, which had become distant during the day.

Thus, after a day of serving clients by looking at the world and interpreting its signs, this late-night listening habit was more a journey of the soul than research into entertainment culture. It made sense to him that listening, in the current age of looking and being looked at, would afford a pathway to the self as direct as any he had followed since college, a practice as serious, and successful, as anything spiritual he had ever tried, like yoga and meditation. So around midnight, after settling into one of his pair of oversized armchairs, dressed, as he did that winter, in sweatpants and a hoodie with the hood up, with a vodka he kept on the little Alvar Aalto table next to him, he would flip through his library of tunes and enter a meditative zone that allowed him to see how precariously yet deliciously he lived on the border between incompleteness and completeness: how his current state of constant longing for a boyfriend mordantly chafed the satisfaction he felt—or was it simply relief?—at having come this far in life without having gone broke or completely compromised his values. Often, a scented candle was involved. That winter, after a favorite Diptyque Cyprès burned out, Peter tried a Belle Fleur candle that Jonathan gave him, Kyara Clove, which he didn't like at first: too heavy with spice and leather, too strenuously opulent in a cliché, so-called Oriental way. But then he decided that Kyara Clove was complex and valid, and used the candle a lot. He'd sit there, feeling the room's scent and shadows, listening and thinking, and sometimes he'd fall asleep, and at four or five o'clock find himself still in the chair, and then get up and go to bed.

His thoughts during these sessions were sometimes about the past, though never about regret. There were surprisingly few thoughts about Harold, which was ironic, since the man had died not five feet away from where Peter sat. Instead, the main thrust was about the future—how where he came from was leading to where he was going. Where he *could* go was still thrilling to Peter: to discover a new city or violin sonata, or revisit a favorite city or violin sonata and now see more in it; to feel the sun again at the end of winter or a chill late in summer, and find the *sensation* in these feelings even greater than before. Also, to find the next lover and possibly a sensational love—which were possibilities that for a long time seemed a betrayal of Harold, despite Harold's explicit approval of them, expressed one day in the hospital, not long before coming home for the last time.

"Peter, I want you to find another boyfriend, after I am gone," he said.

"Now, that's ridiculous," said Peter, as he continued removing dead flowers from an arrangement that someone had brought to the hospital room. Performing care partner duties helped him get through the ordeal of slowly losing the man who meant everything to him.

"I mean it," said Harold. "And I want you to remember I said so. You're gonna need somebody to go dancing with, and I want you to keep dancing."

"We don't need to talk about this now," said Peter. In fact, Harold was a month away from dipping under eighty pounds, two away from dementia, and three from his final, labored breath. Why was Harold talking about dancing, anyway? The last time they had danced together was at a friend's house, the previous winter; Harold had already lost some weight, mysteriously, and everyone said it looked good on him, with the unspoken hope that the compliment would function as a talisman.

"Still, I'm saying it now, while I still can," said Harold. Then he faked a cough and made an extravagantly frail-looking *Traviata* gesture.

"Oh, brav-*o,*" said Peter, clapping slowly.

So where was the next boyfriend? wondered Peter. Why was he taking so long to arrive? How near was he? What was he doing right now? These thoughts were recurring incessantly, especially at night, when he was alone. Unlike a lot of nostalgic literature that Jonathan and his crowd took as gospel, Peter's late-night contemplations expressed a desire not to recapture an old dance but simply to keep dancing. The future had always been golden for Peter, especially since his youth had not been particularly golden, which meant he'd never had anywhere to go but up. He'd often thought himself lucky never to have been particularly cute. He knew that defining one's self by youthful beauty and trading on such things was a trap he'd have been too weak or stupid to avoid. Cuteness then would have meant dealing with fading cuteness now, a drama few can sidestep, if that is their lot. No, his bond with the future was unblocked even by nostalgia, and his chief thoughts now that the present was so golden were about savoring the glow by sharing it with someone. That seemed the best way to use the gifts he'd been allowed at his age—not simply the dark hair and flat stomach, but old age itself and the taste to go on dancing. It was some kind of eternal dance, he realized, that he'd consecrated his whole life to, after emancipation from a fairly inert upbringing in the '50s and '60s, and then immersion, upon arrival in Ithaca in the early '70s, in something called "the movement," which went far beyond politics, to the body itself and the fullness of its moments. His life was still the most beautiful dance floor, not glimpsed from sidelines patrolled by memory, through bursts of sparkle and clouds of mist, but experienced right at the center, the deathless anthem soaring, faces of God dazzling, day after day after day. How could anyone experience the repletion of such a thing, in mere time, alone?

Why wasn't Tyler it? Why hadn't Nick worked out? Where was the man, yet unknown, perhaps, but still so palpable during those late-night séances, whom Peter could almost reach out and touch, and see smiling at him; the man with whom he could go on discovering life, not just a companion for picnic suppers on rolling lawns in the Berkshires during summer and black-tie premieres in town during the winter, but a fellow shooting star with whom to race to the end of the universe and back? Answers were easy—Nick opted out of that approach to life, and Tyler, though seductive, was still faking it—but answers told nothing. Music, on the other hand, told everything. That's where Mr. Right was appearing, for the moment, in all his theoretical, wacky-'n'-wonderful, love-hate/right-wrong/inevitable-impossible glory. (*He's out there somewhere, maybe just around the corner . . . !*) That winter, for when theoretical Mr. Right was making him happy, Peter had Sondheim's "Remember?" quintet, from the original London cast recording of *A Little Night Music,* and Cole Porter's "You're the Top," by Jean Turner with Stan Kenton, on *Anything Goes: Capitol Sings Cole Porter* to listen to; he had Trisha Yearwood's "Hearts in Armor" and Patsy Cline's "She's Got You," for when Mr. Right was making him sad; and he had things like Milton Nascimento's "Dancing," Bill Laswell's "Ethiopia/Lower Ground," and Serdar Ortaç's "Kabahat" for when he wanted to celebrate simply living on the same planet as his theoretical guy. Depending on how deep the hole went on a given night (*Maybe he's not out there . . . !*), there was also Gilberto Gil's "Réquiem Pra Mãe Menininha Do Gantois," Trey Songz's "Can't Help But Wait," and Gergiev's reading of Rachmaninoff's Second Symphony. Alanis Morissette's "Uninvited" or "Another Winter in a Summer Town," from *Grey Gardens,* generally meant that things had gotten too deep (*We all deserve happiness, don't we . . . ?*). And if it came to slow movements from Beethoven string quartets or vocal music by Poulenc and di Lasso, the following morning would definitely bring a kind of spiritual hangover, quite apart from the vodka.

Yet listening this way helped Peter achieve a sense of sheer tenderness and vulnerability that eluded him during the workday. It functioned as a kind of purification, or preparation for something. It kept him primed and clean for love or whatever. And that winter he decided he would be happy even with a little whatever.

A week later, Peter hosted another party at his house. Again, it was drinks and hors d'oeuvres for forty. Will was there, too, only this time as a guest—a guest whose familiarity with the kitchen and desire to be helpful by opening wine led several people to ask Peter discreetly if he had snagged a new boyfriend. Will had come alone, though Peter had explicitly said he might bring someone, and he stuck around after the rest of the gang had left, to help Peter clean up. When they were done, Will asked if Peter wanted to smoke a joint with him. Surprised and delighted, Peter said yes, so they grabbed their coats and some matches and an ashtray, poured two vodkas, and stepped into the garden.

It wasn't too cold outside—and anyway, the chill made a nice change from three hours of indoors. They sat at a wrought-iron table near the black post lamp that switched on during nighttime hours, the light from which seemed to tint the entire garden in microshades of mousy sepia.

"I can't wait until spring," said Peter, as they lit up. "During the day you can smell it coming."

"Mm-hmm," said Will, taking a puff.

"You can't imagine how lush and wonderful it gets back here," said Peter. "The leaves make all this noise; the city sounds filter through them. . . ."

"I'll bet."

"Right now, you can't even see, back here. That planter is brick red," said Peter, pointing. "The siding is green." He paused and there was silence. "What is your coat, blue?"

"Sort of a dusty, dark blue."

"The colors are hidden, in full view."

"Interesting."

The garden, as usual, was quiet. They passed the joint back and forth, relighting when they had to, and started on the vodkas. Unlike the front of the house, a simple brick Federalist façade that was kept as originally built, in compliance with the city's landmark preservation laws, the back of the house showed a bit of fun, with tastefully designed windows, porches, and balustrades that were anything but original, on both Peter's level, the parlor floor, and those of his landlady, the second and third floors.

"Did you and your partner used to have parties out here?" asked Will.

"Not really," said Peter. "When we moved in, the porch and back door weren't even there. She put that in a few years ago. There used to be a weird fifties picture window there. To get to the garden, you had to go through the hallway inside, downstairs, out that door." Peter pointed to the garden door, which gave onto a small sunken patio paved with brick.

"But I have been using the garden a lot recently," continued Peter. "Last summer we had tons of parties out here—well, four or five."

"Yeah?" said Will.

"And she never comes down here, except to garden. And the people who live on the garden level are never in town. So I like to tell people I live alone in a private house with my live-in gardener."

"Nice."

More silence. At a relaxed pace they took hits of the joint, savored sips of vodka. Peter noticed that Will squinted appealingly when he inhaled.

"One year, the people who live *there*," said Peter, indicating the three-story former garage building that abutted the small carriage house on the other side of the fence at the back of the garden, "decided to put a giant HVAC machine right behind this fence, to cool their entire building."

"Hmm," said Will, taking a peek at the spot, over his shoulder.

"It was as big as a motherfucking Buick and sounded like a plane taking off. Seriously—constant noise! Forget the birds; we couldn't even hear ourselves talking back here. We were not happy. He and his wife live on the top floor—see the terrace?—and he has a theatrical prop business on the first and second floors. Anyway, we complained nicely, my landlady and I, and they were like, 'Who says the backyard has to be so damned quiet?' Which pissed me off, right? Then I got all the people on this block, all these gardens, to sign a letter—and these are all rich white people here, who own these houses. Still nothing. Then I got the city involved. Hello! They sent inspectors, noise consultants. And then one day a huge crane comes and plucks the unit up and takes it away."

"Wow."

"Yeah. They relocated the thing on the roof, in a sort of padded shell. And I gather it was *hugely* expensive for them to reinforce the roof, which is why they tried to put it down here in the first place."

Will was looking at Peter in a way that Peter couldn't diagnose.

"I have this thing about quality of life," said Peter. "I'm sort of a crank that way."

"I think it's awesome," said Will.

He asked about some of the people he'd met at the party. Peter explained who was gay and who wasn't, who was in a relationship and who wasn't.

"The white-haired guy?" said Will.

"Straight," said Peter.

"Really?"

"I know."

"But those boots . . . !"

"He's a trend forecaster. What can I say?"

"Is he any good?"

"Uh, only when he steals from the right people."

Will laughed.

"You were funny tonight," said Peter.

"I was?" said Will.

"People were in stitches over that stroller mom stuff."

"Did it sound too mean?"

"It certainly did."

"Oh, good."

They laughed. The joint was gone and they'd finished their vodkas. The night suddenly felt colder.

"Thank you, fresh air," said Peter.

"Brrrr," said Will.

"Go in?"

"Sure."

Inside, before Peter even had a chance to ask whether Will would have another drink, Will, at the freezer, was asking if he should pour them both another vodka. His comfort in his kitchen thrilled Peter. Drinks in hand, they installed themselves in the over-sized armchairs, which faced each other.

"You know, I was sitting here just the other night, thinking about you," said Peter.

"You were?" said Will. "Thinking good things?"

"I would say so, yeah."

"Like what?"

"Well, I'm not sure I grasp the immensity of you," said Peter. "And that's not usually a place I find myself in, with people."

"You mean—you grasp other people's immensity more easily than you do mine?" said Will.

Peter mimed dry amusement with half a grin.

"Other people are not so immense," he said with deliberate sly-ness. "Dope."

"Funny, I don't feel immense. In fact, working at the magazine makes me feel really, really small. Everybody there has such a big idea about themselves."

"How's it going?"

"I've done two interviews. I think people like my ideas. Some-times it's hell. You know."

"But the egos?"

"Exactly—the egos."

"Don't worry," said Peter. "Print will be over shortly and then you can do something better."

Will appeared to take the remark as a witticism, but Peter in-stantly saw how foolish it was.

"I'm sorry," said Peter. "That was a stupid thing to say and not true. It's a good magazine."

"Don't worry," said Will, getting out of the chair and heading toward the bathroom. As he passed Peter, he gave the older man's hair an affectionate tousle.

Holy shit, thought Peter. *Is this really going where I think it may be going?* Now that intimacy might be a real possibility, it seemed scarier than before.

When Will returned, they began speaking of Jonathan. And as they sat, and Will crossed his legs man-style, ankle to knee, Peter noticed what he hadn't been able to see all night, while Will was standing or out in the garden: that he was wearing low-cut white athletic socks with his sneakers, which revealed a few inches of muscular ankle and lower leg, between the top of the sock and the hem of his jeans. Talk about hidden in full view! He looked sturdy, thick, but what of the rest of him? As hairless as the leg? As they spoke, part of Peter's brain began executing some kind of 3-D modeling or mental cloning program, to determine the form of Will's other body parts—feet, ass, lower back, armpits, chest— from the parts Peter could actually observe.

"So he's doing OK?" said Will.

"Sorry, what?" said Peter.

"He's responding to the treatment?"

"Yes, yes. I mean, it's hard on his body. He's pretty weak, lost a little weight. But he's working. That's the main thing."

"Good."

"He's working on a new film."

"About Connor Frankel . . ."

"Yes—oh, right, he was there that night. Anyway, he and I keep talking about traveling somewhere exotic together, a big getaway, but he's so focused on getting this film done. As he should be."

Peter was about to launch into a thought about work being the ultimate therapy, and the way Jonathan was approaching this film—basically, talking on camera until he died—then he thought better of it.

"He's an intellectual, hard-core," said Will. "I respect that."

"Exactly," said Peter. "God knows we need more of them."

"I was amazed by that collection of books."

"Amazing, right? You saw the Eliot manuscript? He collects twentieth-century poetry manuscripts. He's got Millay, Pound, Frost, Sandberg. But the Eliot is his prize. Do you know *Four Quartets*?"

"Not that well. What's it about? Time or something."

"The illusion of time, the eternalness of the present. 'At the still point of the turning world. Neither flesh nor fleshless.' That's how he describes human existence. Though I think the opposite is rather the case."

"How so?"

"I can't believe we're talking about this."

"Should we light another joint?"

"No way. Jesus, you brought another one?"

"The magazine is hookup central."

"No, I'm fine with this," said Peter, lifting his glass. "But you feel free."

"I'm fine," said Will. "So—still point. You think the opposite."

"It seems to me, the person is always in motion, or should be, and the world is what's static. Does that make any sense?"

"It sounds like Buddhism."

"Yes! 'In motion' means being awake." Will grinned. "No one ever talks about this stuff anymore. You know, even as late as the fifties, when I was a kid, we had poets and philosophers as national figures, and they asked big questions. Now what do we have—*Avatar?*"

"*Lost. Battlestar Galactica. Caprica.*"

"Very good, Will," said Peter. "Those are actually much more to the point."

"I like your place," said Will, taking a moment to glance around him. "It's comfortable, but elegant."

"Thank you. You are most welcome here."

"Even your pots are nice. Do you collect cookware?"

"No! That's a funny thought. Well, actually, I guess I do. When I know you better, I'll tell you how excited I was to get that grill pan for Christmas. Do you collect anything?"

Will nodded.

"Beach art," he said.

"Pictures of the beach?" said Peter.

"Paintings, drawings that people do at the beach."

"Wow."

"You'd be surprised at how many of them you can find in second-hand shops, and how many of them are kinda good."

"Lovely."

"You collect books, too, I see."

"Yeah, but nothing like Jonathan. I just don't throw things away after reading them. Actually, I do have a few etiquette books—vintage. The first one I borrowed from my uncle Malcolm, who was very fancy. Then he died and I kept the book, and that got me going. Guess you have to be a good, middle-class boy to fetishize all that."

"I know," said Will. "I got thrown into my mom's school with some folks who were way above me, socially."

"God, does that concept still exist?"

"It does there. It brought out the bad boy in me."

"Good for you. Smoking behind chapel and St. Patrick's Day pranks?"

"Basically."

Was the conversation going anywhere? Peter realized he wasn't in control of it and suddenly wondered if he should be. He couldn't exactly direct the conversation toward the bedroom, yet didn't know how to pounce or whether he was being invited to do so. Pouncing wasn't even his style, nor did he necessarily want pounding-banging sex on a first date anymore. He preferred softer, friendlier play, like kissing and touching while lying on the bed, with cocks that went up and down without necessarily being expected to cum—none of which pouncing exactly set the stage for. Nor had Peter any idea of how to get to that spot by way of etiquette-book talk, even if Will were open to it. Yet again, if Will were more like Peter used to be, willing to have sex just for the fun of it, in a kind of just-jerk-me-off or just-fuck-me manner, then Peter would be willing to wing it and comply.

"Your uncle was gay?" said Will.

"Uncle Malcolm? Yeah, we *think* so. He died in the early seventies. Lung cancer."

"He smoked."

Peter nodded.

"Aunt Ida died of the same thing, a few years before," he said. "They smoked like mad people. They were both very fancy. They had cocktail sets and used them, tiki torches for summer entertaining on the patio. They had the first refrigerator I ever saw with French doors."

"But he wasn't out."

"Not to us. But you know what? This kid showed up at his funeral—a young guy none of us had seen before, dressed in super-stylish, big-city attire, like platform boots and a Carnaby Street jacket. This was, oh, 1972. . . ."

"Carnaby Street?"

"London, the swinging sixties, groovy mod styles."

"Got it."

"The kid shows up looking like a Beatle—big hair—and he weeps and weeps. Later he comes up to my father, Uncle Malcolm's brother, and says he knew my uncle from New York. Uncle Malcolm often went there on business, to buy supplies for the beauty parlor he and Aunt Ida owned, especially after Aunt Ida died...."

"Mm-hmm."

"Right? And the kid has these records with him—like four LPs, vinyl, in a leather satchel—that he says Uncle Malcolm lent him. He wanted to return them."

"Wow."

"So my father says he should keep the records, to remember my uncle by. And that's the last we saw of the guy."

"Was he cute?"

"Yes! And it kind of makes me happy to think that maybe Uncle Malcolm was getting some, even though he never came out, quote-unquote."

"What were the records?"

"Good question. I only saw one of them: the Bee Gees."

"Perfect."

"I know! And I have always kicked myself for not seeing what the other ones were."

"Your uncle blew into town and hung out with the cutest boys."

"And was into the Bee Gees! I wasn't even into the Bee Gees, at that point. They were too pop for me."

"Really?"

"I was strictly classical, back then."

"I'm giving us another vodka," said Will, popping out of his chair.

"Um, OK," said Peter, continuing with his story without compunction, while Will poured, served, and reinstalled himself in his chair. Peter realized not only that he was slightly drunk, but that Will was clearly comfortable with both of them being so; he even seemed intent on it. A good sign? Also, as he went on, Peter realized that the face-to-face arrangement of the chairs, squared off for some kind of interrogation, badly suited a seduction, if that was what was going on. And he hoped that was what was going on, even if Will was driving it and not him. The memory of Will's fingers in his hair and the possibilities of more were proving more intoxicating than the vodka.

"Hey, speaking of cute boys, are you still seeing that guy—Enrico?" he heard himself asking.

"We're just friends," said Will. "We hang out now and then."

"Very cool."

I'm in, thought Peter. *Woo-hoo!*

The rest of the conversation was a blur. The following day, when Peter went over the evening in his head, moment by moment, he groaned as he remembered looking at Grindr with Will, squeezing together briefly to view Peter's iPhone, commenting on favorites and men nearby, then settling back in their respective seats and babbling about friendship and dating, boyfriends and sex, and—ugh!—fuckbuddies. He remembered blurting, ever so casually, that his past exploits included getting simultaneously blown and rimmed one night on the dance floor of the Roxy, surrounded by cheering crowds of shirtless gymbots, but that his sexual practice had evolved into something much tamer—which *of course,* he realized as he said it, would be more palatable for a young prospective bed partner than the risky extremes of gay history's most libertine era. He hastened to mention that most of all, nowadays, he was aroused by a bright, handsome face whose truthful expressions he wanted to watch season after season. . . . He'd wanted to add, "Like yours," but didn't.

And Peter remembered the graciousness with which Will declined to stay the night. It was after three and he had to be up at seven; he said the daybed—toward which Peter had gestured half-heartedly—wouldn't be as comfortable as his own bed. The departure wasn't like an escape and Peter was grateful for that. The two hugged and shared a modest kiss, and Will did give Peter's head an affectionate sort of pat.

"So no consummation?" said Jonathan.

"No," said Peter. "But he did let me steer the conversation."

"And God knows, that's close enough to sex for you."

"I was trying very hard not to be pervy, Jonathan."

They were standing in one of far west Chelsea's most prestigious art galleries, in an airplane hangar–like space with hundreds of other people who'd paid $1,500 a head or more to attend an art-performance event that was also a benefit for an environmental group. The performance took the form of twenty-four models, twelve women and twelve men, dressed in nothing but high heels embellished with rhinestones, processing through the crowd in slow motion, as if in a trance, singly and in groups, stopping occasionally to pose, according to a predetermined choreographic sequence. The result was an amalgam of Vegas show, Japanese butoh dance, and high-end retail display.

Jonathan had been too tired to attend Peter's party, a few nights before, but had agreed to "look in" on the gallery event because he had friends on the committee and the gallery was only a few short blocks from his house. Peter had been shocked, earlier in the evening, when he arrived at Jonathan's door and saw that his friend had lost more weight. Jonathan was noticeably gaunt and joked about it, saying that he had finally lost the seven pounds he'd been trying to dump for years—and Peter did his best to take his friend's cue about the tone of the evening.

"Tyler says it's not about age," said Peter, reaching for a glass of white wine from the tray of a passing waiter. "But how could it not be?"

"Give it time," said Jonathan, who was drinking water.

"He's not into me that way—*claro*. I must be grotesque to him."

"Relax. It was only a second date."

Around them, the gallery's scene-energy was escalating. Guests continued to drink, chat, and laugh ferociously, while the high-heeled models oozed among them, radiating exemplary focus. On hand to preserve decorum between the naked performers and New York's most entitled culture vultures was a squad of art-world security guards, heavy guys in ill-fitting uniforms, whose hovering presence was meant to allow everyone to feel comfortable and wild at the same time.

"Look how clean their feet are," marveled Peter, as they inched through the crowd, gawking at the models in a pretend-blasé way. "Now that's good execution." The boy models betrayed only a hint of the difficulty they were having with the high heels, while the girls looked more at home in the performance, owning their space fiercely on the polished concrete floor—a pretend-simple surface,

Peter knew, that was colored in a precisely formulated shade of warm gray and had cost more per square foot than most Persian carpets.

"You're really into this guy, aren't you?" said Jonathan.

"God help me," said Peter. "He's such a delicious blend of masculine and something else. And why am I being so shy, anyway? Why wouldn't I just put my cards on the table and see what's what?"

"Did you get into top and bottom?"

"I did not."

"It could mean trouble."

"Oh, *no*, darling. Boys are *all* bottoms, these days. You'd know that if you were dating. Anyone born after 1975 is a bottom. Besides, you know I was never into all that. I still don't know what to say when people ask me about Harold and me."

Being free of top- and bottomness was, in fact, a big reason why Peter liked playing around with younger men, though they did wrestle, in their own way, with subtle gender identity issues—a battle that, in Will, seemed like a tension between the Inner Boy and Inner Girl, though not in an artsy way, as with Tyler, who used ambiguity to his advantage in his work at the agency and onstage, but in a more everyday way, with fashion accessories that referenced Affluent White Suburban Mom Realness: the scarves, sunglasses, and tote bag that Will sometimes used to mitigate his Cute Young Guy looks. The new terms of young men's identity exploration felt like progress, Peter told Jonathan: a step beyond the parodies of masculinity adopted by their own generation as a response to oppression. These kids had never known much oppression, which was not only nice for them but also made them nicer to be with. And no, Peter assured his friend, he and Will had not delved into gender theory that night, though Peter did admit being obsessed with a tender lilt that sometimes flecked Will's laughter and a delicate continuity between masculine and feminine grace that Will demonstrated when, for example, handling glassware and pouring drinks.

Was Peter really into the guy? Sure. How—as a friend? That would be nice. As a boyfriend? Maybe, if Will were into it and had no issues with age. But age wasn't a question that could simply be asked and answered. Will might not find Peter "grotesque," just a sexual no-thank-you. Then again, Peter was as unsure about Will as he was head-over-heels. Who was the guy, really, and what would he become? Who was he raised to be, and how would he manage the gift of his parental programming? Tyler's mom, for instance, was only a career waitress, unmarried when she raised Tyler, but she was sharp and progressive, and had imprinted her son with the will to better himself, and that had motivated him deeply. Such imprinting was a kind of hidden color, too, which revealed itself only when the light was stronger.

"You're such a good friend," said Peter, kissing Jonathan impulsively on the forehead. "Listening to me prattle on about boys."

Jonathan rolled his eyes heavenward, which only heightened the fact that his eyes were slightly sunken.

When the performance concluded, the dancers bowed slowly, butoh style, then the evening's chairperson introduced the choreographer, who said a few words about nakedness and nature. Then, as the live auction began—on the block was the evening's artwork itself: a DVD of the performance, plus a pair of used high heels and a certificate of authenticity—Peter and Jonathan made their way to the bar.

The place was a museum of former flings, commented Peter. Julian was there, a journalist whom Jonathan used to see. So were Newsome, a gallerist whom Peter dated for five minutes, and Delia, a dealer Peter had made out with once on a banquette, many years before, when she was at Vassar and Peter got her and some extremely cute classmates, boys, into a hot club. Peter nodded to both, smiling as they passed, continuing to talk with Jonathan in a way that indicated that an interruption would not be cool. For Peter, nearing sixty, the city was never so full of former golden boys, many of whom he had promised the world and many who rejected it. What does one say to a boy who has rejected the world and also lost his looks and now seemed a poseur, a weakling, a dullard, or a fake?

And then Peter saw Nick. He was walking toward them with a guy Peter assumed was a new boyfriend. They were going to say hello and there wasn't time to warn Jonathan, without looking obvious, that he didn't want a protracted exchange.

"Peter, hi," said Nick, leaning in for a perfunctory hug. "Hi, Jonathan."

"Hi, Nick," said Peter. Introductions were made to Benny, the man Nick was with.

"Nice party," said Nick.

"Having a good time?" said Peter.

"Great. Not sure I get the art."

"There's not much to get. Naked young people in cute shoes. QED."

Nick was a tall man in his early forties, with dark hair; huge, dark eyes; and a prominent nose. He had a permanent smile and sparkling demeanor, the latter which now, chastened by sobriety, seemed gentler.

As the four talked, Peter made sure his body language said that he and Jonathan had been on their way to another part of the gallery, and Jonathan, no slouch in social matters, even if at death's door, played along cheerfully.

"How was that?" asked Jonathan, after Nick and Benny had left.

"Fine," said Peter.

"You sure?"

"Jonathan, we did three years of therapy, just to end it correctly. I'm good."

"He's put on some weight."

"Hasn't he, though?"

"But still cute."

"At least he's still alive."

"Who's the guy?"

"A chef, I think," said Peter. "Benedetto."

"Julian is looking well," said Jonathan. "I wonder if he's still hooking."

"What do you mean? I thought he was at *Rolling Stone*."

"He was, back then. He was also taking clients, which is how he and I met."

"Jonathan, you shock me," said Peter. "I did not know that."

"About him—or me?"

"Either of you."

Jonathan smiled weakly.

"You know I've done a call boy now and then," he said.

"I'm not making a judgment," said Peter. "You know I have great respect for sex work."

CHAPTER 10

Peter was more upset over seeing Nick at the gallery than he let on, and he was peeved to be that upset, given all the therapy that he and Nick had been through together, after the breakup. On his way home, as he and a zombie driver rattled down Varick Street in a gypsy cab, toward the Brooklyn Bridge, he kept going over those few seconds of banal party chatter in his mind.

"Not sure I get the art." "There's not much to get."

But Nick was so much smarter than Peter! He often saw more than Peter did in all kinds of art, from contemporary stuff to the masterpieces people knew since childhood. Peter always said so! Yet Nick's background wasn't intellectual. He hadn't undergone the standard art historical indoctrination at home or in school, and never seemed to want to learn more about what he was seeing, as Peter always thought he should do. Peter expected that anyone would want to do that, because . . . Well, all that was ancient history now. The therapist had helped them see that they were two different people, two different stories.

Peter shook his head. *Two different stories.* How to collate past and present, except to unclench and let them scrape against each other like colliding supertankers? Traffic on Varick was light, as usual for that time of night. This was the same route home that Peter had taken for decades, and the city flashed by in the sparse, shadowy, familiar frames of a black-and-white movie, except that almost all Manhattan streets were now hiding too much wealth to bristle with much noir, and the corner of Varick and Chambers, where a gang of bat-wielding children tried to ambush his cab in '78 or '79, now boasted an expensive bistro with sidewalk tables.

Yes, Nick was love, as much as Harold ever was, if love was the switching on of the body's full capacity to process every second of existence with every cell. The man had a great heart, as well as a natural eye for art and ear for music. But Nick was also disaster, because with him, heightened experience came at a high price. He turned out to be an emotional wreck for almost the same reason he was good company and great sex: a messy desperateness to please. Glibly, Peter, as he and Jonathan left the gallery that night, had compared the relationship to the fossil fuel economy: It deadened as much as it brought to life. Blotching Peter's memory of Nick was a massive oil spill that felt important historically, but not exactly a pinnacle of achievement.

How to think about this man? The memory of Nick, which was ultimately a manageable thing, was not the same thing as the human being itself, in the flesh, walking around, showing up at parties. Peter had no other exes, except this piece of living, breathing evidence of a nine-year-long mistake. He had learned in therapy not to think of it that way, but on some level he couldn't help doing so. A dead partner was far more convenient than a living ex! The memory of countless irksome Harold issues that for years had contributed to the normal amount of day-to-day friction between him and Peter dissolved, over that final year, in a voluptuous bath of caregiving and care-getting. Harold's success as a husband was burnished by retrospect and crystallized, after his death, into myth. And what helped the process was the fact that lots of other widows shared similar myths, as after other wars.

The memory of Nick, by the same token, fit into no narrative that Peter could work out. In the story of Peter's life, Nick was a chapter without a number. Even as he told people he was looking for his "third and final marriage," counting Nick as the second, Peter continued to compare all candidates to Harold, admitting only nominally how unfair this might be to himself and others. Nine years? Even that was a point of contention between Nick and him. Nick measured the relationship from the first stay-over sex, which happened a week after the two first met in a public park, late at night, when Nick blew Peter and they exchanged numbers. Peter measured from the first declaration of de-facto boyfriendhood, which took place almost a year later, after a prolonged sexonly thing morphed into friendship and the two started going to parties and clubs together, as each other's first-option dates. It was a status, claimed Nick, that was long overdue. The relationship didn't seem real enough to Peter even then, absent a lightning-strike moment, but he did recognize that a certain momentum had built up between them. And since old friends kept reminding Peter that it was OK to quote-unquote move on with his life, he tried to relegate the Harold figurine to a niche and keep shuffling forward.

At first, Peter was impressed by Nick's embrace of a new life. When they met, Nick was still living in the suburban New Jersey town where he'd grown up, and had just emerged from a relationship with a woman, though since his late teens he'd been sneaking into the city by bus to suck cock. After meeting Peter, and succumbing to sermons about eros and identity, Nick came out and immediately became fabulous. He moved to Chelsea, signed up at David Barton, rethought his hair and wardrobe, and found a job at a top interior design firm that hired him away from the suburban decorator whom he'd been working for since he was seventeen. He was handsome and affable, and for two or three years he did well in his new stratum. He and Peter met each other's families, took some trips together, and started talking about buying a place together upstate. Then Nick became *too* fabulous. The gym and new haircut led to parties and clubs, and then to certain parties that were all about drugs. Nick started hanging out with the wrong people: attractive men who seemed cool and affluent, but weren't as smart as they thought they were—members of some of the pseudo-A-list circles that are always there, eddying with debris, on the edge of the New York social gyre. Peter warned discreetly and smiled when introduced to new faces, but Nick couldn't get enough of these people, nor they him.

And for a while, Peter tagged along with Nick in some of these circles and actually liked being a tourist there. Beyond the clubs and parties, it was drug and sex scenes that Nick brought him to, and there Peter gratefully called Nick his Beatrice—though Nick, of course, hadn't read Dante. On a little K, or coke, or snortable heroin, after an all-night party, Peter glimpsed another side of the city he thought he knew well, a darkly seductive refraction of gay life that felt lusciously poisonous: the hazy, twelve-hour fisting scenes, laced with the acrid-sweet reek of burning rock; the endless and apparently fruitless nipple tugging and cock jerking; the piles of cash and pots of lube and scatter of sex toys; the calls in sick and follow-up messages to people who had *more* and could be there within thirty minutes; the uncertainty whether it was dawn or dusk, and indifference to either.

And as a social observer Peter valued many of the insights he took away from that world: a secret about America's hunger for amusement, yielding one night from a moment of stupid congress with a decorative, sparkle-flecked wall panel inside the elevator of some party-stranger's building; or a discernment between looking and real seeing, such as Peter found crooning one morning, upon exit from a popper suck marathon, from the greenish tinges of a rosy dawn sky. But Peter also liked the social observer's distance he was able to maintain from all that, the permanent outsider position he tended to enforce. More than once—bored, or simply ready to return to reality—he said good-bye to Nick and left him at one of those scenes. Then he stopped accompanying Nick on such expeditions altogether, his ability to do so partly the result of sober parents who'd drastically overwarned against all sorts of evils, during the '60s. *Heroin—it's too good to try even once!* Nick would have heard that tagline as an unironic invitation to party. Monstrous partying for him, in those days, meant monstrous partying again and again and again; and Peter continued to warn gently, again and again, though he also decided that Nick's partying was a parody of the heroic and thus more interesting than mere addiction.

Jesus!

For too long Peter was resigned to the tirades and bad behavior. One morning, when Nick showed up at Peter's house at dawn, he called Peter a "big loser" for having bolted from the party earlier. Peter was hurt, but responded by making breakfast. Nick was swinging wildly from elation to depression by then, and Peter gamely tried to engage with the ills and issues that Nick brought up during those moods. Peter was a caregiver, after all; it was his duty to endure. When Nick became enamored of a whole group of strung-out, steroided, bodybuilder-hustlers, endlessly distracted by their own meth-fueled narcissism, Peter tried to help his so-called boyfriend see the changes in his own personality: Affability turned to pushiness, generosity to insistence, judgments and preferences to belligerence and intolerance. But attempts to question Nick's choices led to shrieking accusations of betrayal. Then Nick started missing work and making excuses; suddenly he was fired. Peter knew the relationship was over when he started hearing through the grapevine about Nick's scuffles with club security and his demented late-night phone calls to friends, to borrow money.

Thank God we never moved in together, thought Peter.

How to talk about Nick? What to call him?

My "ex"? How pedestrian.

In couples therapy—which they entered after Nick's second rehab, as an alternative to demonizing each other for the rest of their lives—they salvaged what they could of the affection and respect they originally felt and started re-parsing their story as a friendship or a family thing. Everything had to be different, if they were to survive healthily, and Peter welcomed the questions that arose for him personally, in therapy, about the premises and purposes of romantic bonding—even if it bothered him that caretaking was so closely related to codependency, that till-death-do-us-part could be as much a rut as a heavenly path.

The cab driver hadn't uttered a word since picking Peter up at the gallery—not even a "yes" when Peter told him his destination. As they crossed the Brooklyn Bridge, Peter sat up and forward, in case the driver should need help negotiating the turnoff at Cadman Plaza, as some did. But toward the end of the bridge the driver pulled smoothly into the right lane, and veered quickly left after exiting. *Obviously the guy knows what he's doing,* thought Peter, sitting back. The plaza was named after a radio preacher from the '30s. It was so safe now, quiet and trim, without the massive bushes that bristled with nighttime cruisers and their predators back in the '70s, let alone the trolleys and elevated trains that bustled up from the waterfront on Old Fulton Street, decades before that. . . .

Old stories—perhaps not so grand, at that.

Since Harold's death Peter had been the sole custodian of their romantic history. Of the mess with Nick, though, there were two custodians, which was much less convenient—especially when it came to Peter trying to tell Will or anyone else where he had come from and where he thought he was going. Maybe the thing to do was coalesce the best parts of one's past into as nice-and-trim a present as can be confected, while wrestling the nastier chunks into a box, jamming down the lid, and hoping for the best.

Anyway, maybe the age of thinking about love the way I do has passed, thought Peter, as the cab pulled up in front of his house. He paid the driver, stepped out of the cab, and watched it tear away. The vestibule of the house was the most inviting one on the block, with his landlady's toile-pattern wallpaper, in crimson and white, visible from the street through double doors that featured large windows. As he mounted the stoop he couldn't help thinking, as he often did—*maybe too often?*—of the day in 1975 when he and Harold entered the house for the first time, after a realtor took them there on a summer afternoon, and of the autumn night years afterward when Harold left it for the last time, his body in the hands of a funeral director.

Love is probably more pedestrian nowadays, thought Peter. *No ascent of Machu Picchu, but an episode of* Will & Grace. *Fine—I guess. Except what if my boy Will and all other gay men under forty really do think of love that way—pedestrian? What if he says "yes" to me someday, but "yes" means only "OK for the moment," fine for an episode or two, and not "yes" the way I wish he would mean it: "I have been joyously aware of your presence in the universe since the dawn of time and will love you completely until the end of eternity"?*

CHAPTER 11

Will's magazine was headquartered in a carefully restored, hundred-and-thirty-year-old brick-and-limestone building in SoHo that once housed a department store whose chief claim to fame was that it was the first such store to put price tags on the goods for sale. The proprietors were seeking to eliminate haggling. The building, whose façade boasted sumptuous architectural detail, faded with the neighborhood itself, after its mercantile heyday in the 1880s and '90s, and stayed faded for almost a century, even through the 1970s and '80s, when SoHo revived as New York's center of art galleries. Then, as the galleries began decamping for Chelsea and SoHo was colonized by high-end retail, the building was reconfigured for a couple of luxury brand shops on the ground floor, and media and design offices on the upper floors. Those who worked in the building now helped move goods with conspicuous prices as effectively as the original department store employees ever did, only now the goods were ideas, notions, fancies.

The magazine's weekly editorial meeting had been proceeding more rapidly than usual, that day in early February, because Colin, the editor in chief, had touched down ninety minutes late at JFK, after a few days in London, and had phoned to ask Herman, the managing editor, to start the meeting as usual. They were assembled in the magazine's conference room, designed in a faux-industrial aesthetic that had required exposing and expensively refinishing original structural elements like iron columns and beams. Seated around a gleaming arc of a table made of bleached recycled ash were key editorial and art staff, with a few representatives from the advertising and marketing departments; perched around the room's periphery, standing against walls and sitting on the floor, was a small band of interns. Herman sped them through the issue plan, with updates on the cover and most important photo shoots, the short articles in the front of the book, the longer features of the main section of the magazine, known as the well, and the back of the book, which included a section devoted to party pictures. The lineup was basically the same as it had been when they last went through it, which, given how messy some issues could be, pleased and relieved everyone, including Will, whose chief interest was his interview with a new Senegalese R&B star named Assetou. The piece was scheduled for a front-of-book section devoted to up-and-comers, and was still slotted for two pages.

It was just before noon and the meeting was basically done. People were surreptitiously checking their phones for time and texts, and hoping to get an early start on their lunch plans. Then the editor in chief swept in, trailed by his assistant, Sebastian, who'd collected him from the airport in a town car, and the meeting basically started over.

"Cheers, everyone," said Colin, plunking himself down at the head of the table, in a spot that Herman had vacated. "Sorry to be late."

A short, conspicuously well-groomed man in his early forties, with a broad forehead and prominent nose, Colin embodied all the energy of a Hollywood studio head. He was known for commanding serious Hollywood instincts, too—for beyond being intelligent and plugged-in, he was gifted at penetrating new cultural phenomena and gathering smart thoughts about them into a bubbly mix that felt essential, issue after issue. A pair of black Louis Vuitton sunglasses was pushed up in his salt-and-pepper hair. As the meeting recommenced, Herman, standing behind Colin, passed the editor a copy of the issue plan, while Sebastian hovered by in the corner, continuing as quietly as possible with the ongoing series of calls and texts that made Colin's hectic life possible.

"We've just been through the issue . . . ," began Herman.

"Good," said Colin, preemptively. "Let's just run through it quickly, since there are a few changes."

This was news no one wanted to hear, yet the kind of thing that was always expected. Herman patiently reported again on the big shoots.

"Good," said Colin. "And Steven is happy?" Steven was the photographer doing the cover.

"He got some good stuff. We're looking at it tomorrow," said Herman.

"Good," said Colin.

Herman gave an overview of the big well stories.

"Good," said Colin. "Now here's the thing, before you go on." He was scratching notes on his copy of the lineup. "I want to drop the water politics movie. It feels like we've done it before—sorry, Eddie"—Eddie was the intern who'd brought the idea to the table and written the story—"and I want to do a story on this amazing filmmaker Elton introduced me to—the guy who did the thing about making chairs, that got all that attention at Sundance. . . ."

"*The Upholsterer,*" suggested Herman gently.

"Yes, *The Upholsterer.* You won't believe this guy. Genius craftsmanship! And you know who he's married to. . . ."

"That actress," suggested Herman.

"Uh-huh! So two pages," said Colin, annotating his lineup, then looking up. "Elton's going to record a conversation with him over lunch tomorrow and send us the file. And we can shoot him in London—Sebastian, you're on that, right?"

Sebastian, on the phone, nodded and pointed to the call he was on.

"So, now . . . ," said Colin. And he and Herman continued running down the new front-of-book lineup, quickly and telegraphically, as if they were discussing it between themselves, yet everyone else just kept sitting there, silently watching, in case they were needed.

"The kids from Costa Rica—one, right? We still love them," said Colin. "The pretty hotel, that's still two. We've got the ad and our party there—good. The writer in prison, OK; the new ballet girl, OK. The fashion designer from Seoul—we love her—that's four pages. The singer from Senegal, one—she's amazing, Will, right?"

Automatically, Will nodded.

"The blind gallerist, one," continued the editor in chief. Then he paused. "One or two? How did the photo come out?"

Herman grimaced.

"Gallerist, one," said Colin, in response. "Wait, isn't this the kid who used to be a model?"

"Yes," said Herman.

"And Carole couldn't get a good picture of him?"

"It's not beauty, is the thing," said Herman. "But it works as reportage. I actually think it's OK that way."

"I'll look at it," said Colin, checking the lineup as a whole and adding up the pages. "And we come out even. Everything else is the same. Good. Oh, and the creative for the new watch . . . ?"

One of the ad people nodded, with evident satisfaction.

"Well done," said Colin. "We're in good shape, people. Thank you."

Everyone understood that the London shoot would take the issue even further over budget, and require time the schedule didn't allow, which meant extra calls and hair-pulling for several people at the table, yet no one said anything—not even the fashion editor who was charged with looking into putting one of the new advertiser's watches on Elton's filmmaker's wrist, for the shoot. The meeting ended when the editor in chief rose and swept out of the conference room, taking Herman and Sebastian with him.

Most of the staff were unaffected by the changes, but Will was hugely disappointed, as he gathered up his pen, water bottle, and issue plan, to know that his Assetou story had been shortened. For weeks there had been a "2" next to it in the lineup, and now there was a "1." Initially, when he first brought the idea to the editorial table, weeks before that, he and the editor had talked about doing four pages. Of course, Will was sorry to lose the real estate—the extra page, the extra visibility for a story of his own. He was also at a loss at how to squeeze his hours of research into Senegalese music, his two-hour interview with Assetou, and his thoughts on her upcoming album, which he'd been listening to, into half the space he needed, a quarter of the space he wanted.

As he left the conference room Will overheard the magazine's editor at large, a slender Parisian dandy named Olivier, speaking on the phone in a soft, liquid-sounding voice about a party the magazine was giving that night at a contemporary art museum.

"The First Lady has checked into her hotel, yes," susurrated Olivier. "She is planning to arrive around nine, I believe. . . ."

It was a benefit for an organization that distributed art supplies to South African children, and several celebrities were scheduled to attend. Will had been looking forward to going, but now he'd have to revise his piece, and he knew he wouldn't be able to accomplish that without major rethinking.

Damn, thought Will.

The door to Colin's office was closed as Will walked past, but Herman's door was open, so Will gave a knock. Herman was standing at his desk, preparing to leave for lunch, and waved Will in.

"*Ow-*ooch," said Will, in two recognizably interrogative syllables.

"Assetou? C'mon, Will, this stuff happens all the time. It'll be great. You'll make it great."

"I'll try."

"A page is better."

"Well . . ."

"The intro was way too long anyway."

"I need to set up all the stuff she says about secrets, and her sculpture."

"Sure, but it's too dense. We need to get right into her words, her voice."

"What I'm afraid of is that we won't see how smart she is. . . ."

"The story is actually too smart, Will. It needs to be lighter."

"Too smart?"

"Light can be another kind of smart."

"Sure, but . . ."

"The art stuff—a lot of that can go."

"But she's very serious about her sculpting."

"Of course, but all the shabazz about hidden colors . . ."

"That's the depth of the piece."

"I don't know what a hidden color is, and you don't have the space to explain it. Besides, the label wants to keep the focus on the music."

"She talks about all these hidden forces in her songs. . . ."

Herman, known for being fierce, was being surprisingly even-tempered.

"May I make a suggestion?" he said. "Flirt with it."

"What do you mean?" said Will.

"Do what I see you doing when you talk to people. You're so smart, but it's light and fun."

"I . . . what?"

"Give it a shot. Four hundred words."

Later, in the hallway, Will ran into Stefan and explained why he was looking depressed. Stefan didn't seem to take the situation too seriously. He talked and talked about the party they were throwing that night—the stars who would be there, the unadvertised, "secret" performance by a young pop star, the appearance, "maybe," of the First Lady.

"Will you be there?" said Stefan.

"I don't see how I can," said Will. "I have to rewrite the piece."

"Can't you do that in your sleep?"

"Not really."

"Ah. Then you're not an editor yet, my friend." Stefan meant the remark playfully, but it stung.

"I certainly don't feel like one," said Will.

"Come late, if you can. Afterwards, we're all going to the new place André just opened. I'll text you the details."

Will stayed late at the office. To rewrite, he completely recast the piece, after walking around his office and chattering about Assetou with an imagined other at a cocktail party, and taking notes. The revised piece would probably work, he decided—basically, it was a "deep caption" to go with the picture they were running. But it was nothing like the gem of cultural journalism that he had been aiming for, with the hidden colors idea he had borrowed from Peter.

Around seven-thirty, as he was leaving the office and thinking about dinner, he decided, on a whim, to call Peter, whom he caught just leaving his office, too. Peter said he had no plans, and Will suggested they meet for a quick dinner. With conspiratorial thrill, they decided to jump into town cars and meet in Chelsea, for a burger at Elmo.

Peter, who had had plans with an old friend but cancelled guiltily, pleading a deadline, was sitting at the bar when Will arrived. Before they had time, even, for the token kiss and ritual exchange of delight in both being available, the friendly young manager appeared and asked if they were ready to be seated. They were shown to one of the best tables in the place, at the end of a serpentine banquette where they could see everything and be seen, yet have a bit of privacy.

As usual for that hour, Elmo was packed and bouncy with attractive gay men and their friends. Peter was surprised that they'd been given a table so quickly, but didn't mention it, except indirectly.

"My friend is the owner of this place," he said. "I don't see him around tonight."

"I like Elmo," said Will. "Good value, good spirit."

They ordered drinks and talked about movies, advertising, and magazines. Will told Peter about the new version of his Assetou piece that he'd written, which was basically done but now "cooking" in his brain before he'd allow himself to commit to it. They flirted with the server, who promised that the sautéed onions and mushrooms, in addition to gruyère, would render the burgers "fantastic." Over dinner they discussed the possibility of Will's going to Fire Island that summer, where Peter often rented a house. As they talked and laughed, Peter saw more of Will's personality in a rainbow of refractions: the sharp-tongued pragmatist, the noble dreamer, the diffident gentleman; and Peter felt happy to be in a crowded restaurant with the man he'd been dreaming about for months, even if he couldn't describe what was happening between them. It could be the start of something big—yet the bouncy atmosphere, light conversation, and stiff drinks were short-circuiting any deep thoughts about eternity or whatever.

When they were done, Peter asked their server for the check.

"The least I can do is buy you a burger," he said, "after hijacking your evening."

"Oh, no you don't," said Will, reaching for his wallet. "First of all, we hijacked each other's evening, buddy, and that's a good thing. Secondly, we're splitting this or it will get weird. And we don't want it to get weird, do we?"

Peter assumed the look of a tranquil Buddha.

"You are indeed wise," he said.

"Besides, I'm making a real living now," said Will. "Even if I have to supplement here and there. You'd be surprised what a boy has to do to get by in this town."

"Uh, no, I wouldn't," said Peter. "But that's one of the reasons why God gave us comps. And you're at a magazine—that should be comp-arama."

So far, Will had been offered a pair of jeans, a suit, a pair of sneakers, a watch, and a trip to St. Bart's, he said. But he hadn't accepted anything.

"Why not?" asked Peter.

"Mmm, not sure I wanna go there."

"The deal is that you say thank you and wear the jeans or take the trip, and do so in view of the right people. It's not just free shit. It's an exchange of value. The assumption is that you, yourself, are valuable, by the very fact of whom you move with."

"Not my actual thoughts about the jeans."

"Those too—*maybe*. But that exists apart from the value."

"And you're a fan of this system?"

"I certainly don't think it's evil. It's like anything, money—it can be made evil by evil people."

Just then, the manager appeared at the table.

"I hope you gentlemen enjoyed your dinner," he said. "We enjoyed having you with us and would like you to be our guests tonight."

Peter's instinct, since this sort of thing was not unknown to him, was to rise and thank the man, shaking his hand. But he realized the manager was speaking primarily to Will, and that Will was already rising. For Peter, this was a shock but also somehow exhilarating.

"Score!" said Will, after the manager had left.

"Why did he do that?" said Peter.

Will gave a kiss to his fingertips, then patted his face with them, while feigning modesty.

"The cute-boy factor? No."

"No," laughed Will. "We shot a story here a few weeks ago and we're giving them credit in the issue."

"Christ, and here I am going on about comps and the owner, and you've got it all hooked up."

Will said nothing. Outside, on the sidewalk, they agreed that it was still early, as dinner had been so short.

"Drink at G?" said Peter.

Will looked at his phone.

"One drink," he said, with a sly smile.

G was packed but navigable. The place was pounding with a sequence of generically energetic tracks. They plowed through the front room into the oval bar area.

"Vodka club, twist of lime?" asked Will.

Peter nodded, clearing a spot for their drinks on the little niched ledge lining the curved wall, while Will squeezed over to the bar.

Wow, this feels normal, thought Peter, until he spotted Will speaking intimately with another guy his own age—a friend?—and felt a pang of jealousy. Do they know each other, or is it just cute-boy camaraderie? Peter also saw Will flirting with the monumentally muscular, tattooed bartender, shirtless, in a pair of jeans hanging so low around his waist that they exposed a good bit of butt crack. The bartender was not just moving around the bar mixing and serving drinks, but somehow making the performance into some kind of muscle-disco-samba.

"I so wanna jump that guy's bones," said Will, returning with the drinks.

"The bartender?" said Peter with as much cheer as he could muster.

"Marcelo."

"Hot."

Will led them in a little toast, then looked out over the bar, sipping his drink and nominally beginning to sway with the music.

OK, he thinks we're buddies, thought Peter. *Well, why not? So I'm the cool, older guy. I can be a wingman. Forget that I am a star in my own world, and an advanced soul. This is his world.* Peter supposed the cool buddy thing was better than the alternative, the old auntie of gay lore. *"Uncle Peter." Maybe that's all I get, at this age, unless I pay. Of course, then I'm only buying a simulacrum....*

Cute guys often came right up to Peter in bars like G—the speed and enthusiasm of their approach revealing what was sometimes their true purpose: hustling—and he'd always blown them off. *Though right about now,* thought Peter, as the music pounded away, *I am very susceptible to theories about simulacra being real things of a sort.*

Will had moved very close to Peter, so they could hear each other speak, and his buoyant chatter was filled with giggles and winks, and little touches to Peter's arm, when making a point.

His eyes really do sparkle—so blue. Can brown eyes sparkle like that?

As they chatted about living in Astoria and the epic N train, which runs from Astoria to Coney Island, Will's face came alive with a range of lambent microexpressions that Peter hadn't taken full stock of before. Little smirks, frowns, and squints, delicious pretend scowls and ironic smiles—all animated Will's sharp observations about his life in New York. And as Peter hung on the conversation as a stream of fresh blessings, he didn't quite know how to accept the new, higher level of intimacy that accompanied it, especially since he hadn't initiated it.

Would I really be content to be just a wingman? wondered Peter. *And what if that's not even the deal? What if I am being summoned into the inner sanctum?*

The only path, he decided, was simply to be good company, as Will was clearly trying to do. *He* was being charming, affable, and as focused on the conversation as possible in a place like G. Peter could be the same. And if people were looking at them, projecting envious boyfriend scenarios, or judgmental hustler scenarios, or ridiculous father-son scenarios, well, what did it matter what *they* thought? Though the boyfriend scenario, every time it occurred to Peter, shot him through with a bolt of warmth.

They were talking about careers and hopes and intentions, a conversation that began in the restaurant.

"My dad is always talking about how this *builds* toward the next thing, how it *builds* on the last thing," Will was saying. "He was always talking about vectors, efforts that, quote-unquote, added up. 'If you know exactly what direction you're heading in, you don't waste any time going this way or that way.' I mean, will my next job be at this magazine, or any magazine? Who knows? I kinda feel like I have to go in a few different directions right now."

"My dad used to talk the same way," said Peter. "There was so much good sense he tried to jam into my skull—life experience from growing up in a small town, stuff he learned in World War Two, in fucking North Africa. All good stuff. But I had to do my own thing, and luckily the seventies were a time when everyone was doing their own thing."

"Some things, you have to learn yourself."

"Amen."

Will shook the ice cubes in his glass, which was otherwise empty. He looked up from them and into Peter's face, tilting his head appealingly, for emphasis.

"I think you would have become what you are, even without the seventies," he said.

Peter felt another bolt.

"I've often wondered that, Will," he said expansively. "And you know what? I don't think so. I think if I had grown up a decade or two before, I would have become a lawyer or something, and probably married a woman—and maybe I would have found out a way to get sumpin' on the side, and maybe not. I don't know that I would have expected my whole life to be *integrated* and the whole world to follow suit."

Will nodded.

"And that's how Jonathan's generation started out," he said.

"What do you mean?"

"I gather he's somewhat older than you."

"Jonathan is only two or three years older than I am."

"Get out."

"Yeah."

Will looked genuinely shocked.

"I would have guessed that he's ten years older, at least," he said.

"Well, bless you, I guess," said Peter, followed by a pause during which neither of them said anything about cancer.

They left G and walked along Nineteenth Street toward Seventh Avenue. A glittering fantasy of dressed-up mannequins with big, big hair occupied the windows of Rootstein's, as usual.

"Barbie, Queen of Outer Space?" commented Will.

"I guess," said Peter. "Window display as glimpse into a magical walled garden."

Stationed outside of McManus's, as usual, was a shabby quorum of desperate smokers.

"Where are you off to?" asked Peter, at the corner.

"I think I'll head back to the office," said Will.

"Another draft?"

"I guess. You?"

"I'm heading home. Check e-mail. Wash face. Go to bed. So glad we were able to do this tonight."

"Me too," said Will. And the two shared a little embrace. "You'll have to come to dinner at my place sometime. We're almost ready for guests."

"I would love that."

As Peter hailed a cab, he realized he'd be going in roughly the same direction as Will.

"Can I . . . drop you?" Peter asked.

"No, thanks," said Will. "I'll just jump in the subway."

"See ya soon, then."

"Definitely."

And the cab sped away.

At first, Will thought he might meet up with Stefan. Several texts had arrived from him, one with a picture of the First Lady waving from a little balcony that overlooked the party space. The after-party sounded like fun, but Will decided to just head home—in a town car, which was an option he'd reserved for himself by taking the subway earlier, to meet Peter. And he'd go via the office, since the pretense of having stayed there all evening, officially after hours, felt like a necessary extra step for someone so low on the editorial totem pole.

As the car emerged from the Midtown Tunnel in Queens and made its way onto Vernon Boulevard, Will was ready for the money shot. There was the Fifty-ninth Street Bridge, magnificent if for no other reason than its having four towers, spiky with finials, instead of the two of most other New York bridges. That allowed the structure's architectural rhythm of drop-and-swag to build up some momentum, as it sprinted leisurely on the air from shore to shore. Will had always loved this bridge, ever since seeing it for the first time in a movie that dated from a few years before he was born, Woody Allen's *Manhattan*. The sheer futuro-Gothic romance of the thing, which emerges, inexplicably, from the naked sobriety of its engineering; its profusion of non-orthogonal lines, speaking of a possible reality unbound by gravity or economy—all made it a monument underestimated, Will thought, by those who lived and worked in its shadow every day. New York, for a California boy, was the place to go and become fabulous in a quirky-sophisticated, Diane-and-Woody kind of way. It's where the individualists were. As he saw *Manhattan* again and again—as a teenager, as a college student, as a young professional in Century City—Will continued to be reminded that New York beckoned, as did a life very different from anything in front of him in California, where people felt processed, preformulated, and—was this too cliché to say?—plastic.

He twisted in his seat and craned to see everything out the car's windows, as they slipped past the bridge's easternmost tower and under its roadway. He wanted to catch all the views he could. In a sequence of wild-angle glimpses, then upside down, as Will leaned way back to look out the rear window, the bridge never looked better.

Will hated the thought of having been groomed, even benevolently, to be a plastic person, vacu-formed in someone else's shape. He respected his parents, but had always reserved the right to pick and choose from among their own lifestyle choices and even from his friends'—from Luz's, certainly from Enrico's, and now from his new friend Peter's, though Peter's, despite the man's age or maybe because of it, had begun to look not just interesting but fascinating.

He looked great tonight, Will thought. The hair looked cute, the jacket was fresh—he looked younger, somehow. Will's parents weren't nearly as stylish, though they thought they were, and they probably were, for Santa Barbara.

Will kept returning to a thought that arose for him at G: What were his parents doing during the '80s, when he was growing up and they were golfing at the Montecito Country Club, when Peter and Harold were visiting Machu Picchu and discovering that the two of them fit together spiritually like those massive, irregular stones that the Incas carved to fit together without a hair's space in between? How did the Incas do it? How was it possible? Will had seen photos of the stones, and Peter told him of trying to fit a credit card between them and finding the task indeed impossible. Why hadn't they visited Peru as a family? Will wondered. And what were his parents doing at the same time Peter and Harold were visiting the Taj Mahal? Touring a four-hundred-year-old garden outside Kyoto with a Zen monk? Were Will and his family at their cabin on Jameson Lake in the Santa Ynez Mountains, downing granola before an early-morning fishing expedition, when Peter and Harold were alone in the Sistine Chapel, after hours, inspecting the restorations with a Vatican curator? Once, Will's family traveled to Belize, via Miami. Could they all have been in the same airport lounge for an hour at the same time, when Peter and Harold were on their way to or from Antarctica?

Peter had told him lots of stories about traveling, about his life. Was it something like the life Will wanted? How did one arrive at such a life? Was the future a walled garden you glimpsed through a gate, for which you needed a key—and did you discover, once inside the garden, that it constituted the entire world, and outside was the prison? Will saw that once in a movie. Peter did seem to be offering some kind of key, and that had begun to seem so different from—even opposite to!—so many of the blessings Will had been raised to enjoy and seek.

Valentine's Day caught Peter by surprise. Not that he didn't know it was approaching; he just didn't realize he was involved. Work was distracting him. The McCaw people had accepted the proposal that Peter and his team sent over. The gig had been secured! But then, the night before the holiday, as he was noting things to do on his calendar for the following day, Peter heard the beat-beat-beat of the tom-tom and realized he should probably use the occasion to say something to Will.

Valentine's Day had always been more of a couples thing than a dating thing, for Peter. Is anyone equal to the holiday other than the partners in a committed relationship—and even then, he wondered, does anyone feel loved enough to join in the yearly hoopla unequivocally, without quiet doubts about the significance of the other or secret regret about having possibly been able to do better? Established couples try to have fun with the day, gazing fondly on what the other has become, honoring each other for time served. New couples, toying with romance, make a game of the day, giggling, then maybe fighting and giggling, then making up and maybe giggling some more—all the while asking themselves, Is it really you, you, you? Nick once made Peter a meat loaf in the shape of a heart and presented it in a red-and-gold-foil, heart-shaped candy box. It was a cute gesture that was also a question about faithfulness. Yes, Peter answered, I love you and am yours till I die, but to sensitive ears—ears attached to an intelligent body that's forever in need of more information about love—there is a thrum of dread on Valentine's Day, hinting at loss, which is a natural condition of life, and isolation, its chief axiom.

At least, that's the way Peter looked at it—though he knew this was not the sentiment he should try to frame into a breezy note to a young beau. *Though Neruda does have a line somewhere about Death being the third party that's always in bed with two lovers. Couldn't that make a funny valentine—funny-smart?*

The next day, at the office, Peter fussed with work for an hour before texting Will. There was a video call with McCaw to gird for, and some personal boundaries to get clear in his brain, before beginning to work closely with a man his friends called a demagogue. Peter had never been one to let a client's personality, even when insufferable, get in the way of a gig; and doctrinal objections were rarely a problem for anyone in advertising. Moreover, the thought of this assignment as a career-defining pinnacle was beginning to loom large in Peter's mind. So as he pondered all this he decided that the text to Will should not go first thing, as if he had been obsessing about the guy instead of tending to business; nor should it go as late as lunchtime, which would make the text look too unimportant. It should look third on a list, Peter decided, after God and country, so it was around eleven-thirty when he managed to thumb a few words to the man who was now never off his mind.

Hey, buddy! A shower of hearts for you today. Cheers! P.

He made it a point to use proper punctuation, to help give the message a more formal, less breathless feel, and he added a burst of shiny, little, red emoji hearts to the message, to connote light fun. For a minute he experimented with a second line—trying to say something about a text message being a poor substitute for "a handwritten note delivered by my man"—but it wasn't working, so he gave up and sent the shorter version.

Then he realized the text was dumb and picked up the intercom.

"Tyler—are you there? May I have a word, please?"

He should have asked Tyler for help in the first place. Ty would have known the right direction to take, if not the precise line to use.

Will's reply came immediately, much more quickly than Peter had dared hope: *Funny! Cheers! You too!*

Peter stared at it for a second. The message seemed warm, but it was so short. Did it mean everything or nothing? Did it represent spontaneous thought or a measured *position?*

"You rang?" said Tyler, appearing at the door.

"Read this, please," said Peter, thrusting his iPhone at his young colleague.

Tyler read and chuckled.

"OK," he said.

"Not too needy, right?"

"No."

"And he's not being guarded or anything, is he?"

"Doesn't sound that way."

Peter sighed in relief.

"How's it going?" asked Tyler. "Are you an item yet?"

"I don't know, I don't know!" bleated Peter.

"And you're tortured by not knowing."

"Yes—like never before! We share constant surprise at the stupidity of other people. We share disdain for people who automatically require you to be *like* them. We share contempt for the wrong kinds of vulgarity, and delight in the right kinds."

"Now that's what I call bedrock," said Tyler.

"Everything seems to be . . . rushing at me!"

"Well, that's life."

"I shouldn't call," said Peter. It was a question.

"To follow up on a text? Not really."

"Can I tomorrow?"

"Sure."

"Ahhh!" Peter pretended to scream, in frustration.

"You could pray, boss," offered Tyler brightly. "Didn't you say you were raised Catholic?"

"Raised but lapsed," laughed Peter. Tyler was either being flip or truly open to any form of magic that might exist. "As a kid I could never pray for personal gain, let alone for a boyfriend. I was taught to pray for starving orphans and earthquake victims—things like that."

"I dunno," said Tyler. "This is turning into kind of an earthquake, if you ask me."

"All set?" said Laura, dropping by Peter's office, shortly after Tyler left.

"For McCaw? Absolutely," said Peter.

"I brought you this," she said. "A little Valentine's Day present."

Laura handed Peter a mock-up of the cover of *Advertising Age,* featuring Peter's face and the caption, *Agency of the Year.*

"Cute, thank you," said Peter. "For inspiration?"

"Just to keep in mind what we're aiming for. People are already buzzing, you know. And can I tell you something? Even the ones who are aghast seem to be jealous of us."

"People are aghast?"

"Some people. You know—people who are bounded by their own prejudices."

"Ah, well . . ."

"Thank God you're not one of those black-or-white types."

"So we're off and running, eh, buddy?" began McCaw, an hour later, on the video call. It was just the two of them.

"We're poised to do some great work," said Peter.

"I'm sure we are."

"You know, I do think we need to explore this 'take back America' thing a little more, so we know what it is, exactly, but we'll discover this together. . . ."

"I know what it is. And it's time. That's all any of us is saying."

McCaw cocked his head brightly and raised his eyebrows in emphasis, and the screen lit up with likable. Video calls were still not all that common, but McCaw was known for using them and Peter saw why. The man who cannily controlled his media image was positioned in the middle of a perfectly composed, and thus perfectly seductive, video shot. Someone had made sure that the picture was professionally lit and contained a family photo, a shelf of books, and a bit of American flag. Peter knew that so much information was being emitted from the shot itself, and received subliminally, that McCaw's words themselves were only part of the call.

"Hendy, let me say this once again," said Peter. "I know it's in the proposal—I just want to be clear. We have to be open about the use of language like 'taking back.' It may come with freight we don't want."

"Sure, Peter, of course," said McCaw. "But I love that you get the underlying imperative here. I mean, look, we both inherited traditions, didn't we—you growing up in the fifties, and me the sixties and seventies? And we both lived through all those transgressions of the seventies, right? We *got* the change. We tore down what we thought was decrepit, fine—that had to happen. But, so far—and be honest—what have we created, beyond freedoms and license? What are we going to bequeath to our successors that's more substantial than what we ourselves inherited? A nation keeping up with the Kardashians? You must ask yourself this, as a gay man."

"I . . . do."

"Then let the great work begin." McCaw beamed beatifically.

Peter knew the last line was a quote, but not, until after the call, from what: *Angels in America*.

Afterward, despite concerns that still lingered in his mind, Peter felt exhilarated. He could manage McCaw, maybe even move him in a good direction, with some smart thinking. The idea of big money was savory, for sure, but Peter had never been much of a careerist, having drifted upward from success to success. The exciting thing for Peter was this opportunity to be a real player, to see his clever little ideas and understandings and mental tricks finally mean something big—get some traction, draw some fire—and push things somewhere on a global scale. Wasn't wanting this, too, like panting for true love instead of boy toys, about being almost sixty—a fruition of the process of constantly opting out of small and meaningless effort, that starts in one's thirties, or should, to afford a steady ascent into bigger realms, toward higher levels, where both love and work are sacramental?

That night, Peter stayed home and ordered in Thai food. He watched *Gentlemen Prefer Blondes* on Netflix and found himself remembering the time he and Harold had once found the movie starting on television and were so excited to see the thing from the beginning that they blew off plans to see a zombie version of *Giselle* at the Brooklyn Academy of Music. Meanwhile, that same night, Will was attending a little Valentine's Day get-together at Enrico's. The tiny jewel-box apartment was packed with stylish young men—they were clumped around the table in the foyer-dining area, where a buffet had been laid under a fall of red crystal hearts, suspended from the chandelier, and jammed into the black salon, which was so full that people could barely move. As a mix of "bitter love" tracks played in the background, compiled by a DJ whom Will had featured in the magazine, Will was explaining to a trio of strangers that he and Enrico weren't boyfriends.

"Oh, we thought you lived here," said one.

"You seem to know where everything is," said another.

"Well . . . everything's, like, two steps away," said Will.

Will was annoyed that Enrico was behaving as if they were co-hosts—asking him conspicuously to find the corkscrew or fetch more ice. Will was attending the party just to be nice; he hadn't wanted to go. For another thing, he was bored with Enrico's crowd, which was comprised of pretty boys Will found markedly superficial, including Olivier, the magazine's fashion director, who had arrived at the party with a small claque of dandies who looked like they were all within three years of each other's age, three centimeters of each other's height, and three pounds of each other's weight.

"Hi, there," said Will, when Olivier squeezed past.

"Hello," burbled the Parisian, looking mildly perplexed.

"From the magazine—I'm Will."

"Oh, yes, hello," said Olivier, producing a slender hand.

They chatted for a moment, about city traffic and the town car Olivier had waiting outside, about Enrico and the party decorations, but it was clear that Olivier's interest was elsewhere. Then Will found himself astounded when Olivier admitted he didn't know that the music track then playing, Femi Kuti's "Sorry Sorry," was a bloody valentine to Nigeria.

"He's lamenting the rape of his homeland," said Will.

"I have this song on one of my Buddha Bar mixes," said Olivier, nominally to Will but for the amusement of his claque.

Pathetic, thought Will. Olivier had never really listened to the song. Wasn't an editor supposed to know more about the world he lived in? It happened to be a song that Will and Peter had taken apart recently, one night after their dinner at Peter's place.

They'd been talking about the course of civilization since World War Two, and the song came up in the mix they were listening to.

"Let's see what won the Pulitzer Prize for music in 1945," said Peter, Googling the answer: *Appalachian Spring.* "Great, terrific piece. But just listen to Femi. Does *Appalachian Spring* contain one-tenth the pathos of 'Sorry Sorry'? Don't tell me that civilization has declined." They'd had a few drinks, but Will was impressed. Peter was right. And since then Will's ears had been a little more open.

Suddenly, at Enrico's, Will realized that he was at the wrong party. Enrico and his friends were as insistent that Will vacu-form himself into their mold as Will's parents had been to theirs. If he stayed too long with this crowd, he would turn into something like the gay men his parents knew, who had always seemed too decorous, too tame, too self-edited. Maybe that was why Peter was so optimistic about the future, so ready to party, for an old man: He was unbounded politically, socially. And that led to happiness. What a goal to point your vectors at!

Will found Enrico and made an excuse, then bolted from the party. On his way to the subway he texted Peter an invitation to dinner at his place.

Can we say next Friday? Luz and I will make something at our place. Please come. Maybe a few other friends. Easy, relaxed. Say yes!

CHAPTER 12

During the week leading up to dinner, Peter thought constantly about Will. He had to make an effort to avoid adding Will-this and Will-that gratuitously in conversations with friends, and was careful, too, to show restraint in contact with the young man himself, texting him only now and then, with a perky thought about some cirrus clouds or a crowded party. He didn't call, because there was little to say that could be said, at this stage. They hadn't yet reached the stage of daily check-in—though that would come soon enough, if they really were becoming close friends. So Peter's plan, for the moment, was to allow the right amount of interest to filter through to Will and hope he would feel something midway between cherished and abandoned.

Filtering was a new mode of behavior for Peter. He had always been quite direct, emotionally, and had used bold, romantic displays to win Harold and Nick—like falling to his knees in the middle of Lincoln Center plaza, one evening before an opera, to beg Harold's forgiveness for being twenty minutes late; or showing up at Nick's office, on their first anniversary, with a bottle of champagne, two glasses, and tickets to Amsterdam. Yet that was then, and Will was now. It was because of his unprecedented age that Peter felt he should commit to a course of second-guessing. He hoped that that would make the infatuation of a fifty-nine-year-old man with a twenty-eight-year-old man a little less ridiculous. This was, after all, the first time he was lovesick as an old man, he told Jonathan, at dinner one night that week, and he didn't know if the condition functioned the same way it had done decades ago. He wanted to explore it a little, before either playing by the rules or breaking them.

"That's a strong word, 'lovesick,' " said Jonathan.

"Yeah, but that's what it is," said Peter.

They were at Jonathan's place, alone in the living room, chatting quietly over pre-prandial drinks. Above them, over the sofa on which Jonathan had installed himself, loomed an epic diptych by Connor Frankel, in pulsing blues, greens, and yellows. The room looked larger and more formal than it did when filled with guests, and seemed better able, when empty and still, to articulate the designer's intended balance between settled and surprising. Beyond, in the dining room, Aldebar, Jonathan's new live-in assistant, hired in lieu of the hospice option, was setting the table and plating the elaborate meal that had been ordered in from a nearby restaurant. Jonathan had invited Peter over as an opportunity to hear his friend gush about his new infatuation. "I want to hear everything," Jonathan said—though it was clear, too, that he didn't want to dwell on his failing health. So Peter gushed.

"I'm fucking lovesick, as much as I ever was with Harold or Nick," said Peter. "I can't stop thinking about him and I can't explain why. And you know how hardly anybody holds my interest nowadays."

"Charming," said Jonathan, whose deteriorated physical condition was hard to overlook. The flesh under his jaw had gone slack, his smile brittle and eyes sunken. He was gaunter than ever and looked lost inside his black cashmere sweater. A day's worth of silvery stubble frosted his normally clean-shaven head. Around the house, where he spent more and more time, he could move about on his own, but in public Jonathan was now using a wheelchair. In order to better focus on his film, he said, he was planning to move upstate, Aldebar and all, to the house in Hudson. There, he would continue working for as long as possible with Connor Frankel, who lived in a nearby town.

"But tell me, Peter, why this one?" said Jonathan. "And yes, maybe it is the documentarian in me who wants to know. What does this one have that your friend Tyler, for instance, doesn't have? Why not any of the men I have set you up with or your friends have set you up with—men so much more, shall we say, suitable?"

It was a good question. Even with men who "looked good on paper," which invariably meant close to Peter in age or salary, there were variables that always got in the way. Peter thought about this for a second.

"Well, darling," he said finally, "damage aside—and you know how many men our age are damaged goods—I need someone who is both decorous and a renegade. You know? I have all the solid citizens wanting to date me, and all the young renegades wanting daddy sex, but each type is boring, in itself. Will is somehow both these types in one, which is absolutely fascinating."

Jonathan chuckled.

"And cute isn't a marker for that, is it?" continued Peter. "I happily register cute boys I see out there, but I don't feel like pursuing them anymore, because it never leads anywhere."

"Except that this one *is* cute . . . ," said Jonathan.

"Well, yes. So I'm told."

"OK, so you plan to go on pursuing. Good for you."

"But that's precisely what I *don't* plan," said Peter.

"What?"

"*No-oo*," whined Peter. And then he whispered, "I think old age has made me shy."

"Shy," repeated Jonathan.

"I'm trying not to clobber the kid with my old tricks."

"C'mon. The way you wooed Harold was no trick. You just showed him how a romantic hero operates. And since then you have only gone from that prime to the prime you were in when you landed Nick, to the prime you're in now. The kid probably wants to see some of that star stuff."

Peter picked up his glass and sat back.

"Well, thank you, darling, but age has made me very specific in my needs," he said, taking a sip. "I want to be known exactly as who I am—not as an operator. Will and I tell each other that we're trying to do something new with our friendship, unprecedented for each of us. We're both promising to go beyond our usual tricks—you know, the cute young man stuff he falls back on, and the older guy stuff I always trot out."

"Hmmm."

"I mean, he gets all the guys he wants, but nothing serious pans out because it's always about the tricks. If, through me, he really owns for the first time how much there is to him besides all that, then that's awesome—even if he does take this new understanding and go find someone his own age."

"Really?"

"Well, you know—I hope not. Anyway, aren't there tons of examples in history of younger men digging older men?"

"I guess."

"The funny thing is, Jonathan, I love being lovesick." Peter shook his head, suppressing a grin. "This damned fever itself is exactly as, I dunno... *useful* as love. Very entertaining for an old man. The fear that usually comes with lovesickness, the feeling that you're gonna die, unless you get the kiss—forget about it! At this age, I know I won't die."

"How convenient."

Peter suddenly realized that Jonathan was looking tired.

"I'm boring you, dear friend," said Peter. Jonathan waved away the comment.

"You're sure it's really love, then?" pressed Jonathan. "Even if there's no possibility of suicide?"

"I'm not sure what it is. I'm not sure I ever knew what love is. No—I *am* sure: I have never known really what love is, though I know I have been loved."

"Fine. But wouldn't real love be better than what you have? I'm just asking."

"I don't know. What can I do but identify it as love and play it out accordingly?"

Jonathan laughed weakly, and Peter sat forward again, putting down his drink.

"I like his tonality, Jonathan," he said. "I like his goofy face, the way he combines grace and klutziness. I fantasize about where Harold and I would be right now and I want to be there with Will."

"Uh-oh," said Jonathan, with a little signal to Aldebar, who had appeared to check on the drinks. The new aide was a good-looking, muscular man in his thirties—a trained nurse, Jonathan had said, but commanding a smile as seductive as a porn star's.

"Sure, I fantasize about him sexually," said Peter, "but I also think about gardening with him and napping with him in the seat of an airplane, the sun pouring through the window, as we're flying off to Rio."

"You and your child *lovah.*"

Peter smiled and took a breath.

"I almost did have a child lover once," he mused. "Did I ever tell you? Dylan Zeleski. He was twelve—a very grown-up twelve. His parents were in a rock band and brought him to dance class, three times a week, on the third floor of Carnegie Hall, near my office. Remember when I had that office at Carnegie Hall? They used to dress him in a little leather biker jacket, with a tight little T-shirt and tight little jeans. Off the hook! And he had blue eyes, and black hair, and, ooh, white-white skin. That kid knew exactly what he was doing, Jonathan. He'd come in and ask for candy, and put air quotes around the word "candy." Twelve years old! And this was precisely the point in my life when I would have had my own twelve-year-old, if I were straight and a parent, my therapist pointed out. We never did anything, Dylan and me, though I talked about it for three years. I thought it went away, but maybe it's here again."

"Boy love?"

"Whatever it was. A certain nostalgia for the kids one doesn't have."

Jonathan raised an eyebrow.

"Have you always wanted kids?" he said.

"Yes—but I probably won't, now," said Peter. "Unless Will wants them."

It was partly a joke, and Jonathan rolled his eyes.

"I'm having dinner there tomorrow night," added Peter.

"Does he know how you feel?"

The question stopped Peter.

"No," he said.

"Ever made out?"

A pause.

"Not really."

Jonathan shook his head.

"Well, protect yourself," he said.

"I know," said Peter.

"What if he's just not into you?"

"I know."

"You have to ask the question and get the answer. That's my advice."

"Even if it's no. I know. And I don't want to abandon him as a friend, if it *is* no. I don't want him to think I've been lying about seeing so much in him and finding him unique among men. I think I could just get through the crisis of his not loving me, if it meant bestowing on him some new sense of worthiness. . . ."

Jonathan closed his eyes, then opened them.

"Girlfriend, you're a mess," he said.

"Oh, how did we ever get this old?" sighed Peter. "Weren't we just twenty-seven and marching in the streets and making history and showing the world how to wear a blazer with a T-shirt? Whatever happened to the timelessness of being twenty-seven?"

"Don't look at me," said Jonathan.

Peter tilted his head.

"Am I ridiculous?" he said.

"No," said Jonathan. "You deserve love and you always will."

"Because we're boomers and entitled?"

"Because you're a human being."

"Thank you, dear friend."

"And speaking of dinner, let's have some," said Jonathan, twisting in his seat and calling toward the dining room. "Aldebar, if you would?"

Winter days had been feeling oppressively dark and short, and Will and Luz had been talking about how trapped they felt in New York. Unable to fly somewhere south for a little vacation, they decided to make "sunny" the theme of their little dinner party. They bought new dinner plates and place mats in shades of yellow and orange, on sale at Crate and Barrel, and created a menu they called "Mexiterranean" that combined a grilled fish with lemon that Luz had learned from her mother, who was Mexican, and a spaghetti puttanesca that Will was creating with Greek olives and Santorini tomatoes he found at a local specialty shop. At six o'clock on the day of the dinner, the two were in their kitchen, busy with final preparations.

"I just remembered: We don't have any coffee," said Luz, zesting lemons for the fish. "You think they'll want some? I could run out and get some, or ask Mrs. Lavris."

"Eh, let's not bother," said Will. He was slicing the tomatoes and arranging them on a sheet pan, for a pre-roast. On the stovetop was a pan in which capers, olives, anchovies, and garlic were sweating in olive oil. "If people want, we can have tea. More likely, we'll just keep going with wine."

"I hope we have enough," said Luz.

"Oh, he'll bring some, I'm sure," said Will. "And speaking of alcohol . . ." Will danced over to the freezer and, with a flourish, took out a bottle.

"Limoncello!" sang Luz.

"A bottle of sunshine!" exclaimed Will.

"Shall we have some?"

"Why not," said Will, opening the bottle and pouring them each a glass.

"We never felt this depressed in L.A., did we, in February?" said Luz, after taking a sip.

"We didn't, did we?" said Will. "But the days are just as short there."

"Was it the latitude?"

"The climate?"

"Something about the desert?"

"You really suffer from this oppressive winter thing, in New York, don't you? Everybody's complaining about it. You see it on their faces."

"We had kitsch, actually—right? That's like sunshine in architectural form."

"Oh, Luz, you're right!"

"I mean, driving into a Mayan palace for a corn dog . . ."

"Dropping off your dry cleaning at a Chinese temple . . ."

"Kitsch against the winter!"

"Kitsch against the blues!"

Finishing the tomatoes, Will threw the pan into the oven and wiped his hands.

"You know what we need?" he said, dashing out of the kitchen.

"What?" shouted Luz.

He reappeared instantly with a pair of sky-blue Havaianas, still new, with the price tag dangling.

"A centerpiece!" said Will.

"Eww!" said Luz.

"No, watch," he said, taking a slender, cylindrical glass vase from a cabinet and attaching the flip-flops to it with some kitchen twine. He removed the price tag, then placed the creation on the kitchen table, which had been set for four, and stood back to admire his handiwork.

"Really?" said Luz.

"I guarantee you one of them will bring flowers."

"Mm-hmm—maybe both," said Luz, slyly.

Will made a face of mock-dread.

"Oh, God, do you think we're headed for disaster?" he said.

"I thought you said having both of them over was the best way to do it."

"I did, but what the hell do I know?"

At the same moment, Peter was standing deep beneath Times Square, on the 7 train platform, the lower-most level of the subway station said to be New York's busiest, where eleven lines converge, on three levels. He had with him two bottles of a good sauvignon blanc, a bunch of expensive, waxy French tulips in a fleshy pink, and a copy of Eliot's *Four Quartets,* wrapped as a gift. Though he was as far from the sky as anyone can be in New York without a hard hat, he was still sporting the sunglasses he'd thrown on just before leaving the house. A Queens-bound train had just left the station, so the platform was almost free of people. An LED display promised the next train in six minutes.

Though he'd set out early, as usual, he was now stressed about time, on top of a certain malaise about dinner that he'd been nursing all day. On arrival at the station he'd found that the N train he'd meant to take wasn't in service between Times Square and Queens Plaza, owing to an accident—though no one could say what kind of accident—so he'd had to figure out an alternative route to Will's house. Now, if the 7 came as promised and the transfer at Queens Plaza happened quickly—and the travel time was really twenty minutes, as a harried assistant station manager suggested—he could still be a little early for dinner, which was called for seven. And that was the way he wanted it, because Peter didn't like being late for important things and was perfectly willing to walk around Astoria or sit in a coffee shop, if he landed there before the dot.

His underlying malaise—now, typically, in the bullying company of an unplanned worry, planted in his mind by New York— was the result of being both sad and happy: sad, because Peter's loneliness made a dinner like this loom larger than it should; happy, because dinner would be fun—though he wasn't sure if it was going to be just Will and him, or Will's roommate, too, or one of those informal dinner parties for a group that young people seem to be able to rustle up on no budget. The invitation said "maybe a few friends"; Peter had been too shy to ask for more details, earlier in the day, when confirming with Will by text.

Even after the much ballyhooed Disneyfication of Times Square in the '90s, Peter's mental picture of the subway station there remained three levels of filthy, crowded, screeching hell. Yet as he stood on the platform he noticed that things seemed cleaner and better maintained than in the rest of the station, probably because the 7 train ran only from Midtown to points in Queens that, for decades, had served the city as solidly middle-class bedroom communities, and the platform was used more by well-trained worker-citizens than by the raucous masses that populated other regions of the "crossroads of the world." The mouse-colored porcelain floor tiles were mostly uncracked; the wooden benches, unscratched; the white tile walls opposite the platform, unstreaked by the mysterious crud you see oozing from cracks in the walls in lots of other stations. The cream-colored ceilings looked freshly painted and relatively soot-free, as did the cream and red of a broad team of overhead pipes that ran a course, bracketed together, parallel to the tracks, above the edge of the platform, into the distance. Or were they electrical conduits? Peter realized that sewage and drainage pipes would have to be larger—and sure enough, he spotted several much larger pipes, vertical ones, attached to some of the station's century-old steel columns and to a bank of massive concrete piers, at least five feet thick, that were at the end of the platform. The piers looked like they could be supporting the tonnage of all of Times Square's buildings.

The place is so massively overbuilt, thought Peter, who sometimes obsessed about such things when nervous. *Is that the way they did infrastructure in the early twentieth century? Will this hole in the ground still be here in a thousand years, even after the skyscrapers melt away or are encased in ice?*

Fluorescent lighting made the whole place shadowless. And, in the absence of a train, it was quiet, too, except for occasional safety announcements and the rumbling that echoed down periodically from the tracks on levels above.

So when it rains, thought Peter, *and Times Square floods, is all the runoff sluiced right through the station, down into some kind of chamber that's even deeper below the surface—a cistern, or a reservoir, or some fractures in the famous Manhattan schist on which this part of the city is built? Is it all drained off somehow to the river, through massive culverts under the city?*

A little girl in a purple parka was sitting with her parents on one of the benches, near where Peter was standing. The parents were talking quietly, their bulging shopping bags from Modell's, Sephora, and Forever 21 between them, at their feet, while the girl squirmed restlessly, periscoping around. The girl caught Peter's eye and smiled, and he smiled back generically: an older guy in shades, with flowers, obviously not from Queens—a guy who meant her no harm. At the end of the platform, where the station gave way to tunnel, was a police control booth, unmanned, with a boxy little chemical or biological detection unit posted outside, like a sentry.

Was the platform even *snug,* as New York places went?

Well, not exactly. It felt peaceful in the bomb-shelter sense of the word, though surely just one bomb that was strong enough— the kind they talked about practically every day in the media, a dirty baby nuke—could transform this bomb shelter into a tomb. Such talk sometimes betrayed an oddly gleeful tone, Peter thought, as if someone believed that the acceptance of the "inevitability" of such an attack was a comfort and the option of dying better than living in a world in which cultural supremacy had shifted away from New York and America itself, toward other continents. Yet . . . *couldn't* the inevitability of death, the idea that the end might be just *there,* coming within reach, be comforting in a way, if you didn't have better things before you, like a dinner party with the man who might become your lover? With no love in your life, wouldn't death be welcome—not a thief, ready to steal something from you, but a loyal sentry, posted somewhere out there on a timeline that was customized for you by God or fate, ready to embrace you at that moment tenderly called "your time"? And if death *were* out there on your timeline, visible in the distance, shouldn't he—and of course it was a "he"—be saluted, despite the prospect of a lovely dinner, so that familiarity could help mediate the impendency of his arrival? For someone looking for love as hard as Peter, the idea of one's own death—as personal as a lover, promising an embrace as specific as a lover's—did afford some shadowy splendor. . . .

Yet *shit,* thought Peter, *isn't it slightly disloyal to Jonathan, for one, to be thinking in this way*—even if death were a fact of life and overbuilding a city futile?

Suddenly, Peter was terrified. He wondered if he could possibly, really, be scoring with Will that night or any other night. Death, he thought with a chuckle, might be easier to deal with than all the work there'd be to do if love truly *were* in the offing—learning about each other, listening to each other, compromising with each other. . . .

Ugh.

Then a train slid into the station. It was one of the new, smoother riding, silver trains, gleaming clean, of a type that would have been hard to imagine back in 1975, when the MTA's rolling stock was uniformly ancient and broken down, and covered with graffiti. The train discharged its passengers and those who'd been waiting on the platform stepped in. Peter settled into a seat and noticed his harshly lit reflection making a ghastly portrait in the window opposite. Then, with a futuristic "bink-bonk," the train signaled the closing of its doors and the little girl in purple uttered a gurgle of delight.

CHAPTER 13

Peter noticed the table was set for four, the minute he walked in. But the tumult of welcome, the introduction to Luz, a quick tour of the apartment, and the jollity triggered by Peter's approving and unprompted description of the color of the living room walls as "paper bag," all kept Will from mentioning that Enrico was the fourth guest—until he received a call from Enrico, whose driver was lost. They were standing in the kitchen, sipping limoncello, while Will finished the pasta and Luz saw to the fish, chatting about Astoria and picking at a *meze* platter, when Enrico finally walked in the door, twenty minutes late. Introductions and subsequent conversation were smooth—more, Peter thought, because he was making an effort to be a good guest than because Will put his mind at ease about this little surprise. Were those two still an item?

"Ooh, pretty table," said Peter, after Will invited them to sit.

"Peter brought the flowers," said Will.

"Sensational presentation," said Peter.

"Nice," said Enrico. He was overdressed in a fitted sport jacket and flashy striped shirt. Peter, like Will and Luz, was in jeans, with a crewneck sweater and T-shirt.

The table was in a dining area off the kitchen, a nook wainscoted in garish panels of the same blond wood that the kitchen cabinets were made of, which was so highly lacquered in acrylic that it looked like plastic. The flip-flop centerpiece did lend an off-beat elegance to the table, an agreeably tropical spree of newly bought china and cloth napkins—charming, Peter thought, and just as entertaining as the tabletop drama his grander friends achieved with gaily mismatched Ceralene, grandmother's Buccellati, and the carnival of glassware one picks up in Venice over the years. On a counter nearby sat a bowl of salad and a stack of salad plates. Will and Luz brought the rest of the food to the table on platters.

"How long have you lived here?" asked Enrico, unfolding his napkin and draping it across his lap.

"Six months now," said Will. "We're still moving in."

"Such big rooms," said Enrico. "Do you have the whole house?"

"Of course not," said Will.

"We have a very nice landlady who lives downstairs," said Luz, serving the fish with the grace of a headwaiter, using a pair of forks. "It's like having our own Greek mama."

"Ah," said Enrico.

"Not exactly like your place," said Will, laughing, filling everyone's glass with wine. "Enrico's apartment is a little jewel box."

"No," said Enrico. And then there was an empty moment during which a gracious remark about the host's apartment could have been added.

Nice guy, thought Peter. *Not worthy of Will.*

After offering a toast to new friends, Will served the pasta. With pleasure, Peter noticed the ease with which Will managed the hosting of his inaugural dinner party. The guy was clearly organized and seemed to have a talent for amplifying the conviviality of a group—asking the right questions, drawing people out, adding to the conversation in ways that kept it going, kept it buoyant. Luz seemed cooler, more serene.

"It's nice to have at least one person in the family who knows how to give a party," she said.

"That always helps, right?" said Peter.

"I can grill fish, but that's about it," said Luz.

"If only life were that simple," said Peter.

"Give a man a fish . . . ," spouted Will—and they all chortled, except Enrico, who didn't seem to get it.

Peter had been surprised to find Luz there when he arrived, but he immediately took a liking to her. She was smart, funny, open; she reminded him of Alanis Morrisette—not just because of the luxuriant, long black hair, which Luz had gathered up into an asymmetrical twist for the evening, but because she had a witchy directness that seemed shot through with something saucy, even girly.

". . . Then I told the guy, 'No, I'm not a dyke, but I *am* nine times the man that you are,' " she said with a laugh, concluding a story.

"*I* am a dyke," purred Will, leaning over and giving Luz an affectionate hug. "That's how much I love women."

"Oh, baby," said Luz, "and you're gonna turn me into one, aren't you."

Talk over dinner ranged from aquaculture and ecology to hunting and firearms, and then to gun policy and politics. Except for a few two-on-two moments, resulting from Enrico's subtle tendency to address remarks more to Will than to the group, the conversation flowed steadily *a quatre*. Twice, when talk touched on the subject of what Peter did for a living, the conversation sputtered—partly because Peter was trying not to be brilliant and outshine his host, but also because Enrico seemed remarkably uninterested in Peter's work or his thoughts. Was Enrico jealous? Maybe those two were still an item!

Enrico was a handsome guy, but Peter suspected it might be the kind of handsomeness that gives way, over time, to a caricature of itself, instead of a fruition. For years Peter had been in the habit of Photoshopping forward people's looks; he always had clear ideas about how they would look, ten or more years on. Thus he had judged Harold, when they first met, as poised to age gracefully; and the changes that did occur in Harold's appearance during the crunch of that awful, final year, even though they were too ungentle to foreshadow actual advanced age, did nothing to dim Harold's beauty in Peter's eyes. Will, too, would only improve with age, Peter knew; and he winced when Will referred to his approaching thirtieth birthday with queeny mock-dread—more because the dread was so obviously unwarranted, than because it was partly disingenuous. Peter knew that the noble proportions among Will's strong nose, brow, and jaw would remain intact, that the classic facial architecture would only be enhanced if the hair went gray and laugh lines developed around the eyes.

"I hear you're going to be working for Henderson McCaw," said Luz. She, unlike Enrico, was very curious about Peter's work.

"Well, I *may* be," said Peter. "We're thinking about it. It would be working *with* him, by the way—not *for* him."

"But only maybe, right?" said Will.

"Right."

"He's only a total monster," said Will.

"Monsters need slogans, too," quipped Luz. "In fact, they kind of depend on them, don't they, Peter? I'm thinking historically."

"Interesting," said Peter, glad to have an idea on the table, along with the unpremeditated lie he instantly regretted. "The slogan itself can be kind of a monstrous thing, I suppose. Anyway, we're thinking about it. I'm trying to determine whether or not I have the stomach for it...."

"Who is this?" asked Enrico, though an explanation did nothing to inspire him to join the exchange. Peter was relieved when the conversation moved on, because he realized he was so ambivalent about his new client, he wasn't prepared to talk about him.

After dinner, Peter helped Luz clear the table and followed her into the kitchen, while Will and Enrico remained in the living room, talking. It made Peter jealous to see them chatting like that, by themselves, though he knew he wasn't really authorized to feel jealousy, since he had never been promised anything and was really only nursing a fantasy.

"Don't worry about them," said Luz, when she noticed Peter glancing back into the living room.

"What do you mean?"

"They're not together."

"Oh, *Luz* . . . ," said Peter, with a pretend shudder. He assumed she knew everything.

"Man, you've got it bad," she said. "I can see it all over you."

"Can you?"

"Mm-hmm."

"Can I be honest?" He spread his arms into as wide a "this much" gesture as possible.

"So what are you doing about it?"

"I'm *doing* it."

"You're not seeing anybody?"

"Anybody *else?* No. Not that I am exactly seeing Will...."

"You're attractive and successful."

"Thanks. I haven't dated in ten years, Luz. I think I'm in some kind of transition. I had two long-term relationships that ended... well, it's a long story. For a long time I haven't known what I wanted, or *if* I wanted anything."

"And now you do."

"I think I do, yeah."

"Why Will?"

"His cooking, of course."

"Seriously."

"I dunno. The men of my generation bore me, and younger guys usually do, too. But Will... he's something else, isn't he?"

"*I* think so."

"But it's all so... confusing. Why am I telling you this? I've had too much to drink."

"It's sweet. It's like you're seventeen."

"Yeah, except I'm in my eighties," said Peter.

"Aw, c'mon."

Then Peter wondered if it were possible that she could believe him.

"Luz, I'm only fifty-nine."

"Whatever."

He had an instinct that she could be trusted.

"So lemme ask you," he said. "Do I have a chance?"

"He tells me everything, of course," said Luz.

"Uh-huh..."

"But in confidence."

"Uh-oh."

"No, no—don't worry. It's not bad for you."

"Oh, good. I guess." A pause.

"I would just say: Step up," said Luz.

"What do you mean?"

She smiled enigmatically.

"I'm not gonna say more than that," she said.

"Step up," repeated Peter. "And you can't say more than that because you're supertrustworthy."

Enigmatic turned to angelic.

"I try," she squeaked.

"Luz, I suspect you are a treasure," said Peter.

"Oh, I'm a good lawyer, too, baby."

"I'll bet you are," he said, laughing.

"That, in there," said Luz, indicating the living room, "if you ask me, it's just a case of VGL, UB2, blah-blah-blah."

"Ecch—really?"

"They're programmed that way."

"He swallows all that crap?"

"I go out with the guy, I see what's out there—all those smiley boy-bots. I guess it's fun—unless you happen to have a bigger idea about relationships."

"Jesus, Luz, what kind of law are you studying?"

"Intellectual property," she said.

"Figures."

"But he's more than that and he knows it."

"I hope so," said Peter.

"He knows *you're* more than that."

Peter smiled.

"You and I, counselor," he said, "are gonna have a big fat drink, one of these days, just the two of us."

"I'm there, buddy," said Luz. "Anyway, I wanna hear more about writing taglines and naming brand extensions."

"Everything I know is yours."

Dessert was figs and nuts, in the living room. No one wanted tea or coffee. Talk was about why people come to New York. Will told his story, which Peter already knew—that he had come more or less automatically, without a feeling of destiny about either the place or his career—whereas Luz said she had come to stake out territory, climb to the top of a heap—like himself and Jonathan and their crowd, Peter thought. They chewed over ambition and power, the good and the bad, and then it felt like the evening was over. When Peter came back from the bathroom, he said he should probably go.

Almost too quickly Enrico was saying what a pleasure it was to have met him.

"I had a great time," Peter told Will moments later, in the doorway, after thanking Luz with a hug.

"Thanks for the book," said Will.

"I was hoping we would have a chance to talk about it."

"Me too. Another time."

"OK."

"Soon."

"Of course."

"Know where you're going? We can call a car."

"No, I'm good with the subway. You going out later?"

"No—Peter! I have an early morning, tomorrow. The rest of the guests will be leaving very shortly."

They shared a genial chuckle and a peck on the cheek, which afforded Peter a waft of rosemary-lavender-scented hair gel—enough of an intimacy to make him feel, as he descended into the street, a little high.

He chuckled again, at himself, on his walk to the subway. On the way out to Astoria he had given some thought to the possibility—a long shot, he knew—of being invited to stay the night. In all other ways, though, the evening was a success. Knowing that Enrico, who seemed so smooth at first, was actually dull, passive, or maybe even lazy, was comforting.

Unworthy.

But the thing that really stuck in Peter's mind, as he rattled back to Manhattan and then to Brooklyn, was why he had denied saying a definite yes about McCaw. It was a done deal, yet he had answered Luz with a "maybe." And the uncertainty seemed to matter to Will. The matter continued to perplex him all the way home.

Soon after the turn of March there was a hint of spring in the air, though not necessarily a vegetal hint. Are the mineral smells released by warming city walls and sidewalks under strengthening sunlight not just as invigorating as reawakened greenery? A fresh breeze, sweetened by sun-kissed brick, was pushing in through a crack that Aldebar had opened in Jonathan's kitchen window, as Peter, in a blue blazer and white shirt, stood there talking with him, leaning on the granite countertop, sipping coffee. It was just before eleven, on a weekday morning. There was little to see out the window—only the building's inner courtyard, though even the difference between a clean, spacious courtyard like that one and the dark, choked airshaft that is more common in New York was another reason why Jonathan's building counted as a prestige address.

"Ted Uppman was the Met's Billy Budd when I was growing up," said Aldebar. "I think he created the part."

"I envy your having grown up in New York," said Peter. "I was stuck in a small town upstate."

Except for their voices, the room was still—the calm of a well-ordered kitchen at rest amplifying the sadness of the occasion: a meeting to discuss Jonathan's will. In attendance, in the library, were Jonathan's lawyer, Mark; Mark's assistant Judith; Jonathan's brother, Ted, who was the chief executor of his will, responsible for Jonathan's real property; and Peter, who was Jonathan's artistic executor and thus responsible for protecting his artistic output. Peter had been asked to step out of the room while they discussed Jonathan's personal bequests of property, artwork, and objects.

" 'Theodor Uppman, the American baritone,' " said Aldebar. "That's the way they always billed him. I guess they wanted to make sure people realized he was American, and not, I dunno, Swedish. They were very proud of the American singers they were turning out, back then."

"What else did he do?" asked Peter.

"Papageno! Pelléas! Sharpless! And contemporary stuff. He was pretty adventurous."

Aldebar was an interesting guy, thought Peter—a trained nurse, an amateur bodybuilder, and a connoisseur in a way that generations of young lower- and middle-class gay boys of various cultural backgrounds learned about, then claimed ownership of, the so-called finer things of life.

"He went on playing Billy probably much longer than he should have," continued Aldebar. "But he kept those athletic good looks that apparently Britten liked so much, and he was terrific in the part. He had all the innocence and trustfulness."

"Have you always been into opera?"

"High school music teacher—Mr. Sternberg."

Judith appeared at the kitchen door.

"Peter, will you rejoin us?"

"To be continued," said Peter, to Aldebar.

In the library, the group was installed in the sofa and chairs that surrounded a pair of midcentury modernist, bentwood coffee tables. The tables were spread with legal papers, notepads, and Judith's sleek laptop. Fingers of late morning sun poked in through the wooden blinds, angling down over Jonathan's collection of antique Japanese pots, which he'd grouped on the built-in cabinet with decorative casualness. Opposite, on a table that was well out of the sunlight, was the Eliot manuscript—something that presumably would go to a museum or a library, sometime in the coming year. The manuscript had been on Peter's mind ever since he decided to give Will a copy of *Four Quartets*. Maybe one day, Peter thought, Jonathan would let us remove the Plexiglas cover and examine the manuscript in detail. In a drawer was a supply of white cotton gloves, for just such occasions.

"One day"?—shit, thought Peter. *We're talking about his will. By this time next year, someone else will be living in this apartment. All the lovely décor will have been dismantled—not even a year old. Has the place even been photographed?*

Peter reclaimed the seat he'd occupied for the first part of the meeting, when they went over Jonathan's wishes for his films and the new grants for documentary filmmakers he was endowing. A foundation was being formed to receive the bulk of Jonathan's estate—around $11 million, excluding the house upstate—and administrate the grants and raise additional funds. Peter was to be a member of the board.

"I think we're in good shape, gentlemen," said Mark. "The only thing that's left to discuss is the directorship of the foundation. Peter, we've just talked a little bit further about it and would love your input."

"Would our young friend be interested in the gig, do you think?" said Jonathan, who had been seated in his chair when they arrived that morning and had remained there throughout the meeting.

"Who?" said Peter.

"Will."

"Will?"

"We need someone who knows the arts and can understand the mission."

"I . . . gather he was planning to stay in magazines," said Peter, slightly flummoxed. "Wouldn't you want someone who could run a business?"

"Well, maybe, but . . . ," began Mark.

"Magazine people have a way of going off and doing something more profitable, eventually—the smart ones, anyway," interrupted Jonathan. "Maybe Will would be interested in going sooner rather than later."

"Maybe," said Peter. "Ask him. You knew him before I did. Are you asking *me* to ask him?"

"No—I'll do that," said Jonathan. "I just wanted to get your thinking."

Ted smiled at Peter and gave an approving nod.

"He's a smart guy," said Peter.

"Mature, responsible?" said Mark.

"As far as I can tell."

"The mission is simple," said Mark. "Give away the money, raise more money. And, of course, protect the money."

"I think he'd be terrific," said Jonathan. "Young blood—you know."

"Then you'll have a chat with the young man and let us know?" said Mark.

"Yup," said Jonathan.

"Good," said Mark. "Then we're done."

The group rose and lapsed into small talk. Aldebar appeared as if by telepathic summons and helped Jonathan to rise, then stood close by him.

"Oh, and I hope you'll all be able to make the screening we're doing next month," said Jonathan. "It's a rough cut—and I hope you won't think me coy when I say I still don't know how it's all going to end."

Peter, who was checking his iPhone, winced when he overheard that.

"Tom and I will be there," said Mark, warmly.

"I'm really proud of this one," said Jonathan.

"Mary and I will fly in, of course," said Ted. "We wouldn't miss it."

"Connor says that art made him miss his calling as a movie star," said Jonathan, with a laugh that turned into a cough. Within seconds, Aldebar was offering him a sip of water.

"No, I'm fine, I'm fine," said Jonathan. "He's really taking to it, Connor is. A big ham!"

At the door to the apartment, after the others had gone down in the elevator, and while Aldebar was tidying up the library, Peter and Jonathan shared a moment alone.

"Wow," said Peter.

"Yeah," said Jonathan.

"How ya doing?"

"Surviving."

"Good."

"I don't really do anguish, you know?"

"I know."

"Probably why I went into documentaries, instead of dramas."

"Interesting."

"One foot in front of the other."

"Oh, yes."

"So Will—huh?" said Jonathan.

"It's up to you," said Peter. "You really think he could do something like that?"

"Of course he could. He's smart and responsible. He could probably do anything he sets his mind to. It's not like it's anyone's destiny to be in magazines."

"I dunno. He might like the glamour of it—the parties, the stars."

"He might—in which case, he'll say no. He might also want to give away vast amounts of money and do some good in the world."

"I marvel that you thought of him, honestly."

Jonathan smiled in a manner Peter thought sly.

"Or is there something else here," continued Peter, "that I'm not aware of . . . ?"

"No," chuckled Jonathan. "I just have in mind that great machine that collapsed in the eighties, that used to shift the power ever so gently from the seniors to the freshmen who looked promising."

"Yeah, that's all gone now."

"Except that I can damned well do what I want with my money."

Jonathan said those words more forcefully than anything he'd said in the meeting, and Peter heard so much in them—sadness, bitterness, resolve. He gazed lovingly at Jonathan and then, on an impulse, gathered his friend into a hug and kissed his forehead. It was a shock to feel the frailness of Jonathan's body and to catch the scent of something scalpy, though not precisely unclean, mixed with Jonathan's Black Tourmaline. As Peter gently released his friend, the idea of losing him suddenly seemed more terribly real, and Peter felt a small shudder in his own breathing and an involuntary twinge in the center of his brow, in that spot where the muscles know, before we do, that worry could give way to weeping.

"My brother is being such a prince," said Jonathan, continuing to steady himself by holding Peter's arm. "Did you notice? He has every right to expect some of that money, but he's being very supportive."

Peter nodded but said nothing, realizing he needed to try and stay composed.

"And you, good friend—so are you," continued Jonathan. "This is . . . a strange time, for all of us. Petey, I've been thinking a lot about you. OK, we've just spent the morning talking about reality. So tell me: Whatever happened to the sexual adventurer? You used to be out there for all of us, long after we bonded with our mates and took it off the streets or gave it up entirely. Even when you had boyfriends, you had adventures, right—you and Nick? You told me. So why are you now . . . courting in this way?"

Peter sighed and slumped against the door.

"I don't know," he said, shaking his head.

"Why prolong this not knowing? Ask the guy, is it a relationship or not? It's so unlike you not to go straight for the answer. If it's not right, let it go. There are plenty of boys out there, if that's what you want."

There was such concern in Jonathan's voice, when he had so much else to be thinking about! In the space of a second, Peter's face melted into a mask of misery. He felt himself tearing up.

"I don't *know* what I want, Jon," he said. "I'm afraid."

Jonathan, surprised, tried to comfort his friend and took his hand.

"But you were never afraid."

"No, I wasn't," said Peter, giving in a little to the sobbing. "But I am now. *That's* . . . age. That's what age has done to me."

They were silent for a moment, then Jonathan spoke.

"Afraid of . . . losing him?"

"No," said Peter, his eyes closed, as if to prevent more tears. "Afraid of the fucking shame and embarrassment when he says, so very kindly, no, but how flattered he is. Confirming that all this time he's been dreading my saying exactly that. Watching him go very politely through the whole rejection thing and then tell me that he still wants to be friends. And, of course, it's all rehearsed."

"Would that be so terrible?" Jonathan asked quietly.

Peter shook his head and said nothing, wiping away tears with his fingers.

"Would it kill you?" asked Jonathan.

"No. It wouldn't kill me."

They stood there for a moment, a dying man comforting a supposedly vital one. And later, when he remembered it, the moment would remind Peter of the time when Harold, home from the hospital for the last time, emaciated and already showing signs of dementia, rose in the middle of the night, in the dark, from the daybed where he'd been sleeping, to bring Peter, who'd awakened coughing, in the bedroom, a glass of water.

He came to the door like a ghost, his eyes closed, meaning to help me.

"Do you need a tissue?" said Jonathan. "Paper towel?"

Peter smirked and stood up straight.

"I'm fine, thank you," he said. "I can't believe I'm walking into a meeting in forty minutes."

"Listen," said Jonathan, "I'm going up to Hudson, from the first of the month on. I'm going to live up there now."

"Oh." It was another seismic shock, though Peter had known it was coming.

"You bring your boy up there for a weekend. Promise you will."

"Sure. That would be nice."

Back in the days when Jonathan's "great machine" was functioning, Peter hadn't understood its workings nor the system behind it. Friends of friends, usually men a little older than he and more successful, asked him to jacket-and-tie lunches and engaged him in genial conversation about this and that; and when they got around to talking about what Peter's career goals might be, other than the poet thing, he never had much to say. He didn't have a plan for his life—though that in itself might well have qualified him for special attention. He didn't know it, but those men were examining him—sometimes in a gentlemanly manner; sometimes lasciviously, as per the loose sexual manners of the time; and sometimes in both ways at once. They wanted to see what he might be capable of, or worthy of, and what they might be able to provide. Yet just as Peter could have become a beneficiary of the machine, the thing broke down, with AIDS. Everyone in books and fashion and antiques and the arts who'd ever taken Peter to lunch died—and he'd often thought that that might be one reason why, having to fend for himself, he'd drifted into his current line.

I'd probably be running some foundation somewhere, myself, thought Peter, as he strode from Madison Avenue into the lobby of his building, a soaring nave of gleaming marble, glass, and steel. *Giving away grants from some ducky little converted town house in the East Sixties. An office full of good antiques; happy enough—but not really in the game.*

The voltage of advertising hit him right in the face that day, as he stepped off the elevator and into the atrium. The girls at the reception desk were smiling a little more magnetically than usual, their voices galvanized as they spoke into headsets, directing calls, while in back of them, on a thirty-foot expanse of video wall, large-scale animations representing the company's biggest clients fluxed with provocative flash. The kids tripping up and down the atrium's jungle-gym stairway and across the main floor seemed a little sparkier than usual. And outside the Gymnasium, a large meeting room off the main reception area, a young woman in dark leggings and a cropped jacket, clearly a member of the client team inside, was standing next to a refreshment table, emitting signals that were apparently terribly important into her cell phone.

It was a big day at the office: Important clients were everywhere. Peter nodded to a colleague, a creative director, who rushed past him with a delegation to greet an A-list television star waiting in the reception area with an entourage. A new series, Peter thought, or a voice-over for some high-profile campaign. Upstairs, in his own private warren of offices, where Peter was headed, key members of McCaw's communications team were spending the day with Peter's top people, led by Tyler, going through an inaugural series of conceptual explorations.

The great work begins.

Peter loved it when the office felt this electric. The sheer energy of being inside a major ad agency at the dawn of the Age of Truly Global Mass Culture was like a drug. Madison Avenue was now the undisputed control room of civilization, whereas Washington and Hollywood were only its rec rooms. Actions like voting and going to the movies seemed quaint, now that the purchase and consumption of the right soft drink or the right body wash promised to put the experience of Life Right Now into focus. More than in politics and entertainment, the higher processes fibrillating the top levels of advertising were charged with the full juice of vast national and global conversations, of the collective unconscious itself; and the people involved in these processes, even when not actually working, existed in a higher orbital, spiritually, than everyone else; they inhabited a better place than Earth, a possible planet where the abundance of everything good was a given. For not only were these young ad execs among the best and the brightest, the most creative, self-actualized, and best-paid individuals of their generation, they could depend on the daily exhilaration of work and play at the font of contemporary civilization, the source of ideas that functioned for consumers like answered prayers.

Being in this line of work, wielding its lightning, was an ultimate privilege, Peter often mused—ten times better than riding to a party in a limo with Nick's one-time friend Madonna and her crew. At the agency, Peter got to create campaigns—movements!—that would sweep whole continents with messages about products and services so beneficial that people would spend trillions of dollars on them; and along for the ride, in that traffic of wants and needs, aspirations and means, came fresh ideas about self and family and nation and world, which brought life on Earth forward, upward. Talk about illuminati! Here was the true elite. Tyler and the rest weren't hoodooing around with naïve, medieval travesties of so-called secret, ancient wisdom. They were serving humanity by generating enlightenment from moment to moment, conjuring new values and powers and orders and blessings—which was the chief thing, Peter felt, that separated him from Jonathan and the gentlemen of their generation, who had devoted themselves to older values and powers and orders and blessings. Those guys were a little less aglow.

In the Den, one of the largest work spaces in Peter's offices, he found things running smoothly. The meeting was the second of two that morning, before lunch. The McCaw team, numbering seven, headed by Sunil, the chief strategist and adviser, and Katy, the speechwriter, were comfortably installed in the room's funky collection of mismatched chairs and sofas, and in oversized beanbag cushions on the floor. Interspersed were key members of Peter's staff. The room's décor, meant to trigger creative thinking, was accented with an array of toys, board games, and indoor sporting goods that would have been at home in the *Brady Bunch* house. With a minimum of fuss, Peter slipped into the back of the room and perched against an old-fashioned stereo console, just as Tyler was beginning.

"What is a big idea?" said Tyler. He was dressed that day for the kind of authority clients expected of him: in an olive-drab suit, much more expensive than it looked, with a pair of Jack Purcells and a plain T-shirt. "We say that brown is big this season—which it is, by the way—but what do we mean by that?" On a flat-screen monitor in back of him was a slide with the phrase, *BROWN IS BIG RIGHT NOW.*

"It's popular; people are feeling it," said Katy.

"The fashion industry is giving us a lot of it," said Sunil.

"All true—fashion, home décor, product design," said Tyler. "People are feeling brown. But we can go deeper. The truths we're looking for are wide and deep—that's the bedrock we want to build on." He flipped to a new slide, featuring three words: *VERITIES, EQUIVALENCES,* and *VALIDITIES.* "So I want us to keep in mind these three kinds of truth, as we think about our goals." Then he launched the group into a discussion of relevant definitions and differentiations.

Peter had seen Tyler conduct this kind of exercise before, with other clients, and it was always a success. And sure enough, the McCaw people were rapt and soon contributing freely and fruitfully. They seemed a friendly enough bunch, Peter thought—not New Yorkers, most of them, but clearly sophisticated and, of course, very smart; no more "other" than other clients, all of whom are teammates until you remember they are also exacting employers. No one on the team was any more of a monster than McCaw himself; there wasn't a wacko, wingnut, or dingbat among them. And as far as Peter could see, there were no doctrinally fueled disconnects in anyone's thinking. Was the monstrous sound of McCaw's "Take back America" message more a product of the media than of the man and his supporters? Was there a more useful way of framing the underlying question—"Whose America?"—than as a backward-or-forward thing, in the context of a posthegemonic nation coming to grips with an approaching nonwhite majority?

"This is how we begin to measure big," continued Tyler. "Now, how big is brown? In what ways is it big?"

The group threw out ideas about what brown could depict or express, what it might be equivalent to, and how it might be particularly valid right now. Tyler carefully guided them to expand or focus their contributions. Katy traced a sequence of thought from "earth" to "dirty" to "natural"; Sunil traced one from "skin" to "humanity" to "diversity"; others suggested "wood," "the environment," and "activism"; "coffee," "stimulation," "self-indulgence." Tyler recorded these ideas on large sheets of paper posted to the walls.

"From 'dirty' to 'self-indulgent'—not bad," said Tyler, looking over the sheets, and the group laughed. "No, really," he said, "very good."

Even from his seat in the back of the room Peter could see, from people's body language, that they were enjoying working together and sparking off one another's ideas.

"And who, again, is thinking these thoughts about brown?" asked Tyler.

"Everyone," suggested Sunil.

"Pretty much everyone," replied Tyler. "Anyone with eyes and a brain, and a few screens or pages of print to look at now and then."

"Can you say the same kinds of things about red?" asked Katy.

"Of course. Red is a huge story, evolving even faster than brown," said Tyler. "Green, too—superhuge!"

"Evolving?" said Katy.

"With the headlines. Through daily experience. Our daily witness and subconscious thoughts. It's always churning. . . ."

"OK," said Katy, "so for green: the environment, saving the rain forest . . ."

"Right. And one story that's emerging on top of that is about Brazil creating all this sustainable farmland in the Cerrado, which is their savannah. Plus, say, the continuing power of *Avatar*—the entire planet was green, remember; and the increasing use of LED displays on food carts and ATM machines; and the herbs they're cooking with on the Food Network; and yes, even our own nostalgia for lawn sprinklers and lazy summer afternoons during the Eisenhower administration. . . ."

Laughter.

"But can't you say this sort of thing about any color?" asked another member of the McCaw team.

"Sure you can, and each story is as deep as *Avatar*. But the point is that each one is as distinct from the others as *Avatar* is from, oh, *Gone With the Wind*. See what I mean? We need to know the full truths of the concepts we're dealing with, or we won't be able to accomplish our task. What is America? What is America *now*? Does

anyone think that patriotism, or partisanship, or simple neighborli-
ness, can function the same way now, among 320 million Americans, as it did in 1776, when we were less than one percent of that?
These concepts are in constant evolution, even if the Constitution
remains intact and we fence up our national borders."

Buy-in, around the room.

"Peter will be getting to some of those concepts this afternoon,"
continued Tyler, with a wink at his boss, "but for the moment, let's
go on." He flipped to the next slide: *HIGHEST COMMON DE-
NOMINATOR.* And for the next forty-five minutes the group
wrapped its collective head around the ideas of "good" and "normal" and the relationship between the two.

When they broke for lunch, everyone seemed buzzed. Several
McCaw people made it a point of telling Peter how useful they
were finding the day's program, and that pleased him, even if he
was still uneasy about something undefined in his mind, regarding
the assignment.

As the group headed off to the dining room, where lunch was
being served, Peter grabbed a word with Tyler.

"Well done," said Peter.

"Thanks," said Tyler. "I think they're really getting it."

"I'm proud of you."

"I'm just doing what you taught me. I remember once you said,
'Don't just think, think it *through*. . . .' "

"I said that?"

"Uh-huh."

"Hmm."

Peter couldn't remember ever saying such a thing, though he
did agree with the thought. He wondered, as Tyler went off, if he
had really uttered those very words—which sounded, actually, like
Jonathan—or only something like them, which Tyler, in his own
brilliant way, had processed into a maxim, giving the idea some
added power. Mentoring worked both ways, Peter knew, with benefits for both parties. He had awarded Tyler a leadership role in
this potentially career-making assignment and had given the boy
some of the tools he needed to ace it; in return for such largesse he
often received from Tyler the perfected version of a thought, that,
while original, might not have been shapely enough to present to a

client; a bit of intellectual refraction that functioned like a mutual gift, since it made them both look good—its exchange more appealing than sex (and perhaps something, thought Peter, that sex would have precluded).

Thank God I never thought it was love, he thought. *Maybe we've both always known what it was.*

It was funny, too, Peter mused, that as he had aged, his work had become a kind of substitute for romance. Career was the place where he was putting so much ardor, recently, so much of the attention and credulity he once lavished on lovers. But had he become stuck? Had he neglected to rethink his habits of affection as vigorously as he did those of clothing himself? Had the situation with Will uncovered a kind of amatory autopilot, set long ago in Peter's brain, when the population was smaller and men were different? Did his ideas about love need refracting for use in the current day?

Or was it time to just retire from the field? Romance itself had changed, too, after all, over the decades. Partly as a result of the social change pushed by Peter's generation, love and sex had shifted away from the sanctified spots where Peter first discovered them and were functioning now as wholly different kinds of common denominators, for a different kind of population. The America that Peter and his generation had built was a place where a rising young man with a Brown education, from a nice middle-class family, could openly use his experience as a rent boy and a performing artist to pull off a major advertising coup. Tyler was "ready to suck cock," he'd said when they discussed the ethics of the McCaw assignment, before signing, "but in a good way."

It was convenient for Peter to have someone like this on his team, of course, so the old man in him could have it both ways: caviling about doctrinal purity while hoping to serve the client well. And since Peter wasn't really ready to retire from romance just yet, he could maybe get a few good clues from Tyler about what kind of love was big this season, even if the boy's wholesome brand of whorishness might have its detriments.

CHAPTER 14

Then, as it got warmer, Peter and Will started seeing more of each other. They got together two or three times a week, for movies and parties, for dinners out and occasionally in, at Peter's place, though there were still no sleepovers. They weren't dating; they were simply sliding into a comfortable relationship as default hangout buddies, with all the back-and-forth texting and phone calling that such relationships entail—a bounty of not-so-idle chatter that Peter adored, since it had begun to subsume those little daily-witness exchanges he had once shared with Harold and Nick: the "I saw a funny thing at Starbucks today" and "I tried to exit at the north end of the Eighteenth Street subway station but it was closed" discussions whose spiritually sustaining nature Peter hadn't fully comprehended, before. He found that such witness had become fundamental for him, even without the connection to sex and other usual boyfriend stuff. It was palpable assurance that another human being, an ally, was huddled nearby and heedful, in the encroaching dark of a frigid cosmos.

Yet there was a casual physical intimacy growing between them. A brush of the lower back or caress of the neck, when they met in a restaurant or lounge, or a warm pat on the knee, as the lights went down at a concert—it was almost as if they were a very old couple or a pair of loving exes, Peter thought. Moreover, less and less, at a party, when the two of them clucked over a cute guy they spotted, would Will want to peel away and go enchant the guy, and less and less would Peter dread that he might do so. More and more, they knew each other's taste in men and enjoyed discussing this at great length, even as the pursuit for other men slipped into some kind of abeyance. When Will mentioned one day that Peter had become one of his "best friends," Peter was thrilled and understood he had to accept this lovely gift for what it was, without wondering if it might lead to a greater gift. If the arrangement precluded Peter from pursuing someone else, so be it, he thought. A stalled romance was better than none.

Why had this comfort developed between them, instead of sex? Did it represent a stage on the way to becoming boyfriends? Who knew? The chief feature of the arrangement seemed to be that both of them accepted it tacitly, which itself sometimes pleased Peter as a very adult form of graciousness toward each other.

It was because of this arrangement that Peter, once more, felt the days pulse with the thrill that comes when tiny, normal moments are also special—the ordinary world of heightened everything, to which he'd found his way before twice in life, and from which he had twice been exiled, too. Now, with Will, for the first time since Nick, dumb little habits that sweetened reality were common again, like texting each other whenever one of them happened to set foot on Eighth Avenue, with messages like *Once more into the breach!* and *OMG, first tank top of spring!* Common were silly nicknames like "Chez Poubelle," for their favorite dumpling joint in Chinatown, and "the presidential box," for their preferred seats at the BAM Cinema; common were "study dates" at Peter's place, when Will would catch up on work reading with his Kindle, while Peter cooked dinner; the repetition of such habits cementing a common history that develops between two people, making the normal of life exhilarating, where it had previously only been tolerable. Suddenly, again, Peter felt he could grasp the full nature of reality in shared moments that would otherwise have gone unregistered: a child's delight in the fluttering of a pigeon he's charged on the sidewalk; the elegance of a lady with long white locks flashing by in the street on a vintage Schwinn; the drama of mid-afternoon shadows from sills and lintels in a row of brownstones on West Fourth

Street, which runs diagonal to Manhattan's grid and thus affords, because of the angle, a different way for light to fall on city architecture.

They came upon the latter one Sunday afternoon when they were walking to a restaurant for a late brunch. They turned a corner onto West Fourth and *boom*. Kindred spirits paused to look, remark, triangulate the sun. And for Peter this kind of thing wasn't just a nice change from the soul-deadening stretch of generic clock-ticking that had filled the days since Nick; it was a reentry into the life of full agency that he'd always desired from the world, since as far back as he could remember, as the baby in a highchair, eager for the thrill of feeding himself; the toddler on a preschool morning, determined to dress himself without Mommy's help; the young adolescent, lying facedown in the grass in the backyard, arms outstretched, desperate to embrace the world's splendor. And the world had given him plenty of splendor, in spurts, over the previous six decades, though each time the cause was an actual person there had been challenges—as there were this time. For one thing, kindred didn't mean "identical." Will had his own mind and didn't necessarily aim to assimilate Peter's. Their first argument, which was perhaps to be expected at this new stage of their friendship, was about a performance they'd recently seen.

It blew up at a party that Peter threw at his place—a big "men thing," as he called it, for friends of a gay writer around his age, who was visiting from out of town and with whom Peter had originally planned only to have a drink. The plan grew into cocktails for sixty, on the second Sunday of daylight savings time—a party also to welcome "the return of the Sun" (said the invitation), with fancy hors d'oeuvres and a staff of three, much more elaborate than the get-together at Peter's that Will had bartended, months before.

After working from home that day, Peter closed his laptop around three and texted Will, as he began to prepare himself for the party.

I can't see myself, wrote Peter.

Use my eyes, wrote Will.

They're too small.

Peter giggled as he threw off his gym clothes and stepped into the shower. The lines were a bit of conspicuously banal dialogue from the performance they'd seen and hooted over, a few nights before.

Peter looked forward to afternoon showers at home, at that time of year, because the sun was again high enough to shaft through the bathroom window and directly onto the shower's white tile walls, making them glow pearlescently through billowing clouds of steam—and, if you looked carefully in that light, you could see clouds casting fleeting, almost imperceptible shadows on other clouds. For Peter, showering midday like that was more than just hygiene; it was therapy—and it was amplified that day by the earthy, medicinal scent of an expensive bar of soap he unwrapped, from a venerable Florentine *antica farmacia* employing a 500-year-old botanical formula originally meant to be "sanitory." Steamy clouds buoyed a grassy, resinous freshness that evoked the healing science of a gentler age. Was it still a science that worked? Peter loofahed his body, exfoliated his face with some costly grit. In a way, the thing he was holding out for, with Will, was therapeutic. Love would be the single most healing thing that could happen in his life—that is, a relationship that included loving sex. Too long, after Nick, he had sex with people he didn't care about, just because it was easy. Sex on the side of something like Harold or Nick was recreational; not on the side of anything, it felt empty. So he had stopped prowling craigslist and Manhunt, though abstinence was far from a satisfactory situation. Too long he'd nursed crushes on younger men he knew could have turned into proper lovers, given the chance—but the chance never happened. Again, sometimes, he felt like he was back in high school, jerking off to the fantasy of guys he liked, with scarcely the prospect of a real sexual experience with any of them.

For a moment, in the shower, since his cock felt full and heavy, he considered jerking off, thinking about Will—something he'd never done. Then he decided against it.

The help arrived at five.

"You can do drinks from here," Peter told the bartender, showing him the kitchen. To the others he gave instructions about clearing glassware, answering the door, passing hors d'oeuvres. Soon they had placed votive candles around the apartment and in the garden, and deployed the food and flowers that had been delivered earlier in the day. Peter had splurged on crab and caviar, since the McCaw account now permitted such extravagance—as it did the new custom-made palomino shoes he was wearing with a pair of old Levi's and a white button-down shirt, untucked. He had yet to find the courage to wear the shoes in public.

When the guests started arriving, around six-thirty, the first cycle of the musical program Peter had devised for the evening, with classic jazz, had already given way to the second: downbeat deep-house stuff like alexkid and De-Phazz—music that was a little composed, a little found, a little designed; more organic than technological, despite its genesis on a computer. One of the servers, a cute guy with a blond crew cut and an Australian accent, commended Peter on the music. Gratified, Peter thanked the guy warmly. He knew the guest of honor might prefer Sarah Vaughan, but he wanted to follow through on a feeling he'd had all day not only about the arrival of spring—the door to the garden was open and the early evening was unusually warm—but *this* spring, when it seemed like something unprecedentedly marvelous might happen. Maybe it was already happening! China was building gleaming new cities every day! Civilizations and boyfriends were always possible! For Peter, laptop music offered the truest, if still hazy, views of the exciting Present, by showing it as a lush, if underappreciated, Past, from the point of view of some wise and opulent Future. It reminded us where we were in history and where we weren't.

Friends arrived and Peter greeted them warmly, bringing them in to meet other friends, then returning to the door. Will arrived with Luz and, after grabbing kisses and drinks, scooted into the garden. By seven both the apartment and garden were jammed, producing an amiable din that rendered the music practically inaudible. The party was a hit! And when Peter saw that food and drink service was flowing smoothly, he began to relax. After what he decided were the last of the introductions, he took a club soda and sidled over to Tyler.

"These all-gay things are as hard for me to host as they are to attend," he confided.

"What do you mean?" said Tyler. "There are plenty of women."

"Plenty?"

"Some."

"You know what I mean. It requires a whole other kind of thought."

"I thought the party was about springing forward or something."

"Ty, did you know that daylight savings was invented by this entomologist from New Zealand . . . ?"

"Stop," commanded Tyler, with a finger to Peter's lips.

Peter chuckled and took Tyler's hand and kissed it.

"Have you talked to Will at all?" said Peter.

"A little," said Tyler. "I *love* Luz."

"She's great, isn't she?"

"Can I have one of those?"

People went on chattering, drinking, laughing. If the evening air was a little cooler than ideal, no one seemed to mind. As daylight waned, and the votives and houselights took over, the party assumed a warm glow.

Peter talked with the guest of honor for a while, standing on the porch overlooking the garden, and as he did so he happened to catch Will, near one of the hydrangea bushes, sharing what looked like a sparkling word with the Australian waiter, who was circulating with a wine bottle. *No biggie,* thought Peter.

"Nice party," said Will, a few moments later, when Peter joined him.

"I've been trying to get over here for twenty minutes," said Peter.

"Fun crowd."

"Yeah."

"And what are we wearing on our feet today?"

"Oh—Belgian Shoes."

"New?"

"Yeah, I guess."

"You guess?"

"They're new," said Peter.

"I thought you hated that stuff," said Will.

"Love-hate, darling."

It was party talk and meant lightly, so Peter thought better of asking Will to define "that stuff." Moreover, he suspected Will had an issue with all the money Peter had been spending recently. The week before, Will had declined Peter's invitation to dine at the city's best Japanese restaurant, claiming a work deadline but also calling the price of a meal there "obscene"—which struck Peter as odd, since Will had never shown an aversion to life's finer things before. Quite the opposite. When Peter reminded him that he could afford it, Will responded with mock-society-lady breeziness that felt barbed: "How nice *for* you."

It was around eight-thirty when Peter found himself standing with Will and Luz near the bar.

"And then she says, 'Use my eyes,' " said Will. He was describing the performance he and Peter had seen.

"And the guy goes, 'They're too small,' " said Peter. They all laughed.

"It was ludicrous," said Will.

"Crazy," said Peter. "But, you know . . . there was kind of a point to the thing."

"Yeah," said Will, "a point in the middle of such intensely un-watchable bullshit that it hardly mattered."

"That bad?" giggled Luz.

"Worse," roared Will. He and Luz laughed.

"Really?" said Peter.

"It keeps *haunting* me," said Will.

"But wait, c'mon," said Peter. "Sure, it was stupid—we made fun—but there was something a little valid about it. . . ."

"Valid!" said Will, incredulously. Then, for Luz's benefit, he went on to describe the performance. "It was totally without shape. There was a little dancing, a little text, a little music, and these projections on the walls of the set—you know, live shots of the street outside and a loop of waves, lapping the shore—all sort of thrown together in a sludge that just kept sludging along, until it stopped."

Luz giggled and Peter stood fixed in a smile.

"It was one of these pieces that's all about the process that created it," continued Will. "There was this greasy straight guy with no shirt and bad tattoos, who kept roaming around, screaming with his guitar; and these two girls who I think were supposed to be into him, but then they were rolling around with each other, on the floor. And the set, where they had obviously been hanging out for a week—which I'm sure someone called a 'residency'—was done up like some random, off-campus crib, with a ratty old sofa and empty beer cans strewn all over, pizza boxes. . . ."

"Ooof," said Luz.

"And on the sidelines, these art-school guys on laptops, presumably controlling the lighting and projections. Technicians of the simulacrum!"

"Wow," said Peter. "Detailed."

Will nodded cheerfully.

"That's right. I'm a magazine editor," he said.

"What about the performers?" said Luz. "Sometimes watching one person can get you through."

"It was just the opposite!" answered Will, before Peter, who was about to say something, could begin. "You didn't know where to look! It was this frenzy of narcissism and misogyny. At one point the greasy guy says he's gonna sing a song about 'boobies'; then he plunks down on the sofa with his guitar and sings a song called 'Booby Trap.'"

"Charming," said Luz.

"It had . . . energy," said Peter.

"It did not. It had *fake* energy," said Will. "It was fake-cool."

"But that guy is pretty well known. . . ."

"So what?"

"He's important, Will."

"I can't believe you fell for that stuff."

Luz chose that moment to duck away to the bathroom.

"You're just not used to being contradicted," laughed Will.

"I was trying to be open to the performance," said Peter.

"So was I. Then I had to sit through it."

"I didn't know you hated it so much."

"I didn't know I had to like something just because you do."

"You don't. But it *is* my job to be open to new things."

"Oh, and it's not mine?"

"I only meant . . ."

"My father used to say that a mind can be so open, it's empty."

"Will!?"

Peter must have looked injured.

"Sorry," said Will. "I just feel that sometimes people can be needlessly tolerant of bullshit."

"People?"

Just then, the Australian waiter passed. Will let him top up his glass, while Peter declined another club soda. There was definitely a smile between the waiter and Will.

"Speaking of tolerance," said Peter.

"You know my heart is always with the worker," said Will.

"He thinks you're cute."

"I *am* cute."

"He wants you, darling."

"He wants an article. He's a singer-songwriter—he wants to give me a CD."

" 'K, now who's naïve?"

"It's OK if someone's interested in me for superficial reasons— someone who doesn't know me *in depth,* the way you do."

"Are you making fun of me?"

"No. But I remember that the first time we met, you didn't even notice me."

"What do you mean? When?"

"The first time you ever saw me?"

Peter had to think for a second.

"At Jonathan's?"

"Yes," said Will.

"We didn't *meet.* . . ."

"Exactly."

"I was probably feeling very shy that night."

"Shy!"

"What difference does it make?"

"Some people are nice to bartenders and waiters."

"Will, the guy was flirting."

"So? It's a party!"

"There's more to life than that."

"I see. That's why you're serving crab and champagne"—Will gestured across the room—"and there's a two-hundred-dollar flower arrangement in the bathroom." He was whispering loudly enough for some of the other guests to look in their direction. Peter pulled him into the bedroom.

"Is that what this is about, money?" said Peter.

"Look, it's no big deal," said Will.

"Tell me, since you have an issue."

"Never mind."

"You brought it up."

"I dunno. Money, display, self-indulgence..."

"I'm a bad person because I'm indulging myself?"

"Peter..."

"I'm a bad person because I'm spending money that I've earned, to give my friends a good time?"

"Peter..."

"Look, I'm just trying to live my life here, Will. I'm a gay man trying to make it up as I go along. I do my work; maybe I have a little success. I'm trying to figure out how to be sixty, which I've never had to do before. Christ! You know, I can't walk down Eighth Avenue and turn heads, and let *that* be the thing that makes me feel like I'm living life at its pinnacle."

Will said nothing, and Peter realized his friend looked stung.

"What I mean is...," said Peter.

"I know what you mean," said Will.

They walked over to the window, to be farther away from the bedroom door and the rest of the guests. On the sidewalk outside, a stroller mom and her payload were parked near the railing in front of the house. The woman was trying to carry on a cell phone conversation, while trying halfheartedly to quiet her squawky child.

"Sometimes it feels...like you think you have everything worked out," said Will, quietly. "It can be a little daunting."

"But I *don't* have everything worked out," said Peter. "I don't have anything worked out."

"C'mon, you do, some things: this house, the way you dress, the way you ingest and process culture. Your approach to living in 'the world of tomorrow'...."

"What are you talking about?"

"First, it was all about sex and love, with your generation. Now it's about work and personal fulfillment."

"So you're objecting not to me, but to my generation?"

"You think you know what it's all about. And, I dunno, maybe you do...."

"Will, I've had two long-term relationships. Both ended sadly. I've seen all my friends die of AIDS—starving hysterical naked. I know what some things are about. On the other hand, my job and the fucking world I live in didn't even exist when I was born. We're all a little certain and a little uncertain at the same time."

Will was nodding, but he was plainly unconvinced.

"Am I...putting some kind of pressure on you?" continued Peter. "Because if I am, I don't mean to. I try to be tolerant, yes. I try to be curious, and that's very important to me. But I'm trying not to be the old guy here, all bound up in standards and requirements and vast experience. I just want to share some enthusiasm. I like you, Will—I'm just trying to be a good friend."

"I know, I know," said Will. "Look, I don't want to ruin your party for you. I don't even know what's going on here. You deserve your success. And I value our friendship, I really do."

"Did you say there was another case of white?" It was the bartender, who had knocked, standing at the bedroom door.

"In the hallway, downstairs," said Peter.

"I'm sorry...," began Will.

"No, no," said Peter. "I'm glad you're being honest. Really. We're friends; friends talk honestly. We can continue this some other time."

"OK."

"Figure it out."

"Sure."

"Good."

"Good."

"Hug?"

"Sure."

They hugged for a moment, silently.

"Then you can tell me more about what's wrong with my generation," said Peter.

Will gave Peter a playful swat.

"I'm sorry if I sounded stupid," he said.

"Callow? Foolish? Immature?" said Peter. "Not at all."

Will made a face and they both stepped back into the living room.

Later, while saying good night, Peter's writer friend gushed about what a great time he'd had and thanked Peter profusely for introducing him to a publisher who'd said nice things about his work. *Well, at least that worked out,* thought Peter. Will and Luz toddled off after Luz probed gently to make sure things were OK between the two men. Tyler bolted for another party. By eleven everyone was gone, including the help, who had left the place spotless. Having one more person than you think you need is the key to entertaining, Peter decided—though with so little evidence of the roaring party that had just taken place, the moment felt a little sad, even futile.

He sat down at the desk and, finding no thank-you e-mails or Facebook pictures of the party—it was too early—started looking through old pictures of himself that he'd posted months before, at Tyler's suggestion, in a folder on his Facebook page entitled "Dim Prehistory." "People wanna see where you came from," said Tyler, and Peter had come to find it useful in the same way—to trace his progress as a human being at a glance, from the *Lone Ranger* fan of 1957 to the high school nerd of 1968, the college radical of 1971, the gay pride activist of 1976 . . . *God, was my face ever that skinny? And that hair—such a perfectly smooth sheet. The amount of work that took every day!* . . . To the young professional of 1986, the advertising star of 1998 . . .

All the styles, and moments, and propositions about life! Peter was contemplating a shot of himself in a hard hat, taken while the atrium was under construction—the empire builder in the new millennium—when a text from Will arrived.

Had a great time. So did Luz. Thx!! Talk tomorrow? We still have to plan our trip!! They had plans to rent a car on the following weekend and drive up to visit Jonathan in Hudson.

He shook his head and took another sip of vodka. He was relieved. The tone of the message was so genial, conciliatory. He'd been hoping he wouldn't have to do the trip alone. Will was such a reasonable soul, underneath the pretty-boy jazz, Peter thought. And his issues, whatever they were, were obviously no less important than Peter's own, which Peter never addressed directly and, to be fair, didn't fully understand, either.

Realizing he could use some fresh air, Peter closed his laptop, grabbed a sweater, and stepped into the garden. He installed himself on the swinging bench at the back of the garden, overlooking the patio, and took a deep breath of the cool evening air, which was fragrant with a rich earthiness. Few of the neighbors' lights were on—and many of those windows would soon be obscured by leaves from trees just now coming to life again. Except for the soft rasping of the bench as it rocked and the ambient *shhusshh* of traffic on the Brooklyn-Queens Expressway, three blocks away, at the edge of the Heights, the night was quiet. The only other sound was the low grind of someone's air conditioner, two or three houses away—probably set on "vent," Peter thought; or had the party been so loud that the neighbor turned on the machine to cover the noise?

OK, they'd had a little scuffle and now it was behind them. The way they had dealt with it was probably more important than whatever the scuffle had been about. Reviewing his mental tapes, Peter thought he had been honest, clear, kind, and understanding. He thought Will had been, too. Both had maintained their humor and sense of respect.

If he were really in a snit he wouldn't have texted.

Peter relaxed back into the bench and took a sip of his drink. By the time he and Will were cohosting summer parties in the garden, their little scuffle would be forgotten.

And tomorrow night the dark will come even later.

What was daylight savings, anyway, but the ritual observance of a cosmic cycle embedded in human life? The practice presented itself as something modern, meaning commercial—because that's the way America did things: It increased farming yields, extended retail hours—yet deep down it was more spiritual, even religious. At least, that was the way Peter savored his excitement about yet another season of warmth and garden parties to come—though the social option was relatively new for him. He and Harold, when they first moved in and before the patio was built and the dogwood and hydrangeas were planted, used to host little pizza-and-beer parties out there for friends, using the landlady's daughter's dilapidated playhouse that was then out there for a buffet. Those parties were nice but always felt a little forced—Harold was the one who insisted on making use of the "backyard," as he called it. Then, over the years, the garden revealed itself as something more than a social opportunity. For Peter it became sacramental—and worth the trouble of dragging canapés and concelebrants into it. If only Harold could have lived to see it!

Peter smiled. *For some, an understanding like this only comes with age.*

It had only been five months since he'd said good-bye to the sun, the previous October, when, in a last grab at the year's outdoor living, he sat out in the garden one afternoon, bundled up in a jacket, scarf, sunglasses, and hat, trying to work. He did mostly calls when he worked in the garden, since daylight made it hard to see his computer screen; and he remembered calling Jonathan on that day to ask for the number of the guy who'd bartended at his lovely housewarming. It was funny to think about how much had happened in five months. Leaves were falling, then. Now, Peter could smell them returning.

And this eternal return of newness was as nice as ever, he thought, but also—unexpectedly—nice in a new way. There was something extra that Peter now found accreted around his experience of spring, something new in his enjoyment of both the season and the idea of it: something weird but delicious that he could describe to Tyler, when they spoke of it briefly, at the party, only as "the weight of springs." If life was sweet once more at this time of year, the sweetness itself was somehow weightier than when Peter was twenty. Perhaps this was always true of an individual, year after year; but it was beginning to register more clearly for Peter, now that there were fewer springs to detonate for him than had already detonated. Back in his twenties, Peter felt each spring as a little dose of a scintillating possibility—new pleasures to come, new poems to read. Now, that part of spring's eternity felt largely expired, enshrined in the memory of decades of scintillation and poetry, and yet—*something* was still there, germinating, pushing up from under the weight of memory itself. And though this feeling was scary and undescribed in lines about "daisies pied and violets blue," it was also thrilling.

I can't see myself. Use my eyes. They're too small.

Risible, yes. And also maybe not. Another sip of vodka.

He remembered adapting willingly to all stages of Harold's decline, and finding new kinds of life and fullness in each one. Then

Harold was gone and nothing more seemed possible, at all, ever. And yet . . .

The air-conditioner grinding had stopped. It suddenly felt colder. Peter got up to go in. From outside, across the garden, the interior of the house looked like a promised land of warmth— lamps, books, artwork, furniture, stuff collected over what was now almost a lifetime. Inside, he shut the door and adjusted the blinds, then fluffed the pillows on the daybed and put them back in the arrangement he liked. The help hadn't got that just right. A group of Tyler's friends had been sitting there for practically the whole party. Peter wondered if Tyler, who knew, mentioned that someone had died on that very spot.

Harold and he hadn't actually shared death, Peter knew—only what led up to it. Some things can't be shared. Of course there were things that Peter and Will would never be able to share—and what of it? Sharing everything implied certainty about what everything *was,* yet life was the ultimate contingency—a terrain whose features looked fixed until the light source changed.

Our issues are not generational at all—they're existential! Peter smirked. *Oh, won't that be fun to discuss!*

It was definitely time for another round of therapy, he thought. This was something he'd been considering for a while. The round of couples therapy he'd done with Nick, lasting three years, had done more than allow them to maintain some civility during and after the breakup. It had allowed Peter to see that the major themes of his life—which he'd examined during past rounds of therapy: a short one in high school, another in college, a long one that started just after he arrived in New York—were still evolving. Suddenly, he was curious: Am I a success as a human being, after working on myself for six decades? What's going on with me and money? Does my mother still matter?

Golly, what's therapy for old people like, anyway?

CHAPTER 15

"Hiya, babe," chirped Will, as he emerged from his magazine's building, around one.

Luz was perched, along with several other people, mostly tourists and shoppers, just outside the door, on the ledge formed by the thick wooden frame of the plate-glass window of the luxury-brand shop that occupied the building's ground floor. With a view into the shop past thirty faceless mannequins lined up in neat ranks, like soldiers in summer dresses, their heads all inclined leftward, the window commanded much of the appeal—and some of the import—of the art that used to hang in the gallery that occupied the same space for decades, before SoHo became SoHo-land. That stretch of Broadway, from Houston down to Canal, was now as crowded with shoppers as Madison or Fifth, though the crowd there felt more hungrily hip than uptown, and the collective mood that April day was particularly ravenous, as it was the first time that season when a bright, warm day had unleashed everyone's appetite for new clothes.

"Hey, sweetie," said Luz, finishing up a text message and rising. They shared a little kiss.

"Amazing, eh?" said Will. He took stock of the street, shielding his eyes from glare with his palm, though he was already wearing a pair of wraparound sunglasses, which he'd donned in the elevator.

"Gorgeous. People are nuts," said Luz.

Will unwrapped the little scarf he'd arranged around his neck before leaving the office and undid the top buttons of his jacket—a crisply silhouetted, black military number he'd been given by a stylist after a shoot.

"Do I need this?" he said.

"It's cooler than you think," said Luz.

"OK."

"See how you feel. We're walking, right?"

"The dumpling place."

"If that's OK with you."

"Baby, I'm all about a dumpling," said Will, and they began walking southward, as SoHo's grandest flight of nineteenth-century commercial-palatial façades canyoned before them—though in his eagerness to stay close by Luz's side Will inadvertently jostled a guy in a gray suit, talking on his cell phone, planted in the middle of the sidewalk. The man accepted Will's apology wordlessly, while continuing to converse haltingly in German. The roar of Broadway traffic made it difficult both to hear and be heard.

"I'm starving!" yelled Luz, veering right and squeezing between a vendor's cart and a family of tourists clumped in front of it. She half glanced back at Will, who was following.

"What?" he said, trying not to bump into more people.

"I said, 'I'm starving,'" said Luz, when they were near each other again. Staying close meant negotiating the flow of bodies rushing at them—a flow made distinctly less laminar by the effects of glare and the protective eyewear everyone was wearing. A herd of blond boys pressed past in shorts and flip-flops, with matching backpacks. A Swedish high school trip, Will guessed.

"Springtime in the Big Apple!" said Luz. "Ya gotta love it."

"What? Yeah . . . and it's a first for both of us, isn't it?"

"I know! Last spring . . . we were both in L.A., and you don't really feel . . . the seasons. . . ." She was piloting while talking.

"I'll take a day like this—it changes everything!" shouted Will. "It's like, you can see how nice the city is. . . ."

"What?" squawked Luz. The current had squeezed her over a few feet.

Will caught her eye.

"Let's ...," he said, indicating the next left. Arm in arm, they steered each other onto Spring Street, where the traffic would be lighter and the noise lower. Then they'd head down Lafayette.

"So your meeting ...," said Luz, breathlessly.

"Yeah, it was great! So I met with Colin, who now loves me, and Herman got raked over the coals, because he let my story get cut...."

"The singer from Senegal?"

"Yeah—though that was kinda my fault, too...."

Just then, a blue-and-white police car turned into Spring Street and sped by, its siren wailing. Then more speeding sirens: a second blue-and-white, followed by a dark, unmarked sedan. Will sighed theatrically.

"I'll tell you over lunch," he said.

And adding to the hellishness of Spring Street that day were two or three idling trucks opposite Balthazar, double-parked for deliveries and roaring—though for a tanned, older woman with flaming orange hair, sitting in a parked limo, it was not hell but picnic time. The limo's rear door was open and the woman, seated half out of the car, in a flouncy peasant skirt somewhat too youngish for her, her sandaled feet planted on the sidewalk, was peeling an orange and breaking it into sections. As she fed herself with exaggerated finesse, she barked intermittently in Portuguese at her driver, who was standing nearby, translating into English into his cell phone. Because the limo door was open, a deliveryman needing to navigate around it, at the curb, had to wait for a moment with his bulkily loaded hand truck while some people passed by, before he pushed on. The lady remained oblivious, her massive gold cuff glinting in the sunlight.

"You know what I'm seeing a lot of?" said Luz, after they'd passed. "Fake genteel."

"Sister! How about no genteel?"

"Ya know? They're rich—fine. They come here to shop—fine. But they're completely absorbed in themselves, and they're fucking in the way."

"Yes! Say it!"

"And the women are the worst," continued Luz. "They have this vacant, amused look on their face, like 'I only brake for Chanel. Doesn't everybody?'"

Will hooted.

"What's up with that?" said Luz.

"I dunno," said Will. "Pride in the distance you've put between yourself and your peasant roots? Pride in living the international luxury-brand lifestyle?"

Luz laughed.

"We're in a mood," she said.

"We're hungry," said Will.

Tucked just below Canal Street on Lafayette, between a sandwich joint and a restaurant supply store, Excellent Dumpling House was a one-story building not much larger than Will's bedroom suite in the house he grew up in, in Santa Barbara. The place wasn't fancy, but Will loved the good food and cheap prices, as did a zillion other people; and indeed, when he and Luz arrived, the place was hopping. Outside, in front of a window neoned with a steaming bowl and chopsticks, one of the restaurant's delivery guys was locking up his bike to a rack, while another guy, laden with bulky white plastic bags, was unlocking his. Inside, customers jammed the tiny reception area, having given their names to the hostess and resigned themselves to a wait—which was always shorter than expected, since the pace of both the serving and the eating at Excellent Dumpling House was so very brisk.

Tables for four lined the periphery of the room, while three communal tables for eight occupied the middle. In the narrow squeeze between tables a team of servers was constantly in motion, delivering food to tables, clearing plates, while customers being seated maneuvered gingerly past those trying to exit. The room was always full at that time of day, and the fluorescent-bright décor seemed to amplify the commotion: a band of mirrors along three walls, above panels of white Formica wainscoting; a series of luridly colored photos of dumpling platters; several China-red plaques embossed in gold foil with some manner of sinographic inscription. Near the cashier's desk, a double-wide, glass-doored, Coke-red refrigerator held, along with soda, unmarked carafes of white wine, desserts pre-packaged in clear plastic take-out containers, and tap water in plastic pitchers so well used that their surfaces had gone from shiny to matte.

Within five minutes, Luz and Will had accepted a pair of seats at one of the communal tables. Within seven, they had been given their water, tea, tableware, and a menu full of pictures; and within fifteen, two of the plates they'd ordered had arrived: house special scallion pancakes and steamed, juicy little pork dumplings.

"I adore this place," said Will. "I come here with Peter all the time."

"You and your boyfriend?" said Luz.

"Not really."

"Really."

"We're like . . . best friends."

"You've been saying that for weeks."

"Uh-huh."

"While you're going out with him and talking about him all the time. . . ."

"And your point is?"

"Fucker."

Will giggled.

"OK, so meeting," said Luz, shifting her chair and elbow so as not to be crowded by a large man to her right. The man glanced in her direction reflexively, but remained focused on his dumplings.

"You ready?" said Will. *"I have a cover story!"* He boomed the news in an Oprah voice.

"No way—dude, that's awesome!" said Luz. They high-fived.

"September issue. The singer I was telling you about—Xiomara."

"Get out!"

"Sixteen pages."

"Fuck me. That's huge, right?"

"Huge."

As Will related the story, his relish was obvious. The meeting had taken place that morning, in the spacious corner office that Colin, the editor in chief, inhabited when he was in town, which was rarely. At other times the office—which was built out in an elaborate and expensive faux-industrial style, like the rest of the floor, with a heavy steel-and-glass-paneled door and beautifully framed transom windows onto adjacent offices—looked like a gift-ware showroom, stuffed with the gaily wrapped packages, floral arrangements, and other tribute that arrived for the editor daily. In the corner, near a window, a large, antique worktable that served as a desk was laden with piles of manuscripts and stacks of new, oversized books on art, fashion, and photography. On the walls hung several contemporary paintings—a Condo, a Marden, and another one by an artist whose name Will could never remember, from the private collection of the publisher, who also owned an art magazine that was housed on the same floor. A wall of books and back issues included a shelf of citations and awards, the latter including the American Society of Magazine Editors' "Ellie" award, in the form of an elephant-shaped stabile designed by sculptor Alexander Calder. The Ellie had been won for general excellence in its category a few years earlier, after the publisher had fired the editor in chief's predecessor and brought in Colin to update the magazine.

Will, whose office was a few feet away, had heard Colin arrive on the floor, hours before. He was used to the commotion Colin's presence caused, even when the editor was working behind closed doors. People constantly streamed in to see him from the art department and publisher's office; photographers dropped by, who had been assigned projects for the magazine or wanted one; celebrity actors and musicians appeared, to be shown into the inner sanctum with quiet ceremony by Colin's unnaturally handsome assistant, Sebastian. That morning, though, things had been quiet, when Sebastian summoned Will.

Will knocked on the door and was waved in. He found the editor in chief installed in a cozy seating area with Herman, the managing editor, who seemed far less pit bull-y, even deferential, that day. Open before them on a low table was the magazine's current issue, containing Will's piece on Assetou.

"There you are. Join us," said Colin. He was dressed expensively in a manner once known as casual, before people started confusing sloppiness with nonchalance. On his wrist were two watches—a gold one that Will knew was a gift from a luxury brand advertiser, and a cheap plastic one that the editor kept set to L.A. time.

"Herman and I have been talking about the fact that this story should have been longer."

"OK," said Will, settling into a chair.

"That's right," said Herman.

"You did a great job, Will," said Colin, "but why on earth did we ever cut the thing so drastically?"

"Thank you," said Will. Herman, looking chastened, kept his eyes on the magazine on the table and said nothing.

"And so what did we lose?" said Colin.

"When we cut it? Detail," said Will, without missing a beat. "Nuance—and, you know, the punch that comes with that."

Herman nodded weakly.

"We talked for two hours, the first time we met," continued Will. "We had a great conversation. She's incredibly well read, incredibly curious—she knows tons about art and classical music, so yeah. . . ."

"You talked to her more than once?" said Colin.

"We did the main interview here—the thing we set up with the publicist—but then she and I had lunch together, a few days after that. I don't even think the publicist knew. She asked me about cool places in New York. I told her I knew where to get some good *cheb-ou-jen*—that Senegalese rice-and-fish thing. . . ."

"Mm-hmm."

"And we're still in contact," said Will. "I just went to this big thing at her friend's place, the other night, a listening party. . . ."

"Good for you," said Colin. "And that's what it means to be an editor, right?" The editor in chief picked up the magazine and looked at the portrait he had commissioned for the story: a beautiful girl in profile, smiling, a graceful hand alight at her sternum, with her head raised heavenward but eyes closed, as if she were savoring the moment privately or perhaps giving thanks. "Well, everybody's talking about her and the album," he continued, "so it's great that we have her, and the issue is on the stands. But, gentlemen, we should have put a few more chips on this square—ya know?"

"Well, I . . . ," started Will.

"We should have tried harder to keep those pages," said Herman, dutifully.

"It was planned at two, right?" said Colin.

"Four," said Will. "That was what I thought, when I first brought it up."

"We said four at first," said Herman, "and then it was two, for months. . . ."

"And then one," said Colin.

"We cut it right after you came back from London, remember?" said Herman. "We needed room for . . ."

"Listen," said Colin, "I'm not blaming anyone. It's a process. There's always the next issue. I just want us to be smart when we're assigning pages. I want us to really support the ideas we believe in. That's what our job is—to fight for our ideas."

The latter was directed at Will, and would have been interpreted by anyone who heard it as a gilt-edged validation—the award of more heft to wield in future editorial meetings, which would soon result in more pages, more access to people and places.

"Got it," said Herman.

"I'm seeing this girl tonight, I'm told," said Colin.

"At the Julian dinner?" asked Herman.

Colin nodded yes, but didn't look at him.

"And I feel like I'm walking in there knowing less about her than I'd like to know," he continued, tossing the magazine back on the table. "Not a feeling I like."

"OK, well, just so you know: She's just as serious about her art as she is about her music," said Will.

"Really? Those sculptures—they're good?"

"They're *assemblages,* made of found objects, and yes, they're amazing. She's shown them in Paris and London. Her father teaches art in Dakar."

"Interesting."

"We had to cut all this stuff she had about the way light changes everything we look at, even as the things themselves remain the same. . . ."

"Huh."

"All about these supposedly hidden colors that you're still subliminally aware of. . . ."

"She said that—'hidden colors'?"

"Well, no, that's *my* phrase—a phrase I used—but that's what we were talking about."

"Do you still have the original?" asked Colin.

"Interview? Sure, on my computer," said Will.

"Send it to me."

"OK."

"Your instincts are sharp, Will. Keep it up."

Colin stood up, as did Will and Herman.

"Meanwhile," said the editor, "I want to bump up your Xiomara story. We just made it the cover."

"Really?" said Will. Xiomara was a Spanish singer and guitarist whom he had proposed for a feature. She was beautiful and young, and had unexpectedly just won a Grammy.

"Yup," said Colin. "Nicole isn't working out. Besides, I'm not hearing good things about the movie." Herman, already at the door, was nodding weakly again.

"Wow," said Will.

"And I'm feeling Xiomara, I'm feeling Latin," said Colin, with an exaggerated gesture that made his watches clink.

"That could be a smart move," exclaimed Will. "She just got a part in that new—"

"Right, I heard—the Judd Apatow," said Colin. "So let's go for it, huh? We'll get Payam or somebody to shoot; you'll do the interview. See where she is. If you need to travel, we'll work it out. But, Will, I want you to come up with a concept, OK? A real direction—and then you and I will talk about it with Payam. Let me see what you're really thinking. Have something for me at the meeting."

"Great," said Herman.

"And, gentlemen," said Colin, "let's protect this one. This is the real deal."

"You're gonna direct the shoot, too?" said Luz. Two more platters of dumplings had arrived and their wedge of communal table was as crowded as it could be.

"Can you believe it?" said Will. "It's major. That's on the level of what Olivier does—the other big cheese."

"Can you do that?" said Luz. "I mean, do you actually know *how* to do it?"

"Of course I do," said Will. "You just have to dream up some concepts, think them through, see what might work."

"Put her in a hotel room, in heels and a bra, crouching next to a steamer trunk, with a naughty bellboy looking on?"

"Better than that," laughed Will. "That's something Olivier would do."

"So is he gonna be happy with this new role of yours, Olivier?"

"Who knows? He stopped by my office, as I was getting ready to step out the door. That's very unlike him. He must have heard it from Herman, like, immediately."

It was the first time the fancy French editor at large had been nice to him, thought Will, as Olivier stood there at the door.

"She is so fabulous," burbled Olivier, in his liquid accent. "This will be such a pleasure for you!" His eyes sparkled and his manner was insinuating. It was the same warmth Will had seen Olivier use at parties with his circle of friends and the celebrities he treated like friends. And though Will didn't particularly like or even respect Olivier, he did feel grateful for the warmth, even if it was fake, because it was so much nicer than the indifference Olivier had thus far shown.

"Yeah, I think so," said Will.

"I saw her just last week at the party and she told me she was going to be spending a few days in Patagonia next month, to recharge her batteries," confided Olivier. Dressed in a royal-blue blazer over a bright green crewneck sweater, with a boldly patterned pocket square, he looked older than Will had thought he was. Had he ever been this close to Olivier's face, ever had a chance to look at it for this many consecutive seconds? The mouth was so beautifully formed, the teeth so perfect, and there were very fine laugh lines at the corners of the eyes.

"The malaria party—I know," said Will. "I was there, too."

"Oh, splendid," laughed Olivier. "Well, I am here to help, if you need." If the editor was surprised or perturbed by the fact that Will was now operating on his turf, he didn't let on.

"Thank you," said Will, whereupon Olivier slipped away with a ladyish *"Ciao-ciao!"*

I bet it'll be kiss-kiss now, when we run into each other at a party, thought Will.

"Do I hear the sound of power shifting?" asked Luz, as she poured them each another cup of tea.

"I guess," said Will.

"So this means you're not gonna take that job that your friend offered you—the guy who has cancer."

"Oh, no, I don't think so."

"I was gonna say."

"I mean, it's sweet of him to try to take care of me like that, but can you imagine? They're trying to see if I can fly down to Argentina and meet up with Xiomara, to go trekking on a glacier. *That*—versus sitting in an office."

A fifth plate they'd ordered impulsively arrived: special crab Rangoon. To make room for it the server placed one remaining shrimp dumpling on the half-empty scallion pancake plate, took the empty dish, and nudged the remaining dishes into a tighter formation—a move noticed by Luz's large neighbor with another glance.

As they tore into the crab, Will told Luz how much his respect for the editor had shot up during the morning's meeting and how happily surprised he was by this development. It was the first time he'd ever been able to talk with Colin at length, one-on-one, and he could see now why the guy was such a superstar. Colin was not only smart and intuitive; he also had backbone. He worked from conviction, and that was inspiring. Herman, on the other hand, though smart and probably good at keeping the magazine's monthly schedule on track, was spineless—clearly unused to thinking for himself or standing up for ideas except for those of his superiors. Olivier was hardly better: the remains of an intellectual enshrined in the urn of a glamorous career. Why did editorial talent not necessarily entail, or derive from, qualities like journalistic valor? That it didn't was one of the biggest shocks that the big city held for a Santa Barbara boy—along with the fact that beautiful people, rich people, and famous people sometimes expect their advantages to dissolve the other criteria by which they might be judged.

"How is the gentleman doing, anyway—the one with cancer?" asked Luz later, after lunch. They were on the sidewalk, in front of

Excellent Dumpling, saying good-bye before running off to their respective afternoons.

"Ugh—not so good," said Will, shaking his head.

"I'm sorry," said Luz.

"He's selling his place—the beautiful apartment. I don't think he's been there even a year. He's moving upstate."

"Really?"

"He has a place there—a town called Hudson—which is beautiful, too, so . . ."

"OK."

"He plans to spend . . . I guess the rest of his time there."

"Do they know how long?"

"Can't be long."

"Jesus."

"That's why Peter and I are going up next week."

"Oh."

"Yeah. And Peter's much more upset about the whole thing than he lets on."

"He's a little uptight emotionally, isn't he?"

"Locked-up, is the way I think about it. And, you know, *I'm* more upset about it than *I* can let on."

"You are?"

"I knew Jonathan before I knew Peter."

"Oh, that's right."

"Remember?"

"One of your *cli*-ents." Luz pronounced the words in her best Locust Valley Lockjaw.

Will smiled wanly. Far above them, his expression was echoed by the wise-ass smirk of the teenage star of a new cable comedy, her face almost filling an entire billboard mounted on the roof of the dumpling restaurant.

"He was the last, before I turned away from my life of sin," he said. "And it's nice that we've been able to stay friends, and that his friend is now my friend, blah-blah-blah. It's just that . . ."

"You still haven't told Peter."

"Nope."

"But you're gonna."

"I guess."

"When the time is right."

"Sure." Not ready to discuss the subject, he was humoring her.

"And when will that be?"

"Oh, my little roomie, I don't know, I don't know," whined Will, gathering her in his arms.

"There's no shame, sweetie," she said.

"I know. And knowing Peter, he may think better of me for it." Will paused. "*May* think."

They gave each other a kiss and then Will released her. Both were wearing shades they had donned upon stepping out of the restaurant.

"Need a cab?" said Will.

"Thanks, sweetie—subway," she said.

The day's slight chill had given way to something almost balmy. All around them, the world looked bright and cheerful—even the piles of recyclables sitting at the curb, bottles and cans bagged in blue plastic, boxes flattened and bundled with packing tape.

"Spring never gets tired, does it?" said Will. "After all these years."

"Uh-*uh*," said Luz.

"Every spring, my mother used to bring *tons* of wisteria into the house, from this grove we have on the ranch. She would open up the windows, and there would be this amazing breeze between the hills and the ocean, and you took a breath and had this feeling that anything could happen—the future would be amazing. Doesn't it feel like that today, Luzzy—I mean, except for the wisteria?"

"So you're coming?"

"Yes."

"Will, too?"

"Of course."

"We're preparing the big guest room."

"We're in the same room?"

"You are and you will deal with it."

"Fine with me."

"I want you guys to become better acquainted."

"I didn't know you cared so much."

"I care about all my friends."

Jonathan was sitting in a wheelchair in the dining room of the Chelsea apartment, speaking on the phone with Peter. Next to him, on a little Shaker table, with his laptop, a legal pad and pen, and a small plastic bottle of diet peach iced tea, with a straw. Aldebar had positioned him and the table near the room's great window, where the light would be pleasant for half an hour or so. Except for Jonathan and his little stand of things, the room was empty. The baronial dining table and its ten chairs were gone; the Hepplewhite sideboard, and mirror, and custom-made rug, gone. There and in the living room, everything was gone—the important antiques carted away to the auction house, along with most of the art, and the upholstered pieces and rugs having been given away. Some of the smaller pieces had been sent up to the house in Hudson, along with the Eliott manuscript, some early-twentieth-century first editions, and most of the other books. As Jonathan spoke, the echo of voices floated across the empty floor from the library, where Aldebar was overseeing a team from Christie's that had arrived to pack up the Asian pots and take them away.

"And how are you?" said Peter.

"Ucch," said Jonathan. His voice was weaker now, and he spoke in shorter sentences, separated by silences that Peter noticed were lengthening—the result of fatigue, perhaps, or heightening discretion as to what merited saying, or some new drift of the mind.

"Working?"

"Oh, yes. Taking apart the house is a kind of work."

"I can imagine. But I meant the film."

"That, too."

Breaking up the home whose creation had taken him and his designers several months to accomplish made an interesting counterpoint for the film he was trying to finish, he told Peter. And it was hard these days to avoid thinking in terms of failure and success, in these and other tasks. Impending death seemed to insist on assessment, he said, but he had never thought about life in those terms before, and he was tired of both thinking that way and trying to avoid it. Suddenly, he couldn't help comparing his accomplishments thus far to what he had always hoped he might do. Without the balance of his lifetime, what could remain? Would his name now wind up in history books? The Oscar nomination that might have come in two years, the Oscar itself in five, the party would have taken place in the very room where he was now sitting—all those hopes were gone. And of course the richest accomplishments to come would have been more personal. Every stick of furniture for the apartment had been selected for the setting of great parties with great friends, and perhaps the appearance of a second great love, and a stage of life when unremitting self-acceptance might have outshone even a golden statuette.

"You've done a ton of important work, Jonathan," said Peter. "It'll certainly stand the test of time."

"Maybe," said Jonathan. "And I do feel proud that I am getting so much into this film, even if it isn't *everything else I have to say*. I mean, I think it's good and honest...." There was a pause, during which neither of them said anything, then Jonathan continued. "At least I am getting to do this house stuff myself. It's giving me a chance to go through everything thoughtfully, reverently, advisedly—how does that go...?"

"Mmm," said Peter.

"The Anglican wedding ceremony," continued Jonathan, rallying a bit more energy. "Anyway, it's odd, because I find myself doing it as carefully as Connor and I are doing the film. Suddenly, everything needs to be done right. God, how many times in the eighties, Petey, did we come across some dead queen's belongings being tossed out into the street by the family? Stuff they didn't even know was valuable: books, clothes, records, invitations to the great parties—historical stuff, remember? Once—I think it was on Bank Street—we literally saw treasure being thrown out the window: this pile of glittery headdresses, like from the Peking Opera. Roberto shouted up, 'Stop! We'll come up and take it away!' A collection some queen had been accumulating for years...."

Peter said nothing.

"I dunno. I've had a good life. I've had some love. I can't complain. I certainly don't feel like a failure, only... I think I *shall* fail to stick around for the holidays this year...."

Silence. Then, from the other end of the line, a sound that Jonathan realized was sobbing.

"Peter, are you crying? I'm sorry."

"No, no . . ."

"Poor thing! I'm so sorry. I didn't mean to get you upset."

"It's OK, Jon, really. Anything you wanna talk about or not talk about is fine with me."

"Well, thank you, darling, but please."

"And here I am, in the office," said Peter, blowing his nose.

"Look, maybe we can cry our brains out some other time, OK? I just don't know if I'm up to it today."

"Sure, sure."

"Maybe this weekend," said Jonathan slyly, as if he were talking about a jaunt to the bakery in Hudson that sold Peter's favorite cheese sticks.

Peter laughed.

"Won't that be fun," he said.

"And poor Aldebar!" said Jonathan, sounding a bit more like his old self. "He never knows what to expect. No matter what I do, he's such a saint. Let's carry on like normal! Let's break down and go to pieces! You know, Peter, he has experience with the dying." Jonathan whispered the last bit, as if it were a secret revelation.

"Oh?"

"I didn't know this before," said Jonathan. "There are blessings and there are blessings."

Peter wasn't quite sure what this meant, but reassured his friend again that he'd be there for him, no matter what.

"Oh, wait, hold on . . . ," said Jonathan.

Aldebar was showing out the team from Christie's, the head of which stopped to exchange a few words with Jonathan. She was dressed in a gray suit, her white hair in an elegant chignon. "Highly important . . . the market is strong . . . especially the smaller of the black raku bowls. . . ." In the fading light, the woman stood in front of Jonathan's chair, holding his hand gently as they spoke, their handshake turning into something like the clasp between a guru and a devotee in a darshan line.

"I'm back," he said, after the team had left.

"Everything OK?" said Peter.

"You should see this place—it's totally empty. The paint job still looks fresh."

Peter was uptown, sitting at his desk on Madison Avenue, looking absently through his office's window into the atrium, as they spoke. A twenty-foot-tall inflatable sculpture of a rat with a crown commanded the space—the latest in the series of art projects installed there, this one by a well-known street artist from the U.K. On Peter's desk were a mug of tea and some deli napkins from the stash Peter kept in the drawer, several of which had been crumpled in his attempt to contain the bawling.

"That persimmon color is so pretty," he said.

"So you guys are driving?"

"Yup."

"Renting a car?"

"Yeah—and you wanna hear something funny? I had reserved a car—a nice one, like I always do—and then he says how much fun it would be to have a van. 'In case we find some antiques.' "

"I think that's a very smart idea."

"A van, Jonathan! Vans aren't very comfortable."

"*Oh . . .*"

"They're noisy and rattle-y."

"Today's new vans are much nicer."

"Ugh."

"But you agreed?"

"Of course."

"You'll be fine. You sit higher on the road, you know—much better visibility."

"Like you know about driving a van."

"I drove one in college. I delivered pizza."

Peter snorted. "I'll see ya Friday, Jon-o," he said. "We're leaving at eight, so expect us before lunch."

"Drive safely."

As he got off the call, Peter noticed that a text had arrived from McCaw. *Call me.*

Christ. The man had been requiring more and more face time with Peter, even as their teams continued to work together.

I need ten minutes of your time, good friend.

Fuck you, good friend, thought Peter. He had so much on his mind, besides work! And now McCaw, who deserved the certain amount of stroking due any important client, was beginning to make Peter feel captive, with constant consultations about image and messaging. How did the man even have time for this? The conversations were always engaging, but Peter chafed at the evangelical ardor that ran through McCaw like a current, which had begun to feel personal between them—as if McCaw expected the two of them to become best buddies as a result of their work together. And now that McCaw had begun spending more time in New York, with his wife at her family home on the East Side, there had been social invitations—opportunities to get closer that Peter, reluctant to get too chummy with a man his friends still thought dangerous, had so far managed to avoid.

Does 3 work? McCaw wrote. It was a command, and Peter saw that the hour had nearly arrived. Resignedly, he cleared the crumpled napkins from his desk, opened his laptop, and scrolled down his Skype contact list to the M's.

CHAPTER 16

Happily for Peter, the chat only lasted a few minutes. McCaw was always prepared with a precise question and quite disciplined about staying focused on it. This time, it was about his upcoming interview with Katie Couric: What should he wear? They settled on a blue blazer and white shirt, with no tie or little American flag pin, but McCaw had been thinking about a cardigan, for a "relaxed" look. Peter advised against.

"What do you mean, 'It won't play'?" said McCaw.

"I mean it'll baffle people."

"People know what a cardigan is."

"That's not what I'm saying. You don't really wear cardigans, do you?"

"Well . . . no."

"So you're trying to make some kind of *Father Knows Best* statement. But the very attempt would function as a solvent to your credibility. . . ."

"A plain cardigan?"

"Look at the reality. You're strategizing about wearing one; you're consulting me about wearing it. You're probably going to send somebody out to pull a bunch of them for you."

McCaw snorted.

"Hendy, I know you want to sit there with Couric, all cozy and dad-like," said Peter, "but I guarantee you, the *formulation* is what will come across."

"Despite my words?"

"It's a costume. People will see that. TV's funny that way."

"Huh."

"It would create one of those subtle disconnects that people aren't even really aware of. But put two or three of 'em in a row, all acting subliminally, and *bang:* The words don't matter."

"OK, then."

"Tell people what you want them to know, absolutely. But play the subliminals, too. Just as much happens on that level. Ignore it at your peril."

McCaw paused to process the information. Then he said: "Once more, I see why you get the big bucks."

Peter laughed. McCaw had a gift for flattery, even seduction.

"If you ask me," said Peter, "the real question is the shirt. Again, people will know the difference between a seventy-nine-dollar one and a four-hundred-and-fifty-dollar one, on some level. Which brings us back to a question we always have with you, doesn't it: How much do you come across as a rich guy and how do we handle that?"

McCaw was nodding thoughtfully.

"And, of course, the underlying question," continued Peter, "which is, 'Class warfare for America, pro or con?' "

McCaw chuckled.

"Right," he said. "Brilliant, as always, my friend. Well, we'll figure it out." He tilted his head slightly. "Peter, I just don't understand why a guy like you is still single."

"What?" A certain modesty, reflexive for Peter, unbalanced his instinct to remain calm in response to a sudden shock. The remark was decidedly off topic.

"Seriously," said McCaw. "You're intelligent, accomplished, good-looking...."

Good-looking?

"I don't know what to tell you," said Peter.

"My wife is planning a dinner thing for a few weeks from now," said McCaw. "I'll see that she invites you. We must know a couple of people you'd find interesting."

Great. He must mean men; he knew Peter was gay, didn't he? Was he offering to set Peter up—the man who had spoken publically against gay marriage? Yet after the call Peter put the matter out of his mind. There was too much life-and-death shit to worry about.

The weather was glorious on the Friday morning when Peter and Will set out for Hudson. It was one of those dazzling spring days that make the city look freshly built. They were a little late in collecting the van from a garage in the far west Thirties, but within minutes they had zipped through the side streets over to the edge of Manhattan and were heading north along the Henry Hudson Parkway, on the edge of the river.

Peter was driving. Having always served as designated driver on car trips with Harold and Nick, he had made it a point to ask Will if he had a preference, but Will seemed indifferent, so Peter hopped behind the wheel. And the van was indeed more comfortable and much quieter than the hollow tin can that he had been dreading. The steering was responsive, and the interior, especially up front, was padded out in a manner commonly known as "luxurious"—which, if not Maybach-level, was at least nicer than not luxurious. Over the insulated din of highway noise, they began chatting randomly about the fine weather, the light traffic, and the final choices each had made after an exchange the night before, about what to pack.

"I did bring the lighter jacket, after all. But with a sweater, so I can layer."

"Jonathan told me it snowed up there last week."

"No! I brought shorts, in case it gets really warm."

"So did I!"

The rising sun had yet to make it above Manhattan's skyline, but morning brightness was streaming in from the right, revealing faint swipe marks on the dashboard's freshly cleaned, black faux-leather surface—which was at least better than not clean. A stoplight poke into the console compartment between the captain-style front seats turned up no dimes or chewing gum wrappers.

"Nice," said Peter, after Will hooked his iPhone up to the van's sound system and got some music going.

"I made a playlist," said Will.

"Goodie!"

"Nothing thematic. Just fluff."

"I like fluff."

"You *are* fluff."

Will had deployed the console's cup holder for the Starbucks he brought for them, and adjusted the air vents in the middle and on his side. Automatically, he popped open the glove compartment to look inside, then popped it closed.

"Remember maps?" he said.

"It's not the same, is it?" said Peter, meaning Will's iPhone, on which Will had plotted the course with Google Maps. He reached over and gave Will's leg a little rub. "My little OnStar," he said. "I'm so glad we're doing this."

Leaving the city via the route they had planned—the Henry Hudson to the Saw Mill River Parkway, to the Taconic Parkway—involved subliminals, too, Peter mused. One minute, content for a moment after shifting into the correct lane for a gradual veer onto the Saw Mill, he felt a bit of city tension easing away, with a long exhale. The next minute, he was aware of all the tiny bits of information from the surrounding landscape that his brain was processing, that cued the easing: a three- to-five-percent decrease in the number of built right angles in his field of vision; the color green replacing shades of gray and brown at the rate of ten percent per minute (which would level off somewhere in Westchester); the increasing sweetness of the air flowing in through the vents, which contained perhaps a part or two less per million of hydrocarbons than the air behind them, a part or two more per million of pollen. Off to the left, along some rolling hills that had probably been cleared for farmland in the 1700s but were now reforested and had been protected since the planning of this parkway, in the 1920s, a bristle of trunks and branches—maple, beech, and birch, Peter guessed—was just at the point of being enveloped in the leafy foam thickening on top of it.

I suppose we'll still see a little more armature as we go north, he thought, as the hills slid by. *Though Jonathan said his maples were pretty leafy already.*

"Great highway, isn't it?" said Peter. They had been silent for a few minutes. Will seemed to be enjoying the scenery, too.

"Nice," said Will.

"Somehow, it's a lot more art-meets-engineering than the Thruway, ya know?"

"Mmm."

"You get the feeling that someone designed the Taconic with aesthetics in mind—the vistas that come into view as you go around a bend, the landscaping and all that."

"I don't know the Thruway all that well."

"It's all business—all the interstates are. Built in the fifties. You can smell the military thinking behind them. Mobilize the troops! Evacuate the cities! But until the bomb falls, enjoy your scenic motoring!"

Will giggled.

"Very postwar. But damn it, the cars didn't all look alike back then," said Peter, jutting his chin to indicate the highway ahead, which ribboned into the distance for an armada of largely featureless little crates in silver, gray, and white. Theirs was silver, and parallel with them in the other lane were two or three other featureless crates.

"You have no idea how it was in the fifties," said Peter. "Cars were sexy then, not efficient. It was all about aesthetics. People had two-tones! They didn't worry about resale value, if they wanted a car that was, oh, turquoise and salmon. When they unveiled the new models each fall, Will, it was like a fashion show: convertibles on turntables, curtains going up, girls in evening gowns! And season after season, those cars were always more gorgeous than the previous models. It was, I dunno, some kind of parade that charted the progress of modern living. And people paid attention to the details! They really looked at those cars—you know, all the new-and-improved swoops and bulges and what-have-you. They really cared about their makes and models."

"Really."

"Oh, yeah! I mean, every fall you saw things like a fender that had morphed into a jet pod, or a tailfin that had turned into a rocket ship wing; and you were happy for that make. Or, please—a bumper that grew a pair of torpedoes!? That enthralled people! It told a story people wanted to hear."

Will smiled.

"I don't think people even look at sculpture that carefully nowadays," continued Peter. "It was like these cars were their friends and they were growing up. The makes, like Chevy and Ford, were finding their way in postwar America—getting nice clothes and new hairstyles that suited them for the times."

"Do you miss all that?"

"I . . . didn't think I did. But now that I think about it . . ."

They both laughed.

Exits flew by, for little towns, and rest areas, and other highways. Peter kept to the right lane, as he usually did when driving, sticking prudently to not more than nine miles per hour over the speed limit, as his father had taught him to do, to avoid tickets; and Will gently kidded him on this "pokey" style of driving. Conversation skittered from snacks, to cooking, to the ideal kitchen, to the idea of Peter moving back upstate someday.

"Wait till you see this place," said Peter. "It's amazing."

"Can't wait," said Will.

"I gather he's done a lot of work on it, since I saw it last."

"You guys never . . ."

"Me and Jonathan? Nope—uh-uh. Woulda, coulda, but we both had boyfriends, and . . . ya know. We've always admired each other from afar."

"Cool."

"He's the best friend I ever had."

Will nodded.

"Harold and I always thought we would get a country house," said Peter. "We all did. Up here or in Bucks County. Somehow, I stopped looking after he died. Yet I feel I'll end up here, someday."

"When?"

"I dunno. When I'm ready. Some charming old place that's been really well cared for. I keep thinking, 'Who's living in my house right now and are they taking care of the pipes?' "

"Funny."

"Which, of course, is the thing: I have no talent for owning property, the way Jonathan does. That's another part of that fifties programming that I sort of rejected. My father came home from the war, built a split-level, and told me that that's what you do. You get a wife and a mortgage and some kids. And a new car, every two years."

"Did he know you were gay?"

"Oh, yeah. I told him, freshman year."

"Did he accept it?"

"No. It was the first time I ever saw him cry."

"Oh."

"But within ten years, Will—and I take full credit for this—he was cutting out clippings from the newspaper on gay liberation and sending them to his proud gay son."

"He came around."

"He did. The same time he switched from Republican to Democrat."

Miles racked up and traffic thinned out. Quiet moments began to stretch between their exchanges, which made Peter realize how comfortable he and Will had grown together. Silences, drivel, and non sequiturs were OK. Baby talk would probably be next. The question of where they were headed, relationship-wise, had subsided somewhat, even among their friends. Their odd friendship had become a given—though Peter still harbored a hope, which he sometimes excused as a form of instinct, that Will someday might announce himself attracted in more of a boyfriend way. Maybe, thought Peter, Will was working through an "older man thing," or an "other man" thing, or maybe even just a "man" thing. Men of his generation were notoriously backward. Lots of young gay men Peter knew weren't especially comfortable being intimate or defined by the term "gay." But whatever the issue—*if* there was an issue—Peter kept this hope silent and feasted quietly in solace on the little things about Will that were part of the relationship as it was: the Starbucks, the travel music, the lilt of his laugh, the endearing way he plucked his shirt away from his chest reflexively, as if to neaten himself.

Peter glanced over. It was endlessly nice to look at Will. He was in jeans that day, with some Nikes and a pair of gray cropped athletic socks. Those ankles were so sexy! He was also wearing a light blue sweater and a khaki safari jacket. So put-together, yet so modern! The posture was appealingly proper, practically military; the hair looked a bit longer than usual, more luxuriant. Was he letting it grow?

Then Will gave his sweater one of those little plucks, as he shifted in his seat; he noticed Peter noticing and smiled, and went back to watching the scenery. And Peter thought, *What is that about anyway, the plucking?* A way to keep the sweater from wrinkling or clinging too closely to the chest—which Peter knew from Facebook pictures, if nothing else, was beautifully formed and smooth? Was it some sort of tell? Were there issues about the body, or sex, or physicality itself that Will was dealing with or needed to deal with? Issues he might not even be aware of, but which, if ever resolved—say, in therapy—would ready him for love?

"How you doin', Boo-boo?" said Peter. "Whaddya say to a rest stop? I think I have to pee."

"You *think?*"

"I have to pee."

"OK."

Peter had thoughts about the difference between today's rest stops and those golden oldies of his childhood, but decided to keep them to himself as they bought water and chewing gum, marveled at the tacky souvenirs for sale, and made fun of an obese family stuffing their faces with cheese fries in the food court. Then they clucked, as they jumped back in the van, throwing their jackets into the backseat, because it had gotten warmer, over how quickly a rented vehicle like theirs, unknown to them two hours earlier, becomes one's private kingdom—a refuge, one's place to stash things.

They arrived at Jonathan's around eleven-thirty, after texting to say they were close and to ask if they could pick up anything for lunch. Just come, Jonathan said. The house was in the hills above the town of Hudson, on fifteen acres with a stream. It was a shingled, Nantucket-style, four-bedroom "farmhouse" built in 1881, with two massive gables and a smaller third one, boasting elaborate diamond- and square-paned windows, and a low, wraparound porch featuring a generously proportioned roof supported by pairs of sturdy square columns.

"Oh, my," said Will as they made their way up the winding drive.

"Yeah," said Peter. "If you had an issue with my shoes, I can't imagine what you'll make of this."

"I *explained* that, Peter . . . ," said Will, giving Peter's shoulder a playful push.

"Hey, I'm driving here . . . ," Peter laughed.

The place was conspicuously well cared for—the landscaping artfully rustic, the windowpanes glinting as they caught the sun. A tastefully coordinated "new" wing, added in the 1920s, now housed Jonathan's film studio. The wing angled off one side of the house to form, around back, a gracious sort of rear courtyard, sentried by two ancient oaks, which is where Peter and Will arrived after following the drive around past the front façade—though the rear of a Hudson Valley house as well situated as this one was hardly less important than the front. Beyond the courtyard to the west was an expansive lawn, a flagstone terrace with a swimming pool, and a 180-degree view of the Hudson River and the mountains in the distance.

Aldebar was stepping down from the stone terrace to welcome them. He indicated that they should park in a little cul-de-sac screened off by some boxwoods, where several other cars were parked, and came over to help with the bags.

"Good to see you again, my friend," said Peter, as they shook hands and embraced.

"Wonderful to see you, too," said Aldebar. "We've been looking forward to having you both." His tight crewneck sweater showed off his compact, muscular build.

Peter introduced Will, as they started walking toward the house. It was good to alight at this aerie after two hours of driving, Peter thought. The midday sun felt warm on his skin—for the first time since October!—while across the river, beyond the foothills of Greene County, a herd of Catskill peaks, majestic if modestly scaled, loped off westward with ponderous ease. The air was pure grace. Yet the moment also released a sad thought that had been squirming beneath Peter's consciousness for days: that some visit with his friend, one day soon, would be the last.

Jonathan was standing inside the kitchen door as they entered.

"Darling!" said Peter.

"Drive OK?" said Jonathan.

"Perfect!"

"Really gorgeous," said Will.

"Oh, good," said Jonathan, clearly delighted at their arrival.

Hugs were gentle, as Jonathan was obviously frail. His neck no longer filled the collar of his shirt. His lips looked drawn, his perfect teeth too prominent. A certain leonine handsomeness that had always been his now hinted at an inner lizard.

"You're out of the chair," exclaimed Peter.

"I'm good around the house," said Jonathan. "And today's a good day. We use it when we go out."

"We have a whole routine," said Aldebar cheerily. "It's fun, now that we've got it down."

"The house looks amazing," said Peter, putting down his briefcase and taking in the room. It was a sprawling, luxuriously homey eat-in kitchen that Jonathan had created out of the house's original kitchen and a bedroom suite that had been attached to it for a century. The custom architectural woodwork, though obviously meant to look plain and simple, was a feast of such lavish design and craftsmanship that it seemed to satisfy a greater hunger for domestic contentment than one had ever been aware of having. A mass of hydrangeas sat in an earthenware pot in a stone fireplace that dated back to the house's construction. A dark Federal hutch that had occupied a wall of the Chelsea apartment sat nearby, between two windows.

"Oh, that's right!" said Jonathan. "You haven't seen the place since we finished it."

"Jonathan got this place—what, fifteen years ago?" said Peter.

"Eighteen. And I only just got around to the kitchen."

"I keep thinking Harold and I used to come here, but you didn't even get the place until after he died."

"Nope. Ninety-four."

"Wow. And I have really not been here for five years?"

"You have not. It's not like I haven't asked you!"

An assuringly beefy cooking smell filled the room. Sitting on the counter of the kitchen's central island, the base of which was articulated with corners in the form of spiraled column legs, were a shallow wooden bowl of field greens and a board with a baguette and a wedge of orange cheese. On the Viking range, set into an arched alcove that was a degree or two too original-looking to look original, was an iron pot of soup or stew that Aldebar uncovered and stirred with a wooden spoon, when he returned to the kitchen after putting the bags in the guest room. The diamond-paned windows of the plush, built-in window seat afforded deafening blue-sky views across the river.

"Nice!" said Peter. "The nook of life." Resting on the window seat was a pile of magazines, a pair of glasses, and a laptop. Off to one side was the wheelchair.

"It is kinda nice," said Jonathan. "There's always something to see—even more in the winter, when the leaves are down. This window is like the best cable channel on earth. Not that I have that much time to watch."

"The film?"

"We're working, like, ten hours a day."

"You film here?"

"We did—Connor and me, the crew. A lot of it is done now, though Connor and I continue to talk on camera. We're mostly editing, going really fast. My editor and the sound guy even bunk here, upstairs over the studio. Connor and I look at footage every few days. He only lives a few miles away, in Claverack."

"Sounds grueling."

"Eh. Keeps me off the street."

They laughed.

"Lunch in thirty, gentlemen," said Aldebar, who began setting the round pedestal table that commanded the area in front of the fireplace.

"Well, then I'll just check e-mail for two minutes, if I may," said Will. "This is still kind of a work day for me—sorry!"

"No problem. He put your things in the room," said Jonathan. "Aldebar, do you want to show him? We'll have a proper tour after lunch; I'll show you the studio."

Jonathan took Peter into the library, where several boxes of art, fashion, and architecture books that had been sent up from Chelsea sat open but still packed—though where the books would go wasn't clear, since the room's shelves were already filled with what Jonathan called the "upstate" collections: film, intellectual history, and literature. The two settled in a seating area near the windows.

"You boys seem to be getting on," said Jonathan.

"Will and me? We're best buddies," said Peter.

"That's all—still?"

"He's complicated, Jon. *I'm* complicated. The whole situation..."

"...Is complicated."

They laughed.

"You know, I'd like to leave this earth with you sorted, darling," said Jonathan.

"Do you know any priestesses in a cave nearby where we can go and sacrifice a goat?"

"I might," chuckled Jonathan. "Well, at least you're companioning. That's nice. You know I think the world of Will."

"Good word for it—companioning. Yeah, and that's not a terrible thing."

"And I suppose...you're getting to know all about each other?"

"Sure."

"Each other's past lives and all that?"

Peter grunted.

"Sometimes I think mine is too much for him," he said. "Revolution, the plague, the agency, my two last duchesses. It's a lot for him to swallow. *His* life—well, college, a few odd jobs, and now the magazine... I mean, he's terribly good at it and really loves it. But I think sometimes he thinks his story can't compare to mine, or something—because there's also much less of it."

"You think *he* thinks that."

"Which is ridiculous, because every life is as full as it is, right? It's not about duration."

"Tell me about it."

Peter frowned.

"Oh, Jon—here I am, prattling on about boys when... I want to know how you are. Tell me everything."

"No, I like to prattle on about boys. It makes me feel good.

That's where I'm at these days—trying to feel as good as I can, as much as I can: doing my work, taking care of my friends. Hey, I'm smoking again."

"You are? You haven't smoked in thirty years."

"I know, but I get to do it now. Why not? Aldebar gets me the Sobranies I like. Oh, they're sublime! Also, helps me keep the weight down."

His face, deadpan—his comic delivery was sharper than ever. Peter shook his head.

"You're amazing," said Peter. "Good thing you have that classic bone structure. Looks good at any weight."

"Like I said, today is a good day. It's funny: I was never particularly naïve about mortality. I'm a Jewish boy, so in some ways the Cossacks are always at the door. And we went through AIDS, right? Which was as good a course in mortality as anyone is likely to get, short of war."

"Sure was."

"But these days, Peter, I have to say that I'm more aware than ever of . . . the need to die. Not my death so much as death-death. Do you know what I mean? Death happens. I get it. The thing is, it's not this unalloyed disaster. Somehow, the awareness *of* the fears, *of* the regrets and frustrations, *of* the joys we still have—all that!—feels more like being alive than anything I've felt before. It's so interesting. I just . . . you can't *be* this alive when you're walking around, taking everything for granted."

As Peter listened he was aware of how quiet the house was, except for occasional cooking sounds coming from the kitchen.

"Of course, it's not exactly a pleasant feeling," continued Jonathan. "But on some level it's almost a kind of compensation—a reward that comes with this state, or *can* come, if you're available for it."

"I see," said Peter.

"And I find myself *desperate* to share this feeling—especially since I'm not going to be able to hold on to it for very long. You know? I mean, the film is partly about this, sure, but I want everyone to feel this way—totally aware! Especially the people I care about, like you and Will and Aldebar—and not waste time being half alive."

"*Oooph,*" said Peter. The sentiment struck him as parental in the most loving way.

"Which is one reason why I keep coming back to Eliot," added Jonathan.

"I see you've kept the manuscript," said Peter. The notebook, in its Plexiglas case, sat on a nearby table.

"I've been rereading the *Quartets*. They make more sense than ever. It's really been helping my work."

"Wow. I guess I should reread them this weekend."

" 'The still point of the turning world.' That's his big idea, Petey."

"I know. You made me read it."

"The days fly by and yet time stands still. And I must say I've been savoring that sense of stillness, while the world races on."

Tenderly, Peter leaned forward, took Jonathan's hand, and kissed it. Jonathan patted Peter's cheek affectionately. Then, grasping the armrests, Jonathan began to push himself up from the chair.

"Something smells good," he said, rising and accepting some help from Peter. "Lunch must be about ready."

"You talk about taking care of other people," said Peter, as they made their way toward the kitchen. "I was just saying to Will, in the car, how much I envy your ability to take care of yourself. Sometimes I make fun of guys our age, when all they want to talk about is their houses and the fancy hotels they stay at. It's stupid of me, I know. But you know how to put a roof over your head. That's a very adult talent."

"Oh, I don't know that there's any trick to it," said Jonathan.

"Seriously. I'm almost sixty, I've got all the money I need, and I'm still renting. I wouldn't know how to get a home like this into my life."

"It's not as hard as you think. You'll see."

Lunch turned out to be a steak-and-mushroom potpie, studded with bits of smoked bacon and laced with ale. As Aldebar served from a baking dish, Peter and Will marveled appropriately. He told them it was easy to make—"just a quick stew, with a crust." It was the four of them, at the table. The cheese was a Double Gloucester.

"A little something to tide us over to dinner," said Jonathan, as they tucked in.

"I'm impressed," said Peter.

"He buys the pastry dough at that bakery," said Jonathan.

"Why not take a little help?" said Aldebar, with a wink. "I'm no cook."

"Oh, right," said Will. "This is fantastic."

A nice family lunch, thought Peter—or *something*. He was glad that Aldebar joined them, since the man's presence at the table answered a question that had been on Peter's mind since they had walked in the door: How should Aldebar be treated? As more than hired help, certainly. A friend of the family? Or something more like a beloved family retainer, which modern gay life sometimes afforded older gentlemen of means, instead of a mate? It was clear that Aldebar and Jonathan had grown genuinely close, which made it less important whether the relationship would have come about without the employment. It was also clear, from little moments between them—as when Jonathan would pat Aldebar's hand, or Aldebar would lay a hand on Jonathan's arm or shoulder—that Aldebar's duties as a nurse-slash-companion extended beyond traditional boundaries, into some distinctly gay realm of spiritual and physical caretaking, where all of Jonathan's needs might sync with Aldebar's skills and generosity in an almost connubial relationship with no precise name. After all, Aldebar bathed and dressed Jonathan, and wheeled him around and saw to his comfort; the operation of Jonathan's body was now largely Aldebar's responsibility. Peter knew that, in happier times, his friend had sometimes hired men, short-term, for similarly intimate duties.

Anyway, it was good to see Jonathan being cared for so lovingly—another extension of his talent for sheltering himself. He looked terrible—skinnier than ever, barely ambulatory—but in some ways, Peter thought, he was thriving.

After lunch, Aldebar tidied up and went out to do some errands. Peter said he needed ten minutes to check his messages before the promised studio visit.

"Go and check your e-mail," said Jonathan, taking Will by the hand and shuffling over to the window seat. "We'll be right here."

The guest suite featured twin beds, as in the past, but Peter noticed the bathroom had been redone. Tile had given way to wainscoting in white bead board, except in the shower and bath area, which was now all white subway tile, with retro nickel fixtures. Will's toiletry kit, in rep-striped silk, had been set out near one of the sinks on the white paneled vanity cabinet, above which, on the windowsill, stood a slender glass cylinder with a few stems of freesia. His toothbrush had been tossed in one of the stainless steel cups on the vanity. Will's laptop was also set out, on the bedroom desk, with the charger deployed; his duffel bag was neatly stowed to one side of the bed he'd apparently chosen, over the end of which he'd laid his jacket.

Roomies, thought Peter. The thought was both delicious and terrifying.

The mountain view outside the windows might well extend for thirty miles, Peter thought—maybe even as far as the town he grew up in, though that was in a different direction. He'd lived there "in the sticks" until the age of eighteen, when he left for college—not long after *Look* magazine published a cover story on "The American Man," featuring the cover line "The sad, 'gay' life of the homosexual."

What in the world ever made me so sure they were wrong . . . ?

After checking his messages and finding nothing urgent, Peter rejoined Jonathan and Will, who were chatting away amiably.

". . . And no cock to speak of."

"Oh!"

"But a very nice guy," Will was saying. "Just not for me, ya know?"

"No, no, no," laughed Jonathan.

They greeted Peter, who didn't have to ask whom they were talking about.

"Enrico," said Will.

"Ah," said Peter.

"The prince of chandeliers," said Jonathan. "I know the type."

Then Jonathan took them, slowly and with a cane, through a passage into the studio wing, where they met the film's editor—a top guy in his field, Jonathan said—and the sound guy.

"I was wondering who belonged to all those cars in the driveway," said Will.

The editor showed them the footage he was working on, featuring two talking heads: Jonathan and Connor Frankel.

"Frankel's never talked so publicly about his sexual identity before," said the editor. "That generation just didn't, right? And now he's coming across with all these amazing insights about his upbringing and his work, the times and the relationship between hiding and creativity, and how America deals with creativity and differentness. Awesome stuff."

"That's groundbreaking," said Will.

"Major," said Jonathan.

"Jonathan's the best there is," said the editor. "A real can opener!"

"You're giving shape to it all," said Jonathan. "Which, I might add, is an impossible task, since for months we just talked and talked and talked, and must have repeated ourselves a million times."

"And you're incorporating shots of Frankel's work?" said Will.

"Individual pieces and installation shots, yes," said the editor. "Some collage, some Ken Burns effect . . ."

"That panning-zooming thing . . . ?"

"Mm-hmm."

"The art photography itself was a whole thing," said Jonathan.

Peter felt a pleasant little shock in seeing the cultural journalist in Will in action.

"Do you have a title yet?" asked Peter.

"We're playing with ideas," said Jonathan, without elaborating.

"Thanks so much," said Will. "Good luck."

"Take care," said the editor.

"That guy has an Oscar," said Jonathan, as they made their way back to the main house.

The rest of the afternoon was devoted to quiet working and reading. Peter and Will each made a few phone calls, off in a corner, so as not to disturb the others. At some point Aldebar returned home and took Jonathan upstairs.

At six, cocktails were served, and at seven, dinner. It was "simple, simple, simple," according to Jonathan: grilled salmon and vegetables with couscous. Aldebar opened a bottle of Riesling and they ate again in the kitchen. In the center of the table was a pair of Depression glass candelabra with stumpy, yellowish candles.

"We don't really use the dining room anymore, do we?" said Jonathan.

"Not since the music society," said Aldebar.

"We did a little benefit here this winter," said Jonathan. "There was a string quartet, we had a nice buffet...."

"You're a big supporter, aren't you?" said Peter. "The Hudson Valley chamber something."

"It's too much now," sniffed Jonathan. "They're in the will."

They lingered over pear cobbler, while Peter and Jonathan talked about mutual friends and old times. They apologized to the others, saying they didn't mean to monopolize the conversation this way, but they did anyway and no one objected. When the foundation came up, Jonathan mentioned that Will had officially declined the position of director—something that Peter hadn't known was a final decision, but that he was happy to hear anyway. Will seemed to know what he wanted, these days. That was great to see. Moreover, something about the boy holding his own in the adult world—chatting with Jonathan's editor, with Jonathan—made Peter proud.

And in a corner of his mind, there was even a half-formed notion to stop thinking about Will in terms of "the boy," language he sometimes used when speaking with close friends like Jonathan. Peter sometimes referred to "boys" jestingly among older gay men for whom terms like "boy" and "girl" had evolved from camp to politically correct, to ironically camp. There shouldn't be harm in framing the idea of a young man occasionally in a witty construct like a Noel Coward song, yet even the glamour of madness about a boy might be detrimental, Peter thought, if one cast someone as the boy too unobservantly.

Right? he telepathically asked Harold, who had been such an apostle of political correctness. *Age has made me lax about the boy thing?* Peter tried to clarify the notion in his mind, and then dinner was over.

When they rose, Peter and Will both started to help Aldebar clear, but Aldebar gently rebuffed them.

"I've got it, thanks—don't worry," he said. "I don't want you to miss the entertainment."

"Oh, yes," said Jonathan, turning to glance outside. "We have to go out on the terrace."

"The sunset," said Will.

"I'll join in a minute," said Aldebar. "Do people want coffee?"

No one did, and the three stepped outside.

The evening was cool but not cold—fine for sitting a little while and "visiting," as Jonathan quaintly referred to it. They installed themselves in the sumptuously scaled deck furniture, while looming before them, over green hills now fading into a mute royal flush of mossy grays, was an evening sky ablaze in orange and gold. The sun's fiery disc hovered just above the landscape, while a spray of altostratus clouds crested up symphonically from the horizon, irradiated from below, edged in mauves that melted into a background of out-dazzled sky blue. It was a scene worthy of one of the noble Hudson River School painters whom Peter had learned to love as a child—Thomas Cole, Frederic Church, John Kensett, and the like: nature's picturesque majesty prompting the contemplation of Wilderness from the edge of Civilization; the quest for the Sublime, by way of the Beautiful. Only this was no painting. And the real thing, as viewed from Jonathan's terrace, came with its own sound score: a profound yet buoyant silence that might be composed of a thousand harmonized echoes of a thousand winds swirling in the valleys surrounding them.

"We're lucky it's clear tonight," said Jonathan. "You're getting a good show. I love this view. It's a view of time immemorial."

"Hmm," said Will.

"If you look the right way, you can see both the glacial and the instantaneous," said Jonathan. "And everything in between."

"OK," said Peter.

"I'm shutting up," said Jonathan.

Aldebar brought out a tray of three cognacs, and no one made a fuss when he withdrew.

"This is truly a precious spot," said Peter.

"You like?" said Jonathan. "This is what I came up here for. Chelsea wasn't really home. This is."

They toasted silently and relaxed back into the terrace furniture's thick striped cushions.

"Getting rid of the apartment must have been hard," said Will.

"Not really," said Jonathan. "Parting with the paintings and the real estate was a cinch. They're only things. Now someone else will get to love them. Same with the furniture. I was only in a line of people meant to own and love and protect these things. And, God knows, the things themselves will continue to demand the protection they need—right? That's what price tags are for. But ya know what I worry about? Things like the rocks I found on the beach at Fire Island. I have one that looks like an emerald when it's wet; and a perfectly round black one, like a big black pearl; and one that's shaped like the head of a Cycladic statue, that I brought back to Roberto when we were dating. I still have that rock upstairs, next to a real Cycladic head. What happens to that, after I'm gone? Does it go back to just being a rock again? After all the meaning it's accrued, the privilege it's enjoyed—it gets forgotten or overlooked when the so-called important stuff gets divided up? There's no museum for cute rocks."

Neither Peter nor Will could think of anything to say.

"Don't worry," said Jonathan. "The rock is in the will, too. My leaving it to someone will probably keep it special for another thirty, forty years."

More silence.

"Sunsets always make me feel unworthy," said Peter. "Like, can I enjoy this *enough?* Can I be present for this sublime thing *enough?*"

Will giggled, and Peter went on.

"Harold and I timed our trip to India—this was during the eighties—so we'd be at the Taj Mahal during the full moon. People do that. And we must have visited the place, oh, five or six times over the course of, whatever, four days and three nights in Agra. Trying to drink it in. One night, we even made love in the garden there—well, we jerked off, kissing, on one of the marble benches."

Jonathan snorted.

"No one was around," said Peter. "You could do that then. It was just this big public garden, barely well kept, and there were maybe six other people in these acres and acres of garden, and this glorious mirage of a Taj Mahal, floating right over *there*. . . ."

"So sweet," said Will.

"He wrote about it for the *Times*—well, except for the jerking off. We used to call it 'our night in the garden of love.' "

"Have you gone back?" asked Jonathan.

"No," said Peter.

"Oh, darling, you must! Going back to places like that is the point."

"Well . . . I don't know. Maybe. I hope so."

"We used to joke about Venice that way, remember? You only went the first time so you could start returning there, and returning and returning. . . ."

Will was about to ask Jonathan if he had ever been to the Taj Mahal, then thought better of it.

The bottom third of the sun's disc was now melting into the horizon. There was no sinking motion to see, even if you stared at it constantly. Yet second after second, at the moment you became aware of registering no motion, you saw the result of motion and the disc was lower! Soon it was gone, and from below the horizon the sun now fueled a further explosion of color: clouds of molten copper edged in iridescent mauve, shot with radioactive purples and pinks.

They talked for another hour or so, as the sky faded, about Indian Point and nuclear power and the sustainability of civilization. Aldebar lighted lanterns and poured another round of cognac. And then it began to feel cold.

"It's gotta be an early night for me," said Peter.

"Oh, me too," said Will.

"Poor boys," said Jonathan. "You must have been up at dawn. Well, to bed, then. Tomorrow we'll take you antiquing."

"Yay," said Will.

"Can we go to the new kitchenware place you mentioned?" said Peter.

"Yes, yes," said Jonathan. "It's right there."

"Kitchen stuff is like porn to me," said Peter.

Inside, at the bottom of the stairs, Jonathan bid Peter and Will good night.

"We alarm but there are no motion detectors," he said, "so feel free to go padding around during the night. Leftovers in the fridge are up for grabs."

"I couldn't eat another thing," said Will.

"Neither could I," said Peter.

"There's water in the little fridge in your room," continued Jonathan, "inside the closet."

"I found it," said Will.

"Aldebar makes a pot of coffee around nine, in the kitchen, yeah? I have mine in my room, but we can all have some breakfast together around ten-thirty. The shops open at noon. How does that sound?"

Peter and Will said good night and went upstairs together. As they entered the room, Peter again felt a pang of excitement mixed with terror.

"Did you have a preference of bed?" said Will. "I didn't mean to preempt a discussion. I just threw my stuff down."

"No, this is fine," said Peter.

"Tout le confort moderne," said Will, as he plopped down on his bed, undid his sneakers, and placed them carefully near his bag. His feet were, what, size eleven?

"It's even splendider than when I saw it last," said Peter.

"Could you ever live here?"

"Well . . . it's not exactly my style, but yeah, sure, of course." Peter poked his head in the large closet on the wall opposite the windows, to take stock. The closet was huge, fitted with a built-in stack of drawers, a cabinet for the refrigerator, and a long rack on which Will had already hung some things—a flannel shirt, a pair of khaki pants, his jacket.

"Well, I love it," said Will, unbuttoning his shirt. Underneath was a crisp white T-shirt, somewhat tight, which emphasized his perfectly proportioned torso. "To me, it's like magic. It's like what my parents' place on Pine Mountain—this place we go near Santa Barbara—wants to be."

"Where you used to go camping?" said Peter, sitting down on

his bed and removing his sneakers, trying not to stare. He was acutely aware of being in a room for the first time with the man who meant everything to him, for the purposes of taking off clothes and going to bed. He wanted to savor the moment but also to give Will the freedom to remain comfortable, in case he wasn't necessarily thinking about ravishing his older friend suddenly with the kind of passion and tenderness that was certainly on Peter's mind.

"Yeah, though it wasn't really camping," said Will. "I mean, there was running water and heat and everything. But I loved it. I was so happy there. I like mountains."

"Me too," said Peter, putting his sneakers and a few of the rest of his things in the closet, including his shirt, which he slipped off unceremoniously. "You wanna hear something funny? There was a bird singing when we got out of the car in the driveway. I don't know if you noticed."

"Uh-uh," said Will.

"It was a bird I remembered from growing up in these parts. I hadn't heard it for decades, but there it was again: *doodle-oo-doo-dweet. Doodle-oo-doo-dweet-doo dwink.*" Peter's gray athletic T-shirt was emblazoned with an orange P for Princeton, where he'd guest lectured once on branding.

"Very impressive," said Will.

"Thank you—thank you very much. I may be known for other things, but I do speak a little bird. But really, the way that sound echoed in the trees—among the leaves, I guess—I dunno, it just brought me back."

Will stood.

"I'm just gonna have one last look online—do you mind?" he said, ambling over to the desk and opening his laptop. "Though I suppose everything is pretty much over for today."

"I'll hit the bathroom," said Peter.

Inside, the door closed, Peter flossed and brushed his teeth, washed his face, peed, and gave his hands another little wash. He looked at himself in the mirror and quietly whispered *"Coraggio!"* Then he stepped out of his jeans and brought them out of the bathroom to the closet, where he hung them on a hook.

"Poor Jon," said Will, quietly, absorbed in his laptop. "He's lost so much weight."

"I know," said Peter. "It's sad." He found himself looking through the papers in a file folder he'd laid next to his computer, on a table near the window, though he wasn't really looking for anything. He was nervous.

"He's such a hero," said Will. "He told me the work was exhausting but that he was worried about letting down Connor Frankel."

"I gather the treatments are pretty intense."

"Chemical castration—that's what he told me it was called. Can you imagine? Testosterone is like fuel for this kind of cancer, so they dose him with the other stuff."

"Ecch."

"And still it progresses. Jesus."

"It's no picnic."

"He said an interesting thing. He said he can't claim that his body betrayed him, because he got through AIDS. But now here he is, old enough to, you know...."

Peter sighed.

"We lived through a war, Will," he said, "and now we get to face the *really* tough stuff."

Will shut down his laptop and closed it, and swiveled in his seat.

"Are you saying that you're made of tough stuff, mister?" he said, with a funny-serious face.

"The toughest," said Peter. "I'm the toughest piece of fluff you're likely to find."

"O-*kay*," said Will, with a triumphant chuckle. He rose and turned toward the bathroom. "Are you finished with the ... ?"

"Please," said Peter.

While Will was in the bathroom, Peter arranged the rest of his things and adjusted the room's lighting, switching on the lamp between the beds and switching off the other lamps that were wired to the switch near the door. He jumped into bed and grabbed a book from the night table and started leafing through it: Edith Wharton's *The Decoration of Houses*. He listened to the water running and imagined Will brushing his teeth, washing his face. And when Will emerged he, too, was in boxers—blue-and-white stripes—and his T-shirt.

Will walked over to the closet to stow his jeans, then draped his socks over his sneakers. He was barefoot. Peter remained cool but felt guilty for stealing even infinitesimally short looks at Will's muscular legs and beautifully formed feet and strong-looking upper arms and thick neck, while pretending to go on casually with the conversation.

"So . . . bedtime, yes?" said Will.

Peter nodded. "I'm bushed," he said. "You know, I think all the books in this room are about décor."

"Oh, nice, cool," said Will, as he jumped into bed. "Alarm?"

"Hmmh—maybe. Just in case."

"Nine?"

"Perfect."

Will programmed his phone.

"I can't wait to go antiquing," he said.

"Are you looking for anything in particular?" asked Peter. And Will began describing some of the things he might be looking for, for his apartment—a table, a lamp—though Peter was too caught up in his own thoughts to concentrate on what Will was saying. *His feet are so fucking gorgeous,* Peter thought. *And his butt is amazing—solid and round and really up there. I can't believe how narrow that waist is.* He continued to flip through the Wharton, but at the same time was mapping all the new bits of physiological information he had gained in the previous few minutes about Will's body onto his old mental picture of it—a picture that had formed over the previous months, when winter clothing had revealed only dribbles of the information about this sacred territory. Now here was a flood!

"Luz said I should be spontaneous, so I'm going to be spontaneous," Will was saying.

Peter closed the book and put it aside. He rolled onto one side, propping himself up on one arm.

"Wait till you see, Will—there's a whole street of shops," he said. "And it's like they come in three densities. There's the junk shop, which is packed with crap that you have to paw through, although there can be some real treasures. There's the nicely arranged shop where everything is clean and nicely displayed, and there are no funny smells or back rooms with old clothes. And then, of course, the highfalutin shop, which is extremely select and set up like a salon in somebody's gracious home, and the owner is a gracious lady or gentleman with whom you have to make gracious small talk. . . ."

"Oooh, I can't wait," said Will, fluttering his legs in boyish excitement, under the covers. Then he slid down in bed and propped himself up on one arm, too.

"Are *you* looking for anything in particular?" he asked.

"I dunno," said Peter. "I suppose I'm always on the lookout for a head of Alexander, like the guy in Egypt I told you about."

"OK," said Will.

"Or maybe a vintage etiquette book."

"For your collection. Same way I'm always on the lookout for beach art."

"That's right—you collect seascapes."

"Sunday painter stuff, mostly—primitives, folk art. I have a few watercolors of the Pacific coast and some little oils I found when I was a teenager."

"But I didn't see them at your place."

Will laughed.

"They're in the bedroom," he said. "And as I recall, you didn't get to spend any time in there."

"There's always next time."

"Yes, there is. Anyway, we have a van, so we can drag back the fucking Lincoln Memorial, if we need to."

"Great."

Did it aid the romantic escalation he longed for, Peter wondered, to be in bed, in the same room together, without even mentioning how absolutely thrilling this was? Or did the very impulse or ability to endure such a thing without mentioning it—let alone without someone making a rashly passionate move, damn the consequences—doom the possibility of romance? Peter tried to quiet his confusion by taking pleasure in the unmistakable domesticity of the situation. Maybe they *were* like an old married couple. That would actually work for Peter, who had, in the previous half century, enjoyed what he often termed "all the sex there was." And if, in some odd scenario, Will were the sexy young guy who happened to want some kind of *mariage blanc* with the right older guy, that included a few discreet fiddlings on the side, well, Peter could deal with that perfectly well. Though signaling the latter to someone under a certain age could come across as pathetic, monstrous, insulting, or worse.

"Lights out?" said Will.

"I guess," said Peter, pushing his pillows into place.

As Will switched off the lamp, Peter slid down in bed and pulled the covers over his shoulders. The room was cool, the quiet, profound. Every rustle of Will's twisty quest to find a good position in bed sounded like heaven.

"I'm a terrific roommate, by the way," said Will. "I don't snore. And if you do, I won't care."

"I don't snore," said Peter. "At least, I don't think so."

Peter realized that he wouldn't know if he had become a snorer. The last person he'd slept with regularly was Nick, and that was ten years before. What if he snored now? These things happened.

CHAPTER 17

The next morning, when Peter awoke, he found that Will was already up. The other bed was empty, semi-made in the same manner that Peter had been taught to leave a bed when a guest in someone's home: the bedclothes straightened and crisply turned down, the pillow plumped.

In the kitchen, Peter was pouring himself a cup of coffee when Will bounded in, winded, in gym shorts and an XL tank top that was patched with sweat. A towel was pulled around his neck.

"Hey," he said.

"Hey," said Peter.

"You know there's a gym here, right?" said Will, grabbing a banana from the fruit bowl. His hair was wet around the edges and he smelled faintly of fabric softener.

"Yeah," said Peter. "I meant to tell you last night."

"I was going to go run outside, but I figured what the hell?"

Will leaned against the counter where Peter was standing. His body was even more luscious than Peter had dreamed, and the sight of more of it was a lot to take in: the big traps and bulging triceps, the surprisingly well-defined deltoids, the smoothness of so much glowing, unblemished *convexity*. Peter giggled inwardly, remembering that this was, after all, a mortal being and also a friend.

No hair was visible on the sternum or the part of Will's chest that Peter could see through the armholes of the tank top. Then Will bent forward to reach past Peter and tear a paper towel off the roll, and the front of his shirt bagged outward, affording a lavish view of the right pectoral. The nipple was small and tender-looking, positioned well to the edge of the pec, and not perfectly round but a little stretched, as if in delicate tension due to the development of the muscle underneath.

"Sleep well?" said Peter.

"Big time," said Will. "And you?"

"Very well, thanks."

"No snoring."

"Oh, good."

"Banana?"

"No, thanks. I was actually thinking about making a frittata, maybe having breakfast ready when they come down."

"Aldebar's up with Jonathan."

"Let's see what we've got," said Peter, opening the refrigerator and peering inside.

"He went out for croissants."

"Plenty of eggs," said Peter, taking stock.

"And fresh OJ."

"Yup. OK—mushrooms, onions, zucchini.... Ooh, Gruyère! I guess we can do it."

"Gimme five minutes for a quick shower," said Will. "I'm totally helping." He tossed the banana peel in the trash and bounced out of the kitchen.

Lord—and well-defined calves, too! I'm fucked!

Cooking together was fun. Moving about in sync in the kitchen was as automatic for them as it had been the previous time, at Peter's place. As they went about prepping and tidying, Peter saw that the level of silent communication and thoughtfully choreographic awareness of each other had, if anything, improved. Will handled the *mise en place* for the frittata without prompting. When Peter put the frittata in the oven and turned to slicing potatoes and onions for the home fries he decided to make, Will took the egg bowl, cheese grater, and the rest over to the sink.

He swooned as he started washing.

"Oh, man," Will groaned. "Is there anything like somebody else's dishwashing liquid?"

Peter grinned.

"Never in a million years would I have bought New Apple Blossom Dawn," said Will. "But right now, it's saying everything to me about my life!" He sambaed in place, as he stood washing.

And as Peter pushed the potatoes and onions around in the skillet, he felt a kind of contentment—not exactly "making breakfast for my best friend in his beautiful home, with my amazing boyfriend"-type contentment, but close. He added some smoked paprika, which he found in the cupboard. Outside, across the river, green hills hummed in unison in the cheery morning light.

Can I have this? Peter thought. *Can I morph my life into this, or do I just go on waiting and drifting, and see what happens? How pathetic I am, to go on and on about love, yet remain so passive, so content without it. Somehow, I used to have more energy to pursue love.*

The aroma of fried potatoes filled the kitchen.

No, wait—I never pursued it. Harold and Nick just . . . happened.

"Looks like we've got an awesome day for it, eh?" gushed Will, toweling his hands and giving Peter an enthusiastic tap on the butt. He hummed a bit of a Stevie Wonder song—"You Are the Sunshine of My Life"—as he began to set the table.

Aldebar and Jonathan were delighted when they came down and found everything ready. The four devoured breakfast and cleaned up as a team. By a quarter of twelve they were walking out the door.

"Two cars?" said Peter.

"We could do one," said Aldebar. "The Navigator has tons of room, even with the chair."

"Why don't we take ours, just in case," said Peter, with a glance toward Will.

"We're hunting big game," explained Will.

They helped Jonathan into the car, while Aldebar loaded the wheelchair into the back.

"We've got this down to a military maneuver," said Jonathan.

"Were you ever in the army, Aldebar?" said Peter, jokingly.

"You know I was in the marines, right?" he said.

Peter and Will were both stunned.

"What—seriously?" said Will.

"Wait," said Peter, "let me get this straight: You're an RN who knows all about opera *and* you were in the marines?"

"It just happened," said Aldebar, laughing, with a wink.

"That's amazing," said Peter. "Jonathan?"

"What can I tell you?" said Jonathan. "He's Superman."

Chartered in 1795 by merchants who ran the place, Hudson was the fourth largest city in New York State by 1820—a bustling port on a major American river. By the end of the nineteenth century, though, river commerce was winding down and the town was flooding under waves of gambling and prostitution. Governor Thomas E. Dewey started busting up the rackets in the early '50s, and throughout the '60s and '70s Hudson was on life support, owing to the same kind of helplessness that still afflicted Peter's hometown, where a long-ago boom in canal- and rail-fueled commerce was never bested. At which point a group of local antiques dealers came together—cue the string quartet!—and ignited a revival. Hudson's new antiques trade at first reflected and then helped fuel a demographic shift in the area, which saw traditional families give way to more young couples, couples without children, retirees, single folks, and weekenders, all of which, of course, meant gays. By the '90s, on Warren Street, the main thoroughfare that climbs up from the river in a battery of modestly scaled commercial blocks, storefronts that once offered quotidian stuff like clothes, shoes, drugs, and hardware now stocked items whose value derived chiefly from their having survived history with a little dignity.

Presumably, there was a mall nearby, where people now went for their hardware—which these days was made in China—and shoes—Brazil. But around noon on a beautiful spring Saturday, Hudson's Warren Street would come alive with well-shod folks from as far away as New York, hankering not for Buster Brown oxfords but for *marvelous* things, *charming* things. And as they began strolling from shop to shop, these folks, whether just-looking-thanks or actively searching for something, would almost visibly charge up with brilliant discoveries about *how we once lived,* and *how we choose to live now,* and *how we survive through our histo-*

ries. And if, just a block or two off Warren, in the part of Hudson that remains unrevived, in a house that was hacked into apartments after Grandpa George's refrigeration business went bust and Aunt Betty died of lung cancer, there was an empty windowsill on which that lovely pink Deco vase had stood for decades, the one that was now close by in a shop vitrine, poised to be snatched by someone who *really values* design and character—well, that was America in the twenty-first century.

Peter and his friends arrived early enough to find parking spots right on Warren, close to each other. And for two hours they explored, sometimes as a full clump of four, sometimes two by two, and sometimes as a threesome, while someone dawdled or peeked into a shop that no one else was interested in. They took turns wheeling Jonathan. Peter and Will just had to poke through a "junk store" that Jonathan disdained; Peter and Jonathan lingered at a fancy shop to chat with the owner about an oil portrait of a young man; they all diligently inspected the place that specialized in prints, the one with the great furniture, and the one with all the books and photographs. Will looked at tables and lamps here and there, but didn't see anything he liked. For $10, he bought an old black-and-white photograph of a college rowing team. The clerk gave him a recycled green plastic supermarket bag, lined with a paper bag, to carry his purchase in.

At one point, Peter and Will were in a gallery looking at seascapes—watercolors and oils from an amateur Danish artist who had died in the '80s. The owner represented the estate.

"This was a little fishing village on the North Sea he returned to every summer," she said, as they inspected a small watercolor. "A place called Lønstrup. Lovely light, as you can see." The piece was primitive bordering on clumsy, but it had the charm of simplicity, depicting a few village houses seen from the hill above them, their red roofs a bold slash between the white and ochre of stone walls and the blue of the sea. The scene was rendered with a genial looseness and lack of pretension.

"That's the way the roofs are there—red," she said. "He was a dentist who lived in Copenhagen." All the works were surprising affordable.

"It's sweet, isn't it?" said Will.

"Absolutely," said Peter. "The price is certainly good. What do *you* think?"

"I dunno. I like it."

"It's nice."

"It *is*. . . ."

"We can keep it on the short list and come back if you want."

"Should I just get it?"

"Up to you."

"Mmm. Maybe I should think about it and see how I feel later in the day."

"Good idea."

Around two-thirty Jonathan suggested lunch, so they went over to a cafe that was owned by a friend of his, who also owned a popular place in New York. The place was busy, but welcoming. The staff knew Jonathan and quickly prepared a table that could accommodate the four of them, plus the chair.

Lunch was relaxed and Jonathan was talkative. As the crowd thinned out, the owner came over with some free desserts and sat with them a while. During coffee, Will asked to be excused. He had received a text that needed to be answered with a call, he said. When he returned fifteen minutes later, Peter noticed that he had his green bag with him, which seemed curious, though Peter didn't give it a second thought. Maybe he went back for the seascape.

After lunch there were more shops, including a high-end kitchenware place where Peter bought a wind-up timer in butter yellow, and then it was time to head home. With endearing tact, Aldebar suggested that "we" might be getting tired.

"Maybe a little around the edges," said Jonathan.

"I'll just take two minutes to circle back to that watercolor place," said Will. "It's only a block or two that way, isn't it?"

"Jon, why don't you guys go ahead," said Peter. "We have to go look at a watercolor."

"Take your time, please," said Jonathan. "I'm going to go take my nap. You guys should go on that drive I told you about. It's only an hour and really worth it. We'll see you at dinner."

"It's good, right?" said Will, when they were back in the gallery, looking at the piece.

"I love it," said Peter. "It's passed the test of time." Red roofs, dazzling ocean. The owner looked on approvingly.

"I'll take it," said Will. And the owner wrapped up the picture and included a brochure about the artist.

Just as they were stepping out of the gallery someone greeted them.

"Peter?"

It took a moment to place the man.

"Arnie—my goodness!"

It was someone Peter had known since college, a composer who taught, Peter thought he remembered, at a community college. It had taken a moment to recognize him because the man had changed so much in the years since Peter last saw him: He'd put on a lot of weight, and his once thick, black, curly hair had gone gray and scraggly. He looked old, yet there was still that diffident, impish smile. . . .

Peter introduced Will to Arnie and asked if he was still teaching.

"Oh, yes—composition," said Arnie, naming the college, which was in the next county. "Which leaves me time to do my own work."

"And you live nearby, right?" said Peter.

"Over in Catskill."

"OK. Yeah, we're just up for the day—you know, doing the Hudson thing."

Arnie rolled his eyes in a friendly way. He was dumpily dressed, Peter noted sadly, in clothes that looked neither vintage nor retro, but worn. The absentminded professor?

"Driving back tomorrow," said Peter. When he mentioned Jonathan, Arnie said he remembered him and knew he lived in Hudson, but didn't see him socially.

They chatted a little about teaching, a little about advertising. Arnie was part of the crowd that Peter moved in, during those early years in New York, only unlike Peter and Jonathan, Arnie had never found financial success. Then again, thought Peter, maybe Arnie hadn't been seeking that.

"Do you get down to the city much?" asked Peter.

"Once in a while," said Arnie. "For a concert or something. It's expensive."

It was an awkward moment. In the mid- and late '70s Arnie was the one who, among all of them, seemed poised for success, and was even a little farther along toward it than the others, with occasional commissions from out-of-town orchestras. The first dinner party Peter had ever attended in a restaurant's private dining room was hosted by Arnie. Yet nothing more had really happened for him, and at some point, during the '80s, he just left town.

The late afternoon sun was making everything look golden. But Peter noticed that Arnie's teeth looked yellow, not because of the light.

"It would be great to catch up," said Peter, "but we're running." And he really did mean that it would be great, since he had always liked Arnie—in fact, had been very close with him, at one point. Inviting him back to the house, of course, wasn't an option.

"Well, look," said Arnie, "did you say you were driving home tomorrow? I'd love to invite you guys to stop by for tea, on your way back to the city."

Peter was surprised by the idea, but not put off.

"If there's time," continued Arnie. "It's right on the way."

"It's an idea," said Peter. "We still haven't figured out the day yet. Can I let you know?"

"Of course," said Arnie, and they exchanged phone numbers. "I'm home, working, all day."

"Terrific," said Peter. "I'll call or text."

"Nice to meet you," said Arnie.

"Same here," said Will.

"Wow," said Peter, as they walked to the van.

"Seems like a nice guy."

"Omigod!" hooted Peter.

"What?" said Will.

Peter halted, grinning, taking Will by the arm and looking around to make sure they were alone.

"OK, here's why I didn't just say no," he said, in an excited whisper. "Arnie and I used to be boyfriends!"

"No way."

"Yes! A million years ago—for about six months, in college. Before Harold and I signed on the dotted line."

"Wow."

"So I didn't want to just blow him off."

"Of course not."

"What a surprise—Arnie!"

"Well, hell, we should have tea with him."

"Oh, I couldn't ask you to do that."

"It's fine with me. I think it would be fun."

"Really? You wouldn't mind?"

"It would give me a chance to see what you saw in him."

Peter snorted, as if he knew well that that could stand some explanation.

"He used to be so cute . . . !"

"No, I'm sure," said Will.

"No, that came out wrong. Arnie's a good composer and a very decent human being."

"He seems cool. Nice smile."

"Well, here's the thing," burbled Peter. "He was the most amazing kisser. Luscious kisser! It was Arnie who made me realize that sex could be sweet. I think it was the first time I'd ever giggled during sex—ya know?"

"Uh-huh."

"Instead of that *grunting* thing—which can be nice, too, of course."

"Very nice guy. Though definitely not as well taken care of, whatever, as you and Jonathan. But so what?"

"Right. So what?"

They settled into the front seat of the van.

"It's not like we're on a fixed schedule tomorrow," said Will.

"I just don't want to get home too late," said Peter.

"Catskill. Where is that?"

"Other side of the river."

"Fine."

"Actually, it might work. Lunch with Jonathan, tea with Arnie, and then we can hop on the Thruway. Which might be better for us, anyway—driving home in the dark."

"There ya go."

The drive suggested by Jonathan took them home on a scenic route that afforded a succession of splendid river and mountain

views. Traffic was practically nonexistent, so Peter found real pleasure in negotiating the road's gentle ups, downs, and arounds
unimpeded, at an appropriately stately speed. Contentedly they ambled over ridges and down into little valleys, along routes that were
so well insinuated into the rolling landscape they could only have
been built upon ancient paths. They glided through quiet junctions
marked by only a house or two; past stretches of field and forest
that gave way to grand vistas.

They said little, perhaps a bit talked-out for the moment.

The road, at one point, after curving along the shoulder of a little mountain, brought them over a bridge that spanned a lush
ravine. The ravine fell away into a valley whose far side was a hilly
landscape entirely of green. It was a view that was more than just
pretty, Peter thought: It was deceptively simple, since it described
the result of eons of erosion and evolution, ongoing processes that
had been basically undisturbed by history. These were hills that
had never been cleared or much occupied, and only sporadically
visited, ever. They looked now the way they had for centuries. Anyone who had ever driven there, or hiked up there before the road
was built, or walked along the Indian path that was there before the
road—say, the young local artist who did a series of woodland
sketches there in 1853, determined to make his native landscape as
famous as Rome's; or the bootlegger who took shelter in a tent
nearby, with a Bible and a bottle of whiskey, after abandoning a
thriving business that was raided by state police in 1951; or the
housewife who stopped there in a Chevy with another woman's
husband in 1963, after dirty dancing to Perez Prado in a riverfront
dive and deciding to drive far from town—all would have seen the
same view. And Peter had always been clobbered by this sense of
conflated eras and possible futures from the views he discovered on
drives he made as a restless teenager and from similar views ever
since. Rome's hills might be more marked, storied, mythologized,
but these—ushering little streams down toward larger ones, and
those, onward toward the Hudson—embodied some of the same
glamour as those on the Tiber, suggesting that opulence can gestate
among piles of earth even without something physical being built
there.

The glamour of a ravine, or a water gap, or a stand of hills derives not only from beauty, after all, but from function—and function can be marvelously unpredictable. Who could have predicted that the hills where Peter grew up, which saw the coming and going of canals and trains and bowling alleys and beauty salons, would also engender Peter and his kind?

This kind of life, this kind of weekend! he kept thinking. *How impossible it would have been for my parents to imagine such things, when I was a kid! Yet in some ways this life was always here and I was simply one of those who was able to see it.*

A little upstate town overrun by antiques dealers, its main street a strip of shops where everyone spoke gay. Men like Jonathan living in great mansions, and still others in shacks.... Peter was almost afraid to imagine what Arnie's place was like.

"Should I text Arnie and say we're coming?" said Peter, breaking a genial silence that had lasted for miles.

"Sure, if you want to," said Will.

"Maybe four?"

"Sounds good."

After a few more miles they realized it was later than they thought.

"It's close now," said Peter.

The sky was managing to hold on to a bit of its glow, but day had already left the depths of woods and hollows they were passing. They were on the final leg of their drive, before reaching the turnoff to Jonathan's road, when they rounded a bend and came upon another valley vista, only this one broader. Far below, in a village at the bottom of the valley, lights were coming on, shimmering through the dusk. A radiant strand of highway led from one end of the valley into a bowl of splattered, glittering filaments, and then narrowed again into a strand that disappeared into darkness at the far end of the valley. It was a view of suppers being cooked, homework being done, TV being watched. And Peter wondered, as they passed serenely above the scene, whether the van's headlights might be visible below, or the echo of its engine audible that far away, across the valley, from someone's back porch or bedroom window—someone, perhaps, who was conjugating Spanish verbs and wondering where his life would lead. Often as a child, Peter, doing homework at his desk or lying in bed on a spring night, with the window open, listened for the drone of vehicles shifting gears, coming from the highway a mile or so away. The sound, echoing over lawns and rooftops and treetops, was a seductive clarion reminding him of all those who must be traveling toward the main road a few miles beyond, which led to New York and untold, glorious possibilities. As he headed home with Will to dinner, the memory of this sound scalded Peter's heart with joy, in a crystalline moment suddenly outside of time, where things past and things to come were dazzling facets of a singularity all to be beheld at once. To be this close to love, in a rented van, on a spring evening, was splendor of a type that Peter couldn't remember the likes of, yet felt he had always known.

By the time they arrived home it was dark. They'd texted ahead, so they were right on time to have a cocktail and sit down to dinner. Aldebar had made roast chicken, mashed potatoes, and apple pie that was served with a locally made ginger-basil ice cream.

After dinner, they all spent a few minutes on the terrace, looking at the Milky Way and figuring out which stars were which, using an app called Planets that Peter had on his iPhone. Then they came in and watched Roman Polanski's *The Ghost Writer* in the "family room"—the other end of the kitchen. Jonathan dozed off in the middle.

"You realize, don't you, that I have to completely reinterpret the stars, because of you," said Peter, when they were back in their room, done with the bathroom and getting ready for bed.

Will said nothing. He was stretched out on his bed, on top of the covers, in his boxers and a T-shirt, examining the seascape he'd purchased.

"This is not a night sky I have ever seen before," continued Peter. "Everything I have ever thought or felt or known about the stars is suddenly off, because of you."

"Yadda, yadda, yadda," said Will. Then he looked up from the seascape and beamed Peter an angelic smile.

"Joke if you want to," said Peter, "but now when I look at the Milky Way, I hear celestial harmonies I've never heard before. And I'm not sure if this is part of a feeling or a memory or something else."

"Mister, if I had a nickel for every time I heard that one...,"
said Will, playfully. And then he turned the seascape around, so
Peter could see it. "C'mon, seriously, come and look at my picture.
It's good, no?"

"It's gorgeous. You did well," said Peter, sitting down on the
bed next to Will and regarding the watercolor with him, though the
picture most vivid in Peter's mind at that moment was of his
friend's muscular legs, casually crossed, and bare feet—possibly the
most beautifully formed feet, by the standards of Renaissance
sculpture, Peter thought, that he had ever seen.

"Oh, and by the way," said Will, twisting around and reaching
down to the floor to grab a paper bag from inside the green plastic
one he'd been carrying all afternoon. "This is for you." He handed
Peter the bag.

"Wow," said Peter. "For me?" Inside was a handsome old volume whose title was floridly embossed in oxidized gilt on a brown
cloth cover: *Our Deportment.*

"Will, I...wow," said Peter, beginning to look through the
book, surprised and gratified.

It had been published in 1882 and was dedicated, according to
the title page, "to manners, conduct, and dress of the most refined
society; including forms for letters, invitations, etc., etc. Also, valuable on home culture and training. Compiled from the latest reliable authorities by John H. Young."

"Couldn't resist," said Will. They had looked at the book briefly
in one of the shops they visited, but put it down when Jonathan
and Aldebar decided to press on.

"It's beautiful," said Peter.

"Look at the stamp inside the front cover," said Will. " 'Number 79' in the library of one E. A. Bacon. 'Purchased in 1884, for
1.25.' That's dollars, I presume."

"Probably, yeah...!"

"I went back and got it for you. I knew you had to have it."

"Will, I'm...overwhelmed. This is so thoughtful."

"Look," said Will, drawing closer to Peter and flipping pages to
a place he had marked with a postcard. "There's a section on calling cards."

"Very helpful," said Peter. With both his pulse and his thoughts racing, he wanted to embrace his friend in thanks, but thought better of it, in case he was too overwhelmed to control the impulse.

"And look," said Will, " 'Receptions, Parties, and Balls'!"

As Peter gazed at the chapter heading, with its extravagant illustration of a silver ewer, and at Will's chunky fingers, holding the book open to the right place, he tried to remember the last time there was so much going on in his mind and body.

"Well, thank you," said Peter. "The, uh, best I can do to express my gratitude is make a reflexively gracious, though hopefully not too embarrassing, gesture." And with that, Peter slid over, took Will's right foot into both hands, and kissed the instep with exaggerated courtliness.

A charge went through both of them, even if both wanted to remain calm.

"Charming, sir," said Will, wiggling his toes.

Peter straightened up.

"Now look, we're not going to make love tonight, are we?" he said, rising from the bed to place the book over on the table, with his laptop. " 'Cause I'm pretty well bushed after all that antiquing."

"Me too," said Will. "I guess we should turn in."

Peter flicked off the desk lamp, then gave Will's hair a tousle and kissed the top of his head chastely.

"You're a sweetie, you know that?" he said.

"So are you," said Will.

Peter went to his bed and sat down, and slowly pulled off his pants and socks.

"But just to be serious for a second," he said, " 'cause we're both so avid about truth—you do know that I'm head over heels about you, right?" He paused, then went on. "I guess maybe I don't want to joke it *all* away. I mean, I know that what we have is special and we're dealing with it in a special way. You're putting aside the games you play and I'm trying to put aside mine. . . ."

"Peter . . . ," said Will, shaking his head in a mellow way.

"OK, OK," said Peter. "Just so you know. No pressure." He slipped into his bed and pulled up the covers.

"No, I do know, and it's not pressure," said Will. "I like you—I like you a lot. But honestly, Peter, I have no idea where I stand on love, on sex . . . with anybody. Maybe you could tell. I think I'm a little nuts that way."

"OK," said Peter, carefully, "I guess I get that."

"No, I don't know if you do get that," said Will. "I don't see how you could. I never talk about it. I just started therapy—big surprise, right?—and I think . . . I'm going as fast as I can. Maybe someday soon I'll be able to talk about this with you. I want to."

"Well, that would be nice."

"I think so, too. Believe me."

Will tucked away the seascape and slipped under his own covers, drawing them up over his shoulders.

"You're an amazing man," added Will.

"Oh, I'm amazing, all right," said Peter, with a big yawn. "And just so you know, I'm not so sure where I stand on love, either— which is, excuse me, a big thing for me to have to parse, since I invented love."

Will laughed.

"You did—you invented it?" he said. "Your generation and the Summer of Love?"

"No, me personally," said Peter. "I, who have stood on the shoulders of giants and personally reinvented eros for the modern age. This was not a game for me. It was some kind of responsibility."

"Oh, I see."

"And suddenly, all this revealed knowledge about eros and civilization and such, which used to be true *for all eternity,* hardly applies anymore."

"Don't worry, you can adapt."

"Can I?" Peter snorted. "The dinosaur surviving the crunch? Will, *you* know: I've gone out a lot and fooled around a lot. But at last I can see how sex and love are this one, whole thing—at least they are for me—which makes dating in today's modern, fast-and-loose social environment a little weird. People don't necessarily go out at night looking for that one, whole thing."

"Funny," said Will. "And I've only had sex with people I didn't love, and am possibly afraid of the whole, real thing. Not that I'd even know it if I saw it."

310 • *Stephen Greco*

They were silent for a moment.

"But c'mon, buddy," continued Will. "You're a little wounded, too, aren't you? It's not just the world that's changed. It's *you*."

"Precisely," said Peter. "I'm the walking wounded. And I love you for knowing that."

"What can I say?" said Will. "I'm immense."

Peter smiled.

"And I love that you remember I once called you that," he said. "It's true, you know—you *are* immense."

"I do remember."

And with that, Peter switched off the lamp on the night table and both of them made themselves comfortable in their beds.

"Therapy?" whispered Peter, after a minute.

"Oh, please, not now," murmured Will.

CHAPTER 18

Sunday was rainy, which was exactly the kind of weather that allowed a more essential quality of Jonathan's house than its beauty to emerge: solidity. In the kitchen that morning, despite the squalling outside, the loudest sound to be heard, besides talking, was the crackling of the fire that Aldebar had built in the old fireplace. Jonathan and Will were sitting nearby, at the big table, chatting quietly over coffee, while Peter was upstairs on his laptop and Aldebar was out looking for fresh tarragon.

"So that's why you're hemming and hawing?" asked Jonathan. "He's 'almost too nice'?"

"Sort of," said Will.

"Bullshit."

"He's not nice?"

"That's not what's going on. I'm too nice, too."

"But you never fell in love with me."

"Didn't I?"

"Oh, Jonathan. You never indicated that you did."

"I respected you and liked you. I still do."

"And that means a lot to me. Thank you."

"But now you know he's in love with you," said Jonathan.

"I do," said Will, "though I was the last person to find out. He's always going on about all the models he's dated and the golden age of gay sex. . . ."

"That's my boy."

"And I respect all that. But every time I was sure he was going to make a move, he didn't. And then I felt relieved, even though I was disappointed, because I'm such a mess."

"Jesus."

"I grew up afraid of so-called 'real' sex, because of AIDS, and I guess I was afraid of finding out he could be just another hand-job guy."

"Ucch."

"Or that I was just working myself."

"Speaking of which, I gather he doesn't know yet."

"Uh-uh."

"You gonna tell him?"

"It's not that big a deal."

"Which is why you asked me not to say anything."

"I want to tell him myself."

"Don't tell me you're still at it?"

"Jonathan! I'm a classy magazine editor now!"

"I've known editors to hook—editors at your magazine, in fact."

"It's over, and I *will* tell him. My therapist says that being honest is part of taking care of myself."

"So what's the big play now that you're an honest man, Will? A career, a relationship? A family?"

"I don't know, I don't know! I never had to know these things. I don't know how to know them."

"Which is pretty much where we were last fall, puppy."

"Even this thing at the magazine, which I was lucky to get—it isn't aligned with any great vector I was aiming for. I just like talking to people. My dad's always talking about vectors—the ones that point in the direction you've chosen to go in, the ones that don't."

Jonathan sighed.

"Forgive me for saying so, but your generation is fucked," he said. "And I don't mean in a good way."

"I know," said Will.

"Completely overprotected and underchallenged."

"I know."

"And you've amused yourselves to death. No wonder all of you sit around watching vampire and zombie stories."

Will snickered.

"I hate that stuff," he said.

"Parodies of life."

"True."

"The hustling wasn't even work. It was a parody of work."

"Fair enough. Though . . . it did feel like work, sometimes, with some people. Not you."

"Oh, man," said Jonathan, "I hope I didn't contribute to your becoming a zombie."

"How so?" said Will.

"By hiring you that way! You know, I've developed some guilt around this, as I've come to know you better."

"Why? What about Aldebar?"

"Aldebar's different. He's full-time. Besides, he has a very special talent for helping people. It's like a calling."

"Anyway, no worries. It's not like you were the first and you *turned* me."

"Well, I did recommend you to Randy and Eric. . . ."

"Helped me pay the rent while I stayed in New York and looked for a real job."

"Still. I should be enriching your mind, seeing to *your* special talent. Maybe I can make it up to you."

Conversation over lunch was spotty. Few topics found any traction. More than once, the four of them agreed that Aldebar's chicken salad, made with leftover roast chicken, was superb. They'd used up all their ebullient small talk about matters past and present during the previous forty-eight hours, and in view of the imminent departure of Peter and Will, exchanges about the future felt forced and sad. Nevertheless, and despite the gray day, they worked up some cheer after lunch, when Peter and Will were leaving, as they all stood on the terrace, the van already loaded, promising to see each other the following month, at a screening Jonathan was planning of footage from the movie.

"Is this the sort of thing you want me to bring people to?" said Peter.

"No, that will come later," said Jonathan decisively. "This is more for family and friends."

Peter understood. By plan, the movie would not be finished until after Jonathan's death. It was to include scenes of him and Connor Frankel talking, presumably, until the point at which Jonathan could no longer endure the process of filming. This screening was only to give Jonathan the pleasure of seeing some part of his work with people who mattered to him most. Attending would be a sort of memorial service in advance of the fact. As they stood there, with Jonathan leaning on a cane, Peter caught himself surprised to hear intention still so strong in his friend's voice. Without knowing it, he had allowed thoughts of Jonathan's frailty to undermine the premise that his friend was still an autonomous adult and artist—which he reckoned was like thinking paper money worthless unless backed by gold.

"Until soon then," said Peter.

"Right-o," said Jonathan.

It took Peter a few minutes to compose himself, as he and Will descended Jonathan's road to the main highway. He had to breathe deeply in order to stave off a bout of weeping.

"He seems in a good place right now," said Will.

"I know," said Peter. "I'll be fine."

The drive to Catskill was quick—a zip down the highway and over the Rip Van Winkle Bridge, a graceless contraption built in the 1930s that is conspicuously unworthy of the verdant hills surrounding it. Clouds hung low in the sky, and it continued to rain off and on—another reason why Peter was glad they would be driving home later on the Thruway, which was wider and straighter than the Taconic. And he was glad, too, to have the van, which in all the blowy wetness felt as safe as a space capsule. The seats were indeed that much higher above the road, the wipers that much more powerful, as they swept away sheet after sheet of rain.

Yet finding Arnie's place was not easy. They had Google Mapped the route, but the house was located up in the hills, where the roads were sparsely marked and the road signs few, and the signs they did see were hard to make out in the pounding rain.

It was the land of many dominions. Mile after mile, they passed homes whose streetside décorismo announced all manner of upstate working-class scenarios: the bland little ranchburger belonging to The Guy Who Knows What's Best For Everyone; the gussied-up bungalow of The Couple Who Seem Friendly Enough But Clearly Don't Want To Get Close To Anyone; the grandiloquent McMansion of The Family Who Seem To Excel At Everything In Public But Argue Violently Among Themselves Every Night In Private. Driveways lined in beds of pansies; property lines staked with painted brick stanchions; yards anchored by exactly symmetrical groupings of neatly groomed shrubbery; chimneys emblazoned with initials of family surnames; shutters pierced with cut-outs in the shape of little pine trees—all of which reflected, Peter knew, strains of Americana that needed to be addressed, and perhaps even cherished, if one was to sell the owners of such places cars and energy drinks and political leaders.

They missed the turnoff to Arnie's road because it was no wider than a driveway, then they missed the driveway itself because the mailbox was obscured by a mass of rain-sagged laurel. When they finally pulled up to the house, in back of a beat-up blue Corolla, Arnie was waiting on the screened-in porch.

"Sort of a shack," said Peter, switching off the ignition and unbuckling his seat belt.

"Be nice," said Will.

It was a modest, one-story cottage tucked into a mass of ill-tended hemlock bushes and old beech trees. The rain coming down on all those leaves sounded like applause over machine-gun fire.

"You made it," shouted Arnie, as Peter and Will dashed up a weed-edged path of stone and gravel to the porch. The yard was a swath of overgrown green that might once have been lawn, patched with humus-layered bare spots under the bushes and trees.

"Yeah," said Peter. "Easy drive."

"C'mon in," said Arnie.

The orange-gingery scent that greeted them inside reminded Peter of Old Spice. Two big brown pit bulls bounded over to welcome the guests eagerly, as shoes were wiped and jackets taken.

"Don't worry, they're very friendly," said Arnie. "Gustav and Alma. Big sweetie pies."

Will knelt down to greet and fondle the dogs, which were delighted with the attention.

The cottage had been a summer place for a New York family, built in the '20s, explained Arnie. It had been winterized in the '60s by the professor from whom he bought it.

"Very nice," said Peter, looking around.

"Thanks," said Arnie. "Look around, make yourselves comfortable. I'm just putting the water in the pot." Though the day was cool and wet, Arnie was wearing a pair of cargo shorts with his hoodie and T-shirt, and a pair of clogs with thick gray socks.

The place was homey in a cute-bordering-on-kitsch way. In the living room, a crowd of mismatched bookcases laden with books, CDs, and mementos was accented with aggressively charming accessories like a blue glass vase in the shape of a violin and a pair of vintage paint-by-number landscapes in shadowbox frames. The room's color scheme—cornflower blue for the painted wood floors, maize for the walls—appeared to be taken from the Mexican folk art retablo that was displayed prominently on a cabinet. The furniture included several handsome mid-century modern pieces, but it was clear from the haphazard way they and the rest of Arnie's things were arranged that he was more of an accumulator than a collector.

He came back with a tray of tea and cookies, and they installed themselves around the coffee table. The dogs trotted off to another room.

"Some of this stuff was Professor Birdwell's," said Arnie, about the furniture. "He and his wife were serious modernists. I just liked it, and it's pretty well made. I see stuff just like this on Warren Street for prices I can't believe."

"It's great," said Will.

"Had to replace the windows a few years ago. The roof is next."

"Eww, big job," said Peter.

"It's always something," said Arnie. "I'd love to do the kitchen one day—not that I'm much of a cook."

Through a doorway Peter could see what must be Arnie's den, with an upright piano piled with sheet music.

"So you guys had a good weekend?" said Arnie.

"Pretty good, yeah," said Peter. "Lots of eating and cooking . . ."

"And talking," said Will.

"Cool."

"We took an amazing drive. Gorgeous country."

"And Jonathan showed us a bit of the film he's working on," said Peter.

"Oh?" said Arnie. "What's it about?"

"Good question. I guess it's about life—gay life. American gay life. Nominally, it's about Connor Frankel."

"What? The artist?"

"Yeah."

"He's lending his name to a gay-identified project?"

"It's kind of about him. He's coming out."

"Will wonders never cease?" said Arnie. "I thought he was pretty closeted."

"He was, for the first eighty years of his life," said Peter. "I gather he's decided to make a change."

"Well, good for him," said Arnie. "The titan takes a baby step."

"People will go at their own pace, won't they," observed Peter.

"I guess," said Arnie. "But I've always felt a little—what?— judgmental about people like that. And *him* in particular. Supposedly such a revolutionary, a fearless innovator!—*pfff!* More like a big coward."

"That could be a little . . . ," began Peter.

"Harsh? I know," laughed Arnie. "As you see, I have a little anger around this." His manner in expressing such a strong condemnation was oddly jolly. Peter remembered this about him—the mixture of cheer and the doctrinaire.

"But c'mon," continued Arnie, "if you get married and are so out of touch with your soul that you wake up to it only when you have grandchildren—I mean, I guess I can have some pity for you and the fact that you missed half your life. Now, if you *know* what you want, like Frankel, and have lovers, and simply choose to keep it secret because of some pact with polite society, then that's reprehensible. I hafta conclude that you don't take your soul very seriously, and I have to wonder what kind of art comes out of that."

"Sure," said Peter, "but you do have to admit, some pretty untogether people have made some pretty good art over the years, haven't they?"

"I suppose you're right," said Arnie. And then he directed an aside to Will: "I came out in 1968 and expected the whole world to be out by 1970."

Laughter all around—which gave Peter a moment to wonder if the cheer in Arnie's manner had given way to a certain kind of smugness in the politically correct. Their generation had forged *politically correct* as a tool of revolution, but now that the revolution had been superseded by something else, those who still wielded the tool without a little irony looked a little pathetic, even if, to an old comrade, the act also nostalgically evoked the heady aspirations of exciting times. In fact, thought Peter, Arnie had probably undermined himself with that attitude, over the years, among New York's cultural elite, despite his musical talent. Smugness, like a hundred other personality traits, can cause someone to pass on a project without ever explaining why, sometimes without their even knowing why. A pass can be as simple as an instinct about the other person— unconscious, yet decisive. And even when people *are* conscious of what they consider to be flaws in other people's personalities, they rarely take it upon themselves to advise or instruct, leaving the others without the benefit of input that just might—if they happen to be open to it—help them improve their karma. Thus, whatever people like Arnie tell themselves about why a project or career didn't work out—"I was too smart!" "I was too nice!"—the explanation remains conveniently untested.

"So you guys know each other from back in the day?" said Will.

"*So* long ago," said Arnie.

"Before New York," said Peter. "Ithaca."

"Mrs. Beddoes's rooming house."

"Oh my goodness, right!" Peter had forgotten the name, but remembered the third-floor room of the big white house just off campus, where he and Arnie had spent a whole day and night in Arnie's clanky metal bed, first getting to know each other. Arnie's hair was long and luxuriously black back then, scented with musk oil.

"And then you knew each other in New York, in the seventies?"

"Yup," said Arnie.

"What was it like, back then? How were things different—I mean, for gay men? I try to get Peter to talk about this all the time, but he's so buttoned-up."

Peter made a face in quizzical amusement, but remained silent. Was this an interviewer's tactic for drawing out a subject? An appeal to the obvious professorial side of Arnie, inviting him to lecture?

"Everything's changed and nothing's changed," pronounced Arnie, with something between a smile and a sneer.

"There must have been this amazing moment right after liberation, but before AIDS," said Will. "Not just for sex, but the whole idea of gay culture. I would love to know how it was—how it changed you."

Peter and Arnie looked at each other, each expecting the other to make a comment. Then Peter spoke.

"Well, it may have changed people in different ways," he said, the slight pause following this diplomatic statement allowing him to register the fact that here, unlike in Jonathan's much solider house, he could hear the rain pounding on the roof and the windows. It had been raining, too, he remembered, on that day in Ithaca when he and Arnie first got to know each other. Under a single umbrella—a broad, striped thing meant for golf, that Peter brought with him to college—they walked back to Arnie's house after a sculpture class. The pounding rain made the umbrella sound like a drum. Their sneakers got soaked and so did the bottoms of their jeans, but that was OK. Then, in Arnie's room, after some mint tea and talk of Rome and a song that Arnie had set to a poem of Auden's, which he rendered a cappella, they lay in bed for hours, naked, kissing and touching, being happy with just being close, because it felt so marvelous. And though the little romance didn't last more than a few weeks, it gave Peter a chance to be himself for the first time in his life and the faith that someone like Harold might be out there. And then, all of a sudden, there Harold was.

"Honestly," said Arnie, "I would say that I was so elated by those first years in New York that what came afterward totally shell-shocked me."

"Really?" said Will.

"It was like the revolution I had believed in failed, or was hijacked by AIDS," continued Arnie. "And then, after we battled for AIDS awareness, the emotional response brought acceptance for gay men on completely different terms from the ones we formulated."

"What terms did you want?" asked Will.

"Oh, you know," said Arnie, looking at Peter, who smirked and nodded. "Against the patriarchy. Certainly not conventional marriage, condoned by church, state, and the IRS. We were looking toward some other bond among men, something truer." He air-quoted "truer."

"Ah," said Will.

"Something more about brown rice and plaid flannel shirts," said Peter.

More laughter.

"How long have you been here?" said Will.

"In Catskill? Since eighty-four," said Arnie.

"May I ask why you left New York?"

"It's complicated," said Arnie, who went on to decry the violence and filth of the city back in those days, and the fear of an unknown killer of gay men that added to the tension of city life. He said he wouldn't have admitted it then, but it was a kind of lack of stamina that caused him to leave New York. Living there and then was "too hard for an unambitious dreamer" who had grown up in modest circumstances in suburban Long Island.

"And I didn't love the kind of gay life I found in the city, either," he said. "It was all about Broadway and Fire Island. And in serious musical circles, then, even if you were gay you had to be a real, quote-unquote, gentleman—preferably Episcopalian, possibly Presbyterian."

"Really?" said Will.

"All that decorum crap," said Arnie. "I have a bit of the Radical Faerie in me, Will. I'm Jewish, my parents were lower-middle class, I wasn't that cute—unlike the adorable creature you see before you now. I didn't fit into A-list circles or any other circles I could find. I knew a few people from college, but I never felt like they were *my crowd*. In fact, what I felt was that I couldn't keep up with the clothes, and the hair, and the accessories of the people who I thought were my crowd. . . ." He paused. "Everything was about conspicuous consumption. Just like now."

"That's what America is," said Peter.

"Is it?" said Arnie. "I didn't think it had to be."

"Sounds like you don't miss New York, then," said Will.

"Not really," said Arnie. "I was priced out of it."

"That place on Cornelia!" said Peter.

Arnie shuddered. "The tub in the kitchen!" he said. "The day I got up and found a dying mouse in my coffee cup, I knew I had to get out of there. And even *that* was expensive, for the time."

"You wouldn't believe what they're charging for co-ops on Cornelia now," said Peter. "A studio in that same building was like a million dollars! It's all renovated."

"Of course it is," said Arnie. "The whole island of Manhattan is. *Mazel tov.*"

"What about the music, the concerts?" said Will.

"We have concerts here," said Arnie, expansively. "And though I still live in poverty, at least my poverty is genteel."

Peter and Will demurred.

"No, I live like I want," said Arnie, "even if it is on the edge of what passes for reality."

"How so?" said Will.

"*The Real Housewives of Fire Island Pines,* or whatever they call it," said Arnie.

Will laughed.

"*The A-List,*" he said.

"That's reality," said Arnie.

Peter felt a kind of pride when it dawned on him that it was Will who was driving the conversation. Whether Will was acting the reporter out of awkwardness or a genuine interest in history, it was nice to see him taking part in this visit between old friends as a peer. And it was nice to see Arnie, for his part, according Will the respect due a friend of Peter's, even a boyfriend. Arnie might well assume they were boyfriends, Peter thought, and if the subject came up and Will felt like going into detail, well, that might prove amusing.

But the subject didn't come up. The three chatted on for almost two hours, about this and that, and then, when Arnie offered to switch from tea to wine, Peter suggested it was time to get going.

* * *

"I wanted to know if he had a boyfriend," said Peter, when they were back in the van, heading toward the Thruway.

"I know—me too!" said Will. "I didn't know how to ask!"

"We're such pussies."

"I could live that way, though. It looks comfortable enough. Quiet. Maybe fewer *things*."

"Right? Underheated rooms, broken-in furniture . . ."

"Floors you have to sweep twice a day, because you keep your boots on inside the house . . ."

"Well, maybe not that rustic."

Will laughed.

"I'd need a mudroom," he said.

"And better china," said Peter. "I don't know what to make of a teapot shaped like a kitty with its paw up."

"But seriously, I'm glad we stopped."

"Good."

"He's an interesting guy. Remember, for you, queer theory is the residue of something you lived through. For me, it's a college course that I always felt should mean more to me than it did. Until today. I mean, it was like meeting someone from Pompeii who could tell you about the volcano."

"Ouch," said Peter.

"You know what I mean."

The rain continued, heavy at times. Night came and took away all views but that of the highway. Traffic was thick and moved slowly—in front of them, a trail of glaring red and, to the left, a surge of piercing white, snapping into focus for a second through the windshield, as the wipers swept across, then instantly blurry. The occasional *thwunk* of spray from a passing truck, hitting the van broadside, punctuated the chorus of *shhsss* from everybody's tires.

The texture of reality felt different, too—and how could it not feel so, at the end of such a weekend? Things were palpably more intimate between Peter and Will, not just because of the specific experiences they had had together, but because they had agreed, tacitly, again and again, to have so many experiences together in so short a time. They had made the Pact of Frequent Reconnection and passed through the Portal of Constant Company, and were now in a dimension that only partly resembled the one they'd left on Friday. They were a *thing* now. The weekend had revealed this.

Now and then, Will fiddled with his iPod and the radio, but couldn't find anything they wanted to hear. Rihanna, Lady Gaga, Massenet, and world news all seemed wrong. Highway noise made listening difficult, anyway. Sporadically, they talked about things like Oscar nominations and tourism in space, but then were silent for long stretches, and Peter liked those stretches. There were plenty of things to say, about work, and summer plans, maybe even Will's therapy, but they would all be said in time, now that they were a *thing*. Silence was good—a new *construction* between them that itself provided a kind of communication.

As he drove, and Will began to doze, Peter fantasized that he and Will were boyfriends.

Here I am returning to the city after a weekend in the country with my boyfriend—my boyfriend who is asleep in the other seat. My tall and handsome boyfriend, with the gray-blue eyes and the amazing calves . . .

The fantasy was as delicious as a comic book yarn. Will's legs were stretched in front of him and his hands were kind of tucked between them.

He's so cute, the way he sleeps. Still so neatly put together! This is precious cargo I'm carrying—my boyfriend. So I have to drive that much more safely. I am responsible for his life, and that's an amazing responsibility to have, all of a sudden!

It was such a different feeling from all the mooning and obsessing Peter had been doing over Will.

What would his family say if we were in an accident and I was responsible for Will's death or something? They don't know who the hell I am. "Who is this guy?" they'd wonder. "What was Will doing with him?"

He was the new boyfriend! They were a *thing*.

Mile after mile, traffic grew heavier. Civilization became denser and traffic signs more frequent—as legible in the bad weather as they were designed to be, those lovely, helpful poems in a typeface Peter knew was called Clearview, floating in reflective fields of Strong Green, also known as RGB #0, 153, 0.

Will woke when Peter took the van onto the shoulder, in a small detour around roadwork. Glare from the banks of work lights outside, as well as from traffic in both directions, now squeezed closer for the detour, lit up the inside of the van.

"Where are we?" said Will, adjusting himself in his seat. Their heads glowed theatrically in the harsh light.

"Yonkers," said Peter.

"Cool."

It was around nine.

"I thought we'd swing over to Astoria and drop you, then I can go on to Brooklyn."

"And return the van tomorrow?"

"Seems easier."

"OK. I don't even know if they do Sunday returns this late. It's not like a car rental."

"I can drop it off on the way to work."

"You're a champion."

Where would they be in a year? Peter wondered. With some lovely memories of their first Thanksgiving and Christmas together, to cherish for years to come? He was glad now that they hadn't hopped into bed together automatically, months before. That would have been too ordinary a beginning for a relationship so monstrously excellent. In the coming months, there would be plenty of opportunities to get beyond all the scripts and tricks, as they said they wanted to do. And yet Peter might also be able to find some satisfaction with a plain, old-fashioned, Damon and Pythias–level friendship, if the romance didn't want to come true—if, say, Will, in therapy, didn't uncover the ability and fortify the desire to love an older man as easily as a younger one.

Might be able . . .

Will tried again with the radio and found a good jazz station, so they listened to Duke Ellington and Ella Fitzgerald as they navigated through the mess of city arteries, toward Queens.

"He kissed your foot?" squealed Luz.

"Mm-hmm," said Will.

"In a nice way?"

"Yeah. It wasn't supposed to be hot. It was sweet."

"So, no tongue."

"Luz!"

"You guys."

"It was lips only, as if he were kissing my hand. It was very courtly, actually."

Luz had been working on a brief, when Will came in. The kitchen table was cluttered with law books, and she was in sweats, her hair pinned up in a plastic butterfly clip. Will dropped his bag, got a can of Diet Coke from the refrigerator, and sat down with her.

"It was a pretty nice weekend," he said. "The house is insane."

"Tell me the short version."

"There's a pool, a full gym, thirty-mile views. Architectural details like you wouldn't believe. And he has his own film studio up there, Jonathan. Which basically means a room where people come with their laptops, and they sit around and view footage, and talk about it, and edit. Two of them stay right there, in, like, these guest rooms that are part of the studio wing."

"Oh, my."

Will listed the things they had done: the shopping excursion, the lavish meals, the visit to Catskill.

"And it was so weird," he said. "We're coming across the Triborough Bridge and guess who he gets a call from?"

"Oh, boy."

"The devil in client-form."

"McCaw."

"Yup. I gather they had a lot of back-and-forth over the weekend, though Peter didn't let me see any of it. I mean, I think he didn't want to bother anyone with work...."

"What was it about? Anything serious?"

"They were just talking about a meeting with some TV people. I think they're developing a talk show. But it's the first I've heard of it. And it sounds like Peter's really close to this guy, and I have to say it makes me feel kinda weird. I mean, you could see that he was stressed or whatever, while he was talking, but he was also sort of sucking up, too, in a way."

"That's his job, dude."

"Yeah, but it was a shock, after the weekend. I really thought we were getting to know each other."

"You are."

"But this thing. He's working pretty closely with this guy—drawing this big paycheck to do something that's probably going to be detrimental to the entire human race. I'm not sure I'm in favor of it, Luz."

"Well, look . . ."

"And you know what? I think part of him was glad I saw him take the call. He never talks about this part of his work, and I think he knows it's a little off, and that I might disapprove, like a lot of people disapprove. So now it's out in the open, though we really didn't have any time to get into it. This only just happened! He said we'd talk. And it's so funny that this was on the same day that we visit his friend in Catskill—the guy who hasn't compromised his principles one little bit, in his whole life, which of course means that he's totally poor and completely marginal. But still . . ."

"Guillermo, with respect, I have to finish this brief."

Will rose from the table.

"I love you," he said, picking up his bag.

"I love you," said Luz.

Then, heading off, Will shook his head. "To live through AIDS, only to be seduced by the dark side," he said.

"Then you'll save him."

"I'm not sure that's my job," said Will.

"Right. Your job right now is to let me work."

CHAPTER 19

"You kissed his foot?"

"I sure did."

"I'm so jealous!"

"Oh, come on . . . ," said Peter, giving Tyler's shoeless foot a playful tug. They were sitting on the wooden floor of a loft in Bushwick, in socks, scattered about the space with twenty or so others, waiting for a dance performance to begin. Or maybe it had begun, since the performers were already sitting and lying on the floor among them, in rehearsal attire, stretching, warming up, and sometimes talking quietly to each other—passively acknowledging the presence of an audience, but not engaging any onlookers too directly.

"No, I know I have to live with these feelings, somehow."

"We must go on."

Audience members continued to chat quietly among themselves, in advance of some cue from the lighting or the dancers that the performance was elevating.

The loft, which was called the Performance Research Collaborative, a name that certainly sounded like it belonged to a public space, was also clearly someone's home. A stove, a sink, and a shelf of provisions were tucked into a corner behind the young woman seated at the door, who was taking people's $12 admissions, asking them to remove their shoes, and directing them to install them-selves on the floor "anywhere in the space." It was in a former fac-tory building that was one of the few structures still standing within those several blocks of Bushwick—the others having been torched during the blackout riots of '77, then pulled down and not replaced with anything. Decades later, that whole edge of the neighborhood was still mostly abandoned. Even the trees were gone, though here and there, amid crumbling pavement, saplings and bushes pushed up boisterously. Where buildings had once been, there were now barely discernable lots, which Peter guessed might not even be technically anyone's property; nor was there much rubble, or even cyclone fencing, or indeed people to be kept out of any particular patch of scraped-bare terrain, except the lone other soul who got off the same train as Peter and headed in the same direction. Peter had thought Tyler was kidding, earlier that day, when they agreed to meet at the performance and Tyler said, "When you come out of the subway, just look for the building." In fact, Peter took the train, instead of a car, only to see what it would be like to emerge from underground into an apocalypscape stretching into the distance, empty except for a boxy fortress a hundred yards away, whose third-floor corner windows beaconed light weakly into the dusk.

"I think he sees that I'm wounded," said Peter. "Which is, you know, a nice starting point."

"I see that, too, Peter," burbled Tyler. "You're a total wreck!"

Peter laughed. Some of the dancers were standing now, but peo-ple were still talking. From his spot on the floor Peter also saw that the loft's windows faced Manhattan. A frieze of Midtown skyline postured above the sill.

"So can you come with me to this McCaw dinner?" whispered Peter.

"I told you, I have a performance that night," said Tyler.

"Please! Can't you get out of it?"

"Of course not. Why don't you take Will, anyway? Or a woman. Wouldn't this be the kind of thing to which you take a lady?"

"That's just what I'm supposed to do! The gay guy brings a ter-rific dame who doesn't mind if he's discreetly introduced to some-one special. That won't give me the protection I need!"

"I see, and I would."

"A man would, yes."

"Take Will."

"I'm afraid to ask him. I don't think he likes McCaw."

"No one does. You don't, even."

"Still."

The dancers started moving, slowly, randomly, with seemingly uninflected, everyday little gestures. Sometimes they addressed each other with simple statements that described their position or perhaps existence itself—"I'm here now," "This is us, in here"—or they addressed audience members the same way. People responded with the kind of smiley, unbroken eye contact meant to both constitute and signal rapt attention. There was no other sound except the occasional creaking of the floor. It was a very quiet, gentle, unfrontal, even ungelled type of performance that might better be described as an exercise or a ritual, Peter thought, since it seemed unguided by any plan of development or complication that would have yielded an actual composition. Instead, the performance seemed to aspire to the state of a *condition*. A peaceable regard among dancers and audience members seemed to be the point of it, a mutual limning and observance of certain rules of conduct in the actual coming together. And in this way, of course, Peter felt the performance, though not theatrically riveting, to be well worth the journey to Bushwick, since it was an advance look at a kind of social research of which the wider world might not receive word or benefit for years—and this could prove useful in serving certain brands, if American behavior continued to move in the bovine direction it had been moving for years.

Moreover, thought Peter, it was bracing to think of this genial ceremony taking place in the middle of such a barren district, in a room that once thundered with industrial knitting machines. Did it represent the end of a great strain of culturally critical performance art, that had begun so disruptively and subversively in the '60s with happenings and such, and was now petering out like a plague that had evolved beyond virulence? Maybe. But it was also fun to sit shoeless on the floor with young folks, as in a kind of religious observance, observing rules of humility that presented themselves as rules of hospitality.

The performance wound down with the dancers returning to

their original positions and becoming still. And then, with a cue that came not from the lighting but from the dancers' faces, reflecting the transition from one kind of presence to another, people knew that the performance was over. They warmly applauded and the dancers warmly acknowledged, then the audience rose and everyone greeted one another warmly.

Tyler congratulated one of the female dancers who happened to be standing near him and Peter, then Tyler directed Peter's attention to one of the male dancers, a lithe, muscular redhead who was talking to admirers on the other side of the room.

"Cute, right?" he said. He had bumped Peter's knee during the performance, when the dancer, in a stretchy T-shirt and knit cutoffs, had come particularly close to them.

"Is that your friend?" said Peter.

"No, no, Leah is over there," said Tyler, turning to catch the eye of a tall blond woman who was with a group near the door. He waved and she waved back, meaning that they would be speaking as soon as the pointedly unhurried, post-performance mingle allowed.

Then the dancer they liked was standing right next to them, talking to a gaggle of gay friends who had obviously come to see and support him; and soon enough he was accepting Tyler's congratulations.

"You guys were great!"

"Thank you," said the dancer, with a shy smile. His hair was in attractively messy ringlets. He suddenly seemed gay himself, and no longer only the generically gorgeous human being that dancers sometimes embody.

"You work with Miguel, don't you?" said Tyler, prompting a few words about a young, it-boy choreographer and his excitingly "transgressive" process.

"He was totally smiling at you," said Tyler, after the dancer went off and they were making their way toward Leah.

"He was not," said Peter. "He was just being nice. Very sweet smile."

"He was into you. You should have said something."

"Nooo . . ."

"He has a thing for daddies. I can tell."

Peter gave Tyler a push. He had always thought of himself as shy, but in truth, since becoming older, Peter had learned to be cautious in dealing with younger men. One was no longer an equal with everyone else. One didn't want to put anyone in an uncomfortable spot with an overture, nor, of course, did one want to be rejected. Yet just as he had been getting comfortable with caution, Peter discovered that some younger men really did like older men. It was a fact he now took seriously, even if it did mean learning how to spot the ones who fetishized an older man in an unconscious attempt, perhaps, to avoid developing their own identity, power, and income.

Leah was still revved from the performance. She said the audience had been larger that evening and the performance "more intense" than it had been the night before. She explained that the text had been developed during improvs, with contributions from the dancers; it was sometimes hard to dance and talk at the same time, she said. And at some point, the conversation was joined by three other dancers, including the young man Peter and Tyler liked.

"Do you see a lot of dance?" the dancer asked Peter, while Tyler continued to talk with Leah and others.

"Yeah, a bunch," said Peter. "You know—ballet, too."

"Cool."

Peter was surprised by the dancer's interest and friendliness.

"I mean, Tyler's a performer, too," said Peter, "so he's always telling me about things I should see."

"I know. I've seen his work."

"They did this thing last fall at Rico's, the company he works with. . . ."

"Right, right," said the dancer, naming the company's director. "You must see everything he does."

"I dunno—I guess," said Peter, suddenly realizing that the dancer might be wondering if he and Tyler were a couple. "Since we're coworkers, I try to see what I can, but sometimes it's hard."

"Yeah, sure . . ."

They exchanged a few more words, then the dancer asked Peter to wait while he went to fetch a flyer for an upcoming performance he was in. When he put the flyer into Peter's hand, he extended a sincere-sounding invitation to come and see the show. Peter said he would try.

Later, on the way back into the city, Peter told Tyler that he would never have approached the dancer, let alone have been able to recognize the dancer's interest in him, without Tyler's gentle hint. And though this thing with Will precluded any additional complication, it was nice to feel in the game.

"See what I'm sayin'?" said Tyler.

The incident also helped Peter see that Tyler's own long-professed interest in him might be more than just a fetish-fueled "boss" thing—which Peter found touching, though he didn't mention this to Tyler.

Peter did ask Will to go with him to Henderson McCaw's dinner party and Will reluctantly agreed. Peter said that a rising editor should include purely social evenings like this one in his busy schedule, if possible, especially since McCaw would undoubtedly be sophisticated enough to surround himself with a wide range of interesting people and not simply fellow ideologues. But Peter was wrong. The guests turned out to be mostly ideologues and funders—a money crowd, more than a social one, though the evening was not a fund-raiser *per se,* but a perk for people who had made substantial donations to McCaw's foundation and were expected to do so again. Except for Peter and Will, it was thirty garden-variety New York blue chippers, skewing toward Palm Beach and a bit toward Palm Springs; and in a sense the evening felt like the anti-Bushwick, in that everyone in attendance was as far from bovine as possible. With scorching immodesty, they smiled and swanned and with the practiced cordiality of their kind bristled with quiet aggression that reveals itself not only through the generic cheer of the salon but the choreography it takes to carry off expensive clothing, jewelry, hair, shoes, and face work.

McCaw's home, too, had been built as the setting for performance, meant, like so much New York architecture, to showcase wealth in action. It was an enormous limestone Beaux Arts mansion on Seventy-third Street, a few doors from Fifth Avenue. Actually the family home of McCaw's wife, Jenna, the house was built by Jenna's great-grandfather, a prominent tin magnate, in 1903, though over the years family members had moved away; and until McCaw and Jenna moved in, a few years before, in anticipation of

McCaw's bid for national attention, the place had been occupied only by Jenna's brother, who lived alone upstairs, in a top-floor apartment. From the street, the house was imposing: a rusticated ground floor whose unframed windows, capped with muscular keystones and voussoirs, contrasted with the more delicately fluted, black-and-white marble columns and balconied cornice of the portico; a *piano nobile* boasting three towering windows with cornices supported by voluted brackets with pendant garlands; a third story of three square windows with punchy, shouldered frames; and above that, for the recessed fourth floor, a balustrade spanning the entire width of the façade.

"Nice place," said Will, when he and Will pulled up in the town car that Peter had hired for the evening.

"Lord," said Peter.

"What did you expect?"

They were both in black tie—Peter in a standard Brooks Brothers tuxedo, Will in a black Prada suit he'd accessorized with a pair of brand-new, blindingly white Chuck Taylor basketball sneaks. Peter had chuckled over Will's outfit when he ducked into the backseat of the car earlier that evening, after the car had gone ahead to collect Will.

"Cute," said Peter, settling in and giving Will's knee a rub and a pat.

"Thanks," said Will. "I couldn't do the standard thing. My tux is so old."

"Very creative. I wish I could get away with something like that."

Will's hair had a bit more pop than usual—a bit more volume, deeper color saturation.

"Are you using product?" said Peter.

"I figured I could use all the help I can get."

"It's just dinner."

"You sure it's black tie?"

"Yes, absolutely."

"OK," sighed Will.

"Don't sound so miserable," said Peter. "It'll be fun. Money! Power! Hors d'oeuvres!"

"Not used to such stuff."

"I thought your parents were rich," said Peter, happy with the opportunity to raggle Will's bugaboo about money and privilege. "Your dad must have rocked a tuxedo."

"He did."

"There ya go. Mine never did."

Peter liked the idea of donning a standard tuxedo again, after so many years of "creative black tie." When he arrived in New York, there were plenty of so-called "formal" events to attend—openings, galas, private dinner parties hosted by gentlefolk who took the old ways seriously—and he alternated between two tuxedos, back then: the cheap one he'd picked up in college and the expensive one he knew he needed the minute he arrived in New York. He was attending so many black tie events at the time, in fact, that he kept a diary of them. The name and date of each one was lovingly inscribed on a fresh page of a little Japanese book made of handmade paper, that he entitled *Formal Evenings*. He knew it was a little precious to keep such a book, but nowadays he was grateful he had done so, for the thing afforded a lovely way to look back on the best-planned birthday and anniversary parties of those long-gone days, as well as events like the Metropolitan Opera's centennial gala, the Broadway opening of *As Is;* a reception for the Cullberg Ballet in the presence of the King and Queen of Sweden. . . .

A butler answered the door, an older man whose proprietary manner made it clear he was family staff, not hired help. He greeted Peter and Will with routine warmth, while off to the side two men whom Peter took to be security stood by with earpieces. The butler showed Peter and Will to the bottom of a sweeping grand stairway, at the top of which, on the house's museum-scale main floor, Jenna McCaw was greeting guests.

She was an overprocessed-looking woman in her late thirties, in a violet cocktail dress and photo-ready hairdo—a former lobbyist for the health insurance industry, Peter knew, who'd given up her career when she married McCaw. Her carriage was a little businesswoman, a little beauty queen. She smiled robotically when she spotted Peter and Will and invited them into the conversation she was having with a white-haired man and woman.

"You must be Peter," said Jenna. "Welcome." Enveloping her was the spicy-floral scent of an exclusive department store. Peter introduced Will, and Jenna introduced the Brinns—Maddy and Don. After a little exchange about the traffic, Jenna continued talking with the Brinns about trekking in Tibet, and Peter and Will did their best to join in, though neither had ever been to Tibet, and none of the tiny observations either tried to add about regional culture or politics seemed particularly welcome. Instead, the conversation was essentially a comparison of high-end tourist experiences, Jenna and McCaw having done the same luxury trek in Tibet that the Brinns had done the year before, with the same "responsible tourism" agency.

"Isn't Raj the best?" said Jenna. She was wearing a tennis bracelet of pretty blue sapphires.

"We were terribly lucky to get him," said Maddy. "He had a cancellation, or we wouldn't have."

"The guide," said Don, for the benefit of Peter and Will. "Highly sought after. Cambridge degree."

"And he cooks!" said Jenna.

"Right there on the trail!" said Maddy. "Though, of course, he's got all that help."

"Bearers," said Don.

"Did he make you that Malaysian thing, with the basil . . . ?"

If Jenna or the Brinns were flummoxed by Peter's choice of date, they didn't show it. Jenna's hostess skills were generic, but the small talk she generated was welcome, nonetheless. Scanning the room and seeing nothing but boy-girl couples of formally attired strangers, Peter knew the evening was going to require some effort.

As the Brinns moved off, Jenna brightly introduced the Sandersons, who had just arrived—Sunny and Bill. The ladies exchanged a few words about Sunny's spectacular pearl-and-diamond earrings—her mother's Bulgari—then Jenna excused herself.

Neither Sunny nor Bill, who was a banker, had heard of Peter's agency or any of the big campaigns he'd created. The name of the energy drink for which he'd done the global campaign drew a blank.

"We stick to water," said Bill.

"Ah," said Peter.

"Huge business, energy drinks," said Bill.

"Well, yes . . . ," said Peter, sorting through a hundred ways to respond to such a statement. Before he could choose one, Will piped up.

"Amazing house, isn't it?" said Will. Beyond an archway flanked by stately pairs of Ionic columns, at the front of the house, lay the main salon, which was decorated with family antiques in a Federal style that looked splendid enough for a public room of the White House. Some of the ladies were sitting, but most guests stood as waiters circulated with trays of hors d'oeuvres and champagne. Like the rest of the house, the salon featured pilasters and moldings whose details were picked out delicately in gold leaf. A pair of ancestor portraits dominated the fireplace wall. Opposite the salon, at the back of the house, through another double-columned archway, was the dining room, where skirted round tables had been set up with china, crystal, silver, and flowers.

"Tremendous asset," said Bill. "It's good they've been able to hang on to it."

"Carrère and Hastings, I gather," said Peter.

"Really," said Sunny, abstractly.

"Henderson told me," said Peter. "And as we're standing here, I'm wondering if that's Apollo and Diana." He directed their attention to the sculptural frieze above the arch.

The Sandersons peered for a moment, but were relieved—Bill was, clearly—when a waiter appeared with a tray of champagne.

" 'Apollo and Diana'?" said Will, after they and the Sandersons excused each other politely.

"What are we supposed to talk about?" said Peter. "Interest rates?"

Will made a face. "I suppose she doesn't have to talk at all," he said, "as the designated earring-wearer."

It was unusual for Peter to feel so alienated at a party. Even at the toniest gatherings he found plenty of people of accomplishment or achievement to talk with, regardless of how much money they happened to have. But with a chuckle, he recognized something chilling at McCaw's that he'd first encountered long ago, a social phenomenon that can happen *en masse* only in a financial capital like New York: The party was one of those gatherings where the guests were only rich, with no particular distinctions or strengths beyond the talent to hold on to their own wealth. By and large, it was a crowd that gave no real service to humanity or contribution to culture—though sometimes one of the ladies in such a crowd would have a pretension around "personal expression," which she felt she could share with a fellow creative like Peter. Now, when someone at a party like this started talking about fulfillment in her avocation of sculpture, painting, or dance, Peter winced internally. Too often, in earlier days, he would follow up such a conversation with attendance at an exhibition or concert whose success, he discovered, could be glimpsed only through the lens of vanity. A question would invariably thus arise in his mind, which was, of course, never to be put to the lady involved: "Wouldn't the first task of someone who wants to be an artist be to get into some kind of critical stance with her own comfortable means?"

Simple experience was what made Peter so sure of this view of McCaw's guests. Sadly, after years of socializing, he knew what to look for: chiefly, a lack of curiosity about ideas that mattered, which seemed to impede the intake of new information and probably expressed the interlocutor's subconscious belief that he or she already possessed all the important information there was. In a sense, these were the people whose lifestyle McCaw meant to preserve, even as that task was bolstered by the sale of a larger myth about "the American community" to anyone who'd buy it—which was, of course, Peter's assignment.

"Is she a real countess?"

"Depends on what you mean by 'real.'"

"They're all so . . . common."

"Can I tell you? I watch that show all the time—secretly, in the den, with the door closed, so Milton doesn't hear."

Peter and Will were chatting about reality TV with the Gladstones, a lawyer and his wife, when McCaw finally found them.

"Honey, Milton, I see you've met our resident genius," boomed McCaw. "Glad you could come, buddy." McCaw shook Peter's hand and clapped him on the shoulder.

"Hendy, this is Will," said Peter.

"Will, welcome," said McCaw, shaking Will's hand.

"Terrific party," said Will.

"It's all Jenna," said McCaw, beaming.

"She's taking good care of us," said Peter.

"Great," said McCaw. "We'll talk later?"

The next forty minutes were a froth of summer plans and redecoration projects, laced with champagne and Pellegrino. Unlike a lot of the other parties that both Peter and Will attended, there wasn't a lot of aggressive circulating, let alone working the room. This was a more ceremonious gathering. The only other folks who didn't seem to fit the mold—despite his black-on-black, foliate-patterned dinner jacket and her sleek aubergine cocktail dress and glamorous heels—were a young, good-looking man with long, wavy hair and a ready smile, and a striking black woman who might easily have been a model. They giggled a lot and touched each other easily, though not necessarily in a romantic way. People seemed to like talking with them. Were they a couple? Upper East Siders? Peter thought he might have seen the man before—maybe on the New York VIP-scape—but he wasn't sure, that type being all too common: young, attractive, rich, straight. Then Jenna announced dinner.

As large and graciously proportioned as the main salon, the dining room was set with four tables of eight. The windows were hung with striped damask, and the walls featured nineteenth-century landscapes in gilt frames. The butler helped everyone find their places, which were marked with cards clipped to holders in the shape of tiny golden hands. Waiters stood by with the first wine.

Peter and Will had hoped to be at the same table as Jenna— "I'm dying to know what *she's* all about," whispered Will conspiratorially, as they walked into the dining room—but instead they got McCaw, which Peter immediately grasped as an honor. Also at their table were Mary, a middle-aged, little-girlish retail heiress, and Nancy, her best friend and, apparently, sidekick; Reynold, a well-known real estate developer, and Peyton, his much-younger second wife; and Fiona, the black woman in the aubergine dress, who turned out to be a London-born and -based attorney working for an American firm.

Peter asked Fiona, who was on his left, whether she had an apartment in New York.

"Oh, I stay right here," said Fiona.

"On Fifth?" said Peter.

"No, no—in this house," she laughed, without further explanation, since everyone at the table was burbling with the small talk of sitting down. Nor was it clear why Fiona wasn't seated at the same table as her long-haired friend—yet there was an art to seating arrangements, Peter knew, and Jenna and/or McCaw would have their reasons for populating each table as indicated by the golden hands.

On Peter's right was Mary, who seemed meek enough at first, in her plain white dress and modest little haircut, and then she spoke, at which point she displayed the gumption of a five-star general.

"What happened to the senator?" she said.

"Last-minute trip," said McCaw.

"Bullshit," said Mary. "Excuse my French. He's afraid of getting too close."

"He sent his apologies," said McCaw, "and promised to come to the next one."

"This is the thing," said Mary, tapping the table forcefully with a beautifully manicured forefinger. "We need to get them to come out in the open."

"Agreed," said McCaw.

"He'll come around," said Reynold, after double-checking whom they were talking about.

"That's why we're so lucky to have Peter with us," continued Mary, suddenly purring and favoring Peter with a big smile. "Helping us *direct* the conversation...."

"Hear, hear," said Reynold.

Peter was surprised. He had met neither Mary nor Reynold before, and wouldn't have imagined either knowing of him. McCaw had obviously been talking about their work. All Peter could think of to say was "Thanks."

They talked of governors and senators, as the appetizer and main course were served and cleared, and of policies and constituencies—with McCaw or Mary generally taking the lead during the moments when the table was conversing as a group. Peter was asked to say something about the way he thought the "national conversation evolved," and he rattled off a few observations that McCaw had already heard, but that worked well over dinner. Predictably, most of the thoughts expressed at the table were conservative, and though McCaw's and Mary's thoughts were anything but unintelligent, those of the others sometimes lapsed into sketchiness. Peyton didn't feel immigration was such a good idea—immigration of any sort, legal or illegal. Nancy wanted the Internet to be more strictly policed, because it could serve as a breeding ground for terrorism. Reynold was tired of being taxed unfairly. Peter thought he might have noticed Fiona reacting with private amusement to a particularly fatuous remark Peyton made about the Islamization of British society. Fiona, in fact, seemed to be keeping a lot of thoughts to herself, much as Peter and Will were doing, as dinner rolled on.

At one point, Fiona mentioned to Peter that she was married to Jenna's brother Miller, and pointed across the room to the young long-haired man, who was seated at Jenna's table. Peter thought, *Oh, OK.*

"I'll introduce you guys later," said Fiona. "I think you'll like each other."

Peter wanted instantly to tell Will what he'd discovered, but Will, on the other side of the table, was engrossed in a conversation with Nancy about growing up in Santa Barbara. As for the person McCaw supposedly wanted Peter to meet, there was no one around who seemed possible, so Peter put the matter out of his mind.

Island Creek oysters, Wagyu beef, Stone Barn asparagus, fleur du sel, Lampong pepper. It was the kind of evening where the specific name of every food eventually got mentioned—not necessarily by the host, who was too preoccupied to do so, but by the guests and, when asked, the well-informed servers.

As the table was being set for dessert, one of the servers, when asked, said she was a native of Colombia. After she'd gone, Peyton said something about the number of "Hispanics" working in food service in New York. Then she admitted, with the comic inflection of a sitcom punch line, that "Latina" might be the right term. Some at the table found this amusing.

"Political correctness! Where did it ever come from?" said McCaw. "Why has it become such a vernacular?"

"Good question," said Nancy.

"Well, think about it," said Will, with another sip of the Pomerol that had been served with the beef, his second glass, though the dessert wine, a nice Riesling, had also been poured. "Think about how people felt in the sixties, when they passed civil rights. They must have felt like they woke up from a dream. You know—'We have television and satellites, but how is it until now that we've lived with the social norms of ancient Rome?' They must have felt like, 'Wow, if we've been this stupid, what else are we doing wrong?' "

"Interesting," said Reynold.

"Huh," said Peyton, pondering.

"We have indeed come to respect each other much more, over the years," said McCaw. "Well said, Will."

Mary patted McCaw's hand.

"I wish more people would open their minds when they listen to you," she said. "I wish they understood that you *get* that certain things are simple and certain things are not. Of course, it sounds so boring, if you say it like that. . . ."

"Not boring," said McCaw. "Just hard to remember." He said he didn't like being misunderstood, himself—it hurt, personally—but that the larger point was the decline of American intelligence. People were no longer being taught how to think. Mary nodded vigorously, and added that this might be an opportunity.

"What about acknowledging this decline frankly, perhaps framing it as a public health issue?" she said. "Peter?"

Peter was now on the spot, or on duty.

"Well, there's always new intelligence, new kinds of thinking," he began. "I mean, in a certain way, Lady Gaga means that music is over, right? But, in another way, our whole idea of entertainment and even the arts is shifting."

There was a titter at the mention of Lady Gaga, but Peter saw that Mary and the others were trying to parse what he'd said—which made him wish instantly that he'd said something smarter and not so dinner-partyish. Each of the other tables, too, he noticed, was in the midst of animated conversation; the room was swimming in chatter and laughter. Was anyone else talking about Lady Gaga? And why was there no music? Had Jenna or McCaw specifically opted for no music?

Suddenly, Will, who had been listening quietly to the conversation, perked up.

"Why not just give people the context with the message?" he said. "What about saying something like, 'Simplify when possible, complicate when necessary'?" That kinda says it, right?"

The line, as it hung in the air, seemed to command attention. It happened to be a line that Will had written for the Assetou article, months before, to describe the singer's approach to composition in her music and artwork.

"Simplify when possible, complicate when necessary," said Mary.

McCaw, after considering the line for a second, repeated it, too.

"I love it," squawked Mary.

"It's pretty good," said McCaw.

"Very deep," said Peyton.

They toasted Will and the conversation moved on. The phrase had merit, Peter thought. It was like something Tyler and he had been working on, during the previous week, but much more elegant.

"Nice job," he whispered to Will later, after dessert, when McCaw got up to visit the other tables and people started table-hopping.

"Oh, thanks," said Will, slightly tipsy. But he was being pulled away by Peyton, who was terribly interested in magazines and wanted to know more about Will's magazine.

As the guests moved back to the salon for coffee and petits fours, Peter stood talking with Mary and an insurance executive she brought over. The man was kind but dim, and Peter delighted himself secretly by glancing across the room as often as he dared at Will, who was looking so sharp, in his Prada and sneakers, and seemed to be doing so well. He was installed in one of the seating areas with Peyton and some of the other ladies. Laughter periodically pealed from the group.

Then, as Peter was excusing himself to go find a powder room, McCaw's brother-in-law appeared and introduced himself.

"Oh, hey," said Peter. "I had the pleasure of talking with your wife over dinner."

"Nice," said Miller. "Hendy said I should find you and say hello."

"Are you in advertising?"

"God, no," said Miller, with a laugh. "Right now, I'm helping some people get a media venture off the ground." Miller described the project, which sounded vague, but Peter saw no harm in responding positively. There was something of the charmer about Miller, even the dilettante. He was very handsome, in an overripe sort of way. Peter realized that he *had* seen the guy around before. *One of those idle pleasure-seekers...*

Then it dawned on Peter: This was the guy whom McCaw wanted him to meet! Fiona probably even knew! Did McCaw really think that Peter would be interested in such a creature? Did he think that an acquaintance with Peter would serve as some sort of corrective for Miller? The possibilities were absurd.

"Are you a partner, then?" said Peter. "Or an investor...?"

"I'm all that—sure," chuckled Miller, with a wink.

Completely unserious, Peter judged. This was a type that Peter knew well. In the old days, someone like Miller might have been called a playboy; and the ambisexual vibe was part of that, Peter knew, not because it represented self-discovery or a philosophy about sexual identity, but because it was easy.

"Cool," said Peter. "Well, how awesome for you to have this place as your home. Fiona mentioned that you live here."

"Yeah, and I grew up here," said Miller. "For a long time, it was just my mom and me. And then she moved to Singapore and I moved upstairs, into the guest apartment. We were going to rent the place out, and then Jenna and Hendy decided to move in. The more the merrier!"

Peter spotted Fiona on the other side of the room, chatting intently with a much older man with scraggly hair. Poor girl, he thought.

"You and your friend might wanna drop by for drinks some time," continued Miller.

"Drinks?"

"Fiona and I try to do a proper cocktail hour, when she's in town. Sometimes we get the Carlyle to send over a bartender and some nibbles and a piano player. It's kinda nice."

"Really?" said Peter. "Wow." *Not in a million years,* he thought.

The powder room was downstairs—a classic chapel in marble and chrome. The details were impeccable: the black-and-white checkerboard floor, the onyx-trimmed faucet handles. Peter guessed the room represented an expensive "modernization" that had been done in the '20s and kept intact ever since. The mirror reflecting a pleasantly buzzed dinner guest in black tie, framed by a voluptuously wrought molding of white marble, had probably already been in place for decades, Peter thought, when his own family's house was built, in the mid-'50s. It seemed so solid, McCaw's powder room, the whole mansion. The walls felt three-feet thick. The tin magnate had undoubtedly called for the finest materials, the best construction. Peter's place was a wood-framed split level, built on the cheap by a gang of locals his father had always referred to as the "Baxter boys." His first sight of the house, as a child of three, had been horrifying, because, as yet only a shell of two-by-fours, it was transparent, incorporeal. His father was proud because the place was so big; all Peter could think of was that it could never shelter anyone from one of the electrical storms he hated so much. His mother explained what it meant to build a house, which helped. So did her asking him to help pick out decorative tile from among the samples the Baxter boys had brought, for the bathroom that would be his.

The party was beginning to break up when Peter rejoined Will, who was talking with Miller and Fiona, Peyton and Reynold, and some of the others. Will seemed to fit right in. Even his sneakers were drawing compliments, though whether this was in genuine admiration or patronizing tolerance wasn't clear. Peter remembered once caring about the difference between the two. Now, he knew it really didn't matter.

Good-byes were the usual nice-nice, as were the promises of getting together again soon. Jenna and McCaw, who were saying good night to people at the front door, were noticeably nice to Will.

"Come back and see us again," said McCaw. Security was now outside, on the sidewalk.

"Thanks, guys," said Will.

In the car, Peter and Will were quiet, in a contented way. There was a lot to say about the evening, but it seemed better to sink into the calm of the backseat and only map out, for the moment, some of the territory that they would undoubtedly be discussing in detail for months.

"Intense," said Peter.

"Ooof," said Will.

"But basically fun."

"It was fine."

"The ladies loved you."

"Ladies usually do."

The car would take them to Queens, where it would drop Will, then take Peter on to Brooklyn Heights. It was around midnight. Traffic on the FDR was light.

"Fiona's a trip," said Peter.

"Right? It turns out we have some music people in common."

"Yeah?"

"Mm-hmm, from London."

"Cool."

If Will were nursing any antipathies toward McCaw, or if some of these had been blunted by his enjoyment of a preposterous party, he didn't let on. Masses of city glittered and glared through the dark, as they slid by.

"She's pretty smart," said Peter. "We talked a lot about her work—global compliance for a movie studio."

"Mm-hmm."

"Though what she's doing with a guy like Miller . . ."

"Ya never know," said Will, settling deeper into the seat's leather plush.

Peter remembered Will laughing at one of Miller's jokes, when they were all standing there in a group, at the end of the party.

"You guys seemed to know each other," said Peter.

"I guess we've met before."

"You guess?"

"We must have run into each other at a party."

"Gay?"

"Who knows."

"Did you know he was there—I mean, before dinner?"

"I saw him."

"You didn't say hello?"

"It's not like we're friends, Peter. Besides, *we* were talking to all those nice people."

"I'm . . . surprised."

Will patted Peter on the knee, shaking his head.

"He manages my funds," said Will.

"Very funny," said Peter. But Will seemed tired—his eyes were closed—and Peter decided not to press.

They were silent for a while; then, when they were crossing the bridge, Peter spoke.

"He's not such a bad guy, McCaw."

Will came back immediately.

"He's evil and so are all those people."

"You think so?" said Peter. "You didn't let on."

"I have manners. And I am capable of thinking two thoughts at the same time."

Peter laughed.

"That's the key, isn't it?" he said. "Two thoughts at the same time."

"I mean, I'm happy to drink the guy's wine and be civil to his friends," said Will, "but did you hear what some of those people were saying, what they think?"

"I know."

"You're working for that."

"I know."

"At some point, my not-boyfriend, it's gonna get real sticky for you."

Peter brightened.

"Did you just call me your not-boyfriend?" he squealed. "That's so sweet!"

Drowsily, amusedly shaking his head, Will gave Peter's knee another pat.

Peter sat back and tried to enjoy the view. Was he really going to help direct the national conversation, as Mary said? It was nice to think he had the power to do so. Advertising had afforded him the power to direct certain kinds of conversations, but this new alliance with political ambition had fostered both the power and the ambition to do something larger with his talent. Peter liked being at the table with players—though of course McCaw and his chums were not the players he would have chosen. And this created a dilemma. Peter had blundered up to this new level of power. He hadn't chosen it, precisely; he had been chosen for it, and accepted. But the real point of playing on this level, he'd begun to see, was to choose the players and to set the agenda. The point was autonomy, and real grace was possible when one's strongest interests served the largest common good. Otherwise, what was talent for? Yet given the position he was in, and the contract he had signed, what was he to do now? Begin charting his own direction more aggressively, which would mean breaking with McCaw and seeking out those with whom politically and culturally he had more in common? This was a much more aggressive mode of living than he had ever practiced before, and he wasn't even sure he wanted that. A sensible course of action, it seemed, would be to play a bit longer at the table where he was, and observe all he could about the way things work there, and about how that kind of power and his own temperament might map onto each other. He was discovering something new about himself every day, through this gig—about masculinity, even adulthood—and it was exhilarating. Couldn't he just keep going and have a good time, and stay aware of all the compromises that were possible, and build some kind of protective structure for himself, to shield him from the dark side?

Will was dozing. Peter would have to wake him when they arrived at his house.

It was a place to visit, McCaw's world, but not necessarily to live in, Peter decided. If there were really insights to be gained there about power and influence, and how these meshed with talent and intelligence, then fine. It would be a growth experience—and how nice to have such a propulsive one, at the age of almost sixty! And there to help him think clearly, and help protect him, if necessary, would be Will. . . .

CHAPTER 20

Laura was furious when Peter told her he'd taken Will to McCaw's dinner party.

"What were you thinking?" she squawked.

"It was a social invitation," said Peter.

"C'mon, honey. There's no such thing as social. This is business."

She was standing at the door of his office, having stopped by to ask how the evening went. As it happened, she knew the Sandersons and some of the others, and was thrilled to hear about Sunny's spectacular earrings.

"It was fine," said Peter. "Will was a big hit."

"You should have taken me," said Laura. She was dressed in one of her power outfits: a black suit whose jacket buttoned rakishly on the diagonal.

"I wasn't aware we were dating," said Peter.

"Seriously," she said dourly. "You represent this company when you attend things like that."

"Don't lecture me, Laura," said Peter. "I wasn't *attending* anything. I was a guest in someone's home. Besides, Will said something over dinner that really tickled McCaw's fancy—something about the simple versus the complicated." He didn't want to tell Laura the exact phrase, for fear of hearing her thoughts about it.

"What do you mean?" she said.

"It was just dinner talk, but McCaw's been really hyping on it."

"Simple versus complicated—what is that?"

"This is one of the directions that we've been working with, that his team really likes. Will hit on a formulation that really adds strength to what we're doing."

"What is it again?"

"We're cooking it, Laura," said Peter. "I'll put it in our weekly thing."

"All right," she said, knowing she had little choice but to let the creative star be the creative star.

"He called Will 'brilliant,' " said Peter.

"And this kid's a bartender or something?"

"Laura, I told you—he's an editor."

"Oh, right," she said, suddenly interested, after Peter reminded her which magazine. "Do we need to hire him?"

"Go away and let me work. You look great today."

Actually, what McCaw had said to Peter, earlier that morning in a video call, was, "That date of yours was brilliant! I like the way he thinks." Which made Peter feel proud and icky all at the same time.

"Gee, I thought that if anything would get you to say something, it would be McCaw," said Will.

The therapist smiled in a kindly way.

"You want me to say something?" he said, after a suitable silence.

Unlike the psychotherapist in Santa Barbara that Will saw briefly as a child, a friend of his mother's who spoke lots and kept asking him if he was comfortable in a bathing suit, this therapist said very little. Still, Will liked the guy, who'd come very well recommended through a friend of Luz's. Will felt he could say anything in his presence—though, despite his best efforts to concentrate and not waste time, Will often heard himself filling sessions with babbly, inconsequential bullshit. His initial account of the McCaw dinner, for instance, had been a list of magazine-article details—the crystal decanters in the bar of the limousine, the daring décolletage of an older guest's dress, the book-matched, veined marble slabs of the powder room wall. . . .

"He's an asshole—a world-class monster," said Will. "Isn't he? Also, little feet. Perfect little shoes—loafers, pumps, whatever. Pristine. Ya know what I mean?"

Silence.

"And Peter is working for the guy," said Will.

"Yes," said the therapist.

"What a *jerk*."

"Peter?"

"McCaw. Despite all the, you know, money and power. I dunno. He treated me well enough, though."

"Peter did?"

"No, McCaw."

"Ah."

"Made it a point of asking me stuff, listened to what I said. . . . Still—he's *hugely* evil. I could feel it, all night. From all of them. And I couldn't *say* anything. . . ."

"Right."

"I kept wondering if Peter felt it. . . ."

"And?"

"Well, we couldn't exactly talk about it then and there."

The therapist gave Will an inquisitive look.

"Did we talk about it later?" offered Will. "No. Not yet."

"OK."

"Maybe . . . I wanted him to protect me? Maybe . . . I wanted to protect him, through this dinner?"

Silence.

"He says I'm 'immense,' " continued Will, "and I have no idea what that means."

"McCaw says this?"

"No, Peter. 'Immense.' He said it again, just the other day."

"It sounds like he sees a lot in you."

"Yeah. Or maybe he's blowing smoke up my ass. Like he does with his boss."

"Do you really think that?"

Silence.

"No," said Will.

"*Could* he see a lot in you?"

Will shifted in his seat, a well-worn leather armchair that faced the matching one his therapist was sitting in, at a slight angle.

"You mean, *is* there anything in there *to* see . . . ?" mumbled Will, with the generic sarcasm of a sitcom character.

"C'mon, Will," said the therapist. "Don't play games."

"Sorry. I dunno. I guess so."

The screening of Jonathan's work-in-progress took place on a Monday evening at a new boutique hotel in Tribeca. The hotel's facilities included a 100-seat screening room attached to a luxuriously appointed foyer, which is where a reception for the invitation-only audience was taking place when Peter arrived at the suite upstairs that Jonathan and Aldebar had also booked for their stay in New York. Because of his condition, Jonathan had decided to go down to the screening directly, and bypass the reception.

Aldebar greeted Peter warmly at the door of the suite and led him into the living area, where he was readying Jonathan for the event.

"Everything set?" said Peter, giving Jonathan a kiss.

"Absolutely," said Jonathan. He was in his wheelchair, where he would obviously be remaining for the entire evening. He was emaciated and looked weak. He was dressed in jeans, a black blazer, and a crisp white shirt, open at the neck. Though his face showed a subtle bit of enhancement from the makeup Aldebar had applied, the toneless flaps of flesh under his chin told a truer tale. Wordlessly, he nodded his assent when Aldebar showed him a foulard pocket square, and sat passively as the nurse inserted the square in his breast pocket and gave it a tender foof.

"We're all organized," said Aldebar, with a kindly wink toward Peter.

"You look great, Jon," said Peter. "I don't know where you get the strength to do this."

"Entertaining a hundred people? Easy," he said, though an attempted laugh was more of a facial expression than a sound—and, actually, the facial expression more a sketch than a fully executed thing.

"Is Connor Frankel coming?" asked Peter.

"He's downstairs already, at the reception," said Aldebar. "They thought it would be better if he ..."

"He's playing host, so I don't have to," said Jonathan.

Nearby on a table with a tray of mineral water and some glasses was an invitation to the screening—a beautifully designed and printed card whose cover featured a stark and probing portrait of Frankel that Jonathan had taken, plus the film's working title, *Shacks and Mansions*. That probably wasn't going to be the final title, Jonathan had said, since it sounded too brainy for a movie. Then again, he admitted, the film was never intended to be commercial, but something more intellectual: an investigation, through words and images, of the life and work of one artist through the creative lens of another, and perhaps something of the times in which they lived. The title derived from a series of snapshots and magazine photos they were using as a kind of armature for the film, to trigger Frankel's recollections—pictures of him in the various houses, studios, and other places where he had lived his life and done his work. Thus the film, as Jonathan explained it, was "about the physical structures and mental constructs we inhabit until the next ones are built."

Gay identity, of course, was one of those constructs.

"Look," Jonathan had once told Peter, "I may not have much to contribute to high-speed rail, or clean energy, or the space program, but I can damned well make America think about the gay culture we got stuck with."

Connor Frankel was an unlikely subject for a project like this, since he'd spent most of his life being discreet—or in the closet, as Peter's friend Arnie had pointed out. Having always been famously taciturn in interviews, though, Frankel was now unreserved. The decorum he'd always observed because of his class, his upbringing, and/or his generation was now out the window. When Peter asked why Frankel had agreed to open up, Jonathan said only, "It was time."

Frankel's work—always abstract and now very large, often with titles that alluded to history and classical culture—was top-of-the-line, blue-chip modernism. It was included in most of the world's major museums and private collections, and was said to embody the freedoms that figures like Rauschenberg and Johns had found in chance, serendipity, and, according to one critic, "the space between reality and imagination." Much ink had been spilled over the relationship between the homosexuality of artists of that generation and their creative strategies. Yet even now that he was talking, Frankel maintained he had nothing to add to this particular discussion. He could only talk about his life.

A native of Bar Harbor, Maine, Connor Frankel was born into a proud German-American family that had been prosperous for generations. Then his father, an insurance executive, lost most of his money in the Crash of '29, just before Frankel was born. And soon gone, too, was the sprawling house on a bluff overlooking great lawns and the water, where Frankel spent the first few years of his life—a place that was always the site, until it became impossible to maintain, of great gatherings of family and friends, long dinners capped with amateur musical and theatrical performances. Frankel's mother was able to keep the family going on her salary as a teacher, and though they moved into a much smaller house in the same town, she and her husband made it a point of preserving for their children—Connor and his four sisters—a sense of family pride that was now largely fueled by their continuing pursuit of music, art, and literature. It was a family priority to secure art lessons for Connor, once he started showing the interest and the aptitude; and sister Fanny had her dancing and sister May her poems. Thus, the formative struggle of Frankel's early years, Jonathan told Peter, was parallel with that of our nation in the world today: to work out a method or an illusion of holding on to privilege.

The film was an artsy project for sure, but since it was widely rumored to be the coming-out story of a major American artist, it was already generating buzz. Senior press types had been applying pressure to get invited to the screening, yet Jonathan and Frankel had insisted the event remain private, only for their friends, families, and colleagues.

"Nice place," said Jonathan, as the three of them went down in the elevator.

"It is," said Peter, who had never included the hotel on his regular circuit. Its "New York–style" trendiness seemed formulated more for out-of-towners than for anyone else. The elevator, with windows onto a grand atrium several stories tall, sounded a sedative chime as it passed each floor.

"Scorsese showed a film here, once," said Jonathan. "The screen's good."

"Uh-huh," said Peter.

"Though I can't say much for the upho-ol . . . upho-ol . . . *upho-olstery*."

Had Jonathan just stammered, or slurred a word? Privately, Peter shot Aldebar a querying look, since Jonathan never did that, but Aldebar shook his head tightly, as if to say, "Not now."

They went straight to the green room to wait while the doors of the screening room were opened and the guests took their seats. Connor Frankel, who had attended the reception, joined them there, accompanied by his quietly genial, middle-aged companion, Wallace, whom Peter had never met.

"Well, they've had their wine and now they want a movie," quipped Frankel, after introductions. At eighty-three, despite the presidential aura he'd taken on as one of the grand old figures of American culture, he still retained the dark twinkle of the dryly quizzical teenager he was in the 1940s, back when such creatures were perhaps stranger to their neighbors than they are now. He hadn't kept much of his hair, but what he had was bright white and smartly cut and combed. Except for the attire of a public intellectual—the shapeless-but-expensive suit, worn with a plain shirt, suspenders, and a pair of pristine trainers—he might have been a retired executive.

"They're gonna need another glass, when they see what we've got in store for them, eh, Connie?" said Jonathan.

"Everybody came," said Wallace. "The house is full."

"Good, we want that," said Jonathan.

Wallace named a few of the celebrities he'd greeted—a Pulitzer Prize–winning novelist, a reigning Broadway diva, a Hollywood action star who'd just formed a production company to make "quality" movies, as well as several boldface artists, dealers, and collectors. Mondays were the preferred evening in New York for a supposedly private little star-studded event like this one, since busy celebrities often had heavier commitments later in the week, and Mondays were usually the only evenings when theater actors and other performing arts types were free. Peter knew that Jonathan's brother and other members of his family were out there, too, as well as Will, whom Jonathan had made a point of inviting, and Luz.

An assistant slipped into the green room to tell Aldebar that everyone was seated. Aldebar told Jonathan, who in turn said to Peter that he was "ready to roll." Graciously, since Peter was officially Jonathan's date for the event, Aldebar was keeping himself in the background, handling the wheelchair and its occupant in the manner of an employee, though he was also clearly the evening's supervising producer.

They went through a door and a small hallway, then mounted the shallow stage. Houselights were on, and applause erupted as Jonathan and Frankel reached center stage. Peter and Jonathan stood to one side as the assistant adjusted a microphone that had been preset on a stand for Jonathan and gave Connor a handheld one.

"Welcome," said Jonathan, in a small voice that amplification made sound only smaller. The crowd became instantly silent. "Thank you all for coming. I'm touched that you all came out to see a movie that's basically just two old men talking." Audience laughter. "I hope nobody was expecting Spielberg." More laughter.

From where he stood, Peter could see that there were no empty seats. It was a nicely designed room, he thought: simple blond wood panels, discreet lighting, nicely arced rows that raked upward at a gentle angle. Then he saw what Jonathan meant about the upholstery. The seats were covered in a ghastly purple plush that was splotched with yellow suns and white crescent moons. At least the room's sightlines were good. Peter spotted Will and Luz sitting in the middle of the room, near the back. When he caught their eye, he smiled, and Will saluted back.

"Most of the time, a film set is like a reactor," said Jonathan—"a hundred people running around like mad, trying to make a place where this nuclear fuel, the performances, can combust. In this case, it was just Connor and me. But I think we combusted a few times, didn't we?"

Laughter, as Jonathan turned to Frankel.

"We're still friends," said Frankel, smiling but not elaborating.

Jonathan, his comedic timing intact, gave his friend a second, then moved on.

"Well, he says it all in the film," said Jonathan. "Just remember, folks, it's a wo-or . . . wo-or . . ."—he stopped, then regrouped—"a *wo-ork* in progress. God—like my ability to speak, apparently."

The audience's reflexive snicker in response to the wisecrack was dampened by the shock of seeing him falter.

"OK. So please enjoy," said Jonathan. "And then we'll have some supper, after. I hope you'll stick around."

The houselights dimmed as Jonathan and party left the stage and were shown to a VIP box on the side of the room. The film started not with titles but a close-up of Frankel sitting silently, apparently thinking about a question he'd been asked, then beginning to speak: "I always knew I was an artist, since I was three. . . ."

The look and grammar of the film was richer and more elegant than Peter had expected. Passages of Frankel speaking, and of him and Jonathan in conversation, seated next to each other, were interspersed with the still photos that Jonathan had collected. Now and then the strains of a Bach partita, played on a classical guitar, would enhance the mood. And those shots of Frankel and Jonathan in conversation were anything but standard talking-head stuff. Jonathan had used not one, nor two cameras, but many. Some shots focused closely on a face, or part of a face, or a hand or gesture, in sequences that seemed to reveal a hidden choreography of emotional "tells"—each moment being the portrait of a thought or a feeling. And the lighting for these shots came from all around the men and was so bright it could almost have been coming from the sun. It was as if their conversation were taking place in heaven.

But the real surprise, for Peter, was that the film's theme was adulthood, rather than age, or coming out, or modern times *per se*—adulthood as a phase of personal fulfillment that Connor contended Americans had been drifting away from since World War Two. It began to come into focus after a question from Jonathan.

> JONATHAN: Can you help me understand who we are today, Connor—you and me? In our twenties we try so hard to become the individuals we think we should be

or really are. Then life goes on and the question becomes, who are we now? Do you think we become more or less ourselves, as we age? Or both?

CONNOR: Hmm. I don't know. Aging, for me, has never been primarily about the physical organism. It's about the mind and what happens to it over time. When we were kids we used to talk about being "big." And that's really stuck with me—big, rather than old, or mature, or successful. Big encompasses not just what you know and have done and may own, but ambition, intention—your understanding of how big life can be and how much of it you want to occupy.

Something about the film's sound design, too, was heavenly. Each of the men's voices was richly textured and utterly resonant, affording full enjoyment of Jonathan's lively New York-Jewish inflections and Connor's muted New England ones. These were voices one wanted to listen to.

CONNOR: The tragedy is that no one is promulgating any ideal these days of what it means to be an adult.

JONATHAN: Are you speaking globally?

CONNOR: No, no—here in America. The Chinese get it. Look at the difference between Shanghai and New York. We're still bumbling around with our Ground Zero site, because of our 9/11 wound, and Shanghai puts up the world's second-tallest building in two years. We may fetishize their lack of human rights, but in many ways the Chinese are more grown-up than we are. The world is theirs, and we're amusing ourselves to death.

JONATHAN: You're equating tall buildings with adulthood.

CONNOR: I sure am. [both men laugh] Infrastructure—you know what I mean.

JONATHAN: I think I do. But we're here to get it on camera, darling.

A snapshot from the mid-1930s of Connor at the "big house" in Bar Harbor, during his family's last summer there. The house, a mass of porches and gables and big windows, is in the background. In the foreground, on the lawn, stands Connor in a summer suit with his regally outfitted mother and his four sisters, all of whom are wearing similar white frocks with oversized bows in their hair.

JONATHAN: That's a beautiful house. Do you remember it well?

CONNOR: Oh, I do, I do. That house was a whole world to us. My sisters and I could be anything we wanted there. And I don't mean just playing. There were books and artifacts. We had a great big globe of the world, and a little one of the moon, and a brass telescope, so we could see the real thing. Father collected fragments of medieval stone sculpture that we used to play with—saints and griffins and such. And there were two pianos—one in the parlor and one in what we used to call the playroom.

JONATHAN: Nice.

CONNOR: Wanna hear something funny? We had several seascapes in that house—oil paintings—including a Frederic Church and a Thomas Cole. Can you imagine? They'd painted them right there, in Bar Harbor. It was quite a little artists' haven, at one time. [chuckles] Those were gone, everything was gone, by the time that picture was taken. The house was practically empty by then.

In the photograph, Connor looks a bit dreamy, despite his very proper attire, while his mother looks proud of her neatly put-together flock. Fanny, the oldest sister, is posing hard; Olive, the youngest, appears to be squirming a bit in her fine garb; the middle girls, May and Elizabeth, seem natural and relaxed. May's smile, which looks illuminated from within, as the camera draws in close on it, says everything about the carefree world that had already been lost.

And what helped a viewer see beneath the surface of the photo was the use of the Ken Burns effect, as the film's editor had explained to Peter and Will on their weekend in Hudson—the strategic panning over or zooming into or out of a still shot, which subtly shifts the focus of an image as it successively recrops it. Used with the right stills, the editor said, the technique can unlock vastly more information per frame than a viewer usually takes in. In a film by Ken Burns himself the technique might reveal, in just a few seconds, the grief of a Civil War soldier whose friend lies dead at his feet, as well as the horror of war itself, as the camera pulls back to reveal an entire battlefield of such losses. And then the shot goes further, and we notice there's snow on the ground and smoke coming from the chimney of a house on the hill, in the background. Who lives there, we think, and what was the nation like for *them* on that day in 1864?

> JONATHAN: You mention this concept of "big." Can you say more about that?
>
> CONNOR: Well—just kids acting big, full of themselves, beyond their years. But isn't that a great thing, to have a big idea about yourself? It's all very well to look, oh, I don't know, youthful, but most American adults these days don't even come across as adults—you know, with any authority or what we used to think of as maturity.
>
> JONATHAN: Gravitas.
>
> CONNOR: Nor gravitas. [pauses] Remember Andy Hardy's father? Can we reference Judge Hardy?

JONATHAN: We can reference anything you like.

Peter looked around. Did anyone know who Andy Hardy was? The audience was rapt, becoming immersed in the world of the film—a world in which ideas were lovingly exchanged, examined, evaluated. One obvious comparison was to *My Dinner With Andre*, though Jonathan's film seemed to slip the viewer even more effortlessly than Malle's into a state of mind in which thoughts can be as compelling as movie stars.

Fascinating.

A snapshot of Connor in the early 1940s: He's standing in back of the garage that served as his art studio, at his family's new house in Bar Harbor; he's dressed in baggy pants and a T-shirt, and holding an abstract painting that shows the strong influence of Paul Klee.

CONNOR: I was trying so hard to be an artist. [chuckles] But of course that's the way you become an artist. The place we moved into had a free-standing garage—a broken-down thing, just a shack—so that's where I made my studio.

JONATHAN: You were clearly taking yourself seriously.

CONNOR: Yes, I was—and I had the support to do that, from my mother and father, and my teachers, and from a world that expected such a thing. I wonder how much support there is nowadays for bringing one's self and one's culture forward and upward? We're encouraged to make a lot of money, aren't we, and carry the right accessories, and live very conspicuously. . . .

JONATHAN: Conspicuously?

CONNOR: America's become one big reality TV show.

The audience giggled—as much at Connor's disdainful tone as at the idea itself. Peter giggled, too, but when he glanced over at

Jonathan, to see if he was enjoying the screening, he saw that his friend had fallen asleep.

Poor dear.

A photograph taken from a magazine, from the mid-1950s, of Connor and a fellow painter, now also quite well known, who was rumored to be Connor's lover at the time. They're sitting at a table improvised with a plank and some cinder blocks, sharing a glass of wine in a studio in lower Manhattan that they occupied together for two years. On the table is an Indian brass candlestick caked with the melted wax of several candles. It's a staged shot, taken by a friend of theirs, and the two are in mid-conversation but the look between them is unmistakable.

> JONATHAN: Connor, I have to ask, though I happen to know the answer already. Were you lovers?
>
> CONNOR: [makes a face expressing exasperation with his own long-standing distaste for talk about such matters] Well, yes. But, you know, then, for people like us, it wasn't all about *making love.* And with Don, it quickly came to be about kindred spirits, which was *much* more interesting and relevant than who does what to whom. [pauses] Though, I mean, kissing is always important, surely.

In the VIP box, Peter noticed that Wallace bumped shoulders privately with Frankel as they sat there and heard the line.

> JONATHAN: It was a great time, then, wasn't it? What was that—fifty-three, fifty-four?
>
> CONNOR: Fifty-four, I'd guess. We were so poor! I remember very often having to decide whether to spend my last quarter on a hamburger or the *New York Times.*
>
> JONATHAN: And what was the outcome, usually?

CONNOR: The *Times,* of course. People would always invite you for dinner, and then, if you'd read the paper, you might have something interesting to say.

JONATHAN: There was a lot going on then, intellectually, wasn't there, in New York? People were doing new things and there was a lot to do. There was a lot of movement among blacks, gays, women, artists. The sixties didn't come out of nowhere, did they?

CONNOR: No, indeed. My opinion—speaking of big? In the fifties, when we were all buoyed up on our triumph in the war, a lot of what you might consider commonplace, like a glass of wine with your friend, took on a kind of importance, on the scale of the war's great mission. We were victors. The world was ours. That felt like something, and we all shared it. America was initiated into a new level of greatness, yet there was so little in our culture big enough to accommodate all that greatness. What did we do? We threw ourselves a victory party that's still going on today. We pumped up Hollywood and Las Vegas and Detroit and Madison Avenue—all the bosoms and glitter and convertibles you could want! Which was terrific, surely, but only parodies, I think, of what a real American greatness, or glamour, or progress could have been. So what if there were a few of us artists, puttering away in the background, just trying to understand what happened . . . ?

JONATHAN: You're right.

CONNOR: Then came the sixties and that generation, who did seek greatness of a more elevated kind, but all that amounted to, ultimately, was Woodstock—another party.

Chuckles from the audience.

JONATHAN: I might disagree with you there, Connor, but often I do find myself wondering whether the value of what we've built since the fifties exceeds the value of what we tore down.

CONNOR: Ah!

JONATHAN: We addressed what we had to address after World War Two—the racism and sexism and all that, right? Tore down conventions. But the other things we tossed out the window, like Sunday dinner with the family—are we going to leave behind anything of as much communal value? Are we even happier now? I mean, as a gay man it's great to be out, to be free of shame, but I have to say—and I'm about twenty years younger than you—I can see there was a certain thrill, a certain value, in the old days, of being included in this very special, secret society; a pride, even, that was embodied in those shadowy relationships. It's true that what we've got today doesn't quite equal that, in color or texture. . . .

CONNOR: No, not at all. But it's not just gay people, it's everyone. As a nation, we've traded in a sense of special for simply being OK.

Another magazine photograph—this one from the 1960s, quite formal, of the stable of artists at the prestigious art gallery in the East Seventies where Frankel racked up his first big sales and established his reputation. Connor stands near the back of a group of fifteen men and one woman, dressed in a very sharp-looking suit, his hair still dark and somewhat long, but combed neatly for the occasion.

JONATHAN: Very dapper.

CONNOR: I bought that suit expressly to be in the photograph. I think it cost eighty-nine dollars, at Bond's. That was an amazing group of people. I was enormously proud to be among them, to have been taken into the gallery. And I started meeting some very fancy people, at that point, and happily they started buying my work.

JONATHAN: You started going places, as they say.

CONNOR: Yes, and getting invited places.

JONATHAN: Such as?

CONNOR: Oh, society stuff. La Côte Basque, Pavillon. Palm Springs, Palm Beach. Not that I ever fit in. Yet I have to say that those people, the great doyennes and moguls, who'd been kids before the war—they did the sixties-international thing with that great, elevated specialness we're talking about. Babe Paley—QED. There's no real glamour around that kind of human being nowadays, only buzz. No more Eleanor Roosevelts or Albert Einsteins, either. No icons worthy of a pedestal. Yet people continue to grow up and become . . . what? Paris Hilton? They're children, with this parody of stardom. And stardom itself, at its height in Hollywood, was only a gold-plated imitation of this precious human capacity for magnificence! [pauses, then sighs] It's like a delicious strain of apple, bred and perfected over centuries, that no one eats anymore, because they're so used to the tasteless, mass-produced thing that's sold in supermarkets. So the orchard lies in waste.

JONATHAN: That's a very fancy image, Connor.

CONNOR: I'm assuming we can look at all this in editing. [glances upward and around the studio, then refocuses] Honestly, I did my share of fleeing magnificence. Even as I put my heart and soul into my work. Which is why I'm doing this interview now—to

embrace, if I can, a phase of growth that for the longest
time simply frightened me. I didn't know how to do it.
There were no wise parents guiding people in the right
direction, toward the right kind of big. No Eleanor
Roosevelts. [shakes his head, visibly moved] I saw the
doors being opened throughout my life—I saw
them!—and just couldn't walk through them.

JONATHAN: Until now. Everything has its time.

CONNOR: Yes. [pauses, as if to control himself] Sorry.
I have some emotion around this.

JONATHAN: Don't be sorry.

CONNOR: I wish it were easier to know what we
want, to know what there is *to* want. . . .

*A snapshot of Connor in the 1970s, now a grand figure in the art
world: He's standing with the leading Park Avenue society doyenne
of the time and a famous boyish novelist, at the pool pavilion of the
lady's Palm Beach estate. Philodendron leaves contrast dramatically
with louvered shutters; bamboo furniture boasts gaily striped cushions. Connor is in a baggy floral shirt and a pair of baggy plaid swim
trunks, while the lady sports chic pedal pushers and a sleeveless
blouse with the collar turned up. Her hair is fashionably big. The
novelist stands by in the skimpiest tank suit possible, clowning for
the camera in an attempt to be alluringly cute.*

JONATHAN: Didn't he have a great body?!

CONNOR: Yes, didn't he? And he certainly wasn't
afraid of showing it off.

JONATHAN: Did he act seductively around you?

CONNOR: Lord, no. He wasn't the least bit interested
in me—I mean, beyond that kittenish thing he did

with everyone. Now the lady's husband—that was a different story.

JONATHAN: Really—he hit on him?

CONNOR: He knew nothing would come of it, but at parties and such he had to let everyone know he was attracted. It was a supremely uncomfortable thing to watch, yet glorious, too, in a way.

JONATHAN: God bless the envelope pushers.

CONNOR: I suppose so. Palm Beach is nuts. It encourages all sorts of mischief. But I'll tell you where I did fit in. I can recall several enormously pleasant weekends up at Sam Barber's place in Mount Kisco—the place he had with Menotti—what did they call it? Capricorn. Now *that* was a special place. Glorious country estate. All the gays of a certain sort went up there—Bernstein, Horowitz, Copland. These were important people. They made music, the authors read their work, we talked seriously about everything. It was fun of an intellectual sort, yes, and there was even some seduction, on some levels. But there was also a code that bound us, a conspiratorial covenant, if you will. Maybe a useful kind of doublethink; maybe even a queer ethics, to use an academic term—all around the collegial and mentorial thing: the sharing and transferring of power. [smirks] Think we have anything like that nowadays?

JONATHAN: You mean doing favors for each other and for newcomers to the fold?

CONNOR: That, yes. But also just this way of understanding and respecting each other's choices about the public and the private. It was a complete and very nuanced social contract among us. . . .

JONATHAN: I'm sorry we don't have any pictures of one of those weekends.

CONNOR: No, well, you wouldn't, would you? I mean, I guess there are some—Sam probably took some—but they're probably in one of those "open in ninety-nine years" vaults.

A photo of Connor as the reclusive master in the 1980s, in the studio of his secluded residence in rural Connecticut. The studio is often described as "a barn," but several million dollars went into its renovation, and it was filled not only with Connor's own work but that of others he'd bought or been given over the years: Johns, Warhol, Twombly, Guston. In the background are several assistants, young artists who also happen to be unusually handsome young men.

JONATHAN: Your crew.

CONNOR: That was a magazine shoot. The photographer was a dream. He really had eyes in his head. His shots were full of meaning. But the writer! She kept pushing and pushing for more information. . . .

JONATHAN: About?

CONNOR: Me; my assistants; Wallace, who had just come there to live . . . ! She was digging for dirt! As if, instead of making art, we were partying all day long. I had to call the editor and say that if that were the tack she's taking, I was going to withdraw.

JONATHAN: And?

CONNOR: The piece turned out fine. [grins modestly]

JONATHAN: She was only hoping to get you out of the closet.

CONNOR: Precisely. Instead of talking about my work.

JONATHAN: It's not as if you've ever loved talking about your work, Connor. And you always do manage to have attractive helpers.

CONNOR: [laughs] No, you're right. I'm just an ornery cuss, Jon—always have been.

JONATHAN: I'm glad we have that on record.

CONNOR: In some ways, the closet was made for me. I'm not happy to say that now, but it's true. For a long time I thought the closet one of the best-engineered conventions of all time, the most towering code of behavior ever constructed, bar none. Christianity, Anglo-American jurisprudence, modern hygienics— none was more useful or elegant or adult. Because it was created and maintained so thoughtfully. And then gay lib questioned all that, and AIDS finally killed it. I mean, people used to pour all this ingenuity into coded appearances, manners, pageantry! Everything heightened. Each relationship, each encounter, was a secret adventure of heroic proportions. Now what we've got, instead, is gay marriage. Well and good.

JONATHAN: Surely you don't miss the culture of shame.

CONNOR: [shakes his head] "Why this is hell, nor I am out of it."

JONATHAN: Funny. [speaks to the camera] Marlowe's *Faust*—Mephistopheles.

CONNOR: [smiles wearily] No, I don't miss the shame. Though I look at Facebook sometimes—

Wallace shows me—and I have to wonder if this is
what pride looks like. Boys dancing around a pool on
Fire Island.... I don't know. I miss Capricorn.

The film, which was about an hour long, incorporated a dozen
photographs in all. Frankel spoke eloquently about all of them, and
Peter was unexpectedly moved by the man's openness in conjuring
a younger, frightened self and letting it share the screen with his
present eminence. In fact, Peter found himself contemplating his
own life in the same way, grateful that he had turned out to be perhaps more of an adult than some others of his age, yet perhaps less
of one than he could still be, at his age—a thought that was both
marvelous and scary, which in turn raised other thoughts. If the
adult in him had been forged during AIDS, almost inadvertently,
then what of the Peter who existed before that, the dear young
Peter who had arrived in New York in the mid-'70s, wanting to
start living? Had he expired without being properly mourned?
Was he still alive today, somewhere in the psyche, still wanting . . .
something?

There was a small wave of applause in the still-darkened house,
as the credits began to roll. *Ah, the guitarist was John Williams,*
thought Peter. *The Partita no. 2 in C Minor—I have to get that.*
Would Will like the partitas? he wondered. Did he like Bach, anyway? Did he like the film? It would be a minute or two before the
credits rolled out and houselights came up, but Peter was suddenly
desperate to gab with Will. *Can you believe what their lives were
like, back then? A hamburger or the* Times! *Would you and I have
been friends in the '50s, do you think?*

And then a thought occurred to Peter: *Shit, I'm kind of in love
on these two different levels, as an adult and as . . . something else.*
Could that be?

When the credits ended, a spotlight appeared on the VIP box.
Peter drew back a bit, so as not to be in the light. The audience responded to the sight of Jonathan and Frankel with another wave of
applause, much heartier, to which Jonathan responded by waving
and Frankel by smiling. Then the houselights came up and people
began moving into the foyer for supper.

A serpentine bar of pink marble and blond wood. A towering

urn of lilies, tulips, and roses. Bartenders serving wine, mixed drinks, and sparkling water. Seating areas of sectional sofas, ottomans, and low tables. In the background, lounge-y music. Across the room, servers ready behind a skirted buffet table, with platters of food set at various heights on cast-glass blocks. Votive candles and little "cocktail" flower arrangements.

Peter and Aldebar positioned Jonathan in a spot where he felt comfortable, then Peter went off to get drinks for the three of them. By the time he came back, a reception line had formed, of quietly animated admirers wanting to share their enthusiasm for the film.

"Marvelous," said a lady in a gray pantsuit and pearls, bending in toward Jonathan slightly, so she could be more at his level.

"First-rate," said a man in a plaid sport jacket and bow tie.

Jonathan, in his chair, looked happy in a haunted way.

"We're going to keep going...," he was saying, when the Hollywood action star appeared at the head of the line and, with overhumble apologies to those who were waiting, stole Jonathan's hand for a shake and said a few words directly into his ear, before heading off with an assistant.

Jerk, thought Peter, watching from one side. Then Will and Luz appeared.

"Amazing, amazing, amazing," said Will, gathering Peter into a warm embrace.

"Really strong," said Luz, kissing Peter on both cheeks when Will released him from the hug. Only Will didn't fully release Peter. He kept his arm around Peter's shoulders as the three of them stood there bubbling on about the movie.

"It really makes you see how much this country has changed," said Luz.

"Exactly," said Peter. "For better and worse."

"You're not going to tell us how brilliant the closet was," said Will.

"No, no," laughed Peter. "Though there was a time in my life when I really didn't expect to be accepted, and that made me think I didn't want to be."

"Things change," said Will. "There was a revolution, which is always better and worse at the same time."

"Really," said Luz.

"We should count ourselves lucky that the gay revolution happened so peacefully," said Will. "That's what I kept thinking. Connor talks about infrastructure. Your generation built an entirely new way of thinking about gay, that both younger and older people have benefited from."

"We did?" said Peter. "Golly."

"Thanks, Papi," said Will.

Peter gave Will a playful push with his hip, but not so hard as to break the embrace. He loved the feeling of Will's arm around his shoulders. It felt protective, endearing, territorial.

"Food?" said Peter.

"Sure," said Luz.

"The music was good, wasn't it?" said Peter, as they moved off toward the buffet. Will and Luz agreed, then starting chattering about a "crossover classical" guitarist whose new album they'd been listening to, after Will was sent an advance copy.

"I'll dupe it for you," said Will. "It's really good."

"Great," said Peter.

"He made you a music mix," says the daughter to Michelle Pfeiffer in I Could Never Be Your Woman. *"That's how boys tell you what's in their heart."* So I get the younger boyfriend? Peter wondered. This thing I want so much—I can have it? It's OK for me to want and have? I merit it?

Daddy and Uncle Malcolm were both in pretty good shape, but looked old by the time they were fifty. They both smoked, they ate the wrong things, and there was no youth culture to keep them common-denominator cool. In fact, just the opposite. They were programmed to turn into village elders.

Peter smiled when he thought of the gap between them and his own generation.

So if you've taken care of yourself for forty years by eating right and listening to new music, and if you're lucky enough to have kept all your hair, then what do you spend your youthfulness on when you're, say, fifty-nine? A boyfriend who's half your age? If sixty is the new thirty, how is that supposed to go down, exactly?

Sex with a younger guy is the easy part, he thought.

But what do you say to him when he refers to the Beatles as "vin-

tage," and the Beatles happened to have rocked your world in a very fresh way in 1964, when you saw them on Ed Sullivan? *You can't reminisce all the time, or lecture about the Beatles' place in history. But you don't want to bottle everything up, either, because then you're not being honest—and you certainly wouldn't want that in the other person, either. . . .*

"The chicken looks good," said Will.

"Mmm," said Peter.

As the server prepared plates for them, Peter told Will that Jonathan wanted them to come up to Hudson for another weekend soon, but that Aldebar had confided privately that a visit would now require special arrangements. For one thing, Jonathan was getting too weak to go out of the house and would soon need to be confined to bed.

"I noticed that he had some trouble with his speech," whispered Will.

"Yeah," said Peter.

"Is it the medication?"

"It's the disease itself, they think, which is spreading. . . ."

"To the brain?"

Peter nodded sadly and took his plate of chicken.

CHAPTER 21

Everyone on both sides of the McCaw project acknowledged that the work was going well. McCaw himself, in his videoconferences with Peter, praised the bulletins he was receiving from the joint creative team headed by Sunil and Tyler. So McCaw decided to make the agency's first quarterly progress report into a presentation that would also function as something of a rally for his top advisers, so they could "begin to absorb the energy and thinking that's being generated." The presentation, which was originally scheduled for the Den, the workspace at the agency where the team usually met, was therefore moved to the Arena, the agency's largest meeting room, which was designed like an amphitheater. And because McCaw was bringing his top people—including Mary, the woman Peter had been seated next to at the dinner party, whom he learned was McCaw's biggest funder—Laura wanted a few of the agency's brass to be there, too. In all, sixty people attended, an enormous audience for a phase-of-work review. Yet as McCaw noted, this was a movement they were building, not just a branding project, "and movements have their own momentum."

"Whatever he wants," was Laura's response, when Peter told her about plans for the event. "What are you gonna show him?"

"We've sorted out the DNA—there's some solid language around that," said Peter. "So we'll give them the big ideas—the five pillars of faith, as it were—and walk them through how we got there and where we intend to go with them. Should be quite effective."

"What about shows? Any treatment, trailers?"

"No, we're not there yet. That's the next phase."

"OK. But McCaw's basically seen the work already?"

"The broad strokes, yes. His people keep him informed. I think he's pretty happy."

"Good. Good, Peter—really," said Laura. "I know I've been pretty hardball with you on this, but I only want us to deliver the best. We're making history here."

"Thanks, Laura. We've got a good team."

The meeting, run jointly by Tyler and Sunil, went smoothly. They spent twenty minutes on each of the five overarching concepts they had developed and showed all work. A telling concatenation of words and phrases, projected onto three large screens that dominated the Arena, was accompanied by a rich collage of contextualizing visuals taken from the mediasphere—"cultural signals" from the worlds of art, music, movies, and fashion, as well as from business and politics. In less than two hours, the presentation told a subtle but powerful story about why the five concepts were inevitably the right ones to drive the branding of McCaw's movement and development of the most persuasive media campaigns, infotainment vehicles, policy statements, etc.

When the presentation was done, McCaw, leading a round of applause, stepped up to the podium.

"This is a great start," he said. "My congratulations and my gratitude to you all. As the client, I'm delighted. But as a human being, I'm proud to see the science and the art of advertising and branding really being used like this to push civilization forward. I've learned a lot from this work—and I'm a pretty smart guy. But that's one of the most important reasons why I'm delighted with the work being done here. There's a lot to learn, a lot that's new, in this world of ours—a lot that's unprecedented. And in this world, what do we know and what do we want, as Americans? We can formulate policy till the cows come home, but how do we mesh this agenda we're so passionate about with the way people process information these days? You all clearly have a great handle on that and I am, really, very grateful. Well done!"

There was more applause, and McCaw beamed his triumphant smile around the room, taking care to project it even as far as the Arena's topmost semicircular row. He had a politician's skill for reaching everyone in a room—though the back row also happened to be where his big funder, Mary, was sitting. She'd slipped in late.

"So let's keep going," he said. "I'll only leave you with a thought that I didn't see expressed here today, because I know 'we're not there yet' "—McCaw made air quotes and smiled at Peter—"but it's already come up and it's pretty important, in my mind, so I want to share it. Simplify when possible, complicate when necessary. It's an easy directive. Some things are self-evident. You just name them—*boom,* comprehension. But some things, important things, need to be explained. You name them, yes, but you tell the story of the name. See what I mean? You describe reality in a way that people can understand. Our thinking has to be appropriate, if we want to reach the hearts and minds of our fellow citizens. And we do want to reach hearts and minds, don't we?"

Shit, Peter thought, as the Arena rang with yet another round of applause. It was Will's line, and Peter hadn't had a chance since the dinner party to figure out what to do about the fact that McCaw liked it so much. Now this—a public pronouncement! The only visual to back up McCaw's comments, of course, was the one left on the screens at the end of the scheduled presentation: a composite of diverse faces meant to represent the population of the United States. But McCaw's powers of oration had overtaken the room and refocused people's attention from the visual to the verbal, allowing the words "Simplify when possible, complicate when necessary" to resonate, as they hung in the air, like a statement of doctrine.

Before this, the questions on Peter's mind had been tough enough: Should he get the creative team to morph the line forward into something better, and just not mention anything to Will? Could the line even be improved? It was already pretty good, as Peter well knew. Or should he approach Will about using it and ask him to approve? Might Will even accept a fee for it? He might even be flattered. Then again, he might not.

Thus Peter was feeling uneasy when McCaw stepped down from the podium and came over to shake his hand.

"Well done," said McCaw.

"Thanks," said Peter.

Mary joined them instantly. She was in a plain black pantsuit with a white blouse and pearls.

"Nice work," she said, thrusting her hand into Peter's, standing shoulder to shoulder with McCaw. Peter didn't remember her as seeming so formidable in a white dress, at dinner.

"Didn't mean to jump the gun by throwing out that catch-phrase," said McCaw.

"No worries," said Peter. "Though . . . we really don't know what it is yet, or how it behaves."

"Sure," said McCaw. "That's for Phase Two—I know."

"Seems to me," said Mary, "it behaves pretty damned well."

Not long after, Will was promoted from associate editor to senior editor, and Peter invited him for dinner at his place, to celebrate. They'd been meaning to do something in the garden anyway, since the weather had turned warmer, and this seemed a perfect occasion.

Peter worked from home that day, and went about his calls and the shopping and prep for dinner in a state of buoyancy. He was proud of his friend, for sure. Moreover, the early May weather was providing that perfect platform for well-being that's bound to boost anyone's mood—a crystalline combination of clear skies, low humidity, and a temperature in the high sixties. Yet something else was going on, too—something Peter couldn't put his finger on, that he felt when they confirmed dinner by phone and Will asked what he could bring.

"Wine?" he said.

"Got it covered," said Peter.

"Dessert?"

"That, too. Just come. I'm making a nice little but possibly amazing dinner for us, including champagne."

"Ooh, I can't wait!"

It was unlike Will to say he couldn't wait, and there was an appealingly impatient edge to his voice when he said it, which suddenly made Peter feel that way, too. With added zip Peter went about steaming shrimp and stuffing mushrooms, and setting out a grill pan for the filets and a pot for blanching the asparagus.

"OK, everyone," said Peter to himself cheerfully, as the orange tea roses he'd bought for the bathroom bunched into a vase beautifully. It was just six-thirty. The table in the garden was preset with Veuve on ice. The kitchen was sorted—the orderly *mise en place* already a still life in Peter's iPhone, ready for possible posting on Facebook. The Château Pavie was breathing. And then, as Peter was repositioning votive candles, half dancing to a pulsing disco anthem with a soaring female vocal, the doorbell rang.

"Hey," said Will cheerily, with a peck on the cheek.

"Hey," said Peter, who continued to dance in his shorts, T-shirt, and apron while welcoming Will.

> *Everything's alive now you and I*
> *Are going to the moon, the way we fly*

"Someone's in a good mood," said Will.

"Someone is," said Peter, taking a small paper bag Will was holding.

"This place near work makes the most amazing biscotti," said Will.

"Great," said Peter.

> *That's the way my heart can rescue you*
> *And you can rescue me*
> *You and you alone can rescue me*

"We doing disco tonight?" asked Will.

"Not really," said Peter, going over to his iPhone and switching the music over to soft jazz. "That was just the score for my final prep. Everything is pretty much ready, actually. Just let me put on a shirt and we can go out in the garden."

"I brought the new issue," sang Will, pulling a magazine out of his tote bag as Peter ducked into the bedroom.

"Thank you," sang Peter.

"I have a piece in it."

"Can't wait to see it."

"I'm just gonna wash my hands."

For Peter, it was between the blue-striped button-down and the orange polo.

"Sorry, what did you say?" he said, emerging from the bedroom in the button-down and seeing that Will was in the bathroom. "Say, can I give you some water?"

Will stepped back into the room.

"Sorry, did you say something?"

"Would you like some water? I should have offered."

"I believe champagne was mentioned."

They went out to the garden and installed themselves in the rocking loveseat, which is where Peter had set up the champagne tray. An intermittent breeze was gently animating the greenery.

"Ah, perfect," said Will, making himself comfortable.

"How was work?" asked Peter, as he poured champagne into two conspicuously heavy Waterford flutes that someone had once given Harold.

"Fine," said Will. "Same ol', same ol'."

"Same office?"

"Oh, yeah. They can't change that. But there's a *lot* more respect now."

"Is there?"

"Major. The publisher came in today to congratulate me."

"Nice."

"I didn't think she even knew who I was."

"Good," said Peter, giving a glass to Will and raising his own. "Well done!"

"Thank you," said Will, clinking with Peter and taking a sip, then scrutinizing the flute. "God, Peter, could these glasses be any fancier?"

"Nothin' but the best."

"It's a lot of crystal to be trusted with."

"I'm sure you can handle it."

Will nodded and looked into Peter's face.

"Did you cut your hair?" he said.

"It's probably still wet from the shower. I haven't had time to do anything with it except push it around."

"It's cute," said Will, reaching up to adjust a bit that was falling into Peter's eyes. The gesture turned into a thoughtful caress of Peter's ear and neck, and then, as Will leaned in slowly to make sure he had Peter's acquiescence, it became a full-on kiss on the lips.

The moment was passionate and real, the kiss deep and probing. And then, after several seconds of contact, Will sat back, smiling placidly, and took another sip of champagne.

For Peter, the moment was seismic. It set him quietly reeling, from his gut and every other part of his body. But it let in so much information, so suddenly, that all he could do was go into some kind of default behavior, which was to continue sitting there calmly as if a kiss between them were the most natural thing in the world. And anyway, it was daylight, and they were in a semi-public place, and all of the other things Peter might be impelled to do as a result of this new information, he knew, should be thought through at least a little bit.

"Am I still breathing?" said Peter.

"You appear to be," said Will.

"Good," said Peter.

"Any other questions?"

Peter took a moment.

"Why now?" he said.

Will shook his head.

"Why not now?" he said. "I mean, why have we not, until now?"

"Ya got me," said Peter.

The garden was looking very lush. The hydrangea bushes that had been cut back too far in error a few years before, by an inexperienced gardener, had grown back vigorously and were looking better than ever.

Then Peter put down his glass and leaned in to kiss Will, slipping one hand behind his shoulder and head, and the other around his waist. It was a waist that belonged to a museum statue. It was the first time, too, Peter realized, that he had run his fingers through Will's hair, and the first time he realized how much he had wanted to do so for months.

"Anything you can do . . . ," Peter whispered as he brushed his lips over Will's ear and began tonguing in back of it sweetly.

Will took a sudden breath and exhaled slowly with a little groan.

"Is this a competition?" he said, finding a place to put down his glass without pulling too far out of the embrace.

"Uh-uh," said Peter. "More of a cooperative effort."

"Oh, OK."

They went on kissing for a while, their upper bodies twisting urgently toward each other in the loveseat. Now and then they paused to look at each other's faces and beam or giggle, then they kissed some more, and more intently, as they placed and pressed and gently pushed their hands on each other's bodies, over their clothes. And then they finally sat back and took up their glasses again. Neither said anything as Peter refilled them.

And for Peter, stunned and exhilarated almost beyond words by the feeling of Will's body so close to his and the taste of his breath on his lips, the challenge was to decide between taking a moment to savor a memory that was now four minutes old but already among the very best of his entire life, and going on right away to create another memory and perhaps another, and another.

"Angela was out here today, trimming and foofing," said Peter. Next to the loveseat was a grouping of three large clay pots that his landlady had planted with ivy and impatiens.

"Very pretty," said Will. "Peter, did I see two pieces of meat coming to room temperature in the kitchen?"

"Yes, two filets."

"May I make a suggestion?"

"Please."

"Can we put them back in the refrigerator for a little while?"

Inside, Peter put away the meat and the shrimp, and had just shut the refrigerator door when Will, standing close behind him, took him in his arms and kissed him again. Then Peter pulled Will to the daybed, where they flopped down amid the artfully arranged throw pillows and continued kissing, this time with more of their bodies involved. Soon they were without shirts.

So this was the outcome that earlier that day, on the phone,

they'd both felt impatient for and knew, without consciously knowing, might happen! The communication between them for months
had been too unblocked and too fascinating, their connection too
effortless and joyous, to be ignored any longer!

And forty breathless minutes later they were lying there on the
daybed in each other's arms, naked, their bellies frosted with dried
semen, talking quietly, and kissing, playing with each other's hair
and brushing nipples, all but two of the pillows having been
pushed onto the floor. Outside, the sky had gone dark, and from
the open garden door flowed a fragrant evening breeze bearing further news of spring.

"It's insane being able to touch you like this," said Peter.

"Mmmm," said Will, touching the hand that was touching him.
"I wanted to, for so long."

"Me too."

His skin was so luminous, Peter thought—the fingers so thick,
the cock so friendly. The idea of unfettered access to all this did feel
literally insane.

"Did you . . . plan to make a move tonight?" said Peter.

Will thought for a moment, then said no.

"Did *you*?" said Will.

"Uh-uh," said Peter. "I always wanted to, I was always sort of
ready to. But I always felt, I dunno, like I shouldn't make the first
move."

"Yeah. Same."

"Really?"

"Yeah. Not that we weren't close enough, or that it would be
weird if it didn't work out. It was more like . . . I didn't know what
I was feeling for you, or why."

"And now you do?"

"Nope. I only realized—Luz helped me realize—that going to
the next level was the only way of finding out about the next level."

"Ah. Good advice. I guess I would have gotten around to being
that brave, eventually—'cause you're so fucking amazing—but I
kept thinking, 'Good manners, good manners! Don't wanna put
Will in an awkward spot!' "

"Please, put me in an awkward spot!"

Peter drew close and began kissing Will's chest and shoulder. When their cocks instantly became hard, they broke into gales of laughter whose force surprised them both.

"May I offer you more champagne?" said Peter.

"Yes, please," said Will.

Peter got up and pulled on his shorts.

"Here, lemme help you," said Will, pulling on his shorts, too.

Barefoot, they went into the garden, gathered the champagne things and votive candles onto the tray, and brought them inside.

"Whaddya say we have a quick shower," said Peter. "Then I can make a little supper out of the shrimp, with some salad. The filets will keep. Unless you're hungry."

"No, good idea," said Will.

But supper didn't happen until an hour after that, because shampooing each other led to kissing in the shower, and toweling each other afterward led to more kissing, which led to the bedroom, where another round of lovemaking—this one slightly more adventurous than the first, though not exactly dirty—took place on Peter's freshly laundered sheets.

It was around ten when they were finally sitting at the tiny table overlooking the garden, shirtless and in shorts again, talking quietly about the real world, over little plates of shrimp and cocktail sauce, arugula salad, and handmade cheddar-dill crackers that Peter had found at a local market. After finishing the champagne, the last drops of which had gone flat, they drank the Bordeaux, since it was open, which, they agreed, didn't make the worst pairing in the world with the shrimp and mushrooms and crackers.

Conversation went from Will's job, and Olivier and Angelina Jolie, to Peter's job and McCaw.

"I don't hate the guy," Will was saying.

"No, I know," said Peter. "That's the wrong word."

"I see that he's human. I just revile what he stands for, like a lot of people do. Like you do, for chrissakes. Though I accept the fact that you choose to continue working for him. . . ."

"C'mon—the word 'revile' . . ."

"You know what I mean, Peter."

"I don't agree with the guy."

"You don't agree with the guy or his agenda, yet you give power to that agenda. Which means you validate it. Now, I know this isn't genocide, but it's not the same as working for, oh, I don't know, Gandhi. I may accept your working for him, but I sure as hell don't approve. And you don't need my approval, fine, but you do need my respect, I hope. And now, of course, I know you need my body, too." Will ran his hand seductively over his pec and Peter giggled. "So, mister, you'd better be prepared for some serious persuasion to come your way."

"Oh, lord, OK," said Peter. "Bring it." He knew this was not the time to bring up the matter of the tagline.

"I'm bringing it," said Will.

"I'm ready," said Peter.

They ate some of the lemon tart that Peter had bought for dessert and then Will sheepishly said he had to go.

"I'm sorry, I planned terribly," he said. "I wish I could stay, but I have a meeting tomorrow morning and can't go in my shorts. . . ."

Peter was disappointed, but said he understood. It crossed his mind to suggest that Will could stay and simply wear something of his, but he decided to remain quiet.

"Later this week?" said Peter.

"Definitely," said Will. "Dinner, sleepover, whatever."

"We'll figure it out," said Peter. "Whatever works."

Everything in the universe had shifted, except the fact that calendars ruled the lives of busy New Yorkers.

Good-byes in the hallway were tender. Then the car that Will called appeared and he went off into the night.

"Holy shit," said Peter, as he walked back into the apartment, alone for the first time in hours, but also not alone for the first time in years. He felt both serene and somehow explosive, as he put away the remaining food, loaded the dishwasher, poured himself a vodka, adjusted the lights, and plopped down in one of the big chairs.

You happy now? he thought, breaking the room's silence with a guffaw. *Jesus!*

How to think about what had happened? Peter knew his usual, analytical mode of thought, as strong as it was, was still too feeble to describe the cosmic reasons for what had happened; nor could it guide a plan for making it happen again, because such occurrences were sublimely elemental. Anyway, a plan was probably unnecessary, since sex seemed sure to happen again—it just *felt* that way. This was no one-time recreation; their bodies had clearly concurred in some massive truth. The only path now was to contemplate what had happened, and, possibly, to thank God for it.

Peter thought better of fetching his iPhone for some music, because no music could possibly be right. So he just sat there in the chair, contentedly, in silence, with the smell of Will still strong on his skin and on his breath. The memory of Will's touch, of the architecture of his scrotum, of his grace in going barefoot up the iron steps from the garden to the house, carrying a tray of delicate things—these things comprised an opulence on which Peter decided to focus, like a mandala, and meditate. They hadn't spoken of love, and maybe they would, someday, though to be loved again—that was an opulence even vaster. Peter had numbed himself to the absence of it for so long that even to contemplate it as a possibility, and not a comic-book fantasy, was going to take some... coaching. If love were in the offing, they'd coach each other.

But it *must* be in the offing, thought Peter. *A man who has stood on the surface of the moon, or on the top of Mount Everest, or at the Rialto Bridge on a late spring afternoon in Venice, must always need to return....*

CHAPTER 22

A few days later, Aldebar called Peter, to update him on Jonathan's condition.

"It's no better or worse than expected," said Aldebar. "He can't be out of bed now. I thought you should know."

"Thank you, my friend."

"The doctor has been coming twice a week from Albany, but there's really nothing left to do. We have another nurse now, around the clock—Sofia."

"Is he in any pain?"

"Not really. We've started him on morphine."

Peter sighed.

"So he can't work," he said.

"No," said Aldebar. "That's all over, I'm afraid. When he can, he talks with Mike, the editor, but he's so weak. Connor still comes over now and then, and they just talk or sit together without saying anything. No cameras. Sometimes Connor reads to him, but he goes in and out."

"Of sleep?"

"Of lucidity."

"Oh."

"It's the brain."

"I see."

"And when he's aware of it, it terrifies him."

"Shit—you mean he can be aware of that?"

"Yes, sometimes, of course. And it's a kind of pain we don't have a drug for."

"Ucch."

"Yeah. So when it happens we talk, and he tells me what he's afraid of, or what he sees out there. And it doesn't necessarily make sense like you and I are making sense right now, but, you know, there's a mind there, and an intelligence. So I listen and try to join him wherever he is, if you know what I mean. "

"God. Aldebar, so what's the prognosis?"

"I'm sorry to say we won't have him for much longer."

"Oh, God."

"It's progressing very fast now, Peter."

"It is."

"I'm very sorry. I know you two are such great friends. We're just doing the best we can to keep him comfortable."

"I know you are, Aldebar. You're an angel."

"We've closed the door to visitors, but I thought . . . you might want to come up as soon as possible."

Peter closed his eyes.

"I see," he said.

"Yeah," said Aldebar.

"OK. Well, why don't I come up on Friday—unless you think sooner. . . ."

"No, no. Friday is fine."

"I should probably come alone, right?"

"Whatever you think."

Before they hung up, Peter made it a point to congratulate Aldebar on being appointed executive director of Jonathan's new foundation. It was the position they'd once talked about for Will; Peter had heard about the appointment from Jonathan's lawyer, Mark, since he was on the board.

"It's a big responsibility, and of course an honor," said Aldebar. "But I believe I understand the mission and will be able to execute."

"Is that the marine in you speaking?"

Aldebar laughed.

"I suppose so," he said. "But I must say it also reflects the vast amount of knowledge and wisdom I've received from your friend over the past few months. He's truly a gifted human being, as you know—I've learned so much from him."

"He *is* amazing," said Peter. "I'm glad you can see that."

"I only hope to have a big enough way to pay him back."

That last comment came to echo in Peter's brain some hours later, when it started to resonate with something else Aldebar had said, about helping Jonathan remain "on his own terms with his body." Peter didn't ask him to elaborate and the conversation moved on, and on some level Peter registered the comment as relating to a patient's right to regulate his own morphine drip, or something. But later Peter began to wonder if he'd missed recognizing an offer, made with elliptical grace, to include him in some end-of-life plan that Jonathan had put in place, which Aldebar knew that some people would find admirable and others might rather know nothing about. . . .

There was a party that week at a newly built private residence in Tribeca, for a new premium vodka that was being endorsed by the fashion-designer daughter of a legendary rock star. Will's magazine was cosponsoring, along with the vodka brand and the high-end realtor that was handling the property. Will invited Luz to go with him, and they decided to dress for the occasion.

Actually, it wasn't exactly a party, remarked Luz, as they arrived. It was more an industry event pretending to be a party. There was no real host—no one truly to see to your comfort and entertainment. There were only girls in headsets at the door with clipboards, and beyond them brand managers, real estate execs, and photographers—the latter, of course, providing the real reason why people had dressed up and were beaming their brightest party smiles. Everyone was friendly, in a chirpy, generic way, and Will and Luz agreed that generic was indeed the kind of fun to be had at a party like this—in the form of spotting celebrities, downing free cocktails, sampling hors d'oeuvres, and maybe getting into a few paparazzi shots.

The house itself, too, had a generically upscale feel to it, made all the more obvious by the fact that no one lived there. Technically, it was for sale—a mutely elegant, glass-and-stone, urban "incursion" with many levels and terraces, designed by a young star architect whom Will's magazine once did a page on. The décor was all staged, the art was borrowed, and the "personal" touches, like candles in the powder rooms, were too contrived to be convincing. Some lucky zillionaire had yet to move in and mold himself into the kind of resident that such a house requires. Meanwhile, on evenings like this, for an hour or two, ordinary people could mold themselves to fit some version of the zillionaire lifestyle.

"It's been on the market for over a year now," Will said, as he and Luz walked down the entry hall and into the soaring two-story living area, which was filled with bubbly guests. Bluish lighting had been specially formulated to dramatize the space's cavernous design. On a sweeping balcony above, guests on an upper level stood with drinks in hand at the metal-railed parapet, chatting and marveling at the larger-than-life-sized projections of gritty, black-and-white, street-scene footage of New York in the '70s that were being live-mixed by a VJ. The music pervading the scene said *Rio, the beach, a few years from now.*

"Someone built this on spec?" said Luz. "That was brave." She looked fiercely elegant that evening. She had put her hair up and fixed it with a glittery costume brooch with big blue stones. The enduring glamour of sapphires set off lustrous black locks.

"Originally, they wanted twenty-nine million for it," said Will. "I hear it's come down, like, five times since then. There's a pool in the basement. Olivier has all the details. It's his party—I mean, he designed and cast it."

"Cast it?"

"That's what he calls it."

"Jesus."

"Come to think of it, I don't think anything's ever happened in this building that wasn't a party."

"So it's a party space pretending to be a house."

"And we're lumps of flesh pretending to be guests."

"This lump needs a drink," said Luz, snatching two cocktails from a passing tray and giving one to Will. *"Salud y amor!"*

"Salud!"

"Mmm," said Luz, taking a big sip. "At least the drinks are real."

"Funny," remarked Will with a snort. "We did a club party last month with a cognac sponsor. The bars were so jammed, I just grabbed a bottle from the display and began pouring for my friends. We were drinking for, like, five minutes before we realized it was just brown water...."

"Here he is—here's the guy," chimed Stefan Turino, arriving with a trio of stylishly disheveled, conspicuously good-looking young men—probably models—whom Will had never seen before. "The newest star in our world!"

They shook hands and Will introduced Stefan to Luz, letting the models go unacknowledged except for a generic sweep of the hand that apparently no one found inadequate. He mentioned that Stefan was the one who'd originally suggested Will apply to the magazine.

"I remember your saying," said Luz.

"I'm a natural recruiter," laughed Stefan. "For the right talent, that is." He was wearing the same model retro-clunky eyeglasses he was wearing on the night Will met him, only this time in pewter, not black.

"What do you do for the magazine, Stefan?" asked Luz.

"Editor at large," he answered, but he was clearly more focused on Will than on Luz. "I hear you're set for Argentina."

"Can't wait," said Will. "Skiing in June."

"Terrific. The issue is selling like crazy."

"The September issue," said Will, for Luz's benefit.

"And you know we're trying to tie in this São Paulo fashion week thing we're doing—same week. So if that happens, we'll get you up there. Maybe Xiomara will be able to come, too."

"Fun," said Will,

"We will talk, *señor*," said Stefan, saluting jauntily, as he and the boys moved on.

"Not fun," said Will, after they were gone.

"No?" said Luz.

"It's hard trying to be normal and social, and get to know this artist you admire, while at the same time trying to function as a journalist. This trip is going to be work. And now I have to be a brand ambassador for the magazine, too?"

"It's glamorous work."

"They should pay me more," said Will. "Actually, I love my job—deciding what's interesting, how to present it to a couple hundred thousand interesting people. I shouldn't complain."

"For a second, until you introduced him, I thought *that* was Olivier," said Luz.

"Oh, God, no," laughed Will. "Stefan at least has some blood running in his veins. With Olivier, it's more like Azzaro Pour Homme or Cool Water by Davidoff."

They wound up on a broad, packed terrace, and each had another few drinks and a nibble of coconut-crusted shrimp, while chatting intermittently with people Will knew. There was no view but the backs and sides of undistinguished neighboring buildings, formerly industrial. At some point the music changed and six dancers in white leotards appeared with ice picks to chip away, in military formation, at a coffin-sized ice block that was wheeled out on a cart—after which everyone giddily applauded, though some perhaps expected the result would be a sculpture of an Ice Dagger, the vodka brand's signature cocktail, and not simply a pile of wet chips. Then Will and Luz decided it was time to leave—which was exactly the moment when Olivier appeared, in a parrot-green suit, with a date in tow, a Ford model named Ilze who seemed sweet but didn't speak much.

"My word, don't you look handsome tonight," said Olivier, sliding a finger under the lapel of Will's jacket. "Lindeberg."

They shared a few words about how well the party was going—Ilze only listened—while Olivier kept scanning the crowd with a smile broad enough for the entire terrace. He complimented Luz on her hair, then waggled a finger playfully between her and Will.

"Say, are you two . . . ?" he said, in a tone Will thought might be described as mock-naughty.

"Nooo," said Will. "Luz is my roommate and my mentor."

"OK, yes," sniffed Olivier. "We all need mentors—so important. Ilze is my mentor, for this evening—aren't you, *chérie?* Help me learn from this party! She's from Estonia."

Ilze was adjusting the strap of her dress, as Olivier spoke. Once it was sorted she refocused her attention.

"I saw your Dolce ad in the current issue," Will said to her. "It's beautiful."

The model smiled in apparent thanks, but it wasn't clear to Will whether she even spoke English.

"A boyfriend, then . . . ," said Olivier. "Why isn't he with you tonight?"

"He's busy," said Will.

"We all want to know who is lucky enough to have this man," said Olivier.

Luz was trying to think of a response, since the remark was nominally directed at her, but then—"Have fun! *Ciao-ciao!*"—Olivier had to fly over with Ilze to greet a young Hollywood star he'd just spotted.

"That was his way of saying he's interested in me," said Will, after they'd gone.

"He's . . . handsome," ventured Luz.

"He's *pretty*," said Will, "which is great, but not for me."

"There is a bit of fey going on there."

"And his cock, darling, when hard, barely peeks above the pubic hair."

Luz burst out in a laugh.

"Shut up!" she said. "You don't *know* that!"

"I have a reliable source," he said.

"Stop!"

"Enrico once said Olivier has vicuña sweaters instead of orgasms."

"I don't even know what that means," giggled Luz. "How many drinks have we had?"

"I had one when I was getting dressed," sang Will.

"Thought so!" she said.

"We're outta here."

"So your 'boyfriend' is busy tonight?" said Luz, when they were outside, on the sidewalk, standing in front of the party residence, deciding what to do.

"What can I tell you?" said Will, shaking his head. "I never

asked for a fucking eighty-seven-year-old boyfriend—I never asked
for *any* boyfriend—but there it is."

"He's a good guy, Will," said Luz. "Very solid."

"I know," said Will. "He makes me laugh, he makes me think, I
like his cooking. And, Luz, his cock..." He used both hands to
make a descriptive gesture.

"Shut up!"

"Those guys in there—they live in a world where everyone has
to be a model. They wouldn't admit it, but they're governed by that
phony lifestyle. And they measure *me* by it, 'cause they think I'm
cute or whatever, and think that's what *I'm* looking for. And maybe
I *was* looking for it, once...."

"And then you met just-plain-Peter."

"He's not plain at all, but yeah. I guess his looks have grown on
me. Can I tell you? I love looking at that face."

Luz's expression combined concern with excitement over what
she hoped she was going to hear next.

"Yeah," said Will, "I'm kinda in love."

"You *are,* baby?!" said Luz.

Guests continued arriving at the party. They stepped up to
check in with the clipboard girls, while others exited or stood by
smoking or making calls.

"Anyway, it's chemical," said Will.

"That's the first time I've heard you say it," said Luz.

"To think how close I came to editing him right out of my life,
because he was so different and I was so...," said Will. "Of
course, there's still a lot to work out."

"Which you will do, in therapy."

"No, I mean with him. Wanna hear something? He thinks he can
be monogamous for the first time in his life, and says he wants to be,
or *would* be—which I think is awesome. But he said he wondered if
that kind of arrangement would be limiting for me—as if I should
be doing all this fucking around, at this stage of my life...."

"Hmm."

"Yeah. It was totally different, back in his day, and I think he's
working that out. Fuck—I *want* monogamy, if we're really going to
be boyfriends."

"If?"

"No if—we are. We are, *yeah!*"

Will started hopping around and cackling gleefully, which because he was well dressed and not particularly drunk didn't alarm any of the clipboard girls or the security guys standing nearby.

"Holy shit," said Luz. "Should I be thinking about a wedding? Am I gonna be a best man?"

"We have a long way to go before that, Luz of my life," said Will, calming down and putting his arm around her waist, with a kiss to her forehead. "Yeah, I feel pretty lucky. But pray for me, OK? You're religious, aren't you? I'm gonna need some help."

"I'll ask my grandmother. She prays for the things I want."

"Thank you, *abuela!* 'Please ask God to smooth the way for my gay roommate and his fifty-nine-year-old boyfriend.' "

"She will!"

"So should we go grab some dinner? Those steaky things were ridiculously tiny. Did you even *get* any more of the coconut shrimp?"

As they began to step away from the door in search of a cab, one of the clipboard girls bade them a chirpy good night, and because they all had their party parts to play that night Will and Luz said good night back to the girl as sweetly as they could. Their part was to be zillionairish and feel sorry for the girl, all dressed up and stuck at her post.

And then, a little while after that, McCaw repeated Will's simple-but-complicated line on TV, during a newscast one night on Fox. Peter heard about it early the next morning, from Tyler, who said it was all over the Internet.

"Why?" implored Peter. "Why is he so attached to it? It's just a little thought. No big deal."

"It was weird, boss," said Tyler. They were standing in Peter's office. "Then they asked him to explain it, which he did, and . . . you know how he gets. The spot is suddenly white-hot—all the stuff we saw the other day."

"Christ."

"Did we give him that material?"

"No, we did not," said Peter.

"I was gonna say. The 'simple' kind of rubs up against the purity thing we're trying to do, right? Though he delivers it well, and it certainly seems to inspire him...."

"Damn."

"So where did he get it?"

Peter laughed. "You don't think he just made it up?" he said.

"Well...maybe," said Tyler. "Did he?"

"*Nooo*. It's something Will said, that night we had dinner over there."

"Really?"

"Word for word, Ty. It's a line from one of Will's articles—a quote, actually, from a Senegalese artist he interviewed."

"So how did McCaw get hold of it?"

"We were talking over dinner, we had a few glasses of wine—you know how it is...."

"You were talking about Senegal?"

"Will was adding to the conversation. He was being a good guest."

"So, I mean... is this part of the work now? Are we supposed to retrofit it into our little process here?"

Peter plunked himself down on his desk chair and slumped into it.

"I don't know," he said.

A glorious opportunity for strategic creative direction—the kind of thing that could cap a career and possibly even make history, as Laura kept suggesting—was morphing quickly into a damage control maneuver. Peter would have to tell Will about the incident and fix things on that level if he could. But he was also losing his enchantment with the part of McCaw that had initially attracted him to the project: the man's intellect.

CHAPTER 23

"So—'love,' " said the therapist. "That's a word you haven't used before."

"I know," said Will.

"Big word."

"I know."

"Tell me what's happening with you guys."

"I told you last week—we had sex. Remember?"

"Of course I remember."

"I'm still trying to figure out what happened."

"How so?"

There was no answer at first. The session had only just started, ten minutes before. Will checked in with some thoughts about work and his parents, and the therapist brought up Peter, in view of recent developments.

"Will?" said the therapist.

"OK, here's the thing," said Will, sunk low in his chair and stretched out. "It's so weird. I realized this thing about love only recently. What is it—only a week after we had sex? Or maybe I should call it 'these feelings that I think I'm perhaps willing to *call* love, though I have no idea what the fuck is actually going on.' But whatever. I think I had some kind of feelings *before* sex—ya know?—only I didn't exactly *feel* them, or know what they were. I think I *had* the feelings, but didn't feel them, but they were in there and maybe they were the thing that allowed me to take that step.... Or something."

"And that's a big change for you, isn't it? Having sex with someone in that way."

"Is that it—I'm changing?"

"It sounds like something is happening."

"I don't know—I guess so. Because, like I said, this was the first time it was . . . like this for me."

"Uh-huh."

"I mean, usually I cruise for a six-pack and then wind up with, you know, a six-pack."

"Uh-huh."

"And I wasn't using any of my tricks, and I don't think he was using any of his tricks. . . ."

"Yeah."

Will thought about this for a second. "This time . . . it's good, right?" he said.

"You tell me," said the therapist.

"It's all pretty new. Yaack! Yeah, I guess it's good."

"Sure. Sure it is. So what happens now?"

Will sat up a bit straighter.

"With Peter and me?" he said. "Oh, you know: a summer wedding, a vine-covered cottage, a white picket fence. Isn't that the way it happens?"

The therapist chuckled.

"Sometimes," he said.

"No way! Absolutely not," bellowed Will.

He and Peter were at dinner, sharing an *assiette anglaise* at a tiny chef-owned restaurant in Boerum Hill specializing in house-cured meats. Peter had told Will about the McCaw incident and mentioned a few options, including issuing Will an honorarium. Will was irate.

"That would add insult to injury," he said. "Don't you see? I already feel stupid enough for opening my big mouth that night."

"There wasn't anything wrong with that," said Peter.

"I know. I was trying to hold my own—fine. But this is actually embarrassing. What if Assetou finds out? I'm probably going to have to tell her, just to be up front."

"Mmm, you wouldn't necessarily have to. It was in print, after all. I'm just saying."

"Well . . . maybe. But the idea of accepting money . . ."

"I only meant that people on my staff who come up with taglines. . . ."

"I'm not on your staff, Peter. 'Taglines'—Christ! As we're speaking, I realize that the deeper issue for me is the fact that you're involved in this monkey business in the first place. . . ."

"Advertising?"

"No, McCaw! And you wouldn't be doing it except for the money."

"This again?" said Peter.

"Yes, this again," said Will. "It hasn't gone anywhere. Using your skills to brand up a guy like this is more than slightly sketchy. I know that advertising involves compromises—so does editorial—but there's always a line you don't wanna cross."

"And you feel I'm crossing it."

"Yeah. I keep asking myself how you can do it. And I have to be honest, Peter: It concerns me."

Peter sighed.

"OK," he said.

"You make such a big deal out of not being like the men of your generation," continued Will. " 'They sold out their principles for middle-class sameness!'—OK, fine, but here you are making this huge compromise for a huge amount of money. And it's gotta be for the money—that's the only thing I can think of. It's not like you believe so passionately in the vision."

"No, but I believe in the work, Will. It's pride. I don't believe in butter substitutes, either, but I can figure out an amazing way to sell them. And when they do sell, I feel proud that I've served my client well and that maybe I've connected with this thing that not everybody can connect with, the collective unconscious."

"Oh, boy . . ."

"No, c'mon—really, Will. This is what I do. . . ."

"OK, I'm sorry. I respect that, Peter. I didn't mean to impugn your abilities."

"And with McCaw, I mean—for my company to have such an important client, for the job to be difficult in precisely this way, yet for us to make a success of it. . . ."

"Sure. But that's just the part that sounds a little prostitute-y to me," said Will. "And I should know."

It was an indication of how defensive Peter was becoming that Will's phrase did not register in his brain.

"We talk about these issues all the time, in the office," said Peter.

"You and your disciples?" said Will. "Come on, they're totally School of Peter. What do you think they're going to say?"

"I think we know what we're doing," mumbled Peter.

Will shook his head. He stopped fiddling with the butter knife he'd been tapping nervously on the table and placed it neatly across the rim of his bread-and-butter plate.

"You know," said Will, "I keep flashing on your friend Arnie, upstate." He was making it a point to keep his voice low, as Peter was doing. "We can make fun of him, for sure, but I happen to admire the fact that he's so attached to his principles."

"Will . . ."

"He might be a little out of touch, but he's got pride, too—you know? Right now, Peter, I'm trying to look at myself very honestly in therapy. I'm trying to be open to my better self, and you've been a big part of that process. You mean a lot to me. All I'm saying is that I would hope you could bring a similar commitment to the table—being open to your own stuff. For us. Though I'm sure you've already had all the therapy in the world. . . ."

He was right, Peter realized—which was as uncomfortable as it ever was when Harold or Nick was right.

I remember this feeling, thought Peter. *It comes with the territory.* Somehow the memory of those moments of vulnerability, resulting from completely reasonable challenges by the two men whom Peter had loved and trusted most, had gone mute over the years. Now it was back. But what was he supposed to do—quit the McCaw job?

The plan for after dinner had been to walk back to Peter's place and spend the night. They'd been sleeping together once or twice a week now, and falling into a semi-cohabitational rhythm that worked for both of them, given jobs and the need for fresh clothing. Yet after their charcuterie, as they stood on the sidewalk outside the restaurant, Will confessed he didn't feel like going home with Peter, and Peter thought it best to accept this without protest. After a perfunctory peck on the cheek, Will headed off toward the subway.

The sky was threatening rain, yet the mood in the Heights wasn't especially foreboding, as Peter walked home. Along State and Henry Streets, a leafy canopy of half-century-old trees sheltered sidewalks where neighbors stood talking and children played near their front stoops. The front doors of several brownstones were propped open, to catch an evening breeze. A pair of cute, skinny men with messenger bags—obviously tourists but maybe not boyfriends—stood on a corner, consulting a guidebook.

Peter cracked a smile, thinking how unaccustomed he was to the state of mind he was in.

"I'm confused," he said to himself, as he walked. Was it the child in him who had been so heedless about the implications of the McCaw job? The parent who'd found no way of saying no to such money and supposed prestige? Reflexively, he checked his phone for a text, since he and Will often texted each other right after leaving each other's company. This time, nothing. And he could think of nothing to text to Will that wouldn't sound cute or manipulative.

He proceeded up Henry Street and tried not to feel sad. How nice the simple pleasure of ambulation! How quaint the slate sidewalks and historic façades, how silly the plantings in some people's window boxes! Harold always made fun of silly window boxes. A child's chalk drawings on the sidewalk. A Dumpster full of construction debris. A dead pigeon in the gutter.

Oh, boy, he thought. But thank God to have no foot issues that would make walking difficult—or hip issues, or weight issues, as some his age did. Thank God, in fact, to *be* his age and not dead, as literally all the people he called friends in 1985 were.

Therapy might be a smart move, he thought. Since ending the ten-year stint of garden-variety gestalt he began shortly after arriving in New York, during which he unpacked what seemed like the entire contents of his psyche, he'd been living on the plateau of functional-enough, though he knew he wasn't *done with* or *cured of* anything. And indeed life had kept coming. His father had died, his mother had grown old, many friends had died, and *he'd* gotten older, too, which meant there was plenty of terrain to survey in preparation for the *next* sixty years of his life—perhaps breakthroughs as transformative as those initial ones. . . .

What a mess.

By the time he reached his house, he'd decided he needed help of some kind. It was a big question to explore: whether the pinnacle of his middle age was going to be defined by the job of a lifetime or a dream-come-true boyfriend.

At least the prospect of therapy isn't as scary as it once was, said one voice in his head.

Yeah, and you can always consult the collective unconscious, too, mocked another.

Days went by and they didn't speak. A few sparse texts informed Peter that Will wanted some "space," but that no, he didn't want to break up, exactly. Peter was both relieved and nervous, and asked Luz if she would have a drink with him. They met early one evening at the bar on the cove at the World Financial Center.

"Hey," said Luz, finding Peter at one of the aluminum tables outside on the terrace, overlooking the marina. She was in a dark suit, as were most of the well-starched, young financial types who packed the place.

"Hey, " said Peter.

"How's it going?" She parked her briefcase and patted Peter collegially on the shoulder, as she sat down.

"Oh, you know, it's going. Thanks for coming."

"No problem. What are you drinking?"

"Vodka."

"Good, me too." She looked around for a waiter.

"I'm feeling kind of in a weird spot," said Peter, after the waiter had taken Luz's order.

"Talk to me," she said.

"I'm in love. I think he is, too, or at least has feelings for me. I think things were going really well between us. I mean, things *are* going well. . . ."

"OK."

"They *are* going well, right? You don't know anything I don't know."

Luz laughed.

"I don't know what you know," she said. "But I don't think he's breaking up with anyone, if that's what you mean."

"Thank God."

"You guys communicate pretty well, as I understand it. He wouldn't just walk away, unilaterally, in silence."

"No, I know. So what's going on, then? What's he doing?"

"He's thinking."

"About what, may I ask? Can you say?"

"Yeah, I can say. He's thinking about whether he has the right to demand anything of you."

"Demand anything?"

"He respects you, Peter. He can't demand that you give up a job, so I think he's trying to figure out how he can coexist with you."

"Oh."

"File it under 'New Relationship Stuff.' It's as hard for Will as it is for anyone to suddenly have this new person to alternately respect and challenge. I should say *simultaneously* respect and challenge."

"Hmm."

"Plus, maybe it's harder for Will. I don't think he's ever been as close to a guy as he is to you, and he doesn't want to fuck a good thing up."

Peter sighed.

"That's a relief," he said.

"I'm glad," said Luz. "Now, it's not for me to say what you should do, Peter, but if you were my client I'd recommend you don't fuck up a good thing, either. I think you and Will are pretty good together."

Peter smiled.

"I know," he said. "I have to do something."

The waiter came with Luz's drink. Peter ordered a second.

"You hungry?" he said.

"I'm fine, thanks," said Luz.

"I don't know what to do," said Peter, handing the waiter the menus. "Except maybe I do."

They made a wordless toast and took a sip.

"I'm a little lost, Luz," said Peter. "Lost for words, lost in time. In the bad old days they used to refer to gay men as 'Peter Pans'— you know, not wanting to grow up or something. But I have to say honestly I feel a bit that way. Always have. Suspended between infancy and old age. Not quite sure what grown-up is. That's part of what's going on."

Luz smiled and nodded.

"I can remember hearing Chubby Checker for the first time and knowing that the Twist was the future," continued Peter. "Very exciting stuff for a boy who was, like, seven. And every moment since then that was also the future, also exciting, I can remember. And all those moments feel scattered in *the middle* of something, not . . . lined up on some directional path. Do you know what I mean? Most of the time I can't see a direction, a spot that everything points to, and most of the time that's OK, 'cause it's all kinda floaty good. But suddenly . . . it isn't good. I'm trying to see a direction now, for dear life. Like when you get knocked over by a wave in the ocean and you don't know which end is up. Even my job, for Christ's sake, in this thing we merrily call 'the media,' supposedly in the middle between the mind and the world. The *media*. Sometimes it feels like that's all there is nowadays, this middle zone. No mind, no world."

Luz patiently let Peter ramble. He spoke of Harold and Nick and his expectation of a "third husband." He explained that over the years, without a partner, he'd distracted himself from loneliness with the achievements of an illustrious career that was built partly on his feelings about the future. In the absence of love, work took over—and that was a kind of direction. He knew he was the luckiest man in the universe to have found Will, and would do anything to keep him, but was having trouble making room for this particular future now, and was shocked and ashamed to find this so.

"In the middle of everything," muttered Peter, "central to nothing."

The sun was low over the Jersey City skyline, barely peeking over a stand of skyscrapers that had cropped up in what some New York chauvinists deemed "the last five minutes."

"Are you saying," said Luz finally, "that you think it has to be between Will and your job, and that you don't know how to choose?"

Peter dropped his head and said nothing.

"Well, let me ask you this," said Luz, "and maybe this is the lawyer in me, too. Can't you just step away?"

"From what, my job?"

"From this assignment. Say you got hit by a bus, God forbid. Would your company lose the account?"

Peter had to think a moment.

"No, I don't think we would lose the account. Though it's me, to some degree, that they want."

"Again, forgive me—I don't want to be presumptuous—but couldn't your team or the process go on without you?"

"Maybe they could. I dunno. I guess they could."

"All I am saying is that maybe there's a way for you to step aside, if you really dislike this guy as much as Will says you do. And, Peter, you've said it yourself—I've heard you, at dinner. . . ."

"I know. I have."

"Anyway, I'm sure you're weighing all the options."

"I'm trying to," said Peter, wistfully. In front of them, in the marina, a small party of passengers was boarding an eighty-foot schooner for some kind of dinner cruise. More young people in the money business.

"You know, advertising is funny," he mused. "You have to create work that answers a client's business needs, always—the bottom line. But to be a real success in this business you also have to get inside a client's head, be able to intuit their deepest emotional connections to the product, the brand, the mission. It's an entirely different talent from the work itself."

"I'll bet."

"I've always been proud to get a little symbiotic with my clients. I love being able to mind-meld with their urgencies. It's a little mystical, this talent, and it tends to foster what we in the industry very smugly assume to be an advanced kind of ethics. . . ."

Peter shook his head and Luz nodded in understanding.

"I never encountered a downside to this talent," said Peter, "though I've often wondered if there could be one."

"Mm-hmm," said Luz.

"I guess maybe I'm encountering one now."

"Maybe you are."

Peter thought for a moment.

"He really likes me that much?" he said.

"He really likes you that much," said Luz.

"Does he miss me?"

"I think he does. Yeah, for sure he does."

Peter made a small, joyous sound like a whinny, then took a swig of his vodka.

"I don't wanna fuck this up, Luz," he said. "On top of everything, it might be my last shot."

"I hear ya."

"So how should I handle it? And I'm so grateful for your help. Do I show up at his doorstep? Do I send flowers to the office? Do I just wait for him to reach out? I mean, I think he and I should be talking. . . ."

"Talking is good. Ask him to talk."

"Again?"

"Again and again. At some point he'll say yes and you'll talk. You could send flowers, too."

"Right."

"Good."

"Thank you, Luz."

"No problem."

The party on the schooner had already started. Even as guests were still boarding, the folks on deck were toasting, schmoozing.

"Did he know you were coming to meet me?" said Peter.

"Of course," said Luz.

"How does he look?"

"How does he look? It's only been a few days. He looks the same."

"I miss those eyes, that little laugh."

"I know what you miss."

"Yeah, that, too."

* * *

Peter drove upstate to see Jonathan alone. Except for a little news from the radio, the drive was silent—no music. Arriving in Hudson early and stopping for coffee at a diner on Warren Street, Peter thought bitterly how odd it was that people could be strolling blithely down the street, looking in shop windows, while someone precious lay dying, under something called "palliative care," just a few miles away. He felt remote from the diner's morning bustle and found himself remembering, as he thanked his waitress with robotic cheer, the way when he was in high school TV sitcoms would roll out normally even on the nights before a test that was destined to annihilate him.

Aldebar greeted him soberly at the door of the house and showed him up to Jonathan's room.

"He's in and out," said Aldebar quietly, before they went in. "The moods come and go very fast."

"OK," said Peter.

Inside, Jonathan was installed in a hospital bed that had been brought in to replace his regular one. He was sitting up, propped by a mountain of pillows, wearing the embroidered red cap he was wearing on the night of his housewarming. There was an IV line in his arm, running up to a bag on a pole. In a chair next to him was Sofia, a kind-looking older woman with a tight-tight bun of black-black hair.

"Look who's come to see you," said Sofia, standing and smiling a greeting toward Peter.

Jonathan raised his eyebrows and opened his mouth slightly, as if ready to greet a guest as soon as someone appeared or was identified.

"Hi, Jon," said Peter, approaching. But Jonathan still didn't appear to recognize him.

"It's Peter, Jonathan," said Aldebar.

"Oh, Peter," said Jonathan. His breathing was shallow. He could barely raise his arm but motioned toward the chair where Sofia had been sitting. "Come . . ."

"If you need anything, we're right here," said Aldebar, slipping out with Sofia.

Peter had resolved to stay upbeat for his friend, but he started sobbing the moment he took Jonathan's skeletal hand, its skin translucent and markedly unpink, and bent forward to kiss it.

"How are you feeling, Jon?" said Peter, sitting back and making an effort to regroup. "I've been looking forward to seeing you."

"Peter . . ."

"Hi."

"OK."

"How are you feeling?"

Jonathan raised a hand feebly, as if to stop Peter.

"Let me say this while I can," whispered Jonathan. "I love you and want to thank you for everything. Your friendship meant the world to me."

The room was very still. Jonathan's voice may have been soft, but it commanded authority. The words were a surprise for Peter, and he saw they must have taken some strength, or resolve, to summon. Maybe they'd been rehearsed?

"No need to thank me for anything," said Peter. Then he paused. It was hard for him to say so little, since the moment was fraught and he had thought of so much else to say, on the drive up. But he wanted to make sure Jonathan could say anything he wanted to say, without the effort of interrupting or waiting for Peter to finish.

"Love you," repeated Jonathan.

"Love you, too," said Peter. "Always."

"Sometimes . . . sometimes I get confused," said Jonathan. "I think Roberto is here." A twitch of the mouth seemed to mark the spot where a laugh would have been. "They know how to handle me, but . . . I like it when he comes."

"He's always right here," said Peter, tapping the center of his chest.

"Yes."

Peter noticed a splendid arrangement of tulips and lilies near the window and asked who sent them. Jonathan said he didn't know. Peter asked if anyone else had come to see him and Jonathan said no—no one but Roberto.

"Aldebar says Connor's been coming to see you."

"Who?"

"Connor Frankel."

"He reads to me."

"What does he read?"

"Oh...," said Jonathan, gesturing toward the night table, where a copy of T. S. Eliot's *Four Quartets* lay next to a box of Kleenex.

"Really? Eliot?"

"I know what to make of it."

"You know those poems very well, don't you?"

"Mmhh."

"I forget which one is your favorite."

Jonathan didn't respond, and after a minute Peter saw that he'd drifted off to sleep. It didn't feel like an emergency, so Peter just sat there. Several minutes passed, during which the only sound was a small click and whir made by a machine attached to Jonathan's IV line, which Peter supposed signaled the dispersal of a dose of morphine.

Peter was shocked at how little of his formerly vital friend remained, yet what Aldebar said was true: Something essential still remained, something congenital. It was a gift to be able to behold it, even in flashes, if under such terrible circumstances.

Presently, Jonathan awoke with an anguished whimper.

"Aaah!"

"Jon, I'm here," said Peter.

"Achh... What?" said Jonathan, grimacing, looking frantically about.

"It's Peter—I'm right here."

Jonathan's breathing was heavier. Then he seemed to focus.

"I dreamed I was at the wrong gate," he said.

"You did?"

Jonathan sighed.

"They told me... they told me I was going someplace that didn't exist," he said.

Peter didn't know what else to do but tenderly stroke the top of Jonathan's hand.

"Well, right now you're exactly where you should be," said Peter. "You're safe at home."

"Water, please," said Jonathan, adjusting his position so he was a bit more upright. The grimace was gone.

Peter looked around and saw a sippy cup on the table.

"Is this water?" he said.

Yes, nodded Jonathan, outstretching both hands in an almost infantile way. Peter inspected the cup, just to make sure it was water, then gave it to Jonathan, who drank and then handed back the cup.

"Help me . . . ," said Jonathan, still trying to adjust himself. Peter repositioned a pillow and smiled sadly when he noticed how nicely Jonathan's favorite Black Tourmaline cologne married with the scent of freshly laundered cotton sheets. The patient was clearly being well taken care of.

"Better," said Jonathan. He sat there for a moment, surveying the room almost contentedly. Then he looked at Peter and said, "OK, present and accounted for."

"You feel OK?"

"For the moment. It's horrible. I know when I'm not making sense, then I slip into it. We don't know if it's the drugs or the disease. It's like a roller coaster."

"Do you need anything?"

"Only my life back."

Peter nodded. "If I only could, dear friend," he said.

"Nice shirt," said Jonathan.

"Oh, thanks," said Peter, raising an arm to model a blue-and-green-striped sleeve. "Paul Smith."

Jonathan nodded.

"My body finally betrayed me, Petey," he said. "Payback for Vietnam."

"What?" said Peter. "How so?"

"I killed people."

Peter knew that his friend had been drafted and seen action during the war, but was uncertain of what kind of response was called for now. Jonathan had never been open to sharing details of the experience.

"I don't think . . . ," he began.

"I never questioned enough," said Jonathan. "I should have gone to Canada."

Where was this coming from?

"It was a very confusing time," said Peter.

"My parents supported the war; we couldn't afford a lawyer. . . ."

"This was all before NYU. . . ."

"I tried to forgive myself," said Jonathan. "I guess maybe the universe didn't forgive me."

Why was he thinking about Vietnam, after all these years?

"You did the best you could, Jon, and you went on to do even better," said Peter. "That's all anybody can do."

"I guess so. . . ."

Jonathan went silent again, and this time, after a moment, Peter saw that he was weeping.

"No Fire Island this year, Petey," he sobbed.

Peter rose and embraced Jonathan gently, leaning over him in an approximation of a hug. They remained that way for a few seconds, and Peter gave Jonathan's ear and the side of his face a gentle caress.

"That place is boring, anyway," said Peter.

Weak laughter emerged out of Jonathan's sobbing.

"I know," he said. "We always hated it, didn't we?"

"Too much alcohol, too many nipples!"

"Well, good-bye!"

Both men were laughing, as Peter resumed his seat and Jonathan adjusted himself further and coughed a bit.

"You OK there?" said Peter.

"I'm fine," said Jonathan. "Morphine is my new best friend."

Vietnam seemed already forgotten.

Jonathan made more sense as they spoke about the daily routine that Aldebar and Sofia had established for him, what he could and couldn't eat and keep down, and how he expected his memorial service to go. Peter initially pooh-poohed talk about the latter, but realized Jonathan needed to talk about it.

"I'm going for High Classical," said Jonathan.

"A string quartet?" said Peter.

"Yes! Have I told you about it already?"

"No, but I know you."

"And a tenor."

"Oh, my."

"Bach, Schubert, and Britten. The details are a surprise."

"OK."

"I want people to have a nice time remembering me, including you and your boyfriend."

"I know it'll be beautiful. Who's the tenor?"

"Don't change the subject," said Jonathan, glaring.

"What—Will?" said Peter.

"Don't tell me you fucked it up."

"No, I haven't fucked it up. I think it's happening, for real."

A gurgle arose from Jonathan's throat that sounded like satisfaction.

"You were so afraid, for so long," he mused.

"That's right, I was," said Peter. "I still am."

"Lose that," snapped Jonathan, sternly. The normality of boy talk seemed to animate him.

"I'm trying," said Peter.

"You went for it—that's good. I never could, after Roberto."

"No?"

"Didn't know how."

"But you're so good at taking care of yourself."

"In some ways."

Peter remembered wondering, when Roberto died, where Jonathan would find another man so matched with him in disposition. Roberto was a cultivated Mexican, from a Jewish family of means. They had met in Paris, while Jonathan was doing a film there, and immediately bonded. Everyone knew their relationship was epically correct. Jonathan may have been from a poor family and Roberto from a rich one, yet the critical mass of arcane interests and refined tastes between them meant a thousand possibilities. Starting with Paris—and a visit to a tiny Grand Guignol museum, which each was thrilled the other knew about—they began turning those possibilities into a life together, and continued to do so for fifteen years.

Love had never happened again for Jonathan, though he hadn't looked for it nearly as hard as Peter had. And when he looked, he said, he had no luck. He once described breaking up with a guy because he'd met his parents and saw, in their commonness and sloth, the kind of "programming" the guy would have to be battling his entire life, which would undoubtedly limit anything the two of them would be able to cook up together.

"Harold was kee … kee … he was *kee*-ping you from it," slurred Jonathan, with some effort.

"Sorry, Jon?"

"You should have asked Harold if it was OK."

Peter was startled.

"Actually, Harold gave me explicit permission, one day in the hospital," he said. "A month before he died."

"Did you listen to him?"

Peter said nothing

"You didn't, did you?" said Jonathan. "Because only after he was dead were you the per … per … the *per*-fect boyfriend!"

Peter didn't know what to say. Though dementia wasn't exactly an either/or thing, he realized Jonathan might be cycling into another episode.

"You didn't listen to him well enough, Peter," continued Jonathan. "But you still can. Here, let me ask him."

What?

Jonathan closed his eyes and was silent for a moment. Then he opened them and spoke with oracular clarity. "He says fine."

The words struck with the force of a supernatural pronouncement, even if they'd been meant partly as a joke.

"Good. Thank you," said Peter. The response was reflexive, yet he searched Jonathan's eyes for something beyond the bewilderment and fatigue that had taken hold there. He remembered this kind of moment from twenty-five years before and other friends. Can the dying see more clearly than the rest of us? Did being close to death afford a view of aspects of life that are normally hidden or ignored? Jonathan might well have connected mystically with some spirit or energy of Harold, and Peter, fighting the urge to ponder the metaphysics of it, thought he should stay open to that possibility.

"Now promise me something," said Jonathan.

"Of course," said Peter.

"Forgive the boy his stuff. People do cra … cra … *cra*-zy things."

Whatever that means.

"OK."

"Remember."

"I will."

"OK."

Suddenly, Peter was afraid he might be wearing Jonathan out. The visit had gone on for some time and must be extremely taxing.

"Jon, when can I come and see you again?"

His friend didn't answer.

"Jon?" Peter said.

But Jonathan had fallen asleep again and Peter didn't want to wake him.

Chapter 24

As Peter drove back to the city, his thoughts roiled like the storm clouds of a sped-up computer model of bad weather. Jonathan would soon die, and so, for that matter, would everybody else. The variables governing the weather in which Peter found himself were few and clear: Life is dangerous, people are fragile, the clock is ticking. Of course, while one computer model saw blobs of darkness swirling messily to engulf everything, another saw them dissipating. Depending on how one chose to weight the variables, a storm could turn out different ways. Oddly, during inclement moments like this, Peter had always been able to "choose" faith in his own survival. Not that he believed he'd outlive anyone or evade his share of suffering; he simply found himself grateful for being called to witness life's true nature, including its menace, and that gratitude helped sustain him. He found it easy at such times—necessary, actually—to remember what a yoga instructor once told him: Blessings are like solar winds; they just keep blowing from the direction of God, no matter what shape the planet or its people are in. You could always lift your head and smile into the wind.

At the age of almost sixty, Peter understood his ability to carry on as a kind of optimism he'd been born with—and yet, almost comically, this now seemed a tinier part of the human drama than he'd ever imagined. Who cared if *he* could carry on? What did it matter if he did? Humanity was more fucked than ever. The torture on Jonathan's face continued to haunt Peter, as he drove. Should he have stayed in Hudson to hold his friend's hand, or would that have hindered the symphony of palliation Aldebar had programmed? Should he try to hope, since there was no other hope, that an end would come soon? Most Americans sheltered themselves from these kinds of thoughts, anymore. That was *their* optimism. Death had been banished from sight, and the blessings we create for our-selves—entertainments and amusements, products and media, totems and fetishes—had pulled our attention away from the eter-nal flow from the beyond.

Funny, thought Peter. People were horrified by the massive planetary transformations of the so-called Anthropocene era, yet weren't the biggest changes not in the environment, but in the species itself? "Lifestyle" was replacing "life," and that was shifting the nature of human nature itself. In the computer model of human evolution, the substitution of variables like "the wrong accessory" for "death," and "the eternal bemusing present" for "time," were transforming everything. When run today, sped-up, the model re-sulted not in swirling blobs of darkness but pretty pinwheels, and daisies, and paisleys that effloresced hypnotically until . . . they flickered into nothingness.

And gays are such a willing part of it!

Even as a child, in the 1950s, Peter knew what he was and under-stood the fucked-up messages about it that were coded into sitcom characters, neighbors' jokes, and books he found in the adult section of the public library. Coming out in the '60s was therefore not only a personal act, but a critique of civilization, too. He'd marched through the streets with hundreds of others, in the first wave of gay libera-tion, his fist thrust high in the air, so he shook his head now, at times, to see a world in which gays were not only accepted but rushed into contract for scoring top Nielsen ratings on reality TV shows in which they did things like pick out colors for their big, fat, gay weddings.

"Peach or apricot? Bra-ad, help *me . . . !"*

Mystical constructions like the gay imagination and ancient tra-ditions of sacred otherness had been kicked to the curb in the race for acceptance as a demographic; it was an old story. The mystical strain could always be dormant instead of dead, yet the point was that gay men, as a culture, had given up acting on that strain, except perhaps to mourn it on some deep, unconscious level, while the party chugged on.

Not dormant here, though, Peter thought. *All that critique stuff still feels pretty adult to me, pretty big. . . . These weddings are like elementary school social studies projects.*

Jonathan had stayed true, in his way. Peter felt so proud of him. Witnessing his decline, though terrible, was also somehow a blessing—the shock of it alone, a salutary thing. Didn't the mind need to reboot periodically? Didn't it evolve that way—reconstituting normal perception and cogitation time after time, following mind-smashing crises like famines and wars? Churchgoing afforded a weak version of the process through denatured, weekly ritual; so, in its way, did all-night dancing and drugging. Except for terrorist attacks and crashes of the economy—behind the fear of which was thus perhaps the wish!—we have precious few cataclysms to cue a restorative reboot nowadays, except the occasional death of a prince.

Peter had only been home for an hour when Aldebar called to say that Jonathan had died.

"It was easy," said Aldebar. "He didn't suffer at all."

Peter was shocked and he wasn't. His face immediately screwed into a grimace.

"What happened?" he said.

"He . . . just fell asleep and didn't wake up. I was with him."

"Did he say anything?"

"No."

Peter sank into one of the armchairs, as a wave of numbness engulfed him. He could hear Aldebar speak and he couldn't.

"It was very peaceful."

"Should I come back?"

"No, no need. We can handle everything. I know he was very happy he was able to see you, at the end."

"Well, yes—I was, too."

"I'm very sorry, Peter. I know it's a great loss."

"Thank you, Aldebar. I know the loss is yours, too."

"Thank you for saying that. I'll let you know about the arrangements. As you know, he made a lot of the plans himself."

"Yes. But let me know if I can help with anything."

"Certainly."

After the call, Peter just sat there, with no music and no beverage, in a state that involved both thinking and not thinking. It was the beginning of adjustment to a world that no longer included his best friend—a process he knew, as with each of the previous friends he'd lost, would take the rest of his life.

Presently, with a vehemence that reflected both rage and the tender memory of love, Peter reached up to the shoulder of his shirt and tore the sleeve half off at the seam, and in doing so popped a button off the front. The button flew across the room and landed on the floor with a soft *tckk* sound. And Peter continued to sit there, staring at the button, the torn sleeve hanging away from his shoulder like some kind of puny, vestigial, blue-and-green-striped wing.

Will was on a photo shoot that day, in a studio complex in the far west Village. The subject was a nineteen-year-old ballerina Will had interviewed a week before, for a feature—a beautiful soloist in a major company, who was getting plum roles and said to be on her way to stardom as a principal. When Will arrived, five minutes late, he was chagrinned to find the shoot already behind schedule. The supposedly hot, new, up-and-coming photographer to whom Olivier had assigned the shoot was still futzing around with boxes on tripods that should already have been set by the time stated on the call sheet. The photographer was bossing around his two assistants imperiously, though with comments too vague to help them know exactly what he wanted, and he was doing nothing to create a collegial atmosphere among the others on set—editors and stylists, hair and makeup people—all of whom seemed uncomfortably idle. The poor ballerina was sitting in the studio's kitchen area, in a robe, her hair and makeup done, waiting patiently to be called, talking with her publicist over little cups of espresso.

"Max, didn't we say we were eliminating the, uh . . . you know," said the photographer, wagging his finger indeterminately at a wide swath of studio. "Isn't there, I dunno, some dead over there. . . . ?"

Max looked confounded, but countered with some specific suggestions that sounded right to Will.

"I mean, seriously, boss. It's the key there, the secondary there, and some backfill—right?" said Max, pointing. "Assuming she's standing there . . . Is that where you want her?"

The photographer, model-handsome himself, looked undecided—a bad sign, especially at the top of a shoot.

"Christine . . . ?" said the photographer. But the stylist, who had the clothes ready for the first setup, wasn't responsible for setting up the shot, nor did she seem happy to note the creative void left by the photographer's lack of direction. She was French and made a very French expression that seemed to combine disdain with readiness to cooperate, once there was a plan.

Will knew he had to act. The words of his former employer, the publishing company head, about stepping up with one's own authority, rang in his head. After a few words with the ballerina, he marched over to the photographer and introduced himself.

"So, Mark, are we ready?" said Will.

"It's not quite working . . . ," moaned Mark, watching Max shift a light slightly to the left.

"What's the setup?" said Will.

"We're almost there . . . ," mumbled Mark.

"The blue Versace," said the stylist. "This is what we talked about. . . ."

"Thank you," said Will.

"OK," said Mark.

"OK, you know what, people?" said Will, clapping his hands. "We're starting." He stepped to the center of the studio and spoke loudly enough for everyone to hear. "I want a ladder set up right here—see? Let the shot include those windows. Max, no seamless, and get some kick underneath—I guess from the right. Otherwise we're fine, OK? She'll climb up to the second or third rung and hold on with one hand, and maybe do something balletic with the other one. Everybody got it? We're shooting a beautiful ballerina who's contemplating the top."

Will turned to the ballerina and asked if she were comfortable doing that, and she said yes.

"A ladder?" said Max.

"Yes, right there," said Will, pointing to the corridor. "There's one right outside the door."

A minute later, the ladder had been set up and Max was

perched on it in the spot where the ballerina would be, so the light level could be metered.

"We go in one minute," said Will. "Mark, are you clear on what we're doing?"

"Yeah, sure," said Mark, as the other assistant quickly handed him another camera.

Will detailed the shot to the ballerina, while the stylist got her into the dress—a frothy blue thing that riffed on the tutu dress of romantic ballet. Then he walked her over to the ladder and helped her up the first few rungs.

"All right, darling, now you're breaking into heaven, yes?" he said. "You're an outsider, you've always been an outsider, and now you wanna be on the inside, and suddenly you see a break in the clouds and you know you're gonna make it up into heaven. . . ."

The ballerina smiled. She totally got it.

The shot went well, and after that one they did two more, which Will also set up with scenarios: "Your luggage has gone missing, but you have to look like a million dollars when you get off the train at Monte Carlo." "The prince who comes backstage after the performance is not the cute one, but his boring older brother." In the latter shot, Max, a skinny hipster with ill-kempt clothes and hair, played the prince, while the ballerina, with obviously lavish theatrical gifts, made the scene come alive by playing against him royally. The contrast worked brilliantly. At the same time, the ballerina made a pair of ridiculously trendy shoes from a magazine advertiser look like the most important footwear in history.

Afterward, Will and the photographer were looking at the results of the shoot on a laptop, with some of the others, when the text came from Peter.

Thought you should know, wrote Peter. *We've just lost Jonathan. Missing you. Call when you can, if you'd like.*

Proper spelling and punctuation, thought Will. The correctness was probably in deference to both the occasion and the gap since their last exchange.

Good.

So so sorry, texted Will. He was sad to hear about Jonathan, of course, and concerned about Peter. For days, he had been looking for the right opportunity for rapprochement, and though he wished he didn't have to make his sympathy do this kind of double duty, he accepted Peter's text as a cue to start talking again. Anyway, it was time. He had begun to see who Peter really was, and why, and how the two of them might coexist. With the help of his therapist, he'd seen through the shadow issues of age and McCaw, to the real one, which was, as he described it to Luz, Peter's awesomeness.

"Seriously," he told her. "Can I use that word in a nonhumorous way? I was in awe of the guy, but in the wrong way. That wasn't good. I was trying to be cool. The awe was, I dunno, too generic."

"Generic awesomeness," she said, trying to parse the concept.

"You know—" said Will, "the agency, the parties, and all that. But now I think I'm in awe for the right reasons. We should be a little bit in awe of the people we love, right? He's an amazing human being."

"OK," said Luz.

"He is!"

"I know."

Will had come to appreciate a part of Peter's history that continued to affect his nature: his childhood as an outsider. And though Will had learned about Stonewall and AIDS through history books, he'd never really grasped what it meant to be a gay outsider in America. It was a mind-set that continued to interact inside Peter's brain with its antidote, the insistence on breaching the inside or redefining the outside as the inside or the middle, or something. It would obviously affect his work. The therapist, who was around Peter's age and gay, helped Will see this—as well as how decidedly unchallenged Will himself had been, as a gay child and a young gay man.

"The outside doesn't even exist like that anymore," he explained to Luz. Anyway, he said, he had finally come to see Peter as the human being he was, not just "a neat older guy who was supercharming, a survivor of a legendary era, and lots of good sex."

Will call you in an hour—OK? texted Will. *On a shoot. Will be great to hear your voice.*

Will already knew about Jonathan, however. Aldebar had called him directly, an hour before, right after he'd called Peter.

CHAPTER 25

"Good to see you," said Aldebar, greeting Peter at the door. The two men embraced. "How are you holding up?"

"Hanging in there," said Peter.

"All set?"

"Absolutely."

The service for Jonathan, which was designed to be something between a funeral and a memorial, took place in the concert hall of the Ethical Culture Society, on Central Park West. Peter knew the place well, having attended several AIDS-related memorial services there in the '80s, as he supposed Jonathan had done, too. Plainly decorated but with a grandly vaulted ceiling and a trio of arched windows in the rear that let in daylight, the hall was both sober and inspiring, ideal for sad celebrations like memorial services. Aldebar, who showed Peter over to the rows reserved for family and close friends, had said he'd almost booked the Society's Ceremonial Hall, a less imposing room that accommodated far fewer people than the Concert Hall's eight hundred, but it was clear that morning, a few minutes before the service was scheduled to begin, that Aldebar had made the right choice. Practically every seat was filled, and the room's vastness was filled with that silence eight hundred people make collectively when trying to remain as still as possible, with no musical prelude to cover a bit of quiet buzzing.

As he followed Aldebar to his seat, Peter resisted the urge to survey the crowd too intently, for fear of disturbing anyone's mood. In passing, though, he did spot and quietly acknowledge a few people he knew: Connor Frankel and his partner, Wallace; Jonathan's brother and his wife; and several of the gray-suit couples whom Peter knew from Jonathan's parties. He was thanking Aldebar with a squeeze of the arm when he registered Will, smiling calmly, already installed in the seat next to his.

"Oh!" said Peter.

"Saved you a seat," Will whispered. They shared a modest kiss.

"Thank you."

"Good to see you."

"Good to see *you*. How are you?"

"I'm fine, thanks—but, you know, very sad."

Peter nodded his head. "I know," he said. They'd shared a brief call on the day Jonathan died and acknowledged they'd be seeing each other at the memorial service, but had made no more specific plans.

"How are you doing?" said Will.

"OK . . . ," said Peter, hesitantly. "OK."

"I've missed you. It was nice to hear your voice, the other day."

"Me too. I've missed you so much."

They were exchanging a few words about Peter's final visit with Jonathan, when the service commenced. A well-known author—a friend of Jonathan's whom Aldebar had asked to serve as master of ceremonies—stepped up to the lectern that had been set up on one side of the stage.

"Talk later," said Will.

"Yes," whispered Peter, reaching for his phone to mute it, when he saw Will doing the same. And he was struck again, almost afresh, by Will's handsome profile and his unaffected elegance in his black suit. A scene from the film *Gentleman's Agreement* danced into his head, in which Dorothy McGuire sees Gregory Peck for the first time in evening clothes and says he looks "good enough to eat with a spoon." It was going to be hard to focus on the service.

"Good morning and welcome," intoned the author. "We gather

today to remember a man, a friend, an artist, who leaves behind a body of work, but more importantly, a body of friends. . . ."

The stage, nobly framed by an arch of dark wood, was also set with four chairs and music stands—for the string quartet, Peter assumed—as well as a piano and a harp. The piano and harp surprised Peter; Jonathan hadn't mentioned them, and it was with something like anticipated pleasure that Peter wondered what musical selections required them. He glanced over the printed program, then returned his attention to the author.

". . . Will be a poorer place without him, but richer for the legacy that bears his name. . . ."

The remarks, though standard, were well formulated and sounded heartfelt, and thus were completely welcome. The room was attentive.

". . . Once, when he adapted a book of mine . . ."

The author recounted working with Jonathan on a film, noting he'd come away with a keen appreciation of the man's thoroughness and generosity, which is why, he said, he wasn't surprised to learn that Jonathan had specified all details of that morning's service himself, including the "casting"—though not, of course, the actual lines he was speaking.

There was some laughter, from those who no doubt fondly remembered Jonathan's elaborate style of hospitality. And as the author went on, Peter stole another glance sideward at Will, who looked so princely in his suit.

Damn, he thought. *Just—damn.*

When Will noticed Peter looking, Peter widened his eyes in mock-sternness and pointed toward the lectern, as if Will were the one who needed reminding to pay attention.

The first musical selection was the trio sonata of Bach's *Musical Offering,* with a flutist, a violinist, and a pianist. The performance was superb—Aldebar had engaged members of a prominent chamber music ensemble. Following was a remembrance by the Oscar-winning film editor who'd worked with Jonathan on the Connor Frankel project. The editor, who was still engaged in daily work on the film's final touches, spoke of Jonathan's fearlessness and restraint, "which need each other, if either is to be useful" in a work of art. Though people applauded after the Bach—following Aldebar's cue, Peter noted—they were silent after the editor, except for some throat clearing. Then there was the second movement of Schubert's *Death and the Maiden* quartet, followed by another remembrance, this from an enduring Broadway and Hollywood star who'd narrated one of Jonathan's films. She spoke of Jonathan's experience and worldliness, which set a benchmark for her, she said, of the kind of "culture-maker" she wanted to be.

At one point during the star's remarks a phone went off, with a particularly inane ring tone. People tried not to look in that direction and the thing was quickly silenced.

"Good turnout," said Peter to Will, after he did twist around in his seat and sneak a peek at the crowd.

Yes, Will nodded.

The *Times* had run an obituary—a meaty one. It referred to Jonathan as "one of the leading documentarians of his generation," a phrase Aldebar mentioned to Peter that he'd suggested was fair when he spoke to the obituary's writer, one of the paper's film critics, who called to update the unfinished piece on Jonathan that was already on file. Aldebar, of course, was running everything, with the grateful approval of Jonathan's lawyer and brother. Throughout the service, he stood off to the side, perhaps not wanting to claim too indelicately a spot among the close friends and family, and, too, to be available as the event's executive producer. In fact, everyone close to Jonathan had known for months that Aldebar had become something more than a nurse, in Jonathan's house. It was clear that something important had developed between them, and that morning Aldebar, in his dark-blue suit, did look like a cross between a widower and a surviving business partner.

As the star left the stage, Will leaned over to say he wondered what kind of service the Ethical Culture Society regularly held in that room. Peter whispered that he'd wondered the same thing during previous memorial services, but that he'd never managed to follow through on the research.

"Let's check it out," said Will.

"Fine," said Peter.

And then, from the lectern, the author announced that a third person, not noted in the program, had kindly agreed to speak before the final musical selection; he introduced Peter.

Peter rose.

"You're speaking?" said Will.

"Nah, I gotta pee," whispered Peter, clapping Will affectionately on the shoulder as he exited the row.

The room became hushed as Peter stepped up to the lectern. *No microphone,* he suddenly noticed—but then he quickly saw that the room's acoustics were a dream.

"You've all spoken so eloquently of Jonathan's creative side," said Peter. "No artist could wish for more loving insights into his work and process. I am so grateful to all of you for sharing these remembrances, and I only wanted to add a few of my own, since I believe I can claim to have known our good friend possibly longer than almost anyone in the room, with the exception of Jonathan's family." Peter nodded graciously toward them.

"We met at what used to be called a consciousness-raising group," he continued. "We were all fresh out of college, it was the mid-seventies, and we were all determined to stay responsible for our own intellectual rigor and progress. We met at our friend Louis's place, a tiny apartment on East Ninth Street that I suppose now we would call squalid. We thought it was homey, and we talked about our fathers, week after week. That's what the group was meant to examine—fathers and sons, masculinity and the gay male identity. I remember Jonathan insisted we tape all of our sessions—three hours at a clip, mind you—and then we realized no one was really in a position to transcribe all that." Laughter. "It was a leaderless group—of course!—but it was Jonathan who came prepared with probing questions and always seemed to get the conversation going and push people beyond their initial impressions, whatever. He was always synthesizing, summarizing, so we could keep building on what we'd discovered. And of course, Jonathan was the most honest one among us, as we divulged our pasts and our secrets to one another. And I quickly came to respect and then like this guy with the big bush of curly black hair." More laughter. "Oh, yes—that was also one of the splendors of knowing Jonathan back then: the amazing Jew-fro. I'll wager very few of you ever saw *that.*"

Peter paused. Light was pouring in through the arched windows, from the unclouded sky above Central Park, outside. Was he really speaking about Jonathan in the past tense? Could he do that? It was a task, all right, to think that way. But Jonathan had done his work, by dying, and now they, in that room, had to do theirs, by speaking and listening.

"He was handsome, that one, and so smart," said Peter, losing his composure for just a second and then, with a breath, regaining it. "He seemed to know everything about New York, since he'd grown up here—where to get the best Indian food, how to get a private carrel at the Fifth Avenue library. And he knew everything about the world—the way it worked, what it meant. He was clearly, even then, a very advanced creature, a very large human being. And he believed the point of life was precisely this kind of enlargement, and that was inspiring."

Peter spoke of Jonathan as being a self-permission-giver for himself, and an enabler for others, in this process of enlargement. It was a "holy talent," Peter said—believing in a bigger sense of one's self to grow into.

"We went through a lot together. We lost both our lovers to AIDS, along with so many other friends, and we were more stunned and grateful each day, Jonathan and me, as we found we were surviving somehow and still had each other as friends. And then for decades we celebrated each other's successes in work, and sampled each other's culinary experiments, and shared complaints about onerous tax burdens and unfair department-store-exchange policies. And we were there for each other, yes, even on Fire Island, through the good seasons and the bad. . . ."

There was a giggle from one of the gray-suited couples.

"Right?" said Peter, in their direction. "That house on Nautilus, with the guys next door who played Donna Summer all day long, full blast?"

The memories kept flooding toward him, making it difficult to stay focused. He was speaking extemporaneously, though from a little outline he had memorized.

"My point is that Jonathan was staunch, and good company, and remarkably kind and tolerant with those who were less intelligent and experienced than he was—and thank goodness he was, because I was certainly one of those."

He looked upward, above the crowd and their faces, toward the windows, because it was easier to continue that way.

"And now, well—you know, this isn't just memorial-service talk—I am a far better man than I ever could have been, because of Jonathan. And I have to wonder, with gratitude and also a kind of panic, where will we ever get another one. And of course I know the answer: We won't get another one. The best we can do is count ourselves lucky to have had him as long as we did."

"Beautifully done," said Will, as Peter returned to his seat. The comment made Peter shudder a bit, as he choked back tears. And then two musicians stepped onto the stage, a young woman in a long dress, who seated herself at the harp, and a handsome young man, who positioned himself near her but not quite at the center of the stage—which probably someone had thought would be too performance-y.

Will elbowed Peter—his way of saying he thought the man was cute.

"Mm-hmm," Peter said quietly. He was trying to put his moment on the stage behind him, and summon full attention for the musical selection.

The work was Benjamin Britten's fifth Canticle—a diaphanous yet distinctly muscular setting for tenor and harp of an early poem by T. S. Eliot, "The Death of Saint Narcissus." Peter tried hard to listen to the words—the poem sounded odd: erotic, obscure, violent—but despite the tenor's best efforts at enunciation, it was impossible to make out the meaning. A glance at the text in the program offered little help:

> *. . . He was stifled and soothed by his own rhythm.*
> *By the river*
> *His eyes were aware of the pointed corners of his eyes*
> *And his hands aware of the pointed tips of his fingers.*
>
> *Struck down by such knowledge*
> *He could not live men's ways, but became a dancer*
>   *before God. . . .*

Peter decided he must be too preoccupied to concentrate. Anyway, the piece was over in a few minutes, and what hung in the air afterward was the delicious memory of a harp and a heavenly voice, not questions about a second-century bishop of Jerusalem who, according to the program note, was accused of committing an unspecified "detestable crime."

At the reception, Peter and Will barely had a chance to speak privately, since there were so many of Jonathan's friends to greet.

"I didn't see your name in the program," said a nice lady whom Peter didn't recognize.

"No, I wasn't planning to speak," said Peter, reintroducing himself. "But then at the last minute Aldebar thought it would be nice to have something personal, to balance all the lovely remarks about Jonathan's work."

"You spoke beautifully."

"Thank you very much."

"Can we get out of here, please?" said Peter, after she'd left.

"Sure," said Will. "I'm only on a lunch break, though. I have to get back to the office, eventually."

"I'll walk you to the subway."

After making sure to have a word with Jonathan's family and with Aldebar, Peter and Will stepped across Central Park West and into the park. They agreed that was the nicest way to the R train at Fifty-seventh and Seventh. But seeing an empty ball field and a set of invitingly empty bleachers, they decided to take a moment to decompress. They installed themselves halfway up the bleachers, overlooking the field and the expanse of lawn between it and the mass of trees marking the park's edge, beyond, above which poked the towers of Fifth Avenue and Central Park South.

"You look good today," said Peter. He noticed Will was wearing a new pair of stylish black shoes.

"Thanks," said Will. "So do you."

"You can't bullshit or get too fancy for a thing like this, can you?"

"No, you're right."

"I'll tell ya who looked like a million dollars—Aldebar."

"Man, didn't he? He must have inherited a million dollars."

Peter laughed.

"I don't know," he said. "I gather they won't be doing the will for a few days."

"Amazing guy," said Will.

The day was warm and they were in direct sun. Will peeled off his suit jacket and draped it neatly over his knee. Settling, he plucked his shirt away from his chest with characteristic delicacy.

"Why do you do that?" said Peter. "It's adorable. I've always meant to ask."

"What—this?" Will plucked again. "It helps me feel neat. I hate feeling crumpled."

"Ah—yeah, I know. So little in this world is neat. At least we can try to be, ourselves, neat."

Will nodded and then betrayed a smile, as if there was something they should be talking about, but weren't.

"What?" said Peter.

"You," said Will.

Peter smiled radiantly. "Me *adoring* you," he said. "That's what you see on this face, if I may say so."

"You may," said Will. But he still looked hesitant.

"What?!"

"OK, I'm just gonna say it."

"Say what?"

"Speaking of Aldebar—I knew him even before I knew Jonathan. He's how I met Jonathan."

"OK. So?"

"He was taking clients on the side, besides his nursing gigs. I met him in a bar one night and got him to talk all about it."

"Clients?"

"As in rent boy."

"Oh—OK. You know, I kind of assumed that. I knew Jonathan hired guys. He told me once, but we never really talked about it."

"Only the best, Jonathan would hire," said Will, with a kind of sly emphasis and a boyish, expectant look on his face.

"What do you mean . . . you?"

"Yeah."

"Jonathan hired *you?*"

"Yup. Once."

"Really?"

"A few nights after that party where we met."

"Wow."

"Yeah."

Peter thought for a moment.

"So you've rent-boyed," he said.

"For about three minutes, yeah," said Will. "Right after coming to New York."

"Wow. OK."

"With an agency, a top one."

"Uh-huh."

"You OK?"

"Sure. Tell me everything."

"I was recruited one night. What can I tell you? The guys who ran the agency were very nice. I needed the money. They took precautions to keep us safe and healthy, blah-blah-blah. I met some boldface names...."

"OK..."

"That's it. Then it was over. I guess I just haven't wanted to tell you."

"Hmm. Well, no problem."

"Really?"

"Yeah. I mean, of course."

And as the information began to sink in, Peter saw that the revelation probably didn't present any problem for him, morally—though he might indeed need a moment to come around to granting Will the respect in that area that he made a point of granting freely to others he knew who'd also hustled successfully—that is, without letting it destroy them with ambition-killing easy money, or soul-killing drugs, or the thousand other dangers that were out there.

"But now?" said Peter. "I mean, you don't still..."

"No, no, of course not," said Will. "I have a job, I have a life. I only did it to pay the rent. New York is a hard place to get started."

"I hear ya. Cool. Believe me, I understand that there are always gifts coming our way, cosmically, and different possibilities for how to accept them."

"It's good to hear you say that," said Will. "It's been torturing the fuck out of me, how to tell you. Whew! So you don't think I'm soiled, then?"

"Will! *No,*" said Peter. "Of course not. But I love the way you put that—soiled. We're all soiled, aren't we? And we constantly struggle toward cleanliness. You've certainly made me think a bit about the bed I have chosen to lie down in, which is pretty goddamned far from immaculate."

"I was so afraid to tell you."

"For Christ's sake! I think Tyler's hustled, and I told him I thought it made his work stronger."

"Well, that's *advertising . . . ,*" said Will, with an impish grin.

Playfully, Peter slapped Will's arm.

"All right, all right," said Peter. "I'm trying, myself, to work toward something better. Just trying to figure out how to do it."

They were silent for a moment. The city was barely audible from beyond the periphery of trees.

"You know, in a way, this doesn't change anything," said Peter. "In a way, it actually just makes the situation between us more clearly what it is. If that doesn't sound too stupid."

"No, it doesn't," said Will.

"But . . . back to Aldebar," said Peter, suddenly more animated in a gossipy way. "Though wait. Now I'm dying to know now if you might have, um, *dated* anyone I know. . . ."

Will smirked.

"I don't think so," he said. "I only did it for a month or two, and by now I know who you know."

Peter nodded.

"Oh, except . . . ," said Will.

"Who?"

Will leaned in, as if to share a scrumptious secret.

"McCaw's brother-in-law," said Will.

"Him?"

"Yup—big fag. You must have gotten that."

"Well, yeah."

"Not very nice, on the inside. Not at all."

"Ew."

"I'll tell you all about it someday."

"Interesting. Now that's a whole story I cannot wrap my mind around: McCaw wanting to set me up with—what was his name . . . ?"

"Miller."

"Miller!" Peter cackled. "And Fiona! Can you imagine?"

Will giggled.

"She was terrific!" he said. "What's that about? I mean, she must know everything, right? I assume she figured me out, that night—or maybe she keeps out of it. Who knows? I don't really get it, but then again, I don't have to get it anymore."

"OK, so back to Aldebar!" said Peter, gossipy once again. "So he's much more than all that—you get it, right? A nurse, a marine, a connoisseur of opera—come *on!*"

"I know. The minute I met him I knew he was beyond something amazing. We never connected on a sexual level—though I kinda wanted to—but I really saw he's like this angel in human form, some entity from the Gorgeous Planet."

"So do you think he pulled the plug on Jonathan—I mean, in a nice way?"

"Omigod, do you think so, too?!"

"I think he once tried to tell me that he and Jon had discussed the matter and decided something, and I was too obtuse or scared or immature to go into it with him."

"Peter, I have thought about this again and again, and I have to wonder if maybe it was the most exquisite, loving, complete gift that anyone could have given Jonathan, in that situation. . . ."

Peter paused to think about this. Then he took a deep breath and exhaled calmly.

"I think you're right," said Peter. "It was a gift. Wow. Sitting in a ball field in Central Park and discussing euthanasia."

"And prostitution," said Will.

"What Aldebar did or may have done, what you've just told me about—they deserve finer names than that, don't you think?"

Will reached over and took Peter's hand in his.

"Absolutely," he said.

They sat there quietly for a moment, then Peter spoke.

"So we're fine here, Will, really," he said. It was perhaps the caretaker in him speaking. "But just so I know, for the future: Who knows about . . . ? I mean, are you open about it? What about Luz—does she know? Your fancy magazine friends?"

"People know. Nobody cares. The magazine people think it's fun. God knows, some of them have done the same thing, or dealt drugs, or worse. I was only afraid to tell you, because . . ."

"Because I'm such a prude—I knew it."

"When I began to feel the bar being raised with you, Peter, I wanted to play the game correctly. Why do you think I started therapy?"

More silence, then Peter piped up.

"Harold and I once went to a very fancy dinner party right there," he said, pointing at the Sherry-Netherland, whose gracefully proportioned Gothic spire rose sublimely above the trees at the southeast corner of the park.

"You did?"

"Yes. A big-deal illustrator we knew, who did all the big-diva album covers in the seventies and eighties, invited us to a soirée hosted by his best girlfriend, a lady who was one of the first television weathergirls ever, in the fifties, who became a talk-show host and then married well."

"Interesting."

"A very elegant lady—a pioneer of live television, I learned later. The husband was long gone, of course. It was like, seven gay men and her—all formal, we gentlemen in tuxes, the lady in a long skirt and an iridescent metallic blue jacket, cropped just so."

"Nice."

"She had the most amazing enameled gold bangles—Schlumberger; she was impressed that I knew that—and a staff of two who looked like they'd been with her forever. I remember the guy's name was Pedro; he served dinner. I don't remember the wife's name, or even if we got to see her. No, wait: I think she appeared for a second in the dining room after dinner, so we could compliment her on the food. I still remember these crispy, miraculous tarragon potatoes."

"Right there?" said Will, looking at the Sherry-Netherland.

"Right there," said Peter, pointing. "Corner apartment, thirtieth or whatever floor. High up. For all I know, she's still there. She was probably sixty then, so maybe she's eighty-five now and still in the same apartment, wearing her fabulous bangles, no longer receiving guests."

"Or maybe she's still receiving."

"Yeah, maybe so, God bless her. And after dinner, Will, we all repaired to the living room and she wound up telling stories from her early days in television. I seem to remember her saying she was just a cute girl from Texas or Oklahoma, who happened to be smart enough to come up with interesting ways to fill hours and hours of live morning talk show. I think she invented the interview or something. Anyway, her stories were really funny, and at one point she laughed so hard she spilled her wine on her jacket. And I swear, the lady just stood up and excused herself graciously, and returned to the living room not five minutes later wearing another elegant little formalish jacket of *exactly* the same cropped design, only this one was, like, a stiff, transparent, magenta crinoline."

"Amazing."

"Yeah. Harold and I just looked at each other silently, our eyes bulging. She probably had six more where that came from!"

Will giggled silently.

The sky was bright; the day felt open. There were a few lunchtime strollers far beyond, on the lawn, but no one on the ball field.

"The lady really . . . valued herself," mused Peter.

"Evidently," said Will.

"It's a talent I could probably better cultivate in myself."

"Oh?"

"It's been hard for me to . . . give myself the thing I wanted most. Needed most."

Peter gazed at Will fondly, with a smile suggesting sadness but also a new hope for the possibility of relief. Part of what Peter felt at that moment—one of two little figures in a long shot of an otherwise empty set of bleachers—was what he always felt in Central Park: quiet elation in an open patch of land in the middle of a great metropolis. Not that the plot was natural, in the sense of being a part of the forest primeval that had survived until the present. In fact, the park had been constructed along with other great works of the nineteenth century, and some settlements were destroyed in the process. But the place—the *work*—did allow the earth and its inhabitants to breathe together, and it had been there, so often, on walks and picnics with Harold, that Peter had been able to hear the music of the earth and the other spheres.

Spring was turning into summer, and Peter wondered what the season would bring. Would he go to Fire Island this year? He hadn't yet rented a house, but there were openings he knew about. Would Will want to go, or would they by then be creating their own summer style in a different place—Provincetown? Upstate New York? Some lake in the Berkshires that Harold had never heard of? Travel plans made via text or Facebook or some other medium that Harold never knew? Something primal was indeed asserting itself that day in the park, even if it were cloaked in the innocent possibility of ball games and picnics and strolls across the lawn.

Peter squeezed Will's hand.

"I have grieved for Harold so long," he said slowly, his voice suddenly shaky. "This service made me realize what a high-functioning widow I've been, all these years. In a way, I think I was afraid to love someone again, because that would destroy him. So I went on achieving, and grieving, and being very proud that I was carrying on."

"You did the best you could," said Will. He saw how serious Peter was.

"But Harold died a long time ago, didn't he?" said Peter, his face contorting as tears came.

"Yes, he did."

"And now is the time for something else, isn't it?"

"Yes."

Will gave Peter a peck on the cheek, and Peter's words gave way to soft tears. Peter brushed Will's lips with his, but they both knew that it wasn't the time for that kind of embrace. That would come soon.

For a few minutes longer they sat on the bleachers, as Peter recomposed himself and they clucked over the drably formal outfits the musicians wore, and then they walked to the R train, arm in arm.

CHAPTER 26

"And as Peter says, it will be business as usual," said Laura. She punctuated the sentence with a practiced executive smile that no one in the room could have mistaken as heartfelt. Still, she was doing her best as a corporate officer to project confidence; and the point of meeting was, beyond logistics, to rekindle confidence in all the factors required for the success of the McCaw project other than the one once deemed most important: Peter.

Sitting around the conference table in Laura's office, besides her and Peter, were McCaw, Sunil, and Tyler. The latter two said little, though Tyler's new title of creative director conferred new clout that he'd be expected to start exercising immediately. Now that the group had acknowledged Peter's bow out, they all had to affirm that they wanted it to work, that they were sure it would work, and that until now the results had been splendid. The unspoken assumption was that, anyway, they had no choice, since the project was so far along.

"Business as usual," reiterated Laura. "Except, of course, that Tyler is your man now." She smiled at Tyler briefly, and in doing so looked at him for probably longer than she had ever done before. Laura was pouring on the charm aggressively, and had dressed for the task in another of her power lady outfits—this one, a blue pin-striped skirt suit that shouted "Alexis Carrington."

Where does she get these things? thought Peter. He was doodling discreetly in a notebook, as the meeting progressed. There were really no notes to take in a meeting like this.

Funny, he thought. The phoniness of Laura's warmth reflected exactly the kind of robotic state of mind that the designers of the office complex had sought to counter, a few years before, when they transformed the agency's floors in that building from cubicle farms into "an inspiring hive of nontraditional work spaces clustered around a multistory atrium in which creative connections can take place serendipitously." Laura's office and the rest of the executive suite, on the top floor of the complex, though, had ironically been left out of the hive. Her office was the standard fuck-you glass corner, with generically expensive furnishings like those to be found in every four-minute-old glass tower in new business centers from Berlin to Shanghai. Yet the place did seem to suit Laura's style, which Tyler once called "Executive Medusa Realness." And compared with the agency's other "environments," Peter knew, Laura's office was indeed the correct one for a sober occasion like this, where the participants should probably not be enveloped in overstuffed bean bags or trying to balance on giant koosh balls.

"The good news is that Peter's most critical input is already part of the process," said Laura. "And these guys are running with it." Tyler smiled modestly. In addition to the new title he'd received, he was now making a lot more money, some of which had been earmarked for Peter.

"We value our clients, we honor our contracts," added Laura. "But the point is, we're only thinking about what's best for you."

Afterward, there was a cordial send-off by Laura, and a brief, gentlemanly good-bye among Peter, McCaw, Tyler, and Sunil, at the elevator.

"Just keep me posted on the date for the next review," said McCaw, making it a point to address Tyler.

"I will," said Tyler, shaking McCaw's hand firmly with his own kind of Boy Executive Realness.

"I know you believe in this one a lot," said McCaw, to Peter.

"He's the rising star here," said Peter. "For me, that's one of the discoveries of this project. I know it's going to work for you both."

"You're gonna be so proud of me, boss," said Tyler, after McCaw and Sunil had gone.

"I'm already proud of you, Ty."

"We're gonna kill."

"I have no doubt."

And it felt to Peter like the drama of the entire McCaw encounter had unfolded correctly. Tyler deserved the title and the money. He was unmistakably a rising young star and was poised to lead the McCaw project to success. It was good that his ascension hadn't been blocked, even a minute, the way such young-star ascensions can sometimes be, by their so-called superiors. Gladly, Peter had suggested the financial arrangement to Laura—giving up a bit of his own McCaw take and adding it to Tyler's. The happiness of their young star and his success in the mission would only increase the value of Peter's financial stake in the company, anyway.

The meeting had been routine, but the real drama had taken place in the days leading up to it. After deciding to step down, which he did on the day of Jonathan's service, Peter did what he considered to be the manly thing and called McCaw. The conversation, via videoconference, was brief and friendly. Peter said he couldn't continue for creative reasons and was handing the project over to Tyler. After an expression of disappointment, McCaw accepted the news with the kind of old-fashioned WASP coolness that Peter had expected.

McCaw only pushed back a little, at the end of the call.

"Nothing I can do to change your mind?" he said.

"Henderson," said Peter, "I want to be honest with you. Part of me just doesn't believe in what you're doing, and my faking it would be a bad idea. This business is like acting. The audience can detect the slightest funny business. Tyler . . . knows better how to give everything to the project. I thought I could do it, but I can't. Simple as that."

"I appreciate the honesty, Peter."

"Well, thanks for understanding."

"Let's stay in touch."

Whatever that means.

"Sure."

Then Peter went up to Laura's office and told her. As he expected, she went ballistic.

"That's totally irresponsible!" she shrieked.

"Don't tell me what's responsible," said Peter. "I've brought millions in billings to this company. I've done my best to make this project work, and it's totally secure, because of me. Now I need you to do your part."

They went back and forth on it for half an hour, then Laura came to accept the situation. She had no choice, really. Grumbling, she even suggested they lie to McCaw and concoct some explanation around a personal or medical issue—which Peter found unconscionable and also reminded him that Laura didn't really understand the nature of the work itself. Which is why he had called McCaw first.

"Honey, if you ask me, it stinks," said Laura. "Seamless confidence is the only way to go, with a client."

"I know it is, Laura," said Peter. "But here we are. We can repair the confidence."

"Clients don't like it when questions like this are hanging in the air. You know that. If this kind of thing happens, what else can happen? That's the way they think."

"I agree. So I recommend we emphasize our creative ethic and the best practices way we do business. And you know very well that McCaw is happy with everything we've delivered so far."

"It still stinks. I hate it."

"What you hate, Laura, is not being able to control the client's thoughts. But in this case, I've controlled him, so you can fucking relax. We'll get through it."

She shook her head disgustedly.

"I know we'll get through *this*, Peter," she spat. "It's the next job I'm worried about—the next client, and *their* confidence. Word gets out. You should be thinking about that, too."

"I *am* thinking about it, Laura. I'm also thinking about integrity."

They were getting nowhere. Anyway, there was a plan on the table and the next step was to talk with Tyler. Peter looked around Laura's office and was suddenly hit by the thundering banality of it, as a "cultural sign."

"I keep forgetting that places like this still exist around here," he said.

"Well, they do," said Laura, testily.

Peter was still giggling over her ire a few minutes later, in his own office, as he texted Will.

It's over. I just pulled out of McCaw. You busy later?

When you drive through some parts of upstate New York at night, down a winding, tree-lined country road, illuminated only by the headlights of your car, you can feel like you're coursing through a tunnel, ever farther into a leafy vortex that keeps regenerating itself hypnotically before you, moment to moment; and even if you're driving slowly, you can begin to feel like you're fast-forwarding not just down a country road, but past some illusion of the here-and-now, into an ethereum composed of every moment and all the leaves in God's imagination.

The route that Peter and Will chose to take up to Hudson that weekend was an alternate one. Since they were forced to get a late start, on Friday after work, they'd decided the smaller roads would be less congested and make for a nicer drive.

Peter was behind the wheel, and in the moments of silence between them, once they were north of suburban lights and structures, he found himself thinking again how pretty these roads looked at night, and how gently the darkness opened in front of the car, even as it closed up instantly and inexorably behind it. In the rearview mirror was nothing, which was surely a lot to think about, while in front of the windshield was always more than the brain could even process. All those billions of leaves, and all the billions of billowing, three-dimensional bunches they made, in the direct beams of the headlights and in light reflecting from leaves and filtering through them, and in their shadows—all of which, simple physics said, were in shades of green! An almost infinite number of shades of green—all passing by too quickly to see! Wouldn't an elephant, walking along this road, be able to remember the position of each leaf, each bunch of leaves, each color green and pattern of shade and shadow—all of them!—mile after mile? Elephants could do that, people said, though they always made it sound stupidly as if this was some useless capacity for registering meaningless nothing. Whereas Peter always thought how absolutely content elephants must be, remembering minute details of all the leafy paths they have ever trod, and perhaps seeing magnificent patterns emerge in a composite retrospect huger than anything humans could even imagine—which might eclipse the memories we form for smaller-scale things, like the sound of a Chopin étude or the sight of a Poussin landscape.

He and Will had been determined to leave on Friday so they could spend the night at the house, get up early, and have the whole day to plan the things they had to plan, now that the house was Will's. The bequest had been among others that were revealed when Jonathan's will was read, earlier that week, in a meeting they both attended at the lawyer's office. Aldebar and Jonathan's brother were each given $100,000, while the bulk of the estate went to the new foundation; and though everyone was surprised about Will's bequest, they were also delighted, especially Peter, who saw it as an extension of Jonathan's talent for providing and sheltering.

"For reasons well known to my executor and attorney, and knowing that my brother and my dear friend Peter are secure in their own residences, I leave my house in Hudson, New York, to my great friend William. . . ." And the will went on to explain that Jonathan hoped Will would occupy the place and find the security there in which to blossom. By that morning, too, Will had told Peter how kind Jonathan had been to him in other ways—like getting him bartending gigs as a way of helping him earn money, especially after Will told him he wanted to ease out of rent-boying.

The drive was all headlights and dark hills, infinity. . . .

"So much to figure out," said Will, suddenly, after staring out the car window for minutes.

"I know," said Peter.

"Are you going to live there with me?"

"At the house? Are you asking me to?"

They hadn't discussed the matter until then.

"At least we wouldn't have to move the paintings," said Will. Jonathan had left Peter the remaining Frankels, the ones that didn't go to Christie's, the Eliot manuscript, and both the Cycladic head and the little beach rock that looked like it.

"Well, I *have* thought about moving upstate one day, as you know...."

"Yes, I did know, dear."

"So ... you're gonna live there *and* continue at the magazine?"

"Yeah, of course. I don't see why we shouldn't live in Brooklyn Heights during the week and come up here on the weekends. Starting when I return from Argentina. Then we'll have the place for when one or both of us want to pull out of the city for good."

"Oh, is that what you're thinking?"

"Luz has already started to look for a roommate."

"Poor Luz!"

"She'll be fine. She'll be making good money next year."

"What about the whole studio thing? Have you thought about that? That *wing?*"

"As a matter of fact, I have. I thought it would be great to let Aldebar use it for the Foundation. Whaddya think? They need a place. And some of the filmmakers can come there for a residency. Unless you think that's too busy and public."

"No, I like it. It's your house."

"I was kinda thinking of it as *our* house," said Will. He went back to staring out the window. "Aldebar told me he's been wanting to get out of town, too. He really liked being up in Hudson. I gather he's looking for a place to buy."

"It's so interesting," said Peter as the landscape slipped by. "There's so much in plain sight that we just don't see, or can't see, and maybe even don't need to see. It balances all the stuff we do see, like dark matter does—allows the stuff we see to *be* the world, to *think itself* the world. You know what I mean? Aldebar and Jonathan—those final arrangements: unseen, yet reality. And it also makes possible another reality, the one I was living in, in which people don't pull each other's plugs. You know? Why did McCaw think he should set me up? What's in back of that?"

"Ya got me."

"I don't even want to know. I want that to remain eternally dark matter."

Will smiled, but Peter didn't see, since he was watching the road.

"Aldebar and the power of life and death," mused Will. "Could be."

Outside, infinite shades of black that were really hidden greens.

Peter realized he'd fallen in love with Will as part of a story that began before Will ever set foot in his house that night, to bartend. It began, as far as he could tell now, at Jonathan's housewarming, when he was standing right there beside Will and ordered a drink from him, without knowing the guy would become his boyfriend. He'd asked for a vodka from the most extraordinary person in the universe and got no particular vibe from it. *So much for my intimate acquaintance with Fate,* thought Peter. And then Jonathan and Will hooked up; and Jonathan took Will up to Hudson, but they had no more sex. And then there was that weekend in April . . . when Will *already knew the house*! It was the same for the little towns they were passing through—abandoned by industry or flooded by new waves of antique-shoppers. How could even the wisest city or regional plan scale up to counter massive forces slouching in full view—*like one of these hills*—but invisible, impossible to know?

They'd agreed on monogamy, but for different reasons. Peter wanted to avoid dangers he said he knew well; Will said he wanted to avoid those he knew nothing about. Each referenced "experience"—and that was as much as they ever said about the so-called generation gap between them. Marriage, children, and old age might require some further discussion, but not yet. And about the other parts of the story that could also be looming invisibly in front of them—illness, random accidents, acts of God—there was little planning to be done. They agreed only to create a story together.

"Music?" said Will.

"Sure," said Peter.

Will fiddled with Pandora on his iPhone, and after a minute found "Moments in Time," by N'souciance.

"Don't laugh," he said.

The car was filled with a wash of lush synths, uplifting a heartfelt female vocal. It was as much a lovely, warm bath as a song.

> *The moments in time that our hearts make together*
> *The moments of love that we dream for each other*

These moments of love that I make for you, and you
  make for me
The moments in time, my darling, that we make eternity

"Ooh, I love this," said Peter.

"They were a duo back in the nineties, eurodance. I interviewed the girl once, when she was trying to make a comeback. The guy had already died—plane crash. I know it's supercorny. But gorgeous, the way Prince is gorgeous."

"It's totally effective."

By the time the song arrived at the final chorus, which modulated up a half-step, to amplify the splendor, Peter and Will were singing at the top of their lungs, "These moments of love that I make for you, that you make for me; the moments in time, my darling, that we make eternity. . . ."

They were still giggling about their performance when they pulled into a gas station convenience store, a little while later. The exterior was mundane, but inside was a kind of Oz. Obviously brand new, the place was clean and brightly lit, with aisles of pretty snacks, sparkling banks of refrigerated drinks and frozen foods, vivid display shots of pizzas, tacos, and burgers. Far cheerier, Peter thought, than such places used to be when he was a boy. Gas stations were tawdry then. They all seemed to have the same beat-up aluminum-and-glass dispenser from which, for a nickel, you could get a handful of stale cashews. And it made Peter proud on some level—as a self-proclaimed hick—that that little patch of upstate, only forty-five minutes from where he grew up, had not missed out on a half-century's progress in roadside culture.

He was looking at magazines when Will brought an energy bar over to the register.

"That it?" said the register guy. He was a mild, plain-looking man of a certain age.

"It's all together," said Will, indicating Peter. "He's getting some stuff."

"No problem."

"Where's the men's room?"

"Back there," said the guy, pointing and reaching for the key.

After a moment, while Will was still in the men's room, Peter stepped up to the register with two bottles of water and a copy of *Elle Décor.*

"Hi," said the counter guy.

"Hey there," said Peter. "How's it goin' tonight?" Peter instantly thought the guy might be gay. There was a certain softness about the eyes, even a womanliness.

"Great, thanks," said the guy.

"Just this," said Peter. "The water and the magazine."

"All righty. And I think your son wanted the Clif Bar."

"Oh, sure. But . . . he's not my son. He's my boyfriend."

The counter guy smiled warmly. The store's bright lighting made him look older than he probably was.

"Oh, sorry, buddy," he said. "My mistake. Big age difference."

"Yeah," sighed Peter, handing over his credit card. "Like *that's* a big deal. . . ."

ACKNOWLEDGMENTS

For moral support, cultural insights, and thoughtful conversations that helped me clarify many of the ideas that went into this book, my thanks to Matthew Bank, Victor Bumbalo, Anicee Gaddis, Philip Gallo, Deborah Gimelson, Sharon Gluck, Claude Grunitzky, Ted Henigson, Lesley Horowitz, John Jahnke, John Jenkinson, Frances Kazan, Eric Latzky, Sam J. Miller, Derek Nelson, MaryEllen and Dr. John Panaccione, Ira Pearlstein, David Anthony Perez, Michael Raver, Angela Rizzuti, Tim Smyth, and Sarah Van Arsdale.

For generous help in preparing the book for publication, my thanks to Larry Ledford and Steven Salpeter.

And for a wealth of guidance and patience without which I (and this book) would have been lost, my deepest gratitude to my editor, John Scognamiglio, and my agent, Mitchell Waters.

In loving memory of K. J. Dinnhaupt and Barry Laine.

Please turn the page
for a very special Q&A
with Stephen Greco!

How did this novel come about?

It's my fourth novel, but the first I've written to take its cue from events in my own life. For a while I was dating a guy who was much younger than I am. Actually, "dating" is the wrong word. We were hanging out a lot, doing stuff together, and I kind of fell in love with him, half secretly. I started the book as an exercise in wish fulfillment, to take some pressure off the relationship.

You were in love "half secretly"?!

I didn't profess my love as fearlessly as I would have done when I was younger. And maybe I should have done that, even though I suspected my feelings were unrequited. Anyway, I think the message got through.

You guys never went further?

No. Then one day he stopped taking my calls and never explained why. And I had tried *so* hard to be a good friend and not put my fantasy in front of everything!

That's so sad.

Yeah—disappointing. Then again, the book worked out.

Is it true, then, that like Peter, the character in the book who is around your age, you've had two long-term relationships, one of which ended with your partner's death and the other with your partner's drug addiction?

Yes. Though I would hope I'm not quite as wounded and twitchy as Peter is. And yes, I do date younger men—because, as the novel says, "that's who's out there"—but no, I'm not seeing anyone in particular, at the moment.

Why is that?

Why aren't I seeing anyone? I don't know—bad luck. Plus the fact that I had to learn how to do it all over again and how things work now. Love is the least immutable thing there is, in my view. In a way, adjusting to being older was a lot like coming out. Only it's not just about *who* I am, but who I am *now*. Thank goodness there are plenty of young guys out there who seem OK with an older man and are willing to go beyond the daddy thing—which is a perfectly fine fetish that I don't happen to like being squeezed into.

And the other aspects of the novel—the advertising world setting, the references to upstate New York—those are autobiographical, too?

Largely, yes. I was born upstate, I've worked in advertising, I used to write poetry.

Can you describe your journey into writing novels?

I studied architecture at Cornell in the late sixties, at exactly the same time that all those revolutionary forces were swirling about. I came out as gay, started writing poems about identity, and got into magazines when I arrived in New York, in the mid-seventies, to earn a living. But though my friends were mostly gay novelists and "serious" writers, I continued to stick with commercial pursuits—out of fear, I suppose, that I didn't have as much to say as they did.

Then, around 2000, I was partner in a media company focused on youth culture, and we needed someone to script out a serial animation we were planning. But we couldn't afford a writer, so I did it. I started inventing characters and situations, and a story began coursing out of me like lava. It was almost scary, yet I couldn't believe how good it felt—to have this story *erupt* and then to work on it, craft it, make it better.

What happened then? Did the animation get made?

No, but I kept going with the story and it became *Dreadnought,* my first novel.

Wait—I thought your first book was called *The Sperm Engine.*

The Sperm Engine was mostly nonfiction, erotica—essays, reminiscences, and the like. Though I did need to knock out some fictional pieces to round out the book, and writing those was thrilling. That's what gave me the courage and curiosity to go deeper with *Dreadnought.*

And *Dreadnought* was self-published?

Not exactly. The publisher of *The Sperm Engine,* Green Candy, passed on *Dreadnought,* and I had no agent at the time. When I asked my younger writer friends who their agents were, they said, "Get modern. Publish it yourself." And just then my friend Dave King, the novelist, helped get me into a pilot program with Amazon that he was part of, called Amazon Shorts, which published original short fiction for direct download. This was around 2005. Amazon took one of the parts of *Dreadnought,* since it was a novel composed of relatively independent sections; and then, once that began selling, they took the rest of the parts.

What is *Dreadnought* about?

Predictably enough, youth culture: who wins and who loses when a fictional biggest-brand-in-history stalks a planet-wide youth market of a billion souls. You see the workings of it in six tales, like Mount Fuji in Hokusai's *Thirty-six Views.* "Everybody loses, but the party's fun while it lasts." I'm quoting jacket copy here.

Sounds interesting. How did the novel do?

You mean how did it sell? Not too badly, thanks. Some parts of it got up into the thousand-most-popular Amazon offerings during the weeks when they launched. I got two film options out of it, too, from an independent producer who found the novel online and liked it. So it was natural for me to do my next novels, *The Culling* and *Other People's Prayers,* through Amazon, too—though for the current one, *Now and Yesterday,* I wanted to go a more traditional route and give the novel the best possible advantages in design, marketing, distribution, etc.

It sounds like you came to writing relatively late in life.

I started writing fiction only after I was fifty, yes. But between twenty-five and fifty I kept a journal that's pretty good, I think— you know, hopes and fears, love and loss, thunderingly telling details of life during AIDS and the time leading up to it. Parts of that have been published.

Let's get back to *Now and Yesterday*. Am I right to feel the influence of Victorian literature in this work?

Yes, actually. I had *Middlemarch* quite particularly in mind, in fact: a supposedly little story of people in a little world, embedded in a larger world where society is lurching forward. I wanted the pace of my novel, too, to be stately and Victorian. I thought that would work well for the situation Peter is in—kind of *stuck* and crawling ever so slowly out of it.

In your novel, what kinds of things in the larger world are "lurching forward"?

Oh, new forms of consciousness and identity; the shift away from those noble, citizenship-driven values of Peter's father's generation, toward the consumerist, brand-driven values of today. The latter is what the younger character, Will, grew up with. Seems to me, that shift in values is just as seismic as the one in *Middlemarch* associated with railways and the Industrial Revolution. In fact, it was all I could do to resist lapsing into long, righteous passages like those in which Eliot halts the narrative in order to lay out another fifty yards of moral vision.

Whom did you have in mind as your reader for *Now and Yesterday*?

Well, to quote Richard Howard, who was speaking of poetry, the book is not for *every*one, but it's certainly for *any*one. That is, it's not just for gay readers. I had general readers very much in mind—including fans of what some people call "women's fiction," where feelings and emotions and memories really matter.

Do you still work in advertising?

I do. I often consult with major agencies and am also a partner in a media company, in addition to my various writing projects.

Are you working on another novel?

I sure am. After *Now and Yesterday* I wrote a deliciously dark, *noir*-ish science fiction romance set in 1947, a straight love story that I'm very proud of. It turns on a neat idea about World War Two and human evolution. Currently, I'm working on a new novel that takes off from the appalling gap between rich and poor in this country right now. The hard part is to keep the thing from becoming *The Grapes of Wrath*. I have something funnier and more buoyant in mind, but biting, like a Preston Sturges film. Wish me luck.

NOW AND YESTERDAY

Stephen Greco

ABOUT THIS GUIDE

The suggested questions are included
to enhance your group's reading of
Stephen Greco's *Now and Yesterday*.

DISCUSSION QUESTIONS

1. Peter is fifty-nine and Will is twenty-eight. To what extent does the age gap between them affect the development of their relationship? Are there examples in the book of Peter and Will attending a social event or performance together and experiencing it in different ways, because of their age? What other factors, besides age, prevent Peter and Will from getting together sooner?

2. How do Peter and Will change over the course of the novel? Does one change more than the other? (Make reference to the decades in which Peter and Will grew up—respectively, the '50s and '60s, and the '80s and '90s—and the kinds of "programming" they would have received from their parents.) Does Peter learn anything from Will? Does Will learn anything from Peter?

3. By the end of the novel, Peter has realized he is still wounded by the loss of his first long-term boyfriend to AIDS, and that that wound has kept him from embracing new love, with Will. What does it mean to "heal" from such a wound? How is Peter on his way toward healing, as the novel ends? In what ways, historically, have events like plagues and wars left whole groups of people wounded psychologically, and how do these compare with AIDS?

4. Some older gay men find they don't fit comfortably into today's "post-liberation" gay culture, where issues like AIDS and coming out are less central than they were in past decades. In what ways does Peter fit in and/or not fit in? Does Will, a much younger man, fit in any better?

5. How does the novel treat the fact that Peter's friend Jonathan has survived AIDS only to be exposed to another disease associated with men of the age that he and Peter are

now? With irony? Sympathy? How do Jonathan's actions reveal the way he has chosen to embrace his fate? How are other gay men of Peter and Jonathan's generation depicted in the novel?

6. Because of AIDS, older single gay men like Peter face an extremely limited dating pool of available men of the same age. What romantic and sexual options are open to Peter, other than dating younger men? How do these compare with the romantic and sexual options for straight men of that generation?

7. Peter and Will are both affected by their road trip upstate, to visit Jonathan. What happens to them, emotionally, on that trip? How are things different between the two when they return to the city, and why?

8. Is Peter fooling himself to think that the McCaw assignment is "just another job"? Is he a sellout, by the standards espoused by his upstate friend Arnie? Is Arnie noble for still holding on to his old-school, politically correct standards? Are those standards obsolete? Have they been superseded by newer forms of political correctness?

9. Discuss the way gay life in New York and life upstate are depicted in this novel. Are Peter and Will typical gay men? Do they, because of their work in the media or other privileges, wield special influence over gay culture and contemporary culture at large?

10. Peter is a member of the "baby boom" generation. In what ways is he typical of the baby boomers and in what ways not? Historically speaking, how might the expectations of gay baby boomers have helped fuel the Stonewall rebellion and other liberation movements? How have boomer expectations shaped culture at large?